SWEET HUSH

ALSO BY DEBORAH SMITH

Miracle
Blue Willow
Silk and Stone
A Place to Call Home
When Venus Fell
On Bear Mountain
The Stone Flower Garden
Alice at Heart

SWEET HUSH

A NOVEL

DEBORAH SMITH

LITTLE, BROWN AND COMPANY
Boston New York London

First Edition

The characters and events in this book are fictitious.
Any similarity to real persons, living or dead, is coincidental
and not intended by the author.

Library of Congress Cataloging-in-Publication Data

Smith, Deborah.
    Sweet hush : a novel / Deborah Smith. — 1st ed.
      p. cm.
    ISBN 0-316-80650-1
     1. Apple growers — Fiction.   2. Women farmers —
Fiction.   3. Children of presidents — Fiction. 4.
Mothers and sons — Fiction.   5. Single mothers —
Fiction.   6. Widows — Fiction.   I. Title.

PS3569.M5177 S94 2003
813'.54 — dc21

                          2002073010

10 9 8 7 6 5 4 3 2 1

Q-FF

Book design by Oksana Kushnir

Printed in the United States of America

FOR
Chelsea, Amy, Patti, Trisha, Susan,
and all the other First Daughters

SWEET HUSH

In your orchard, you welcome all blooming souls,
Green spirits, gold dreams, red passions —
Sour Shaws, Auburn Delilahs,
MacLand Tarts, Osmo Russetts, Candler Wilds;
A thousand whispers of trees long gone —
Forgotten apples, lost in the earth.
But yours survive, my dear, strong Hush;
Your hopes beckon, soft and sweet;
Your trees grow forever, where two hearts meet.

A poem written for the second Hush McGillen,
1899, by her husband

PROLOGUE

I'm the fifth Hush McGillen named after the Sweet Hush apple, but the only one who has thrown a rotten Sweet Hush at the First Lady of these United States. In my own defense, I have to tell you the First Lady threw a rotten Sweet Hush at me, too. The exchange, apples notwithstanding, was sad and deadly serious.

"You've ruined my daughter. I want her back," she said.

"I'll trade you for my son," I answered. "And for Nick Jakobek's soul."

After all, the fight wasn't really about her or me, but about our sorely linked destinies and our respective children and our respective men and our view of what we were put in the world to accomplish with other people watching—whether those people were a whole country or a single, stubborn family. There's a fine line between public fame and private shame. For those of us who have something to hide, holding that line takes more of our natural energy than we want to admit.

So, standing in the White House that day with liquid, festering apple flesh on my hands like blood, I realized a basic truth: The world isn't kept in order by politics, money, armies, or religion, but by the single-minded ability of ordinary souls to defend all we hold dear and secret about our personal legends, armed with the fruit of our life's work. In my case, apples.

I walked wearily down one of the White House corridors we've all seen in magazines and documentaries. For the record, the mansion is smaller than it looks on television, but the effect is more potent in person. My heels clicked too loudly. My skin felt the weight of important air. History whispered to me, *Hush, go home and lick your wounds and start over with your hands and your tears in the good, solid earth.* I followed a manicured sidewalk outside into the winter sunshine, and then to the public streets. The guard at the gate by the south lawn said, "Can I help you, Mrs. Thackery?" as if I'd strolled by a thousand times. Fame, no matter how indirect or unwanted, has its benefits.

"I could use a tissue, please." I only wanted to wipe a few bits of rotten apple off my jeans and red blazer, but he gave me a whole pack. Hush McGillen Thackery of Chocinaw County, Georgia, rated a whole pack of tissues at the White House guard gate. I should have been impressed.

I put my mountaineer fingers between my lips and whistled up a cab. I took that cab to the hospital in Bethesda, Maryland, where in the 1950s President Eisenhower's doctors hid his heart trouble and in the 1980s President Reagan's doctors hid the fact that our old-gentleman leader had gone funny. It was a safe place to keep family troubles close to the soul and away from the rest of the country. I slipped in past a crowd of reporters with the help of the Secret Service, who hadn't yet heard I'd splattered you-know-who with an apple.

I went to the private room where Nick Jakobek lay recuperating somewhere below the shore of normal sleep, his stomach and chest bound with bandages that hid long rows of stitches, his arm fitted with a slow drip of soothing narcotics, which he would sure as hell jerk from his vein when he woke up. I sat down beside Jakobek's bed and cupped one of his big hands in mine.

People had sworn he was the kind of man who could do me no

good outside of bed. A suspect stranger, not a Good Old Boy or a swank southern businessman, not One of Us. A man who had never tilled the soil for a living or sold a bushel of newly picked apples to an apple-hungry world or sat around a campfire drinking bourbon under a hunter's moon. A man who knew more about ways to die than ways to live. A man so cloaked in rumors and mysteries that even the President couldn't protect his reputation. Without a doubt, people said, Hush McGillen Thackery would never stoop to love that kind of man, after loving such a fine man as her husband.

I'm here to tell you I did, he wasn't, I wasn't supposed to, but I do.

"This was never about you and me," I whispered to Jakobek. "People just have to grow where they're planted. That's the last apple analogy I'll offer you until you decide to ask for more. If and when. Just remember. Just believe me. *You have earned your blessings.*" I kissed him and cried a little. His mouth eased, but he couldn't wake up.

"I hear that you and my wife had an unhappy meeting," someone said. I turned and found the President gazing at me from the doorway.

"I hit her with a rotten apple." Not something you really like to tell a man who has his own army.

But the President only nodded. "She probably deserved it."

I tucked a small crucifix of apple wood inside Jakobek's unfurled hand, bent my forehead to his for a long, hard moment, then left the room. It was time to go home to the fertile, wild mountains of Georgia, where I and everyone I loved — except Nick Jakobek and his presidential relatives — belonged.

We all make ourselves up as we go along, until the tall tales of our lives grow around our weaknesses and humiliations like the tough bark of an apple tree. Call it public relations for the country's good or call it making the best of a bad situation in a family or a marriage or a love affair, but either way, we root our lives in other people's ideas of who we are, both public and private, both great and small.

But an apple, of course, never really falls far from its tree.

PART ONE

Earn the blessings. We McGillens had always had to earn our blessings on the cruel grace of the seasons and the hard red hope of ripe apples. Our legacy started in 1865 with Hush Campbell McGillen, a young Scottish woman whose husband, Thomas, died in pieces at the Battle of Bull Run. We suspect Thomas McGillen was a Pennsylvania Scotsman in the service of the Union Army, but Great-Great-Great-Grandmother Hush never admitted such a notorious thing after she came to enemy territory in the Appalachian South. She brought with her four half-grown sons and daughters, a mule, a wagon, fifty dollars, and a bag of apple seeds gathered from every orchard she'd passed between Pennsylvania and Georgia.

Hush the First had grown up growing apples in the old country, where her daddy managed an Englishman's fruit trees. Hush knew how to site an orchard, how to make a graft take life on the rootstock, how to draw bees covered in pollen every spring, how to store apples for months every winter. She understood an apple tree's need for warm soil and good water and clear, cool skies, and the apple trees understood her. Like them, she had a yearning for land, the kind of good orchard land even a dirt-poor widow could claim for nothing. That land lay in the cradle of a wild mountain paradise called Chocinaw County, Georgia.

Hush the First found her way to a broad creek valley at the base of Chocinaw Mountain and Chocinaw's sister mountains, Big Jaw and Ataluck. That valley was called the Hollow by mountain people, like the mysterious hollow at the base of a great, towering tree. It lay so deep in the laps of Chocinaw, Big Jaw, and Ataluck that it could only be reached on foot and was so far from civilization that nobody but a desperate person would want to try. The Hollow sat ten miles west of Dalyrimple, the courthouse seat of Chocinaw County (where everybody was unashamedly glad the war had ignored them), twenty miles south of shell-shocked Chattanooga, Tennessee, a hundred miles north of burned-out Atlanta, and a thousand miles west of the Scottish lowlands where Hush had been born.

"Nowhere" had a better chance of being found on a map.

To add to its mystique, the Hollow was shunned by local folk as a valley of the dead. There, in a glen along the creek, lay buried the corpses of nearly fifty Union and Reb soldiers. They'd killed one another in a nasty mutual massacre only the year before Hush arrived. The mind-your-own-business mountaineers of Chocinaw County had buried the soldiers in shallow graves, right where they'd fallen. Dalyrimple's most educated man, town founder Arnaud Dalyrimple — bartender, gambler, minister of the gospel, and newspaper columnist — wrote in the *Dalyrimple Weekly Courier: The gloriously wild Hollow is as haunted as Mr. Abraham Lincoln's own most personal Hell.*

But Hush looked at the Hollow and saw apple country. The mountainsides protected it from high winds and gave shade from the blistering southern sun; the mountain springs seeped water down to the Hollow's big creek in a dependable supply. Most of all, groves of wild crab apples draped the lower hills like oases among the granite cliffs. Those tough little trees clung to the crevices between laurel shrubs and rock, blooming like mad. They knew a good home when they found one, and they knew the Hollow was meant for apples. "Apple trees do no' mind a few bones, and the dead do no' mind a few apples," Hush said. She gave her fifty dollars for a deed to the Hollow's two hundred acres, set up camp, cleared the soil, and planted her seeds.

Now, apples are the same as people. No two seeds are alike. Plant a hundred seeds and you'll get a hundred unique apple trees — some good, some bad, but most ordinary, like anybody's children. Hush knew only time and fate would sort out the curious mix she'd planted Vandermeers from Pennsylvania, Coleridge Yellows from Maryland, Spirit Reds from the Carolinas, and many more. There were hundreds of apple varieties in the cool eastern half of this country then. Every small farm had an orchard, and every county had a breed of apple to call its own. Farmers waited to see what each season's bees would bring them on fuzzy bee legs covered in pollen. They studied every offsprung seedling like pilgrims searching for a holy leader.

Maybe this one will be special. Maybe this one will be the queen mother of all apple trees.

Hush watched her trees for ten years, then twenty. By then her children had grown and gone, and she'd added a room to her drafty log house, established a small lot of cattle and chickens and pigs, built a barn, and bought two new mules. Her sons had hacked out a muddy wagon lane over to Dalyrimple and named it McGillen Orchards Road. Hush earned a meager living selling wagonloads of apples to the townsfolk every fall. But still, no special tree. Every spring she watched the bees flit back and forth between her tame orchard and the wild, seductive crab apples on the mountainsides. A daughter who had moved to Atlanta wrote to a friend: *Mama still believes God in His Heaven will smile on the marriage of her trees and His.*

As she grew older, Hush taught a granddaughter, Liza Hush McGillen (known as the second Hush McGillen), to help her in the orchard. Together, they studied each year's maturing young trees for the One. In the fall of 1889, they found it. There it was, in its first season of fruit—a strong, proud young tree standing right in the middle of the old burial ground of the dead soldiers, sprung up from their bones, bearing apples so sweet the juice burst in the mouth like sugar.

Hush and Liza Hush fell to their knees, crying and laughing and eating that wondrous fruit. Over the years that followed, they slivered twigs from the young tree's branches, trained them onto rootstock, and cloned the marvelous mama tree a hundred times, then two hundred, and more. Word traveled like love-hungry apple bees; people came to buy. Hush sold apples, and Hush sold grafted seedlings, and Hush sold Hush—her legend, that is.

Redder than an Arkansas Beauty, as long-keeping as a Ben Davis, juicier than a Jenny's Eureka, sweeter than a Blush Delilah.

The Sweet Hush apple.

Every generation before me earned the right to the name, and I'd had to as well.

I WAS TRAINED TO GROW the Sweet Hush by my great-aunt Betty Hush (the fourth Hush McGillen), who had owned the Hollow before my father. Betty had learned the apple business from her elder cousin, William Hush McGillen (the third Hush McGillen and the only one who happened to be male), who had run the famous Sweet Hush orchards during their first heyday, between 1900 and 1930. According to all the family stories, William Hush McGillen had been endowed with the expert business sense of a preacher pumping sinners for nickels. I liked to think I inherited his knack.

All of Chocinaw County sported Sweet Hush apple orchards during the reign of William Hush, and the widely seeded McGillen clan basked in comfortable homes with fine iron stoves in the kitchens and fast Model T cars in the yards. William Hush and all his cousins sold apples by the ton and illegal homemade apple brandy by the barrelful. Down in Atlanta, William's sister, Doreatha McGillen, started the Sweet Hush Bakery Company.

Every year the mountain McGillens sent thousands of the best Sweet Hush apples by mule wagon and train down to Doreatha, who stewed and pureed and spiced them into fillings for all manner of baked goods. Those delicious products were hand delivered to the city's finest homes by white-suited black men in handsome, horse-drawn wagons with SWEET HUSH BAKERY on the sides in scrolling Victorian letters. Sweet Hush deep-dish apple pies regularly appeared on the dessert board at the governor's mansion.

Then the Depression wiped out Doreatha's bakery. Federal revenue agents from the Roosevelt administration broke up the McGillen liquor business (and our families, too—my proud grandfather and one of his cousins, both deacons in the Dalyrimple Baptist Church, were caught with their liquor stills and killed themselves rather than serve time on the chain gang). But worst of all, the rise of modern refrigeration and long-range shipping turned local apples into a novelty, not a necessity.

Most of the great southern orchards were gone by the time of my birth in 1962—chopped down, burned to their stumps, forgotten, unwanted, unloved. Potter Prides, Escanow Plumps, Sweet Birdsaps, Black Does, Lacey Pinks—all were extinct from the earth, and hundreds more like them. Gone forever. We McGillens continued to suffer one streak of bad luck after another (my own father died young of a heart attack while chopping briars in the orchards), but we and our Sweet Hushes hung on by stubborn stems, refusing to give up in a world that had turned us aside for cheap Wisconsin Winesaps and ice-cold Japanese Mutsus.

As a child, I became determined to make people taste us again.

THE FIRST ELEVEN YEARS of my life, before Daddy died, were perfect. Mama sang as she worked in the orchards beside him; Daddy was always cheerful, or at least seemed that way. And I was their apple princess, the fifth Hush McGillen of Sweet Hush Hollow, the prettiest place on the face of the earth. It bloomed in the spring, ripened like a womb in the summer, fed our souls in the fall, and slept in the kindest dreams of sanctuary all through the cold winters.

McGillen orchards paraded across the broad creek valley and up the feet of Chocinaw, Ataluck, and Big Jaw Mountains, covering terraces built by generations of backbreaking McGillen labor. We had a saying in the family: True Sweet Hush apples can only be grown by God and McGillens. There was something dark and rich and haunted in our soil, the old folks whispered.

"That kind of earth always produces the most satisfying fruit," Daddy said.

I had no idea we were poor, and I had not yet begun to understand what our relatives meant when they mourned the last evidence of our family's grand past—the monogrammed silver pitcher Daddy polished lovingly and displayed atop an old pine table. *There was a time,* I heard old aunts say, *when our family didn't have to sell off its fine heirlooms.*

As far as I was concerned, all the fine heirlooms were still with us. They grew in splendid, blooming beauty around me on our hillsides and were recorded in the dusty agricultural texts in the living room's simple oak bookcase. On the wall, in a place of glory above our sag-backed plaid couch, hung the one, the only framed piece of fine art in our home: a 1909 botanical rendering, in full color, of a Sweet Hush apple.

"It was first published in the big federal agricultural references of the time," Daddy explained, telling the story repeatedly to me when I was a child, as if it were a fable or a favorite ghost tale. I loved the look of pride on his face when he spoke of our former grandeur. "A pair of men were sent here from Washington. They sat in the orchards with the whole family watching as one painted a perfect specimen of a Sweet Hush apple and the other one studied dozens of apples and made notes."

Then Daddy would open our very own aged copy of the resulting glorious government tome and read the men's conclusions solemnly, as if reciting from the Bible: "The ripe Sweet Hush fruit is deep red in color, bordering on burgundy; the fruit is uniform and round in shape, of medium size; the stem is thick and long in an acute, blackish, unlipped cavity; the basin large and shallow, unfurrowed; the flesh extra crisp and very white. The apple ripens from September to December; it stores well over winter, and holds its flavor in cooking." Daddy always paused at that point, gathered his breath, then recited the most important part of all in a deep, profound drawl. "The taste is like pure fresh honey mixed with the finest cane sugar. There is no acidic aftertaste in a Sweet Hush. Every bite seems to melt on the tongue. A truly spectacular apple."

Truly spectacular. Imagine. Government men using superlatives like that, without being bribed.

Mama, being a small part Cherokee, would stand beside Daddy and offer her Cherokee grandmother's advice. " 'The Sweet Hush is the best apple for what ails you,' Granny Halfacre said. 'Because sweet apples settle the stomach and clean the intestines and soothe the heart.' " Years later I would think back on those words with a certain wry sorrow. Surviving as an apple farmer did indeed take heart, guts, and a strong stomach.

But as a child all that mattered to me was the miracle of our association with one of God's finer gifts, which, by no small measure of pride, was my namesake.

"My own little prize apple," Daddy called me. "Just like your mother."

I had Mama's angular face and long, knob-tipped nose, her wide, downturned mouth and Cherokee cheekbones, but Daddy's strong chin and deep green eyes. No haircut or perm ever kept my rust-brown hair from shagging around my face like a horse's forelock. People never said I was beautiful, but they always said I was a looker. But then, so is an albino calf. Daddy said I had green-apple eyes. I turned a raw, unripened stare on the world outside Chocinaw County, daring that world to take a bite out of my happy, hardy self.

Until finally, it did.

AT THE START OF apple season in 1974, while Mama was at her backbreaking job waiting tables at the Dalyrimple Diner, I poured cider from the silver pitcher onto the gnarled roots of the first Sweet Hush tree and cried until I thought my head would burst. Daddy had died while working in the orchards the summer before with Mama holding his head while I ran for help, and I would never stop missing him. I was only twelve years old and still so in love with my own daddy that the world began and ended with his passing. "You'll own the Hollow one day," he'd told me not long before he died. "I know you'll make it proud of you. You're the fifth Hush McGillen. Don't ever forget that."

I had to do *something,* or the farm would be lost. The fame and fortune of the old days were no more than a moldering Studebaker in the main barn and the remnants of the silver service we'd had to sell. I understood, now.

All we had left were our apples.

I lugged two empty bushel baskets, a plank, a handful of paper sacks, a cardboard box full of freshly picked Sweet Hushes, and my baby brother, Logan, through the orchards and up the long dirt lane from the farmhouse to McGillen Orchards Road. I set up my homemade table and stood beside it, holding a big sign I'd made on a square of cardboard using red house paint.

THE ONE, THE ONLY, REAL SWEET HUSH APPLE
NO WORMS, NO ROTTEN SPOTS
55 CENTS A BAG
2 BAGS FOR ONE DOLLAR

I had noticed that people from Atlanta had started driving through the Hollow. They'd come up the new spur off the interstate, then turn right on the state route, meandering through the mountains to look at the scenery before heading home to their subdivisions and shopping centers. I had been counting the number of Atlanta station wagons that parked every Saturday and Sunday in the tall joe-pye weed near our weathered mailbox.

People got out and took pictures of our farm. I walked up to the paved road once and looked back at the Hollow to see what intrigued them. I saw the broad valley filled with rows of apple trees, the round mountains rising behind them, and the pretty roofs of our farmhouse and barns peeking from a grove of huge beech trees on a shady knoll. All I saw was home, but I loved it dearly.

If I wanted to keep it, I had to make it pay like it had in the old days.

Within thirty minutes, I got my first customer. I've never forgotten her — an old, silver-haired Atlanta lady driving her sisters through apple country in a Cadillac with a fading NIXON FOR PRESIDENT bumper sticker. "Why are these the 'real' Sweet Hush apples, Honey?" she asked, smiling.

"Because, Ma'am, ours are the only Sweet Hush apples in Chocinaw County that are grown over the bones of about a hundred Yankee soldiers —" I made a dramatic gesture toward the orchards — "who were killed by Rebs on the back side of our Hollow during the Battle of Dalyrimple, in 1864." I paused for effect. "My great-great-great-grandmother Hush McGillen the First said apple trees don't mind the dead. So she planted her first trees right over the dead soldiers' graves. And ever since, Sweet Hush Hollow has grown the best apples anywhere. Because bones are roots and roots are bones. That's what my mama says, and her mama was part Cherokee Indian, and you know that Indians know the spirits of the earth. What they say is true." I took a deep breath. "That'll be a dollar for two bags of apples, please. And a quarter if you want to take any pictures."

The old lady and her sisters laughed and bought my whole box of apples. "I'd pay just to hear you tell tall tales," she said. She touched my red-brown hair. It was long and impossibly wavy, and I'd bound it up with a string from the pocket of my overalls. "You look like you were grown from the earth inside a farm-fairy's ring. You stay this pretty and this lively in using your imagination, and people will buy apples from you right and left."

After she drove off, I put Logan in a wheelbarrow and pushed him back up the farm lane to get more apples, frowning and chewing my tongue as I went. "Logan," I said, "people will buy apples if you throw in a story they can take home with 'em." From then on I would relate the gloriously weird story of the Civil War dead beneath our orchard's heart to everyone who stopped. It sold apples.

Two hours later I'd moved forty bags of Sweet Hushes and collected somewhere in the neighborhood of twenty dollars. I pulled the wad of bills out of my jeans pockets at every opportunity to count it with trembling fingers. In 1974 it was a fortune.

I heard a motorcycle and looked up the paved road between the deep trees and rhododendrons. Davy Thackery cruised over a knoll. His sister, Mary May "Smooch" Thackery, hung on behind him, her dark-brown Thackery curls waving like mad in the wind. Some families never quite catch the brass ring of respectability. The Thackerys were that kind, though most of them had sweet, placid natures and worked hard to stay middle class. They were known — and to tell the truth, revered by many — for their legacy of illegal liquor and their wild talent with fast mountain cars. After all, professional stock-car racing had its roots in the southern backroads of the 1940s and 50s, when bootleggers in souped-up sedans packed with whiskey outran government agents. Thackerys were a Chocinaw County legend in that regard. No Thackery had ever been caught in those old days — alive, at least — by the revenuers up on Chocinaw Mountain.

Davy grinned at me under his own set of girly Thackery curls, and my heart beat faster. He was only thirteen, a year older than me, tall and lanky and quick to punch anyone who bothered him. But his eyes were sweet and blue whenever he looked at me, and I was desperate to love and be loved by a new fellow, now that my father was gone. Davy's daddy had died young, too, racing stock cars on the southern dirt tracks, and then his mother deserted him and Smooch. Smooch had turned eager-to-please and needy. Davy had turned reckless and angry. They were being raised by a sickly grandmother in town. She couldn't control Davy. But I could. I thought.

"Hey, Beautiful," Davy said jauntily. "What crazy thing are you up to now?"

I blushed. *Beautiful.* His bullshit was my one weakness. "That's Mr. Jetters's motorcycle, you thief."

"The dumb old bastard won't miss it for at least an hour."

Smooch hopped off worriedly. "You said he let you *borrow* it!"

He chucked her under the chin. "Well, Sis, I lied." Davy sat sideways on the cycle's leather seat, surveying my ramshackle baskets and boxes. "Your mama sent us out here to see what's goin' on. Somebody told her you're sellin' apples like a gypsy. She's afraid you'll get run over or knocked in the head. I told her I'd take care of you."

I pulled out my wad of bills. "I believe I'm doin' just *fine,* thankyaverymuch."

Smooch gaped at me. Her eyes gleamed. "Oh, I wish I were rich, too."

"Mama can buy a lot of groceries with this money."

Smooch picked up my cardboard sign and studied it. "I'd leave off the part about the worms and the rotten spot. That only gives people bad thoughts."

"I'll redo the sign later."

"Let me, oh, let me! I want to help, please, please! I'll make you a new sign with fancy curlicues on the corners."

"Okay, thanks." Smooch had a talent for drawing, plus she spent a lot of her time figuring out what people wanted to hear. I felt sorry for her, and I could use her public relations advice. I looked at her and Davy. "If y'all help me sell apples to the folks from Atlanta, I'll give you two dollars each for the whole day."

"I'm hired!" Smooch said.

But Davy only looked down at me with his troublemaking, sky-blue eyes. "I'll help out just because you asked me. But I'm not gonna kiss anybody's ass from Atlanta. They're all Jews and niggers and snotty rich shits."

This was the kind of moment in which smart girls turn stupid and blind. I should have gotten in his face and read him my personal riot act. I should have recognized that there was too much anger in his view of the world, but I was already in love with him, so I let it go. But I knew: Words mattered. Ideas mattered. Reputation mattered. My mother was one-fourth Indian and I'd heard people call her names and say Daddy shouldn't have married her. Even my own uncle Aaron and his damned kids. My own cousins. "Would you let people call me nasty names like you use?" I asked Davy somberly.

He bristled. "Anybody calls you a nasty name where I can hear, I'll kick his ass."

"Then please, please, Davy—" I smiled—"you're such a *fine* person. Don't talk that way *yourself*. Promise me."

"All right, all right. If you don't like it, I won't say it."

"Good."

"Not where you can hear, anyway."

I bristled and almost said something back, but then a yellow Volkswagen van came up the road. "Look friendly," I ordered.

Smooch, Davy, and I lounged by the roadside. Smooch waved, and I held up my sign. The Volkswagen stopped. A man got out carrying a pair of cameras with long lenses. "Man, oh man, this is *the* most beautiful place in the mountains," he said. "It's really got the whole back-to-nature thing going for it. Garden of Eden. I can feel the *chi*, you know. The good energy. Wow." His lip sported a mustache, and he wore his hair in long sideburns. We gaped at him. Men in Chocinaw County religiously shaved their faces and kept their hair in God-fearing crewcuts.

"That man's a hippie," Smooch whispered.

"That man's a *customer*," I countered.

Davy stepped ahead of Smooch and me, balling up his fists. I dodged in front of him, holding up my sign. "Sir, welcome to Sweet Hush Farms. Parking's free if you buy apples, but if you're just here to take pictures, it'll cost you a quarter."

"That's a deal, Gorgeous." Grinning, he handed over the quarter, and I pocketed it. "So can I take a picture with you in it?"

"Hell, no," Davy said.

"It's for the newspaper in Atlanta."

"The big one?" I asked.

"That's right. I'm a photographer."

"This'll sell apples," Smooch said in my ear.

I nodded fervently. "Yessir, I'll be in your picture, but only if my friends can be in it, too."

Smooch squealed with delight. Davy scowled until I linked my arm through his. I held the sign up with my free hand, but Smooch took it from me. "I'll hold the sign, and you hold up the cash," she whispered.

"Good idea." I plucked the wad of bills from my jeans and raised it high.

The hippie photographer laughed and began snapping photos.

That Sunday, thousands of people saw our color photograph on the front page of the Atlanta newspaper's "Dixie Living" section. I didn't tell Ma about the photographer. In Chocinaw County, good girls didn't talk to hippies.

People gathered at the diner after church, bringing their "Dixie Living" sections with them. Ma was working the lunch crowd and hadn't caught on yet. Davy, Smooch, and I loitered in the kitchen and exchanged worried looks. People didn't get their pictures in the Atlanta papers unless they were wicked or in politics, or both.

"Doris Settee McGillen, look here, are you deaf, dumb, and blind?" a customer said to Ma. The woman held up the paper, laughing. "Your daughter has been consorting with the great wide world without telling you. What goes through that child's mind?"

Ma stopped in the middle of the restaurant, her lean arms full of dirty plates, her blue polyester waitress uniform speckled with cream gravy, her long braid of brown-black hair bobbing as she ducked her head and stared at my picture in the state's biggest newspaper. She read the words below it, mouthing them silently.

Life is sweet for "Sweet Hush" McGillen and her roadside apple business. Ma looked stunned.

"I'm up shit creek," I whispered. Smooch moaned.

Davy put an arm around me. "I'll kick anybody's ass who calls you 'sweet.' "

I leaned into the warm crook of his arm and peered harder out the kitchen door, watching Ma. Slowly she lifted her chin. Gravy dripped off a dirty plate onto her stained white tennis shoes. She stared at the grinning neighbors looking up at her from their tables, dressed in their Sunday clothes, able to afford a fancy fried-chicken lunch after church. "I'm not blind," she said loudly. "I see that I got me a daughter who knows how to sell apples. She's Hush McGillen the Fifth all right, and she's earnin' the name. Y'all will sure see, too — the Sweet Hush apple ain't done for in this county. I am flat sure that one day my Hush will prove it." Ma paused. "Now, 'scuse me, I have to yank her up by the hair and yell at her."

Everyone laughed and applauded. I burned. They thought I was a joke. That's when I knew I'd become somebody just to spite everybody else. They'd have to take me seriously.

Ma and I sat at the farmhouse that afternoon with a framed snapshot of Daddy on the old wooden table between us and the amazing newspaper picture beside it. She bounced Logan on her lap. She didn't really look angry, just bewildered by my ideas. The first hint of redemption began to spread over my chest like the warm menthol salve Mama rubbed on me whenever I had a cold. I burrowed my head on her shoulder. She smelled like breast milk and apples and Marlboros. "I know I'm a strange bird," I said. "Everybody says so."

"Well, well," Ma said. "Well."

She smoked a cigarette and pulled up her T-shirt so Logan could suck at her right nipple. She looked from Daddy's picture to the newspaper clipping to me, connecting us by line of sight as if asking him what kind of McGillen charm he'd bred inside her twelve years ago. She was only twenty-six years old, with dark,

SWEET HUSH

tired eyes. You could see the Cherokee in her high cheekbones and strong mouth. She cursed when she thought I didn't hear, drank beer when she thought I was asleep at night, whipped me or pinched me purple on the back of the arm when I needed punishing. She sang solos at the tiny clapboard Gospel Church of the Harvest in Song, prayed like a preacher but worked like a dog to keep food on the table. She was mourning Daddy, and she was scared.

"Yesterday, while you were at work," I told her carefully, gauging her reaction, "I made another forty-two dollars selling apples up at the road." I pulled that secret stash from my jeans and laid the bills and coins on the table. Ma's mouth opened, then shut.

Tears slid down her face. "I don't want my children to have to grub for a living. I want to provide for you-all decently."

"I'm not grubbin'." I swallowed hard and leaned close to her. "Ma, I have to tell you something. I'm meant to sell apples. I can do it. I know I can. Because . . . I've got *sugar skin*."

Sugar skin. Most people said sugar skin was only a tall tale McGillens had concocted in the glory years to gild their own legends a little more. But old folks in my family claimed sugar skin was real magic and that all the Hush McGillens so far had been endowed with it. Mama sucked in a deep breath. "Have you tested yourself?"

"Yessim. More than once. I didn't want to scare you, so I didn't tell."

"Oh, my lord. You coulda been stung to death."

I nodded. There was only one way to know if a person had sugar skin. You went outdoors in the fall, when the bees and the yellow jacket wasps were swarming, looking for trouble with their red-hot stingers full of poison, and you found one of their nests in the ground, and you walked over to it.

And then you held your hand down to them.

"They lit all over me, Ma," I whispered. "I bet I had a hundred on me. But not one stung me. They . . . licked my skin, Ma. They really did. I've got sugar skin."

25

"Oh, my lord," Ma said again.

"Ma, I'm gonna set up an apple stand *every* weekend, and I'm gonna make us rich, and I'm gonna go to college to learn how to sell even more apples, and nobody's ever gonna laugh at us again."

"You promise me. College. You promise." Mama had quit school in the eighth grade. She'd married Daddy when she was fourteen and he was thirty. I was born six months after the wedding. She had kinder dreams for me, and for Logan. College dreams. "College," she repeated.

"I promise. I swear on Daddy's spirit." I clutched his picture to my chest.

She hugged me, hard. We both cried. She pushed me back and looked at me fiercely. "I don't doubt you've got the magic, the sugar skin. And I don't doubt you can sell apples. But I also don't doubt wasps and bees ain't the only creatures who know you're as sweet as an apple. *You keep that damned Davy Thackery at arm's length or he'll take it all away from you.*" She shook me a little. "*Promise* me."

I looked at her in confusion. "But Davy's good to me, and he wants to take care of me—" The harsh disbelief on Mama's face stopped me. "I promise," I said.

I really believed I wouldn't break that vow.

And that she'd live to see me prove it.

She didn't. A mother can only protect you so much before she leaves you to protect yourself.

TWO

The week before my sixteenth birthday, Mama died of an infection from a ruptured appendix. I remember sitting under the original Sweet Hush apple tree on the icy winter night after her death, just sitting there in the dark with a blanket around me, one arm hugging Logan and the other hugging the old tree as if she had become our mother surrogate. I cried to that old tree, I talked to that old tree, and I began to believe, in that pit of desperate loneliness, that she — I called her the Great Lady — listened and answered.

Hold on to the earth, Hush. Hold on tight to me and sink your own roots alongside mine.

I will, and I'll never let go.

Forces beyond all my circle of experience began to crowd in on me. I found myself sitting in the small, pine-paneled courtroom of the Chocinaw County Courthouse while lawyers debated my and my brother's future and the future of the farm in Sweet Hush Hollow.

"Your Honor, there is simply no way a child of Hush's tender years can maintain proper control of a large orchard and a home with amenities," lawyer Mac Crawford intoned, leading the cause for a cousin Daddy had loathed. *Aaron McGillen is a greedy son of a bitch*, I heard my father say many times.

"Now, Mr. Aaron McGillen is a well-known merchant with a stake in the Pancake Diner franchise over on the new interstate, and he's prepared to buy the entire Sweet Hush Hollow from his late cousin's estate at a fair market value that will give young Miss Hush and her poor little orphaned brother a nice amount of money to live on."

My attorney, the ancient and cheap Fred Carlisle, who drank bourbon in his office near the courthouse and wore a bad red hairpiece to hide a dent in the top of his graying head, stood with arthritic melodrama. "Yo' Honor," he drawled, "Aaron McGillen cheats his own waitresses out of their flapjack tips."

The audience of McGillens and McGillen relatives nodded solemnly. I had a lot of support among my extended family. But the judge grunted, unimpressed, and I stiffened even more at the defendant's table. Mr. Carlisle's mentholated and bourboned scent nearly gagged me. Sweat slid down my small breasts, and the discount-store blazer and dress I'd bought itched on my skin. Behind me on a front pew, Logan wiggled between Smooch and Davy. My chubby, good-natured little brother whispered loudly, as any bored five-year-old would do, "Hush? Come on! Hush! Let's go *home*." Finally I turned around and whispered, "Bubba Logan, I'm doing the best I can to get us back home and keep us there, just like Mama and Daddy would want." That made several of my female relatives cry.

Judge Redman, a red-faced, portly old man who smoked filter-tip cigarillos during the proceedings, waved old Mr. Carlisle aside and pointed at me. "Miss McGillen, I would be a fool to let a sixteen-year-old girl keep control of that Hollow, now wouldn't I?"

I stood. Resting my clammy hands atop a small briefcase I'd bartered for at the Dalyrimple Flea Market, I said very clearly, "Yes, Your Honor, you'd be a fool to do that, if I was an ordinary sixteen-year-old girl. But since I'm not ordinary, you'd be a fool not to."

People gasped. His eyes narrowed. He smoked his cigarillo until the ash tip dropped on his desk. "Tell me how you're gonna ease my fool mind, Miss McGillen."

I opened my briefcase, turned it to face him, and dumped the contents on the table. Bundles of twenty-dollar bills fell out. Stock certificates fluttered against Mr. Carlisle's suspiciously mentholated water glass. Government bonds tumbled atop the pile. "Here are my assets, Your Honor. Earned from selling apples by the road over the last four years. My mother wouldn't take much of my earnings. She insisted I save the majority. So, I did." I pointed to various piles. "Cash. Stocks. Bonds. A total of five thousand, two hundred eighty-five dollars and twenty-seven cents in value, based on the closing market prices as reported in yesterday's *Atlanta Journal* newspaper, Your Honor."

The courtroom came alive with whispers. The judge rapped his gavel. "Miss McGillen, you are plain amazing. Everybody says so. I don't disagree. But you've got to get an education and care for your baby bubba here. Your mama wanted you to go to college. How you gonna sell apples and do all that?"

"I'm graduating a year early from high school. I have a scholarship from the League of Farm Women and another one from the Kiwanis. Enough money to get me through my freshman year commuting over to North Georgia College. Smooch and Davy Thackery's grandmother has agreed to baby-sit my brother while I attend class. And I'll be able to work full time at the farm, too."

Mac Crawford snorted. "This girl is well intended, Your Honor, and nobody doubts she's an outstanding young citizen. But it's just not sensible, Your Honor, to let her retain control of two hundred valuable acres of orchards. Why, that Hollow is a sacred place to the McGillen family. It ought to be in the care of a grown male McGillen who—"

"Who cheats his waitresses out of flapjack money!" Mr. Carlisle repeated. Everyone laughed. My heart sank.

The judge leaned on an elbow and eyed Mac Crawford. "Tell me, Mr. Crawford, have *you* ever managed to save five thousand dollars?"

"Your Honor, that's beside the point—"

"No, I'd say it's pretty much right smack *on* the point. How about you, Mr. McGillen? Can *you* produce that much cash and stock right now?" The judge pointed at Aaron, who sat on a front pew, skinny and stern, dressed in a nice suit. I had marked his name in a ledger I kept. He would never set foot in the Hollow again, if I could help it.

Aaron shifted uneasily. "I have investments, Your Honor. Not a lot of cash flow, but quite a nice income."

The judge smiled. "Maybe I should call your waitresses up to testify about your management techniques."

People guffawed. Mr. Carlisle said, "Here, here, I told you so!"

"This is a joke, isn't it?" Aaron said stiffly. "Nobody but an ignoramus would leave the Hollow in the hands of a sixteen-year-old girl with not even a farmhand to help her pick the apples."

"You callin' me an ignoramus?" the judge asked.

"Oh, no, no, Your Honor! But poor young Hush doesn't have any reliable help—"

"That's a damn lie! I'm her help!" Davy said loudly. He leapt up like a soldier coming to attention. I twisted in my seat to stare at him. Seventeen and six-foot-two, lean as a post in jeans and leather, he had long-lashed eyes and dark, luxurious Thackery hair, plus a glorious brand of rowdy charm but hopeless bullshit. He made a serious show of straightening the half-assed tie he wore with a plaid shirt beneath his leather jacket. "I'm a grown man," Davy announced. "And I'm damned sure serious about apple farming."

Most of my relatives rolled their eyes. The rest of the audience laughed outright. Even the judge couldn't repress a smile. "Mr. Thackery, I know you way too well. Words are cheap, Son, and you dole 'em out by the bushel."

Davy went very still. Usually he seemed to swagger even when not moving, but not that time. He looked Judge Redman straight in the eye — calmly, beseeching, promising. God help me, a trill of excitement and adoration went through me. At that moment I believed in him, and I fell in love just enough to set my fate. "Your Honor," he said in a quiet, manly drawl, "I swear to you on my soul, I'll work my fingers to the bone for Hush McGillen. I'll never turn away from her, and I'll never betray her trust, and I'll be there every time she needs me. I know I've got a lot to prove, and I'll prove it, for her sake. Just please, Your Honor, let her keep the Hollow. She'll die without it. And if she dies, so will I."

Goosebumps went up my spine and tears came to my eyes. I brushed them away. Smooch gaped up at her brother as if aliens had replaced him with a sentimental stranger. The whole courtroom sat stone-silent, awed.

A long ash smoldered and fell from Judge Redman's cigarillo. He laid it in an ashtray, steepled his hands to his lips, and spoke between his fingers. "Miss Hush, my reputation for not bein' a fool or an ignoramus is ridin' on your shoulders. Don't you and your helper here do anything to *ruin* that reputation, or we'll be right back here again. You understand?"

I stood, breathless with hope. "Yes, Your Honor."

"All right, then." He scowled at Aaron McGillen, nodded to the assembled McGillen audience, then raised his head for a proper oratorical moment. "Control of the Sweet Hush Hollow property is hereby left to Miss Hush McGillen!" He rapped his gavel.

The crowd applauded.

I turned around and looked up into Davy's gleaming eyes. He blushed, frowned, and restored his everyday persona with a shrug. "How's that for shovelin' some deep shit?" he whispered. I reached up and touched his cheek, making him blink and suck in a startled breath.

At that moment, I was sure he loved me with all the faith and honor in the world.

NO ONE SERIOUSLY BELIEVED I'd keep the farm. I was so sunk in grief and worry I barely looked up — but every time I did, Davy was there. A charmer, a bullshit artist of the old school, driving too fast and cheating his luck. Most men, women, and children couldn't help but grin back at him. At the racetrack, he was already an idol. Hard-toothed, big-haired women wore his number — 52 — on their sequined T-shirts. Men placed bets on him to win. Girls flirted with him endlessly. I knew about them. He said they were just his fans. I believed him.

But he worked alongside me in the orchards harder than he'd ever worked before in his life or would ever work again, although in his spare time he howled at the moon and tried to charm me into howling with him. "I don't like the racetrack," I said bluntly. "I'd rather read a book."

"Aw, hell, Beautiful," he drawled with just the slightest sinister hint of unhappiness in his eyes, "reading won't win you the jackpot."

"Not just reading. Education. Education will make me more money than all the jackpots in the world. Being smart pays off."

"You're already smarter than any other girl in the world. And prettier."

He had a way with words.

But not with me. Not yet. I couldn't risk getting tangled in the sheets with him.

Not yet.

"I'D BE A FOOL to give a sixteen-year-old girl a construction loan," the bank president said. He was a newcomer to Dalyrimple and didn't know a thing about McGillens in general or me in particular. A big Atlanta bank had bought out the Farmers Bank of Chocinaw County that year.

I replied with my best line. It had worked before. "Sir, I'm no ordinary girl, and the Sweet Hush is no ordinary apple, so you'd be a fool *not* to give me a loan."

He gaped at me. "Just exactly *what* do you want to build?"

"A little apple barn up in the front of the Hollow where people driving by can see it. With a kitchen for making baked apple goods, and a graveled parking lot." I paused. "And I want a big Sweet Hush Farms sign by the entrance. Smooch Thackery is going to design it, but I'll need a professional sign man to make it." Another pause. "And I'll put another sign over where people turn off the interstate. My mother's cousin owns a strip of land along that road, and he's given me permission to set a sign there."

"A sign asking people from Atlanta to drive ten miles over Chocinaw Mountain just to buy apples?" The banker shook his head.

"No, Sir. Not to buy apples. To buy Sweet Hush magic." I went off on a long, rambling explanation of nostalgia and heritage and the Hollow and dead soldiers while he sat there, smiling ignorantly.

When I finished he said, "I'm sorry, but I need proof that your business plan will work, Miss McGillen, and you have none."

I stood up, set a basket of Sweet Hushes on his desk, and said, "Then I'll get you some."

I STOOD AMONG the apple trees in the full fruit of determination — theirs and mine. Smooch watched in horror from fifty feet away, but Davy, white-faced and balancing a video camera on one shoulder, stood only a few yards from me. He'd *borrowed* the camera from the so-called media department at Chocinaw County High. With a flick of one finger, he turned on its scalding white light. "Let 'em rip," he said.

I clutched a microphone in my right hand. Beads of sweat ran down my face and stained the armpits of my red-checkered shirt. I smiled. "Come to Sweet Hush Farms," I intoned, "and see why Sweet Hush apples are so good they charm the bees." I'd decided there was no point in trying to explain that yellow jackets were not bees, but wasps. *Bees* was a good, generic advertising word.

With my right foot out of camera range, I toed the lid off a five-gallon tin can. Hundreds of furious yellow jackets swarmed out. Within seconds they covered my sleeves, my hair, my face. I barely breathed. "Let me tell you all about the McGillens of Chocinaw County and their Sweet Hush apples," I went on finally, gazing at the camera as yellow jackets crept around my eyebrows. "And let me tell you all why you'll love visiting me and my bees, and why you'll take home bushels of the best southern apples bees ever kissed."

I rambled on, covered in wasps. I had learned to see them as purposeful trouble — the thorns around the rose, the poison that went with the sweetest fruit unless you held your breath just right when you reached for a taste — another of life's prices to pay for a good harvest in apples or matters of the heart. There were always hurts that stung so badly I thought I'd die. Mama. Daddy. Logan calling for Mama when I was the only one there. Too much pride. Too much responsibility. Loving Davy Thackery so much I couldn't think straight around him. But I kept on living.

We took the videotape down to all the Atlanta TV stations and left copies — along with a florid press release written by Smooch. And then we waited.

It worked.

I was interviewed by two news crews. Clips of me covered in yellow jacket *bees* were shown on the Atlanta TV stations. "Hush McGillen and Her Hypnotized Bees" were famous.

That weekend I sold five hundred bushels of apples to Atlanta visitors and took orders to ship nearly four hundred more.

And I got my bank loan.

"I'd be a fool not to do business with TV's Bee Girl," the banker said solemnly.

"Thank you. And by the way, Sir, when I make my first million dollars, I'll give it to you to handle. But only on one condition."

He could only shake his head and smile. "What, pray tell?"

"That you use it as seed money to start the Farmers Bank of Chocinaw County again. Because money grows money, and I want to keep all the seeds right here where they have the best chance of helping people I care about."

After a moment spent just studying me, the man nodded. "I do believe I'd be a fool not to agree."

And we shook on it.

DAVY AND I WERE pruning dead branches in the orchard that winter when he fell off an icy ladder and knocked himself out. When he came to, I pressed my fingers to the bloody cut on the back of his head. "How much beer did you drink before you came here?" I demanded.

He laughed. "Not enough to make me bounce, dammit."

I guided him to the house, letting my guard down, breaking another of the rules I'd sworn to Mama I'd keep: *Never let Davy Thackery get you alone indoors.* Smooch had taken Logan to her grandmother's for the afternoon. The weather that day was cool and rainy and ripe, smelling of an early spring when animals would begin to breed and the bees to seek the eager, damp blooms of my trees. I was well aware that Mother Nature encouraged mating and survival above all else. "Open a window and let me smell some of that fresh rain to get my wits back," Davy groaned dramatically as he stretched out atop the old quilts of my parents' creaking double bed.

I flung the window open and let cold air rush over me like protection. "Don't bleed on my mama's good pillow." I tucked a towel under his head, then sat on the edge of the bed and studied him with more sympathy than I'd admit. He was dirty, damp, and bedraggled, like me. "Got any beer?" he asked.

"No."

"Mind if I smoke me a joint?"

"Yes."

He groaned. "Then I'll just have to lie here in the most terrible pain and hope your sweetness eases the misery."

"I doubt it." But I tenderly wiped his hands and face with a warm, damp washcloth. He grew quiet and watched me through slitted eyes. "You're too good to me," he whispered. "I mean it."

"Because I'll never be able to pay back all you've done to help me."

"I don't need any pay." A lie if I ever heard one, but effective. He clasped my hands at the wrists, smoothed his fingers down my palms, and held my hands atop his chest. I shivered. Everything seemed gray and miserable except the heat of his hands. He gently tugged me toward him. "Poor sweet Hush. Tired. Cold. Worried. Com'ere. Just put your head on my shoulder and I'll put my arms around you. That's all. I swear it."

I knew better, but I was so alone, except for him, and he was so warm. I leaned over, still sitting on the edge of the bed, and rested my head in the cusp of his hard, lean shoulder. He had the strongest arms. When he held me up close to his chest and flipped one side of the bed quilt over the two of us I couldn't help sighing at the cocoon of solid comfort the quilt made in league with his hug. When he stroked my hair and my back through my shirt, it felt too good to complain. When he slid his fingertips under the waistband of my dirty jeans and caressed the soft skin near my navel, I began to grow damp and warm and relaxed.

"I love you," I whispered.

"I love you more," he whispered back.

And I was lost.

A few hours later, with him asleep among splotches of semen and blood on the white cotton sheets my mother and father had shared, I dressed and staggered out of the bedroom in the cold twilight. I made my way downstairs on womanly legs, fixed a pot of coffee, and sat on the edge of the back porch clutching an old ceramic mug so hot it burned my fingertips. The gray winter mountains faded behind silver mists and deep, blue-purple shadows. The orchards made a melting watercolor of naked gray trees. I shook until my teeth chattered.

I was a smart girl; I told myself I wouldn't make any mistakes. In the fall, I'd start college. Davy, who had barely finished high school, would keep working for me. I'd keep sleeping with him. I loved him, and he loved me. I did like going to bed with him. He made me forget every fear, every worry, every chore.

I goaded him into using condoms. I was also strict about attempting to calculate the fertile days of my cycles. I would have sex with him only at certain times of the month. He laughed and said I had crazy mountain ways, but in fact I'd driven the farm's old pickup truck down to a big bookstore in Atlanta and bought some kind of feminist-earth-mother book on natural birth control, which was all I could afford as a backup for the condoms. I douched with herbal concoctions and parceled out my nonovulating days to Davy as best I could figure them.

But Davy was potent, and I was careless in love.

That spring, when I realized I was pregnant, I sank to my knees under the branches of the Great Lady and shook my fists at her. "Why? Why give me more responsibility to handle? What did I do to deserve this punishment? I give you everything, but you give back nothing but *another* baby to raise! I've already got my brother to take care of! I don't need or want another youngun'."

I cursed my own unborn child, sat thinking about ways to pay for an abortion, then dully admitted I didn't have the courage to risk the hellfire preached by every mountain minister who'd ever pointed a finger at evil women. But I'd already thought the thought and wished it. I raised my face to the apple tree and the blue spring mountains. "So kill me and send me straight to hell!" Nothing happened. No lightning bolt struck me, no rush of wind indicated the hot breath of unhappy angels, nothing. I stretched out on the grassy spring earth and beat the dirt and sobbed.

Davy found me there. White-faced but clueless, he crouched beside me. "What's wrong, Hon, what's wrong?" I sat up, wiping tears and dirt from my face, going as cold as the spring ground. "I've let you knock me up, that's what."

I'll never forget the look that came on his face — hopeful, scared, but then excited, as if I'd promised him a faster car or a six-pack. "We're gonna have a kid!" He tried to pull me to him. "*You're gonna have my baby!*"

"I'll lose the farm over this. Judge Redman will take it away from me. He'll say I'm irresponsible. And he'll be right."

"No. I'll marry you! Don't you understand? I love you! You love me! It's okay!"

That was true, but it was dull comfort that day. I finally let him pull me close and held on to him desperately. How could I love him but be so miserable? "You're happy to have our baby. Admit it," he urged. "You're really happy."

"Yes. Yes, I am."

I hugged him but felt nothing growing inside my belly except that lie. *Say good-bye to college.* I put my face against his shoulder and moaned. I'd spend the rest of my teens sitting at the kitchen table like my own mama, young but worn out, with a baby nursing at my breast and no place to go but outdoors to pick apples.

The old tree spoke to me.

Even the finest fruit isn't always easy to bear.

I SCHEDULED MY MARRIAGE to Euell Davis Thackery at the county courthouse on a cold spring Monday without inviting anyone except Smooch, two old-lady McGillen cousins who thought I could do no wrong, and Davy's kind, half-crazy great-uncle Henry Thackery, a World War II veteran with scars, inside and out. Smooch was thrilled to serve as my maid of honor. "Oh, you and me will be sisters now!" she cried. "I won't feel so alone in the world!"

Davy wore a new blue suit, smiled constantly, told everyone he was about to burst with excitement, but watched me with a worried look in his eyes. I think he already suspected I was sorry to be there. He just didn't want to admit it, yet.

I put on a white skirt and stern white blazer and insisted I was happy, too, at least in public. We went to Judge Redman's chambers for the ceremony. He shooed Davy out and shut the door.

"Have you lost your mind, Miss Hush? He's ten cents' worth of value in a two-dollar bag. He's puttin' on a mighty good show of respectability for you, and I don't doubt he'd walk over hot coals for you, but I wouldn't place any bets on his long-term prospects. I can only surmise that you don't mind that he smokes dope and guzzles beer and sneaks over to the dirt track to fight with no-accounts and race old beat-up jalopies?" The judge paused. "And dare I mention," he finished gently, "that he is a good-looking boy who never tries very hard to look the other way when girls look back?"

I hid my trembling hands behind a homemade bouquet of bright yellow jonquils. Jonquils bloomed even with frost on their petals. So would I. "People like to gossip, and he *is* the best-looking boy in the county, and that naturally makes people envious —"

"Hush, you only have one rotten apple in your personal barrel, and he's it."

"He's always there to help me and always has been. There's nothing rotten about that."

"Will he support you while you go to college?"

"I've decided to put college off a year or two. Concentrate on the farm."

He squinted at me. "Miss Hush, I have two granddaughters your age; thus I'm not a complete dunce when it comes to the evasive answers and dumb shenanigans of the current generation. So just let me put this bluntly: Are you carrying Davy Thackery's apple pie in your oven?"

I sagged. "Yes, I am, Your Honor."

"Oh, my lord." He bowed his head as if in sorrowful prayer, then sighed and wiggled bushy white brows angrily. "I should've made staying away from Davy Thackery a condition of your keeping the farm."

"No, Your Honor. I chose him, and that's that. He'll do right by me, and I'll do right by him."

"Hush, you can't make an honest man out of Davy Thackery just by marrying him."

"I'm marrying him because I love him. And I'm no fool. Yes, he's *the father of my baby*. I realize that girls are having babies without getting married these days. Free love and all that. But I'm not playing by those rules. I'll do what's right for my good name. So. Me marrying Davy ought to take care of any questions about my sense of responsibility and my ability to manage the farm like a grown woman." I said no more and waited stiffly, terrified he'd argue some more. Everything he'd already said about Davy swarmed in the back of my mind like angry bees I couldn't tame.

He sighed. "I'm not gonna take the farm away from you, Miss Hush. You're gonna have enough troubles without me addin' to them. Pride is your downfall, I fear."

"Thank you," I whispered.

He shook his head. "Nothing to be thankful for."

Fifteen minutes later, thankful or not, I married Davy.

I WAS FIVE MONTHS' PREGNANT that August, starting to look as if I'd swallowed a bowling ball, and sucking on Sweet Hush apple slices soaked in saltwater to fight morning sickness that lasted about twenty-four hours a day. I sweated through that summer in cheap T-shirts and baggy shorts I bought at the Chocinaw County Flea Market and Movie Drive-In. Most everything and everybody in Chocinaw County served at least two purposes, out of necessity and practical mountain ideals. The old drive-in the-ater showed movies every Friday night, mostly Disney films, since everything else broadcast curse words or sex scenes too far for public decency outdoors. But on the weekends, the owner rented ten-dollar flea-market booths — meaning you got a pair of folding tables in a space that fit inside a parking spot. I hung my SWEET HUSH FARMS sign on a speaker post, then sold apple jam and apple baked goods. I also bartered those apple products for baby clothes and a crib. The whole county knew I was pregnant by then.

But people didn't know Davy had a girlfriend.

I cornered her behind the drive-in's concrete block concession stand one Sunday evening when nearly everyone else had already packed up their flea-market wares and gone home. I tracked her and the scent of her fake designer perfume like a coon dog as she sashayed along in the hot dusk filtered by a yellow security light. Moths and small bats swirled above us, dipping so low I swore a bat or two aimed for her Farrah Fawcett haircut. Farrah was falling from favor in Hollywood by then, but her hairstyle would live on in Chocinaw County for years to come.

"Turn around," I called in a quiet voice. The girlfriend had an armload of stuffed paper bags. She'd been shopping for fake designer jeans — even tighter than the ones that made her butt move like two balloons about to pop. She swung about, surprised to find anyone there. "Oh, my gawd," she said.

"God isn't here. Just me and the wrath of married women everywhere." I raised a service revolver my father had carried in Korea, and I put the tip of the barrel right between her eyes. "Oh, my gawd," she said again, and began backing up, clutching her packages and making soft shrieks under her breath. I followed her, keeping the tip of the gun to her skull so hard I could see the indentation on her skin.

"Shut up," I ordered, and to my impressed pride, she did. I kept the gun in place as she flattened herself along the concession stand's back wall between a discarded DRINK COCA-COLA sign and a fifty-gallon oil drum filled with half-burned garbage. "Please don't kill me, please, don't," she mewled.

"Stay away from my husband. If anybody asks, you never fooled around with him. He never so much as looked cross-eyed at you. Hear me?"

"Please, don't kill me —"

"You touch him again, and people won't even find your body. Not even pieces of it. I'll gut you with a ten-inch blade I use to carve apple wood and feed your carcass to Tom Willis's hogs over on Castleberry Road. Those hogs'll squeal your name when they're slaughtered."

Her knees went weak, and she sagged. "I swear, I won't ever again, oh my gawd, don't, don't —"

"Good. I've got your word. Now, beat it." I lowered the gun, and she ran. As I watched her scramble into a little pickup truck with pink vinyl seat liners, I tucked the gun back inside an old burlap sack filled with trustworthy jars of apple preserves. My hand shook a little, and a wave of nausea rolled up my throat. I quickly plucked a wet, salt-soaked apple slice from a jar I kept in the top of the bag. I sucked hard on it, and felt better.

That night, when Davy came home from a trip to North Carolina — where he and some cronies raced motorcycles occasionally — he found me standing in the rutted driveway at the farm. He owned a jazzed-up, rust-red Impala sedan for dirt-track events. It was the fastest car in four counties. I had parked the Impala in the farm road, surrounded it with bales of hay, and doused the hay with gasoline. I waited there in the headlights of his truck, my face swollen from crying but stiff with pride. I held the gas can in one hand and a cigarette lighter in the other.

He got out of his truck. "What in the hell?"

"I know about your girlfriend."

Davy sagged. In that first, quicksilver moment, I saw how much grief he'd caused himself — how much he knew it. He couldn't do more than stand there with his hands out in supplication. "She doesn't matter. I don't give a damn about her."

"Then why did you break our vows?"

"Because you don't want my baby."

"Don't you dare twist this —"

"You think you can pretend? You think I don't see how unhappy you've been since the day you told me you were pregnant? I thought you'd get over it, but you haven't! You think I don't know you only married me so people wouldn't talk?" He was yelling by then, and crying. "Do you know how low that makes me feel?"

"I love you! But I can't help it if I don't want a baby this soon! And I can't help it if I don't want to be married this young!"

"You can't really love me and feel that way!"

"Yes, I can! I have to do what's best for this land and these apples!"

"That's it. That's the problem. You love these goddamned apples more than you love me!"

"Yes, I do!"

We both froze. I bit my tongue. Those words changed our marriage forever. Changed me. Changed him, changed us. In that instant, I broke his heart as much as he'd broken mine.

I dropped the gasoline can and the lighter, walked to the house, and locked the front door behind me. I cried at night for weeks, but never let Davy know. He slept in the barn until September, when I needed him to help with the harvest.

"I'll never touch another girl," he promised. "I apologize."

"I accept." We were cool and formal with each other. I didn't believe him, and I was right not to, but I needed his help to pick the season's apples.

And we had a child still waiting to come.

THREE

Because I lied about my due date to hide the fact I was two months' pregnant on my wedding day, I was alone on the rain-soaked November night when our son was born. Smooch knew the truth about my date and kept Logan for me that week, though she was scared to death. Davy knew it was my time, too, but couldn't resist heading to the dirt track that day towing the Impala. "They're running the Mudcat Five Relay," he told me. "I stand a chance to win big — two, maybe three hundred bucks. We need that money. I figure I'll bring home the jackpot and buy a go-cart. You watch — our kid'll be racing go-carts before he's able to walk."

"What if he's a girl?"

Davy snorted. "Girls can race, too. Hell, she'll be the first girl on the NASCAR circuit. The first woman to win the Daytona 500, if I get my way about it."

You won't, I said to myself, but dropped the subject. I'd never ask him to stay with me because I was afraid the baby was coming. I never admitted fear or need to Davy. I tried not to notice my giant stomach or think about the baby inside it. Boy or girl, I only wanted it out of my body so I could get back to business. "We have two acres of late-season apples left to pick. I've got a wholesaler who'll take them all if we can get the crates filled by next week. Apples are money in the bank. We have bills to pay. Stay home. Pick apples."

"Apples can wait. Life's too fast for apples."

"I said *stay home and work*. I mean it."

"I'm just a hired hand to you, right?" His voice rose. "That's the only reason you let me lay a hand on you. To get more apples picked."

"If you'd picked more apples and kept your hands off me, we wouldn't have a baby coming that we can't afford. Having a baby before we're even eighteen years old and able to make ends meet."

His blue eyes went to ice. "I've been *making ends meet* since the day my old man died and my bitch of a mother left me and Smooch to fend for ourselves. You had it a lot better than me, so don't complain. And you *let* me put my hands on you. I didn't make you. Just say so: I'm not smart enough or fancy enough to be the daddy of Hush McGillen's baby. Go ahead and say it. You don't love me and you wish you'd had an abortion. Say so."

"Don't tell me what to do. Get out of this house. I'm through talking to you. I intend to educate myself and think fine thoughts and learn about the world — even if I *never* get to live anywhere but this wild old ghost-dappled Hollow. And I intend to have money in the bank and nice things around me and the respect of this whole county — no, the whole state — for me and every McGillen who's too poor to piss right now. Just like the old days. And I'll do it with or without your help — and even with my brother, Logan, to raise and my own squalling baby dragging me down."

"See there, goddammit? You don't care about my kid any more than my goddamned mama cared about me and Smooch."

"Don't you talk to me like a redneck. I'm a McGillen, not a truck-stop whore. I'm *having* this baby, aren't I? I could've got-

45

ten rid of it, but I didn't." I gestured fiercely at myself. "I do the right thing! I have honor!"

"Bullshit! Only because you're too scared of what people might *think*."

"What people think is more important than the truth! I'm a McGillen! I have a reputation to hold up!"

"God didn't create McGillens second to Adam himself, no matter what the hell you say! You're poorer than any Thackery and swollen up like a cow. You've got a loan to pay off and we haven't even started building the apple shop or whatever-the-hell-you-call-it—and who's gonna supervise *that*, while you're laid up with our baby? *Me*. I'm the one who'll take care of you now and always." He thumped his chest. "Me. Euell Davis *Thackery*. And I expect some respect!"

"You'll take care of me? No, you'll take care of your six-pack and your bong pipe and your cars. *And your girlfriends*. I'll take care of *myself*." I turned and began to walk away. We were in the farmhouse's ramshackle kitchen at the time, a room not even an old stone fireplace could keep warm. I reached the door to the drafty back hall when Davy yelled, "At least I can scare the shit out of you," then grabbed a pair of cheap gas-station glasses off the dish rack, and threw one right after the other. The first glass cracked on the fireplace rocks and sprayed me with sharp chunks. I screamed and threw up both hands. The second shattered on the door's hard oak frame, and a sliver of glass caught me just below the right eye.

It was as if he'd cut me with a razor. I pressed a hand to my face. Blood streamed down my cheek. I turned toward him—pregnant, bloody, trembling.

"Oh, God," Davy said, and bounded toward me. "Hush, Hon, oh, God, I didn't mean to—"

"Get out of my house. Get out. And don't call on God. He doesn't listen."

"You're hurt. Let me—"

"Get out or I swear I'll kill you with my bare hands. Nobody treats me this way. Nobody — not you or anybody else — threatens Hush McGillen."

His face went stark white and stony. "Hush Thackery," he corrected in a low voice.

"Only on the marriage license. Get out."

I went upstairs and shut myself in a bedroom. He shouted hoarsely, "You're gonna believe in me someday!" and slammed the front door behind him. The farmhouse shook. It was rundown, and I had no money for repairs. The floor joists sagged with termites, the doors hung crooked on settling joints, the roof leaked. I lay on the bed for an hour, holding a washcloth to the nasty gash below my eye and rubbing my enormous stomach. I stared bitterly at a water stain spreading across the slatted ceiling.

You can either lie here and bleed and wait for the place to fall down around you, or get up and pick apples.

I covered my wound with a rectangle of dime store gauze held in place by gray industrial duct tape, stuffed myself into a salvage-store army coat of Davy's and a big yellow rain slicker, tied my father's old slouch hat on my head with one of Mama's scarves, and waddled out into a gray day misting cold rain. Anger and sheer determination gave me energy. I drove the farm pickup truck through the orchards to the last area of unpicked fruit, parked under a tree, and hoisted myself into the truck bed. Standing there, I could reach most of the lower limbs.

By God, I began to pick apples.

Four hours later, the truck was nearly full. That was no small accomplishment, considering that the bed had five foot-high wooden sides. I stood on the tailgate, reaching and plucking and groaning with effort. A mountain of apples was piled nearly to my shoulder. Rain dripped from my hat brim. My slashed face throbbed and seeped watery blood from beneath the bandage. I was so tired I choked on my own bile. My back throbbed, my ankles were swollen, and a weight like an iron stew pot settled low in my belly.

When the labor pain hit, my knees buckled and I staggered backward into my apple pile. Cushioned by ripe Sweet Hushes, I lay there gasping and clutching my stomach. Fluid soaked the legs of my overalls. The pain subsided, and I crawled, shivering, from the bed of the truck. I staggered toward the driver door. I had one foot on the running board when another pain put me down on all fours. I crawled under the tailgate, out of the rain, and stretched out.

Two hours later, as darkness fell, I managed to sit up, unlatch the bib of my overalls, and shuck their soft blue denim down to my knees. Using a pocketknife, I sliced my white dime store panties at the sides and pulled them off. Then I propped myself against one of the truck's back tires, and, shivering in the cold, began to yell as the baby slid out of me.

"You will not destroy me! You will not!" I screamed at the top of my voice to some unknown fate, at the same time thrashing and clutching at the soggy earth. Darkness and rain covered me; my hair hung in soaking, tangled streamers around my face, and I began to sob as one last, great pain nearly tore me apart.

And then, it was over. I was empty, heaving for breath, half-fainting, but breathing only for myself, after nine months of double duty. I blinked and wiped rain from my eyes. Something wet and warm moved between my thighs. I hunched forward and reached down. My hands formed a shield around my baby's wet face and soft, vulnerable head. He mewled.

And in that moment, I was transformed. What was left of my girlhood and self-pitying misery fled before a rush of love and devotion. The dim light shadowed us both; he was as alone and as needy as me, and that made him mine. The end of a wet November day in a secluded hollow of the Appalachian mountains can convince a person there's no one else on earth. But I wasn't alone anymore; I had this astonishing little person, this fruit I had borne in my own orchards, on my own ground, beneath one of the great tree's children, like mine. From a random and imperfect match had come perfection, just like a Sweet Hush. I pulled the rain slicker over us as a tent, tied off his umbilical cord with a shoelace, then cut the cord in two with my pocketknife. I scooped my son into my arms and held him warmly.

"I do want you, and I do love you, and I'm so sorry I ever said otherwise," I sobbed. "And your life *will* be fine and rich and full of everything I missed out on. I promise you. *I promise you.*"

By the time Davy finally came home late that night, drunk, stoned, covered in mud, and waving two one-hundred-dollar bills, I was burrowed upstairs in bed on old sheets smeared with my blood, our son asleep on my breasts. "I told you, I told you I'd bring home the jackpot—" Davy began as he leapt into the room, drenched and dirty, slinging rust-colored rainwater. "I told you . . ."

His voice trailed off. He halted in the middle of the linoleum floor, staring at me across the shadowy space lit only by a small stone fireplace and a kerosene lamp on the bed table, because our electricity had been cut off earlier that week. The year 1979 was nearly upon us, but I had built my own heat and lit my own light. Men had gone to the moon more than once, computers were beginning to hum in the world, and we were entering the era of prosperous baby boomers dependent on Volvos and Bon Jovi albums. But I had borne my son without drugs, doctors, or a hospital, just as my pioneer ancestors had. A hard but proud occasion. I learned more about my own strength that night. And I knew what was real.

I looked at my husband as if I were some mother animal in its winter den—not trusting even the male who had seeded this cub inside me, very still, guarding my young. My face hurt almost as badly as the rest of me. Slowly Davy tiptoed to the bed, reached down with muddy fingers, and pulled the quilt aside a few inches. When he saw our son, he uttered a low sound of awe and sat down beside us as if his legs had given way. He touched his fingers to the baby's face. Tears slid down his muddy cheeks. "We got us a kid," he whispered. "I got me a boy."

No, he's mine. I brought him into the world all by myself, I almost said, but the tender look on Davy's face stopped me. I had important battles to fight for my child, and I was stuck with that child's father. Davy wanted his son. I could manage him, but I had to pick the battles very carefully. "We'll name this little boy after you," I said. "Davis Junior. But on one condition."

Davy went very still, his dark, drunken eyes boring into me. "Name it."

"You swear on the head of your son. You *swear*. That however you live your life — no matter what you do when you're away from this farm — he'll never have reason to be ashamed. He'll never hear anything but the best about you."

Anger and defense and disappointment rose in Davy's face, but he was no fool. He didn't argue. He knew his own weaknesses and my strengths. He sealed my expectations of him — and his expectations of himself. Davy laid a muddy hand on our son's head. "I swear it."

Then he bent his head to mine, and cried.

So did I.

"THE NEXT PHASE of Sweet Hush Farms' apple business is about to commence," I announced. It was a windy April day the next spring; the fertile air soothed and excited me. Logan and Smooch sat stoically on cheap lawn chairs, her a nervous, energetic little teenager, him a chunky six-year-old with rusty hair and green eyes, holding my handsome, cheerful baby, his nephew, Davis. Davy Senior was off at a dirt track somewhere. Four of my somber, polite McGillen and Thackery elders sat in their own lawn chairs. I lifted the silver pitcher and poured a ceremonial splash of apple cider on the pine siding of a small, barnlike building surrounded by a parking area of red clay and fresh granite gravel. The building was squat and simple; a metal vent marked the side where the small kitchen waited for apple pies and apple fritters and other manner of baked products to be made. The building's other end would be a market and gift shop, where apples and apple crafts would be sold. Dried apple granny dolls. Apple-wood thimbles. Apple-scented candles.

I explained my plans to my kind but worried-looking relatives, trying not to give up on fake calm and twist my hands the way Smooch was doing. I was young enough to be these people's daughter or even granddaughter. "I'm asking y'all to work for me," I blurted. "Part time at first, full time later. I've got no money for salaries this spring or summer, but if the harvest is good, next fall I'll catch you up with back pay and a bonus."

Silence. I was just seventeen years old. They needed real jobs, not promises of future paychecks. "I know it's a big chance to take this year, and I'll understand if y'all tell me you just can't—"

"Are you going to make us rich or just proud?" My gruncle Thackery stood. He was only in his late fifties then but squinted and leaned like an old man, bent more by his quirky mind than his years.

I blinked. "Pardon?"

"Rich or just proud?"

"Not rich, Gruncle. But well-off. And proud, yes, the way our families were in years past."

"Then I'll work for you. And so will these others."

As if they'd just been waiting for his signal, the rest stood and nodded. I put a hand to my heart in wonder. Sweet Hush Farms had its first commercial building and its first employees. I gathered Logan and Smooch to my side and held Davis in my arms but did not shed a single tear of joy. Not then. I let the hard, cold truth settle down deep inside me, where it lived its own sad life, without Davy's support. I bowed my head to my son's. *I'll make you and everyone else proud of your father and me no matter what. I'll give you what I wanted from him — all that love. But none of the pain.*

I kept that vow as long as I could.

God help me.

FOUR

Twenty-Three Years Later

On a cool September dawn, the first day of what should have been an ordinary fall apple season for Sweet Hush Farms, I knelt in the heart of my orchards, unaware that the next few minutes would change my plain, everyday worries into an extraordinary drama. We live most of our lives in those quiet times just before tragedy or victory upends everything we thought we knew about ourselves and the people and the places we love. Sweet Hush Hollow was still one of those places.

Davy had been dead for five years that autumn. And yes, I mourned him. But over time he'd done worse to me than even at the beginning, and the secrets I had to hide about our life together weighed me down. I had become the seasoned incarnation of the tough, ambitious girl who'd do anything to be somebody, who loved apples more than her own husband, and so I mourned Davy but couldn't swear I *missed* him.

We'd built Sweet Hush Farms together, people said, and that was true when I considered Davy's knack for showing up when I needed him — most of the time — and putting on a good display of hard work. Sad to say, but there had been people who wouldn't have done business with me in the early years without my husband in the mix. As Davy polished himself into some semblance of a businessman — even investing in a local truck dealership as long as the partners agreed to put his name on it — people assumed he actually managed the farm's accounts, thought up the new promotions, and supervised our employees. He didn't, and we both knew it.

For one thing, I'd sent Smooch to marketing classes down at a university in Atlanta, and she handled our promotions. I'd helped a McGillen cousin get training in accounting, and he handled the books for me. A Thackery cousin went to commercial cooking school on my nickel, and she managed the farms' kitchens. A Halfacre cousin, from my grandmother's family, taught himself all about the mail-order business, and set up our shipping department. And Davis, my own brilliant son, had early on proved himself a savvy little businessman and a computer programmer to boot. He'd designed an inventory tracking system that won awards.

As for me, I'd worked like a dog at every chore on the farm while getting a bachelor's degree in business over the years at night school. I drove an hour and a half through the mountains over to North Georgia College at Dahlonega, with Davis beside me. By the time he was ten years old, my son had sat through so many college classes that I awarded him a certificate: BACHELOR'S DEGREE IN WATCHING MOTHER LEARN.

"I like college," he proclaimed solemnly. "I'm going to Harvard someday."

He said that at only ten years old. And he meant it. And for the past five years, he'd done it. I was so proud. My son had not turned out like his father. He and Davy had shared little in common except a love of cars, thank God. No son and father had been closer over a hot engine or a rebuilt chassis.

And no son had ever been loved more. No matter what else I could say about the deteriorating state of my and Davy's marriage as the years passed, he never wavered as a kind and devoted father, and he never gave me any doubt that he worshiped the ground Davis walked on.

But he wouldn't let me forget that I hadn't wanted our son at first. That raw wound never healed. We hid it for Davis's sake, and the miracle was, he never suspected that we fought behind closed doors, that we often slept on opposite sides of our big bed, and that his father slipped further every year into a separate life at the racetracks and the bars and the casinos far from the Hollow. Because when Davy Thackery was at home, all anyone saw — including our own son — was a happy family.

When Davy died, I thought Davis would grieve himself into the grave with him. Nothing I did could help. Only one discipline kept Davis centered during that dark time: a curt but loving rule his father had hammered into him all his life.

Never let your mother down. She'll need you someday.

Davis hadn't glimpsed the pain or sarcasm in his father's words. And Davy, to his credit, had never said it to our son that way.

Now, bathed in long morning shadows that receded like soft fingers into the earth, I poured apple wine from my small silver pitcher onto the grandmotherly roots of the Great Lady tree. I steepled my forehead to one fist, and I prayed a private prayer for Davy's soul and my own. I prayed to keep our secrets from our son, and I prayed for forgiveness. Then I raised my head and opened my eyes. "Please, let this be the best season yet," I finished. An old ritual, a smaller prayer, a ceremony.

There was nothing prettily ceremonial about *me*, however. As owner, company president, and chief apple polisher of a family business that grossed two million dollars a year, I was dressed for hard work. My standard apple-season uniform consisted of jeans, a red pullover sweater embroidered over the left breast

55

with a small SWEET HUSH FARMS apple logo in white, and thick-soled hiking shoes. I would be on my feet eighteen hours a day for the next few months. On my red braided belt I carried a cell phone, a pocket calculator, and the keys to an old-fashioned iron safe I'd bought from the Bank of Chocinaw County at a charity auction. There are two kinds of business in a small southern town: One is personal. The other is more personal. My fellow merchants prospered. My neighbors prospered. My family prospered. And so did I.

In my hip pocket I carried a packet of herbal energy pills from the Mother Nature Health Food and Christian Gifts store in Dalyrimple. I'd turned forty the month before and had begun to take better care of myself. Give me enough ma huang extract and good percolator coffee, and I could get by on six hours' sleep every night until New Year's. Then I would lock down the whole farm and crawl into bed with the season's accounting records, a bottle of chardonnay, and a shiatsu massage pillow. I would tuck that undulating electric friend under the nape of my neck, beneath my lower back, and near places lonely young widows don't discuss in polite company. I would heal from the autumn strain, and I would begin to plan the next year. I was always planning the next year.

But, at the moment, two hundred acres of apple trees filled with ripe fruit waited for me like red-and-green landmarks on a map of my life. Half their crop had already been harvested into big, refrigerated bins at the storage barns; the other half would be picked over the next several months by crews of McGillens and Mexicans. The Mexicans would find their place in Chocinaw County, just as the Cherokees and Scots had, the English Dalyrimples and Thackerys, the Africans who came first as slaves but stayed as farmers, and every other creed or kind who made up our people. I didn't hire anyone to do work so hard no McGillen would do it, nor work I hadn't done since I was old enough to climb a tree myself.

A soft autumn breeze made the ancient apple tree beside me seem to nod her aged limbs as if remembering. I patted the Great Lady's trunk. The wind smelled of warm fireplaces and wood smoke, of ripeness. The big farmhouse—which I had restored to its previous splendor—sat in solid comfort on a knoll beyond that creek, overlooking the rest of the broad valley that made up the Hollow. Beneath my feet, the bones of the soldiers still rested where they'd fallen in battle, long before the first Sweet Hush tree wrapped loving roots around them. They waited in gallant silence.

In a few hours I'd open the farm's front gates, and the first of more than twenty thousand autumn visitors would arrive. About thirty employees—most of them my kin—would put enough money in their pockets and mine to keep body and soul together for another year. After taxes and operating expenses, the rich preserves of two million dollars would be reduced to a modest jelly, and I always spread it thin. My personal take made me comfortable, not rich. *Comfortable,* considering my childhood, would more than do.

One more prayer. I was pushing my luck. "Give me the strength to earn my blessings. And please get Davis through Harvard for two more semesters with his honors average intact, and let me make enough money this season to pay for the rest of his senior year without mortgaging the front orchard again."

Family and home and love and death and pride. Apples still meant all that and more to me. They weren't just the fruit of temptation, but the ripe result of my planted dreams and harvested fears. I grew the finest apples and the finest reputation as a mother, a widow, a businesswoman, and a McGillen in Chocinaw County, Georgia. "Hush McGillen Thackery," people said, "is a legend in her own time."

Wishful thinking. People want something or someone bigger than their own woes to believe in. That's why we have actors and politicians and preachers. But like most ordinary legends, I was real flesh and blood, and I dearly wanted to keep my private shames private. Due to my careful and hard work, people believed a lot of pretty fantasies about me and mine. But sometimes we rise to the occasion of ourselves. On a day like that, our legend becomes a truthful hint of who we really are.

My life had come to such a day.

I took the cell phone off my belt, checked my wristwatch, then looked at the phone and waited. I needed only one more tradition to complete my ritual. Davis always called from Massachusetts to wish me a good first day of the season. The phone rang. All right, to be honest, it didn't ring; it played the opening bars of that old 1940s tune "Don't Sit Under the Apple Tree with Anyone Else but Me." Thanks to Smooch, no one would ever accuse us of subtle advertising. We had learned through long experience that apples, like most victuals of life, sold better with a side dressing of hokum and nostalgia.

I quickly put the phone to my ear. "How's my big, smart Harvard-educated son —"

"Mother, hold on, I've got to get around this curve. I'm up on Chocinaw." Wind rushed in the background, and I heard the soft roar of a powerful engine.

I stood quickly. "What's wrong? Why aren't you at school?"

"I can explain later. I'm heading down into the Hollow, maybe ten minutes from home. I've been driving since yesterday. Fourteen hours. I'm bringing you a surprise."

"*Why did you leave school?* Listen, now, what — Davis, what in the world —"

"Hello, Mrs. Thackery!" a voice called out. A female voice. "Davis, tell your mother I'm looking forward to meeting her, and —"

"Eddie, get back under that blanket!"

"They obviously *know* I'm in this car. Hiding me under your rowing-club blanket won't fool them any longer."

I clutched the cell phone so hard my knuckles hurt. "Euell Davis Thackery Junior," I said slowly. "*Why are you hiding a girl?*"

"Mother, I can explain . . . hold on." I could hear him rustling around, the hard whoosh of air, and a low yell from the unknown girl named Eddie. "They're right behind us again," she called. "Speed up."

"No. No," I said. "Dammit, Davis—"

"Mother, wait for us up by the gate, and get ready to shut it after we pull in."

"Who's chasing you and this girl?"

"Can't talk! Have to drive! Love you, Mother!"

Click. I held the empty phone away from my face and stared at it. My legs started to shake. In the next second I was running for the house, leaving the silver pitcher and all my protective prayers and traditions spilled at the base of the old tree.

Mother, I've got a surprise for you.

I raised my son to call me Mother instead of Mama or Ma, and I called him Davis, never Davy, like his father. His father never grew up. My son *had*. I wouldn't accept any compromises. And no unpleasant surprises.

I leapt into a big red van we used for deliveries to local grocery stores. IT'S NOT AN APPLE UNLESS IT'S A SWEET HUSH, the van's logo proclaimed beneath a delicate white silhouette of an apple tree. Driving too fast out of the yard, I ricocheted off tumbled fieldstone borders of iris and daylily beds that had been old when I was young. The farm road twisted a quarter of a mile through our front orchards before entering a broad, open area we now called the Barns.

My first little building remained as our gift shop, but its kitchen and market had been moved to much larger structures, and the shop's wares now included crystal and silver knickknacks, gold jewelry, fine linens, and other household items—all with apple themes. Among the Barns were climate-controlled storage facilities and a rustic pavilion for our outdoor market and bluegrass

59

music. All were surrounded by acres of graveled parking lots and carefully authentic split-rail fences.

The bumpy dirt lane vanished into the parking area, then snaked out of it on the other side like a woman after a makeover, smooth and asphalted, rising up a knoll between an alley of apple trees and clipped boxwoods until it reached a handsome, white, double-sided gate at the civilized pavement of McGillen Orchards Road. Our red-and-white sign loomed between big, gray, stacked-stone posts. SWEET HUSH FARMS, OPEN DAILY, 10 TO 6, SEPTEMBER 1 TO DECEMBER 31. IT'S NOT AN APPLE UNLESS IT'S A SWEET HUSH. WWW.SWEETHUSHAPPLE.COM.

I pulled my cell phone off my belt as I unpadlocked the gate and swung one side back, staring at a spot where the public road disappeared into big firs and pines, hardwoods and laurel, slicked by trickles of water that seeped from exposed rock faces at the base of Chocinaw Mountain. "I need you out here at the Hollow," I said into the phone. "Pronto. There's trouble."

"I'm there. Ten minutes." The deep male voice asked no questions, and I clicked the phone off. My baby brother, now Sheriff Logan McGillen, parsed out words like diamonds—a few fine ones were all he needed. To Logan, life was simple and easy to sum up. I had raised him to protect our world, and he did.

I waited.

Waiting is the hardest part of all, for a mother.

UP ON CHOCINAW, Davis—a twenty-four-year-old senior in Harvard's school of economics, meaning he was smart enough to know the price of his own choices—careened down the mountainside in the black 1982 Trans Am he and his father had lovingly rebuilt with an oversize engine when Davis turned sixteen. The Trans Am was everything a muscle car should be, right down to a license plate that said 2FAST. Davis kept an old picture of himself and Davy in the glove compartment. Covered in grease, their arms looped around each other's shoulders, they grinned beside the Trans Am's then-disassembled carcass. The car was a work of father-son devotion. It wouldn't let Davis and his mystery girl down.

Behind him, three black SUVs disappeared in a curve of the mountain. Davis tossed the cell phone aside. "My mother knows we're on the way, and she'll take our side!"

The girl peered at the back of his head from beneath a blanket in the Trans Am's backseat. "Davis, you didn't even tell her what 'our side' *is*. You scared her to death."

"My mother, scared? No way. I've told you, nothing rattles my mother. She'll be ready to defend us."

"All she knows is that her son is driving like a crazy man and he's bringing home a stranger."

"I have a cousin who brought home a stripper from a traveling carnival. This is nothing."

"Your logic is very reassuring. Look, I'm not staying back here any longer. I don't intend to arrive at your ancestral home this way and let your bewildered and upset mother see me cowering in your backseat beside your Garth Brooks CDs and a box of mildewed donuts."

"Stay put. It's safer back there. The donuts are like little airbags."

"I'd rather pitch face-first through the windshield when we do a Thelma-and-Louise off one of these cliffs. It'll sound so much more dramatic on CNN than being squashed between your front seat and the trunk, right?"

Edwina Margisia "Eddie" Jacobs — a law student at Harvard, meaning she was smart enough to know better or at least understand *why* she ought to know better — was accustomed to limousines and yachts, motorcades and military tanks, and even, during a recent jaunt with her mother through the Middle East, a sheikh's ceremonial camel caravan. Eddie pawed her way out of the cheap Mexican blanket she and Davis had bought the night before at an interstate Gas'n'Go after they left Massachusetts. She stuck a foot between the front seats. She wore thousand-dollar suede loafers with solid gold buckles.

Davis gripped the steering wheel. "Eddie, dammit, don't —"

"Don't distract me. I'll fall in your lap and then we really *will* run off this mountainside."

She clambered between the Trans Am's bucket seats as Davis held the fast car to a turn that edged a creek ravine thick with boulders and giant rhododendron. The first tints of fall colored the wooded valleys flashing by on the Trans Am's left side, and the Georgia mountain's sharp granite shoulder rose like a mossy wall on the right. He'd been trained to drive the mountain roads by his father; he knew one wrong twist of the leather-covered steering wheel either way could kill him and Eddie.

Eddie fell into the passenger seat, then snapped the car's webbed seatbelt over her lap. Davis glanced at her. "How's your stomach?"

She put a hand over her abdomen. "Not good." Her freckled face went whiter, but she pushed back streamers of shoulder-length chestnut hair and forced a laugh. "This is the first time in years I've ridden a roller coaster without the men-in-black on-board to protect me. I like it. Even if I throw up."

"Brace yourself."

"Don't worry, I know how to stand shotgun on a runaway stagecoach. Or whatever that saying is." She smiled at his profile. "I wish I could make love to you right now. You look wild."

He flashed her a tight smile. "My room has a bed full of home-made quilts and down pillows. We'll get naked and burrow like rabbits."

"Promise?"

"I promise. Life in the Hollow is that simple."

They heard a noise behind them. Eddie twisted in the seat and frowned out the back window. The black SUVs zoomed around a curve not more than a hundred yards behind them. "Houston, we have a problem. They're gaining again."

Davis glanced in the rearview mirror. Forget the perfect SAT score and the trophy shelf full of leadership awards from Chocinaw County High School and the sterling record at Harvard. He came from a long line of Thackerys who couldn't resist a dare on wheels. No one could catch a Chocinaw County racing man. Not alive, at least.

He thought of his father. And downshifted.

Eddie shook her head. "Don't you dare give up now! You told me nobody can outrun your family on Chocinaw Mountain."

"And I told you I wouldn't get you killed, either." He eased one foot onto the brake. "The game's over. We made it this far. All the way from Boston. Nobody thought we would. My mother'll never forgive me if I do something stupid. I'll never forgive *myself*. I couldn't even begin to ask you to forgive me, either. That's all that matters."

"You've told me your mother is the strongest person you know. You told me she'll support our right to lead our own lives. How is it going to look to her if we give up when we're this close to her doorstep? What kind of girl will she think you've brought home? A loser!" Eddie clutched the sides of her seat. "I'm not giving up! I love you, Euell Davis Thackery Junior, and I trust you with my entire future! You said your father taught you how to drive this car faster than any man in your county. Now, *drive!*"

The fragrant autumn wind whistled through the car's open sunroof like a song of defiance, luring all the souls of the men and women who'd braved old Chocinaw to settle in the fertile valleys below. Davis swallowed a lump in his throat, took one look at Eddie's adoring face, and decided a man didn't let his woman down on Chocinaw.

"I love you, too! Hold on to your cute little ass!"

Eddie gasped as he floored the gas pedal and gave a yell. The

Trans Am spiraled down the sides of the old mountain. Davis drove with a light-fingered skill his father would have admired. The car was doing ninety by the time Davis and Eddie passed a handsome wooden sign that welcomed them to CHOCINAW COUNTY, HOME OF THE FAMOUS SWEET HUSH APPLE. The tires squealed like a mountain haint as Davis swung on to a shady two-lane heading into Sweet Hush Hollow. He flashed by a green metal sign that proclaimed it MCGILLEN ORCHARDS ROAD, then a white metal sign pointing out it was also STATE ROUTE 72, and finally a second big wooden sign set up by the state park service.

NOW ENTERING THE SCENIC SWEET HUSH APPLE BYWAY.

Davis yelled again. He'd made it. He was carrying his woman home to a legacy of faith, sacrifice, hard work, and the finest southern apple ever grown. Home to live like an ordinary girl, home to stay, home to be welcomed by his mother, the most famous Hush in a line of Hushes since Hush the First said a Scots-Irish Presbyterian prayer and planted an apple seedling over the bones of soldiers in the wild Hollow.

Me. Waiting.

Without any warning.

I HEARD THE LOW ROAR of the Trans Am coming up the road. I was as sensitive as a mother cat—I recognized the sound of my kitten. Clenching the gate's top board, I said a prayer in favor of the low-slung car, though I hated the damned thing. I had nothing against racing, just something against my son dying before me. The Trans Am flashed into view, going at least eighty and fishtailing a little. I dug my fingernails into the gate and braced my legs. *He's his father's son, too.*

Davis looked calm and determined. He had the Trans Am's windows open, always loving the feel of the mountain air. His short, dark hair moved wildly in the rush of wind, but nothing else about him registered any chaos. My son. Methodical. Smart. Sensitive. Honest. Kind. Adored by girls and manfully respectful of them, as I'd taught him and his father had demonstrated to him, at least in public. A strong leader. State Star Student.

He'd won Georgia Junior Entrepreneur of the Year as a high school senior. I swear to God I didn't push him to be an overachiever. All right, so maybe he'd sensed my urgent need for him to make wiser choices than me. At any rate, he was my wonderful son.

Please, be careful. Please, God, don't let him get hurt. When he was a child I'd actually made a secret list titled THINGS I COULD NOT SURVIVE. At the top of the list were these words: *Seeing Something Bad Happen to Davis.* I wouldn't let myself be more specific. Some superstition told me it was bad luck to put a worst fear into writing.

The girl (at that moment I was thinking of her as the *Damned Girl Who Has Lured My Son into Some Kind of Trouble*) sat up straight in the passenger seat, holding on to the dashboard with both hands, looking forward, her face calm, too. They were two of a kind. Somewhere, her mother must have listed that moment as a worst fear, too.

Davis braked expertly, whipped the Trans Am through the gate, slid it to a stop, then leapt out and strode to me, making sure he put on a smile. Tall and lanky and darkly handsome like his father, he was dressed in khaki trousers, good dress shoes, and a rumpled dress shirt with onyx cuff links. I blinked in surprise. My unpretentious, jeans-wearing son, in onyx cuff links. "Such a grown-up young man," people had said since he was a child. But when had he really become a *grown man*? I suddenly had a *grown* son. I knew women my age still raising babies. Crazy women, but still. "Talk to me," I said.

"Mother, there's nothing to worry about. Eddie and I aren't in any particular kind of trouble. We're here to make a point of principle." He hugged me in passing as he reached for the open gate. "Let me get this closed. Just bear with me and watch the road. We're taking a stand."

"It's hard to take a stand on a point of principle without getting stuck. Have you broken any law?"

He laughed tightly. "No."

"Is this some kind of research for a class?"

He laughed again and shook his head. "We don't do road trips in economics."

"So you risked your life and this . . . Eddie's . . . to make some kind of point about what? Driving too fast and ditching classes and showing up with trouble in tow on the most important day of the season?"

He frowned. "I didn't risk—"

"Don't even *try* to justify racing down Chocinaw. Don't. Your father *died* on that mountain."

He halted. His throat worked. Even five years after Davy's death, we had trouble talking about him. God knows, I had my reasons for avoiding the subject.

"Mrs. Thackery?" the girl interjected. I turned to find her standing calmly by the Trans Am. Tall and slender, with golden brown hair and a good, clean-boned but sickly pale face, she had big blue eyes smeared with worry. "Davis is my best friend and I trust him with my life. He's not in any trouble, I promise you. He's my hero."

I didn't know what to say to that. Finally, "Do you need a hero's help?"

She looked even more exhausted, and began to wobble in place. "A little bit, yes." Davis hurried to her and put his arm around her shoulders. She wound her arm around his waist and clung like kudzu on a pine tree.

I stared at their interlocked embrace. "My son's scared you sick, I think."

"No, he's been nothing but wonderful to me." She turned and

tilted her head upward, giving Davis a look of adoration that rang alarm bells in me. I wanted some girl to love him like life itself, and him to love such a girl back. I wanted his wife to become the daughter I'd always wanted but had never risked birthing with Davy Senior. I wanted grandchildren someday. Just not before my son turned forty, ran a Fortune 500 company, and won a Nobel prize. "I'm afraid we need to be introduced," I said slowly. "And I really need to know what's going on here."

Davis frowned. "I'll explain everything, just give me a little time."

Eddie nodded. "Plant your dreams with passion and honor, and your roots will hold you firmly in any storm —"

"That comes from a book about Johnny Appleseed. I read it to Davis when he was a boy. I carved that saying on a plaque for his bedroom wall."

"Yes. Davis has told me all about you. And all about his wonderful father, may he rest in peace." She crossed herself. *Catholic,* I thought. My son had brought me an exotic Catholic girl? She had strict Catholic parents, I'd bet. Good. They'd haul her back home, wherever home was. "And you should be proud, Mrs. Thackery. Davis has tried very hard to live up to the creeds you and his father taught him."

Clueless. Just like my son, she believed in the fantasies I'd created. I pivoted toward Davis. "What exactly have you done? Talk. *Now.*"

"There's no time. The posse is here. Circle the wagons." He managed another laugh as he looked up the road. Three large, black SUVs roared around the bend. They swerved into the entrance of our road and squealed to a stop, lined up in perfect formation. All the doors opened, and over a dozen people — mostly men, but also one woman — got out. They tried to look casual in wrinkled slacks and golf shirts. Even the woman. All wore shoulder harnesses with guns.

"Federal agents," Davis said in my ear. "Eddie has bodyguards. I'll explain more later."

Federal agents? Bodyguards? I slowly lowered my hands to my sides and faced a gun-bearing crew in golf shirts. Armed golfers.

"Everyone, please, be calm," Eddie said. Davis kept an arm around her protectively. She lifted her chin. "Lucille, I'm sorry I put you and your people through this. But I had to."

"Eddie, we've always been fair to you." So spoke Lucille. She was tall and muscular, midthirties, maybe, with shoulder-length blond hair and freckles and squint lines. She held out both hands to Eddie in a friendly gesture. "I know why you're upset. But this isn't the way to handle it."

"Lucille, it's *exactly* the way to handle it. My mother responds to actions, not words. Now she's paying attention."

"Be reasonable. We'll call in a helicopter, and we'll take you and your friend Mr. Thackery to a secure location, and then we'll talk. Your mother's postponed her schedule in England. Your father's waiting by a phone in Tel Aviv. They do want to listen."

I frowned. England? Tel Aviv? Helicopters? Who were her parents? International flight attendants?

Eddie stiffened. "My *father* wants to listen, but my *mother* wants to destroy every shred of my privacy. Nothing excuses what she's done to me. Nothing. Nothing."

"Now, Eddie, it's not my place to discuss that issue —"

"Do you report to her, too? Were you one of her spies?"

"No. You have my word."

"I only believe one person's word right now." She looked at Davis. "And I'm so sorry for what my mother did to you."

"Shhh. I'm a big boy. This is about you. Doing what's best for *you*."

"No. For *us*."

He kissed her. Every antenna in my brain went on high power. "Whoa," I said. "Excuse me, but what did your mother do to Davis?"

Davis shook his head. "It's not actual, personal damage. I can deal with it."

"Fine. Then just tell me what she did, and I'll help you *deal* with it."

"Davis, let me," Eddie said. "I'm sorry to have to admit this, but my mother has been spying on me. She started when I left home for Harvard, and now she has files of information on all of my closest friends. Including Davis. We found out yesterday."

I clutched a fist to my stomach. A hundred fervent questions popped into my mind, but by that point this Eddie had turned away from me and looked firmly at Lucille again. "I hereby decline all further services from you and your office. I'm an adult of legal age, and it's my right to reject formal protection."

"I'm sorry, Eddie, but we're like the tax department. You can't just tell us to leave you alone."

"Then *I'll* tell you," Davis warned.

Lucille inched forward.

I stepped in front of her, leaned over my gate, and held up a hand. "What part of 'private property' do you not understand?"

She stopped, scowling.

"*Mother*," Davis said with affection.

"Thank you, Mrs. Thackery," Eddie whispered. "Davis *said* you'd defend us."

"I'm defending my *gate*." Lucille and I fought a silent, primal battle over the whitewashed boards.

She blinked first. "Ma'am, you don't know who you're dealing with."

"My son tells me he hasn't broken any law."

"Not exactly, but —"

"Has Eddie? What — did she escape from some witness protection program? Is her father a mob boss in hiding?"

"No, but —"

"A mob boss in hiding," Eddie repeated under her breath, and almost smiled.

69

"No, but—"

"Then I don't give a damn who you are. You're not coming on to my property."

Lucille looked even more unhappy. "We do actually have the authority to intercede if we feel the situation warrants it."

I was a stubborn McGillen by birth and a fighting Thackery by marriage. An anthem rose in my mind: *I Saved this Farm with Backbreaking Work and No Government Handouts; I'm a Tough One-Eighth Cherokee Mountain Farmer Whose Grandfather Shot Himself Because of Government Agents Who Confiscated His Liquor Still.*

"I've got two dozen dead Union soldiers in my apple orchard who made the mistake of invading Sweet Hush Hollow during the Civil War."

Lucille's eyes went cold. "Is that a threat?"

"You better believe it."

Davis pushed in front of me. "I'm going to drive Eddie to the home my family has lived in for over a century—" he jabbed a hand behind us, indicating the big farmhouse peeking from the orchards in the distance— "and that's where she's going to *stay.*" He pivoted and took Eddie by the arm. "Let's go." She nodded fervently.

"*Eddie, it's my job to come after you,*" Lucille warned. She laid her hands on my gate.

I pulled out my cell phone and punched a number. "Smooch? Call Asia Makumba and ask her to get back to me right away."

"Okay. Anything wrong?"

"Nothing a little media coverage won't help."

"Huh? I'll be there in an hour to go over the radio spots for opening day—"

"Get Asia for me right now. I'll have to call you back. I'm in the middle of something."

I clicked the phone off. "Asia Makumba. Local girl. Used to be named Alice. Alice Jones. Married a Nigerian and decided to honor her African roots. Changed her name. Now she works for one of the Atlanta TV stations. Investigative reporter. I have a feeling you people don't want cameras and an audience."

Lucille turned an angry red. I leaned over the gate and crooked my finger. When she leaned toward me, I spoke very softly. "*Move everyone else in your crew back from my gate, and then you get to come in. Just you. Is it a deal?*"

Seconds ticked by. Lucille didn't move. I had to give her credit. My phone sang. I put it to my ear. "Asia?"

"What's going on? How can I help you, Mrs. Thackery?" A job at my farm had helped Alice/Asia put herself through the University of Georgia.

"I've got a story for you. Here. I'm going to let you talk to Lucille. She's a federal agent of some kind who's about to—"

Lucille suddenly held up her hands. *Surrender.*

"Asia, let me call you back. It may not be worth your trouble."

"All right . . . but you're sure?"

"No, but I'll get back to you if I need to." I returned the phone to my belt. "This is what the world has come to. To get anything done, you have to threaten government people with television people."

"All right, Mrs. Thackery, you win," Lucille said slowly, and eyed me with a certain respect. "My *people* will wait across the road until they get your permission to enter."

"Good." I opened the gate for her, then turned to Davis and Eddie. "Lucille comes in. Just Lucille."

Lucille sent her group across the two-lane into the mown weeds, then walked back and entered the gate. I locked it behind her. Eddie looked relieved. It was clear to me that she liked this Lucille and didn't want to cause her any more grief. "Thank you, Mrs. Thackery. Davis said we could depend on you. He was right."

Davis nodded. "Thank you, Mother."

I gave him a look that made him duck his head. I had a business to run. Our livelihood and the incomes of most of our relatives depended on it. Ten of his McGillen cousins were headed to college with my money as backing and Davis's example as inspiration. "I want some answers and I want them fast."

"I don't blame you for being upset, and I know it's apple season, so I'll keep this basic, for now." He cleared his throat. "I'd like to introduce Edwina Margisia Nicola Jacobs. Eddie, this is my mother, Hush McGillen Thackery."

Eddie held out a hand to me. "You do recognize me, don't you, Mrs. Thackery? I can see it in your face. You do. So you understand why I'm in a difficult position? Mrs. Thackery? I'm *Eddie Jacobs*." She studied my face. "Eddie. Jacobs."

"*Eddie Jacobs*," I repeated with mild bewilderment, but shook her hand. Her palm felt clammy. She swayed in place.

Davis suddenly picked her up. "Shhh. You can relax now. We're home. The Hollow is the safest place in the world."

Her long, skinny, bell-bottomed, Gap-trousered legs dangled in the mountain air, ending in feet clad in what looked to be very fine loafers with gold buckles. She clutched a hand over her mouth. "I may throw up again. This isn't the dignified entrance I wanted to make for your mother."

"I'm calling a doctor," Lucille said.

"No. I'm fine."

"You have a stomach virus. Or food poisoning."

Davis shook his head. "She just needs to rest. It's been a long night."

Eddie looked at me wearily. "Mrs. Thackery, I'm sorry, but I seem to be a complete sissy."

I laid a hand on her arm. "Calm down. We'll get you to the house and I'll feed you some salted Sweet Hush slices. That'll cure any upset stomach." I pivoted toward Lucille. "Lucille, I said *back off*."

Lucille frowned. "You don't have a *clue*, do you? You don't understand the situation at all."

"Then somebody tell me. *Right now*." I looked at Davis.

His jaw worked. He raised his head formally and held Eddie a little tighter against his chest. "Eddie and I met at Harvard this summer. We've been dating ever since. In secret." He paused. "Because her father is the President."

I arched an unimpressed brow. After all, I was a president, too — of Sweet Hush Farms, Inc. "The president of what?"

Davis waited one beat, just enough to let the moment take root in our quiet lives. "President of the United States," he said.

FIVE

In the middle of a tornado, there's no time to think before the wind sucks you headfirst up your own chimney. Suddenly the world outside the Hollow — a world I invited into my home every fall but only under my rules — invaded with no invitation.

Most of my family believed Al Jacobs wasn't handsome enough to be President. Or tough enough. Or smart enough. Or "like us" enough, whoever "us" was. He had been a lawyer for the poor in Chicago, then a judge, then a congressman, then a senator, and finally, the first Catholic President since Kennedy — and the only President from a Polish-American background. His election single-handedly restored the dumb-Polack joke to its former glory. There was no evidence Al Jacobs fit the stereotype, but people who hated him didn't care.

"The country's elected a damned dumb Polack," Aaron McGillen said loudly during a family reunion the spring after the election.

I turned to Smooch over the fried chicken buffet. "Cousin Aaron is still manning an outpost on the Road to Stupid, I see."

Editorial cartoonists often drew Al Jacobs's pointy chin like a gull's lower beak, and portrayed his thick, graying hair as a crazed Einstein bouffant. "Roosevelt didn't look like some wild thinker," Gruncle complained, citing his favorite President. "Who'd be willing to die for Jacobs like we did for Roosevelt? Would Al Jacobs inspire men to kill poor German women in the name of war? I don't think so." Gruncle Henry, now completely ancient but still tormented by memories of the great war and his part in it, had no sympathy for any President since FDR.

It didn't help that Al Jacobs always billed himself as *Al,* reducing his importance with the casual acquaintanceship of his name. But his given name was Aleksandr, after a family tradition, and that was too tricky a business for red-blooded Americans to accept, much less spell. His immigrant relatives had been Jakobeks when they came over on the boat at Ellis Island, then turned themselves into Jacobs sometime before my gruncle's great war — fully Americanized, fighting for their new homeland, working as mechanics and butchers and secretaries, building up their American dream until they produced plain, solid Al. Al Jacobs. Good ol' Al Jacobs. As American as kielbasa and apple pie. In my opinion, he'd won the presidency because he had kind, dark eyes and radiated a brand of decency no one could ignore, love him or not. Most of the residents of Chocinaw County, who tended heavily toward thorny survivalists and hellfire conservatives, hated his tender, liberal guts.

As for his wife, Edwina Habersham Jacobs, she was either the answer to a modern woman's prayers or a loudmouthed, big-butted East Coast blue blood hiding her feminist colors behind designer suits and a "friend of the working mother" campaign promise her enemies didn't take seriously for one second. Her family had come over on the *Mayflower* and been rich country clubbers ever since. She'd ranked tops in her law-school class back in the 1970s, then earned a reputation in the Chicago DA's office as a tough prosecuting attorney, which bewildered the hell out of everyone who said she and Al were bleeding-heart Socialists. Her admirers insisted she had the style and class of Jackie Kennedy, only in a larger panty size. Dammit, no woman, not even the First Lady, could avoid being sized up by the size of her behind. I checked my own size twelve in the mirror more often than I'd admit.

During Al's campaign, the nation got its first good look at Edwina. Short and pear-shaped and deadly blond, she took over the podium at her party's national convention without a single nervous blink of her ice-blue Maryland Pilgrim's Pride eyes. "I'm not here just to tell you that my husband will make the finest President ever elected," she announced. "I'm here to tell you that I will make the finest *First Lady* ever elected."

The convention delegates went wild with cheers. Once the rest of the country finished swallowing its spit over her drop-dead candor or unbelievable gall — depending on the point of view — she commandeered our attention like Patton in imported pumps. She knocked supermodels off the covers of magazines for months to come. She named her own terms for interviews on all the major cable and broadcast TV networks. The press followed her like lovesick puppies.

But the polls said most regular Americans — including many in her own party — wouldn't touch her with asbestos gloves. Too mouthy. Too ambitious. Not modest enough. I watched sympathetically as she tried to fix her image by hawking homemade cookies. "I make these from my favorite recipe — they're cinnamon nut crunchies," she told Jane Pauley on *Dateline*. "That's what Al and I call them."

Tops in her law class, smart as a whip, managed her husband's political career from day one, but she had to do that cookie routine to make people trust her as a woman. I could see the hard decision in her eyes. I'd held up my share of womanly cookies, too.

"I expect she threw those things down the nearest commode the first chance she got," I told Smooch at the time. "Have you ever seen anybody ask a *man* to prove he can bake cookies, just so we'll believe he's no threat?"

"But those cookies appeal to the soccer-mom voting demo-

graphic among her husband's voters," Smooch pointed out, bewildered by my disgust. "That's what my professor in marketing
class says. And what's wrong with baking cookies? I'd bake cookies if some man asked me to." Tears welled up in her eyes. "But I
can't even find a good man to marry. Much less bake cookies."

I said no more on the subject, but I knew. Edwina Jacobs
would do what she had to do to get herself and her man into the
White House. She'd even pretend to be a sweet little girly girl at
fifty-something years old, if she had to.

The act didn't last long. Standing on a windy stage in front of
a crowd in Des Moines, Iowa, Edwina leaned too close to a microphone that was supposed to be turned off and said to one of
her assistants, "That bitch from the *L.A. Times* is here. Go tell her
that if she hurts my daughter's feelings again by calling her 'a
skinny nerd,' I'll cut her head off and defecate down her exposed
windpipe."

God, MSNBC, and everyone else heard every elegantly ob-
scene word.

Well.

No one in the entire country talked about anything else for the
next two weeks. The other candidates and their wives didn't stand
a chance in the battle for public attention. One presidential candidate's wife was reduced to assuring Larry King, "Well, I say a
good healthy *damn* and *hell* occasionally," and then every righteous blabber in the country began debating the value of cuss-
words and Edwina Jacobs's potential influence on our Precious
Children. All right, so Edwina Jacobs wasn't a sweet little cookie-
baking wife or a demure Jackie Kennedy. She apologized, but you
could see she had to grit her teeth.

The strangest thing happened. Her poll ratings soared. People
decided to love her for a while. She was a fighter, by God. A
woman who stood up for her child and was willing to threaten
people to do it. She *would* stand up for other women's children.
She understood. She *was* a working mother.

Thanks to her, Al Jacobs won the Iowa primary, and the rest is history. I didn't vote for him, but then I never voted in presidential elections. I considered myself an independent with libertarian leanings, meaning the pickings were few and far between. I had given up hope on national independent candidates after Ross Perot went bat-ass silly.

But if I had voted, I would have voted for Edwina.

All through the campaign, there was one thing no one could dispute: Al and Edwina Jacobs had done a damned fine job as parents. Their daughter, Eddie — that skinny nerd — supported them with the wholesome sincerity of a Girl Scout doing a hard sell on leftover cookies. Not one dark whisper tainted her reputation as a sterling daughter, a dedicated student, and a fine young citizen. She didn't drink, she didn't smoke, she didn't do drugs, and she told girls it was okay to keep their legs together.

Everyone should have known that she was only waiting for the right chance to run hog-wild and that a woman with Edwina's personality was the brand of stage mother who'd make a daughter want to bolt for the nearest exit.

I was just sorry Eddie picked my son to bolt with her.

EDDIE THREW UP in the kitchen sink. I fed her freshly sliced apples soaked in saltwater, just as I'd promised. She ate the crisp, salty slices politely. "Holistic medicine is so admirable and down-to-earth. Davis has told me your maternal grandmother was a Cherokee apple farmer named Fruit Halfacre. I admire the Native American traditions so much."

"Thank you." My grandmother Fruit was a tough old lady who downed a shot of hundred-proof homemade liquor and a chew of rabbit tobacco every morning, not a slice of apple. I smoked a soapstone pipe she left me. But I told Eddie none of that. Unnerved, I ate several medicinal apple slices myself and debated whether a glass of wine at 7:00 A.M. would look suspicious.

Within five minutes our runaway First Daughter fell asleep with her head on her arms at my antique pine harvest table. Davis bent over her and stroked her golden brown hair lightly. "Get some rest, Honey," he whispered. "I'll be nearby."

I motioned to him to follow me. We sat down across from each other in the cool dawn light of the farmhouse's large dining room, a place of good carpet and old beadboard ceiling and white wallpaper embossed with fine golden apple leaves, a room filled with crystal and china and good antique furniture I'd put together over the years, piece by hard-earned piece. No apple wholesaler or grocery chain VIP or apple lobbyist or state tourism official would ever sit at my table thinking the McGillens of Chocinaw County had not returned to their former glory, or that I was an unsophisticated Daisy Mae with a few apples to sell. By God, they took me and my fine china seriously. I faced my son over a cut-glass crystal bowl filled with handsome wooden apples I'd carved with my grandfather's whittling tools in the farm's workshop.

"Let's get something out in the open," Davis said. "I love her. And she loves me."

I had seen that announcement coming, but it still hit me in the stomach. The best I could manage sounded like a worn-out song lyric. "What's love got to do with it?"

"I love her the way Dad loved you. He *lived* for you. He'd have done anything to take care of you when you were upset and needed him."

He had no idea. "What are you trying to protect Eddie from, besides a meddling mother?"

"She's a prisoner in her own life. Death threats, hate mail, stalkers—you name it, she gets it. If she sits down alone in a coffee shop or a bookstore or a theater, some loudmouth mouths off about her parents. You can't imagine what her life is like. What the *world* is like out there, for the daughter of a President."

"So you feel sorry for her and you think you can take care of her without the help of a whole troop of highly trained professionals who'd give their life for her if they had to. So you voted to get rid of them and do it all yourself. Makes sense."

"It's not that simple."

"You could have counseled her to talk to her parents. *You could have told me you were dating her and I'd have talked to her about her problems.*" I looked at him mournfully. "Why didn't I deserve to know about you and her? Should I hire myself some spies to find out the most important things in my own son's life?"

"Eddie was *afraid* word about us would leak out. The last guy she dated ended up on the cover of the *Enquirer*."

"You think I can't keep a secret?"

"We just wanted privacy." He paused. "I know how it feels to grow up under a spotlight, with expectations."

I went very still. "What?"

"I didn't want you and a hundred McGillens and Thackerys debating whether she was good for my future."

"Is that how you feel your life has been?"

"I'm only saying I understand the pressure on her."

"I see. You don't trust *your* mother, either."

"Mother."

"She's young. She doesn't know what she wants. And neither do you, at the moment."

"Oh? You gave me a bank account and a computer on my tenth birthday and taught me to help you run the business. Dad gave me a rifle and a dirt bike and taught me to stand up for myself. You told me I was a genius. He told me I was a man. Neither of you ever said I was too young to take care of myself."

"We lied."

He stood. "Do you want Eddie and me to leave?"

"No. Of course not. This is your home. She's your . . . guest. My guest."

"Good. Then please don't ask me to explain every decision I make."

I got to my feet, too, fighting mad. "But school has to come first and girlfriend trouble comes second. I don't care if Eddie's parents *are* the First Family of the United States—they could be the Royal Wazoos of Wazooland for all it means to me. I won't let you jeopardize your future and drag our family's name into the mud. I've worked too hard to keep it clean."

"What's *that* supposed to mean?"

I went off on a long tirade outlining the nasty gossip about presidents and their relatives. Hadn't the media swarmed down to Plains and pried out every odd-peanut relative and ugly family tale among Jimmy Carter's people? And look at what Clinton's family had been put through. And the Kennedys, bar none. And Betty Ford's drinking problem — all over the news. And Patti Davis's I'll-get-you-Mother antics. And her mother's little astrology secret, for that matter. I stood there yelling about all that to my son because the more I thought about it, the more I realized people demanded to look at every single shovelful of shit and innuendo in every presidential household going all the way back to where Washington slept. And I was terrified.

"Mother, calm down," Davis said grimly, watching me. "I don't understand what this has to do with us and our family. We've got nothing to hide."

"I just don't . . . want to see *you* on the cover of the *National Enquirer* as Eddie Jacobs's kidnapping boyfriend," I finished lamely.

"You think our family's good name isn't safe with me?"

"I just want you to go back to school and graduate next spring and have options I never had."

"Oh? My mother is the finest apple farmer and the best businesswoman in the state," Davis replied hoarsely. "She brought her family name back to prominence despite everyone telling her it couldn't be done. My father loved her and believed in her and devoted himself to helping her make her dreams for us come true." Davis halted, cleared his throat, and pinned me with his father's heartbreakingly handsome blue eyes. "I'd be honored to live my life as successfully as either one of you. Because the two of you inspired me, and you still do. But on my own terms."

I stifled a need to cry. Tears, I had learned over the years, only watered the ground that wanted them. "All right, then tell me what happens next."

"Eddie's parents are sending a relative to bring her back. I don't intend to let him. I'd appreciate your support."

"Who is this mystery man?"

"His name is Nicholas Jakobek." Davis paused. "And he's already killed one man on Eddie's behalf."

SIX

Nick

I was fourteen in 1972, when I first met my uncle John Aleksandr Jacobs, the future President, in a dirty hallway outside the morgue of a hospital in Mexico City. The *policio* had taken my mother's body there after she overdosed on heroin. Julia Margisia Jacobs had been kind and beautiful, but easy to break. She didn't know who my father was, only that he must have been one of the boys she'd dated during her freshman year at the University of Illinois. Margisia Jacobs had been the first college girl in the history of the Jacobses in America.

"Everyone was so proud of me," she liked to tell me, crying. "Until I got pregnant."

She never understood how that sounded to me, her son. I lay in bed at night, swearing I'd be worthy of every breath I took. Telling myself I had to earn the right to live. Telling myself if I could save her from herself, I'd deserve to be loved. The Mexican diplomat and drug addict who had been my mother's last boyfriend called her Dreaming Margarita. She told me her little brother, Al, back in Chicago, had called her Margee. By the time she died, I called her nothing. It hurt too much to call her *Mother*. She'd stopped playing that role as soon as I was old enough to take care of myself. She thought she was taking care of me, and didn't realize we'd switched. The drugs told her she was in control. I knew better. I took care of her as much as she'd let me and I never hurt her feelings, but I never called her Mother either.

And toward the last, she never noticed.

I was handcuffed to a metal bench late that night at the hospital, with blood on my hands and my clothes, my knuckles swollen and bruised, my head down. I stared at the floor between my tennis shoes and tried not to think. The hallway was empty. My mother had been well known in society as the diplomat's drugged American mistress. I had hurt him badly.

I heard footsteps on the tile floor, but didn't look up immediately. I'd spent a lot of years on the streets, and I could gauge the proximity of trouble by sound and smell and even the feel of the air, like a dog. When the hard-soled feet came within range, I flicked an ice pick from the cuff of my jacket, and, hiding the sharpened point inside my palm, raised my head. "Stay back," I said in Spanish.

The guy halted, and he looked as startled as I must have. I knew at first glance, on some instinct, that he was there to see me. He was young, maybe just a year or two out of college, but looked serious as shit. He had dark eyes and hair, like me and my mother. I pegged his build for middleweight boxing, or playing shortstop. His hands were big but clean, like the pants and dress shirt he wore with a broad red tie askew at the collar. He was over six feet tall—my height, and I was still growing. His face looked ordinary and smart and honest. It surprised me when I thought that. Honest.

As I sat there in a daze, looking at him, he walked all the way up to me and dropped to a squat inches from my knees. I straightened quickly and curled my fingers around the hidden stiletto.

Who was he—a goddamned snake charmer? "You don't fucking listen," I said in English.

"I hear what I want to hear. I only care about one thing: I've finally found you." He paused, his throat working. "And your mother."

"I don't know you."

"But I think I know *you*. You look like her. You have to be Nick. You call yourself Nicholas Jakobek. Jakobek is an old family name. The name your mother's family brought over from Poland." I said nothing. Didn't know what to say. My mother and I had moved around a lot. As far as I was concerned, I had no family I cared about, other than her. I took the Jakobek name because she had liked it. Thought it was elegant and romantic.

"Stay back," I repeated louder, and lifted my hand, flashing the ice pick.

"Impressive. I had one of those when I was a kid." The stranger's voice was gentle. "My father found it in my sock drawer. He threw it away and made me clean chicken carcasses for a month after school every day, at his butcher shop. 'Here,' he said. 'You punk, you want to draw blood? Cut the guts out of chickens.' He looked like John Wayne. I loved him, but he scared the crap out of me." The stranger paused. "He never got over your mother's disappearance. He died young."

I drew a long breath. My ribs hurt. I couldn't cry in front of him. "Who the hell *are* you?"

He hesitated. His throat worked again. "I'm Margee Jacobs's little brother. I'm your uncle. Uncle Al."

AL JACOBS MIGHT LOOK clean-cut and all-American, but he didn't hesitate to bribe a policeman, who unlocked my handcuffs. I stood in the morgue while a bored-looking attendant pulled my mother's body to us, draped in a sheet on a rattling gurney. When the attendant started to toss the sheet back, I said in Spanish, "Don't touch her." He looked at Al, who said, "Do what my nephew asks, please," in awkward but earnest Spanish, too. The man held up his hands and backed away.

I stood close beside the gurney with my fists against my thighs, not moving, daring anyone to touch my mother, daring her to stay dead and leave me feeling as if I'd been gutted. Daring her to leave me with this brother of hers, this uncle who had shown up after all these years.

"Nick, may I have your permission to look at her face?" The words came to me down a dark tunnel. My newfound uncle was speaking to me, his voice a low rasp. We were alone in the morgue, the only two living souls. My mother had told me a little about him when she was sober. He was still a kid when she ran away from Chicago, but they had been close. She had loved him. "Nick, please, it's your choice," he went on. He spoke to me with respect. He asked my permission.

"She never forgot you," I told him. "It's all right for you to look at her." I walked over to a wall and sat down on my heels with my back against the cold tile behind me.

I heard the rustle of the sheet, and then his low sobs as he cried over her bloated body. I didn't look up, just stared at the floor, dragging the back of one bloody hand and then the other across my eyes. After a while he grew quiet. I heard his footsteps. He dropped to his heels beside me. We shared a view of the floor in silence. Finally, he spoke. "I know you don't think you have a family anywhere, but you do. I want you to come live with me in Chicago."

I wanted to tell him he was a piss-yellow do-gooder, and I didn't need his charity. I should have told him I had no idea how to live among his kind of people, and that his family must have done something deliberate to drive my mother away when she was pregnant with me. Since he'd been gullible enough to let me out of the *policio*'s clutches, I could walk out of this hospital anytime I wanted and disappear into the Mexican night. He'd never find me again, if I wanted it that way. The threat formed like blood on my tongue, and I started to say so.

He held out his right hand. My ice pick lay in it. "Don't underestimate me," he said, "and I won't underestimate you. You have one chance to stay out of a Mexican prison. They don't care if you're only fourteen. Don't even think about running, or you'll be arrested. Keep quiet and follow me. I'm taking you back to America. We're going home. To Chicago. That or a Mexican prison? You choose."

I swallowed my pride, took my stolen weapon back, hid it in a pants pocket, got up, and went to my mother's body. I covered her face carefully, tucking the sheet around her dead, dark hair, touching it with my fingertips one more time, whispering to her without words.

I wanted to save the world for you, but I couldn't.

"THERE'S SOMETHING I NEED to tell you about my wife, Edwina," Al said, the first time we walked into their big apartment building on a snowy winter day in downtown Chicago. "She's a little obsessed with appearances."

"Yeah, me, too," I grunted. I followed him past a doorman who stared at me as we stepped into an elevator. I carried a duffel bag filled with my worldly possessions. Not much, including a pair of coyote skulls I kept as talismans for my own loneliness. I didn't have to look in the mirror to know I was big and skinny and homely at fourteen, with patches of acne on my cheeks and a boxer's nose and silences so deep people assumed I didn't know how to talk. Al, on the other hand, was a solid, squeaky-clean citizen. He talked all the time, and he carried a fine leather overnight bag with his initials stitched on one side. The elevator lifted off.

"What did you mean about your wife?" I finally asked. He pointed to his satchel. "This was my twenty-sixth birthday present. Edwina gave it to me last year. It cost a thousand dollars. She bought herself one just like it. I said, 'Honey, we're rookie prosecutors in the district attorney's office. People will think we're taking bribes from the mob.' She answered, 'Honey, no mobster could afford this leather.' Her family's rich. The Habershams. Of the Maryland Habershams. They're in shipping." He smiled beneath dark, gaunt eyes. Yeah, we definitely had the same eyes. "The first Habersham came over on the *Mayflower*. They were very, very English. Edwina's descended from a duchess."

I didn't know why he was telling me all that. I kept handing him the I-don't-give-a-shit treatment, but he kept luring me in. He forced me to keep listening. "The *Mayflower*," he repeated.

I shrugged. "So what about the fucking Jacobses? How did our family get here from Poland?"

"On a steamship in 1902, bunking one level below the goats and chickens. I think our most famous ancestor was a bricklayer named Ludvig."

"Then why'd Edwina marry you?"

"Because she thinks I'm brilliant and honorable and special, and we're going to save the world together. Boy, have I got her fooled."

Save the world. Right. Bribing Mexican policemen to save *me* was one thing. But saving the world? No. He was too soft for that. That was my job.

"Now, about Edwina," he went on. As the elevator rose, he told me they'd met in law school. There had been only five women in their 1970 graduating class. Al had been the one guy who took Edwina Habersham seriously and who didn't feel threatened by her. She was rich and mouthy and smart — she ranked at the top of the class. Al was near the "low-middle," he said diplomatically. When one of their professors called her a ball-busting lesbian, Al threatened to punch him. Edwina defended Al before the law school's administrative board, and won his case.

"We went out on our first date that night," Al told me. "It was love at first defense."

Suddenly we reached his apartment door, and an irrational sense of panic set in. I debated shoving Al out of my way and making a run for the emergency staircase. He was only twenty-seven years old — hell, how could I take him seriously as my uncle? And Edwina sounded like trouble. "So what'd she say when you told her about me?" I demanded suddenly. "Lemme guess. She said she didn't want some piece-of-shit punk nephew of yours stinking up her fine life."

Al slapped a hand on my shoulder. I froze. His eyes bored into mine. I'd finally pissed him off. "Are you planning to rob us?"

"Hell, no."

"Refuse to take a shower?"

"*What?*"

"Kill us in our sleep?"

I shoved his hand away. I was furious. "Fuck you! No! You think I'm like that? I may not be a fucking college boy like you, but I have my own kind of honor—"

"Easy, Nick. I'm just asking questions. If you don't intend to cause us any trouble, then why shouldn't we be glad you're here?"

"I . . . what? You're trying to confuse me! Look, all I can do is give my word. Take it or leave it."

"Okay, I'm taking it. I have your word that you're honest and trustworthy. So why are you yelling at me?"

I looked at him morosely. "Because you play fucking mind games with me, and you're good at it."

"I'm glad you're here. No mind game."

"Yeah, well. Anytime you *change* your mind, I'll leave."

"I won't. You'll just have to stick around and see if you can prove I'm a sucker, won't you?"

I didn't know what to say to that. I shifted awkwardly. "What about Edwina? You can't make me believe your fancy wife wants me here. That's all I'm saying."

"You don't know her. Just be honest with her, too. Keep your hands clean and your mind open, and don't say 'fuck' out loud unless you want to hear how well she says it back."

I stared at him. He unlocked the apartment door and shoved it open. "Honey," he called, "we're home."

I followed him into a luxurious living room of oriental rugs and stuffed bookcases, gold-trimmed furniture and paintings of half-naked European women surrounded by cherubs. At the center of that room stood Edwina Habersham Jacobs, small and chunky and perky-blond, with a slit-eyed expression on her face when she looked at me, like a Persian cat studying a bird. She was dressed in a white pantsuit with bell-bottomed legs and a gold belt dangling around her butt. I had to admire a woman bold enough to emphasize a big butt. At the same time, I drew up in a tighter knot, expecting nothing but the cold shoulder from her. How many rich girls would invite their husband's nephew to move in?

"Welcome home!" She kissed Al quickly, then studied me. "Good work. I see you got your weapon-wielding *bandido* to join our little gang. I'm proud of you."

"He's got a solid defense, but I wouldn't give up." Al took me by one arm. I was too surprised to pull back. Me coming there was his wife's idea, too? "Edwina, may I present my nephew, Mr. Nicholas Jakobek? Nick, may I present my wife, Edwina Habersham Jacobs? Okay, you're both duly presented to each other. Now, go for the throat." He stepped back. I offered her a handshake. She wrapped her strong little fingers around my big ones with a grip like a truck driver, and she continued to dissect me with her calm, cat eyes. "Nicholas," she said firmly.

"Edwina," I said back. I nodded at the cherub paintings. "Von Hosterlitz, right?"

"Why, yes."

I shrugged a long, narrow case off one shoulder and laid it atop my duffel. Her gaze went to it. "Your machete?"

"My flute."

All the air in the apartment seemed to suck up through her flared nose. Al put a hand to his mouth and began to cough. She scrutinized me from the tips of my old western boots to the hand-clipped dark hair I wore long enough to hit my shoulders. She reached out suddenly and took one of my bruised hands, turning it, examining the fight marks. "You're too smart to act this stu-

pid. We'll have to teach you better ways to fight for what you believe in."

"Some people only understand one thing." I held up the other
swollen fist.

She and Al traded a look that said I was raw material with a
more entrenched philosophy than they'd expected. "That's a debate for another night," Al said.

With Al bringing up the rear, Edwina led me to a frilly bedroom that looked as if only girls would sleep in it. "My mother
and sisters usually stay here when they visit. But it's yours now.
We'll redecorate as soon as possible." She pointed to my duffel
bag. "Do you have anything you want to put on the wall tonight,
to make it feel less girly in here?"

"Skulls."

She didn't miss a beat. "Human?"

"Coyote. I found them in the desert."

"Oh, good. I'll tell my decorator to think 'Southwestern.' Or
perhaps, 'Pagan Sacrifice.'"

I was embarrassed and said nothing. Behind me, Al made snuf-
fling sounds and finally laughed out loud. "God, I can't believe you
two. I'm sorry. Sorry, Nick. It's not appropriate." His laughter became a strained groan, then faded. "Sorry. Oh, God. Sorry, for your
mother. My sister. Margee. Sorry. Margee. Sacrifice. That's what she
was. A sacrifice to her own worst impulses and to social stigmas that
didn't make any sense." He put his face in his hands. "If I'd only
found her sooner. Nick, I'm sorry. You needed help with her and
you didn't get it. I'm glad you're here, but I'm so sorry that she's
not." Edwina went to him and put her arms around his neck. He
swept her into a hug, and they held each other. I was just this
stranger who couldn't cry, couldn't ask for help, didn't know how. I
stood there outside the circle of their comfort, envying them.

"Come here," Al ordered suddenly. He wiped his face and
reached for me. I didn't have a chance to back away. He wrapped
an arm around me and kept the other around Edwina. "If anybody deserves sympathy, it's you, Nick, not me."

"I don't want any fucking sympathy." My voice broke. But I didn't move away either.

Al only hugged me harder and nodded at Edwina. "Tell Nick how it is in our home, and how we want the world to be."

She nodded. "*All for one and one for all.* It's that simple, Nicholas." The benediction, the rules, the expectation. If I wanted to stay, I had to do my part.

I shrugged. "If it makes you happy, I can keep the coyote skulls in a drawer."

She smiled thinly. "You bet your ass you will."

AL AND EDWINA PRESENTED me to Edwina's relatives, the Habershams. "Call it the out-of-town tryouts for your social debut," Edwina said wryly. "In other words, if you're going to be a jerk, Al wants you to practice your jerkhood on *my* family first."

We flew to Maryland. Al bought me a suit. I ditched it in the airport men's room and wore jeans with a frayed denim jacket stamped with *Diablo* on one shoulder. Al got a hard look on his face but forced a smile. "No problem. I'm a firm believer in bucking tradition and celebrating your own personal style."

Edwina, however, cut me no slack. "You owe us two hundred dollars for that suit."

"Like you need the money. I didn't ask for the suit. I didn't want the suit. It's not my style. I don't want to be dressed up just so Al isn't embarrassed by me."

"Look, Diablo, let's understand the Sturm und Drang of the family dynamics, here. Al bought you the suit because he thought it would make *you* feel more comfortable. He did it for *your* sake, all right? Not his."

I didn't know what to say to that, and pretended not to care.

The Habershams were easy, as it turned out. They all took one look at me, shit on their silk underwear, and headed for the martinis. At least that's how it felt to me at the time. I *was* a jerk, and I did do my best to sound tough, even speaking with a sinister hint of the *barrio* in my voice, which only made me sound like Cheech Marin in a bad reefer movie.

Edwina drank two gin-and-tonics on the flight back to Chicago, and even sucked the gin from the olives. "I'd say that went well."

Al looked out the plane window and said nothing.

I felt bad, but of course would never admit it.

The Jacobs family came next. Al talked me up as if I were a treasure he'd found in the attic. What guts. Most of the Jacobses were middle-class midwestern types, down-to-earth, either very conservative or very Catholic or both, and I figured out quickly that Al was the odd one. Not conservative, that is. Not particularly religious either, at least not in a public way. I had to give Al credit for keeping a straight face when he stood by me in the hall of a downtown hotel where he held my so-called homecoming party. Weird Al and Diablo.

But this time, I wore a suit. Edwina made me. It didn't help.

Half the Jacobses looked scared of me; the other half cried and prayed and thanked various saints for helping Al find me. Either way, I wasn't won over. But I kept my mouth shut and didn't upset Al's pretty party by asking the one question I wanted answered: *Why couldn't my mother depend on any of you?*

Finally, a hunched little old lady in black gabardine and a flowered hat cornered me. "You hate and fear us all," she whispered with a thick Polish accent. "Do not lie to me, I can tell."

After a moment spent considering my options, I nodded. She grasped my hands with her blue-veined claws, pressing a black-beaded rosary in my palms. "These I brought all the way from the old country. These belonged to my mother and her mother before her. These hold the prayers of our family. Have *faith* in our family — *your* family," she whispered, "and when you have the courage to hear the truth about your poor mother, ask me. Do not ask the others. I'm the only one who knows."

She was my great-aunt Sophie, the last of the immigrant Jakobeks.

And she was right. I was so rattled I didn't have the courage to ask her then.

And not later either, the more I thought about it.

Noble arrogance is a hard nut to crack.

AL WAS THE QUIET, serious type, but Edwina was a firecracker. Prissy and vain and smug. But no bullshit or hidden agendas. She yelled at me in Latin, and I learned enough Latin to yell back. She dragged me to court to keep me under surveillance, so I spent the first few months of my life in Chicago watching her and Al work. They had a mission. They stood up for ideals that mattered — truth, justice, the American way, whatever that really means in the trenches of real life.

You have to picture Edwina in court, dressed in prim little jackets with big, bow-tie scarves and those calf-length skirts women wore in the 1970s. She looked like a ferocious blond librarian. But she was great. She snapped out complex prosecutorial punches in her blue-blooded Maryland accent so quickly people didn't know what hit them. I loved to watch badass defendants gape at her. The dumb bastards never stood a chance. Al was just as impressive in his own way. He turned his summations into speeches on behalf of humanity. At the end of a typical trial, the jurors might not be certain Lonnie the Loan Shark deserved ten years for breaking a man's kneecaps, but they sure as hell knew that every American had a constitutional right to life, liberty, and a pair of legs that bent in the right direction.

Every night after dinner, I sat with Al and Edwina at their gilded dining room table, where they debated the cases they won and lost. "What do you think, Nick?" they asked me all the time, and eventually I began to tell them, as politely as I could, that they were naive and had no clue how bad most people really were. Most people, I said, deserved worse than they got.

"Nicholas is a hanging judge," Edwina liked to say. She thought my eye-for-an-eye philosophy was quaint.

But Al didn't. "Civilization is built on higher standards than revenge. People of good conscience have to *maintain* those standards even when their emotions tell them otherwise. Even when the object of their ethical consideration hasn't earned it. Society as a whole deserves better than our basic instincts."

To which my basic response was always: "Some fuckers are evil, and they need to be killed." This would set Al off on a table-pounding crusade to convince my higher conscience otherwise. I just let him talk. We had grown up on different sides of the sewer that runs through the lives of good people. I never said so, but my motivations always boiled down to a simple misery.

If I'd killed all the men who had turned my mother into a stoned, high-class whore, she might still be alive.

Al and Edwina believed in the *system* — that vague *system* by which people agree on all things good and holy. They believed in each other, and they even believed in me. Although I didn't make it easy for them.

I was hanging out in the back of a nearly empty courtroom one day, watching Edwina try to convince a jury to convict some loser whose idea of fun was slapping his wife around. She was giving them one of her feminist rah-rah speeches. Behind me I heard some guy mumbling, "Yeah, blah blah blah. Your pussy-whipped husband needs to slap *your* fat ass a few times, Lady."

I turned around and looked at this fleshy little turd who was scribbling in a reporter's notepad. He felt my stare and looked up with a greasy expression. "You have a problem, Punk?"

"You're talking about my aunt and uncle."

"Oh? Hey, that means you're Al Jacobs's punk bastard nephew." He smiled. "I heard about you, Kid. Righteous Al's nasty little family secret. Didn't your mother croak down in Mexico with a needle in her arm and her legs wrapped around some rich spick?"

I sucker punched him. Blood bloomed between his teeth, and as I watched, a front incisor slid neatly from its socket and fell out. His eyes rolled back, and he swayed forward hard enough to make a loud smack when his forehead hit the back of the bench where I sat. Edwina, the judge, the jurors, the bailiffs, the wife-beater, his lawyer, and the wife all rushed to the scene. They weren't sure what had happened.

"Haywood Kenney," one juror whispered. "Crime reporter from the *Tribune*. Maybe he's dead."

"I hope so," another whispered back. "He lives in my apartment building. He's a jerk."

Haywood Kenney lay sideways with his head against an elderly black man who happened to be sitting near him. The old man pushed Kenney away. "Nasty white boy," the old man said.

"What happened here?" the judge demanded. He prodded Kenney with his gavel. "Kenney. Don't bleed in my courtroom." He didn't like Kenney either.

I looked straight into Edwina's worried eyes and started to admit I'd hit the asshole, when the old man spoke up. "Man fainted, Your Honor. I saw the whole thing. Just passed out and fell forward and whacked himself in the mouth. This young man here tried to catch him, but it was too late."

The judge gave me, the old man, and Kenney a shrewd assessment. "Sounds reasonable," he said. "Couldn't happen to a more deserving member of the press." Edwina nodded. The jurors applauded.

"Quiet," the judge ordered. "Somebody check his pulse."

Edwina pressed her fingertips to his throat. "He'll live."

"Too bad," the old man said.

When Kenney came to, he took a long, woozy look up into the warning faces of the unfriendly judge, the smirking bailiffs, the stubborn old man, Edwina, and me, then picked up his tooth and clamped his bloody mouth shut. But one day not long after that he walked by Edwina and me in a courthouse hallway and said, "Just give me time. I'll get you and Al and your rat-bastard charity-case nephew, too."

Edwina arched a brow. "You're about as frightening as the Wicked Witch of the West. 'I'll get you, Dorothy, and your little dog, too.' At any rate, I can't imagine what you mean, Mr. Kenney, but next time, you'll need more than one tooth repaired." Then, pulling me by the arm like a little blond tractor, she breezed by.

"I think it's time we insisted on channeling your energy away from the courtroom," Al declared. "Edwina can take care of herself, and you need something to do that's more constructive than punching reporters. There are too many Haywood Kenneys in the world to devote yourself to rearranging their teeth." He said all that with an arm around my shoulder, then added, "So it's time, Pal, for us to incarcerate you. In high school."

I couldn't stand that — I'd never attended a real school for more than a few months here and there, and none at all after my mother moved us to Mexico. "I'm ditching this shit," I muttered to myself after the first week. I took a bus to the south side, lied about my age, and got a job skinning steer carcasses at a meat-packing plant. When Al found out, he was mad as hell.

"You lied to me. Don't ever lie to me again. Sorry, Pal, but you have to go to school."

"I don't need to sit in a classroom listening to teachers who've never been anywhere or done anything except take care of their own little pile of shit. You can't turn me into a monkey in a cage."

"Before your arrogance completely overwhelms your view of life, Mr. Monkey, at least take a few tests and show us how well you can count your own bananas."

"Try me."

I took their damned tests. They didn't know that my mother, when she was sober, had kept me in the company of smart people, educated people, and she'd pushed me to learn from them. Plus I liked to read. And I'd had my share of helpful women as tutors, not that I was going to tell Al and Edwina about them. A mathematics professor from the Universite del Sol had taught me algebra and trigonometry, then took me to bed. I was twelve when she made a man of me, so to speak. By

God, I knew how to solve an equation in bed. Some lessons you never forget.

So I took the tests, and everyone was shocked. I qualified for college-level courses, especially in math.

"Our teenage monkey has quite a brain," Edwina said to Al, prodding me with a finger as she talked, as if testing to see whether I had monkey fur under my shirt. Then, to me: "All right, so what do you want to be when you grow up, Monkey Boy?"

"I don't have a clue."

"You won't get a clue by skinning cows."

"I'm not like you and Al. I don't know how to save the world the way you do at the DA's office."

"You don't even know how to save the *cows.*"

That was true, but I got my high school GED without ever sitting in a classroom, and I refused to listen when they encouraged me to sample a few early college courses. I worked at the meat plant and kept to myself, saving money, insisting on paying Al and Edwina rent, pissing them off but earning their respect, grudgingly, the same way they'd earned mine. I lived a hidden life between their wide circle of educated friends and sophisticated interests and the dark, bloodstained world of the meat plant, where even the toughest SOBs on the factory line left me alone after I knocked out a few of their teeth.

He's hopelessly violent and isolated, everyone told Al. *Your charity will come back to haunt you.*

Why do you still keep those awful coyote skulls in your dresser drawer? Edwina's elegant sisters asked me nervously. Edwina had shown my skulls to her sisters without my permission. At the time, it felt like a major violation of my faith in her and Al.

Because they're the only family I can really trust, I said.

I WAS SEVENTEEN, still working at the meat plant, with no big plans and no idea how to decide what or who I should become.

Al and Edwina had almost given up trying to soften me, or polish me, or convince me I might learn the secret to peace of mind in a college classroom. I'd saved a lot of money but with no real purpose other than to buy myself a new flute and a 35mm camera with darkroom equipment. I took pictures of buildings and beef carcasses and good-looking girls and men on the factory line who threatened to cut my balls off if I *snapped that fuckin' camera one more fuckin' time,* which gave the whole hobby a dangerous edge I liked.

But underneath I hated myself and hated the dark void of uncertainty that wouldn't tell me where I fit in. So I planned to save the world in my mother's honor? How? When? Hell, not so far. I had blown off Great-Aunt Sophie's melodramatic hints, but deep inside, I wanted to know the truth that would change my life.

And then we got a call.

Sophie was dying, and she wanted to see me.

And I went.

I sat by her bed while a great-granddaughter hovered, casting worried glances from me to Sophie's wizened face. Like I might hurt the old lady.

Sophie finally looked at her with as much disgust as she could muster. "Leave the room; you bother me," she ordered. "What do you think — Nicholas scares me? Don't be a fool."

The great-granddaughter sighed and shut the door on her way out.

Sophie and I looked at each other for a minute. "Thank you," I said gruffly.

"You keep my rosary beads hanging on your mirror. I asked Aleksandr. He told me so."

I clenched my hands on my knees. "You told me to have faith in our family. I've tried for three years now. But I still don't fit in."

"But you *want* to fit in. You're loyal to Aleksandr and Edwina. Anyone can see that."

I shrugged. "They put up with me. I put up with them."

99

"Not good enough. Ask the question you fear the worst. Open your heart."

"What really happened to make my mother leave here?"

Sophie struggled for a moment, then lifted a tiny, decrepit hand and put it over one of mine. "Your mother and Aleksandr were raised by their father, and they adored him. But he was very strict."

I nodded. "Al's told me all about him." My grandfather had been dead for years when Al found me. Al said he was a great man. Had his portrait on the living room wall. Said the old man had the courage of his convictions.

"Everyone tried to find her when she ran away," Sophie went on. "Her cousins, and poor, worried Aleksandr, and all the other relatives. They looked for years. No one could understand why she thought she had no choice but to run away and never come home with her baby. Sins such as hers are easily forgiven by kind people. We *are* kind people. Margisia was a beloved girl. *Why, why, why did she run?* the family asked."

"My mother only told me she couldn't go back. That she got pregnant with no husband, and she knew she wasn't wanted."

"Poor Margisia." Sophie paused, struggling for strength. "No one but me knows what I am about to tell you. It is your choice whether you tell Aleksandr and the others. It would break Aleksandr's heart. And I know what I have to say will hurt you, too, but you will be hurt much more if you go on blaming your family for her sorrows."

"Tell me," I said.

Sophie shut her eyes, then opened them and looked at me with hard, sad resolution. "Her papa told her she could not come home unless she gave her baby away. He called her names. Said she ruined her life. Said she broke his heart and he'd never forgive her. Said he would rather take her child and throw it in the river than raise a bastard under his roof. He said if she wouldn't give the baby away she should leave and never come home again. I know. I was there when he spoke all those terrible words to her."

I sat for a long time with my head bowed. I said nothing, wanted to *feel* nothing, because at that moment I knew how much my mother had sacrificed to keep me, no matter how badly she'd managed the rest. In a sense I *had* been given away as a child, and I hurt enough to do justice to the truth. When I looked at Sophie again, she was wheezing lightly but watching me with shrewd eyes. "After your mother disappeared, your grandfather never spoke her name again. His regrets killed him. No one knows why he died of a broken heart but me."

"Everyone in the family honors his memory. And Al thinks he walked on water."

"Yes. Now it's up to you to decide whether to tell Aleksandr the truth, or if you need to tell him anything at all. But no more bitterness toward this *family,* all right?"

I stood, bending over her as if I were bowing to her, holding her frail hand like a bird. "You're my great-aunt Sophie," I said simply, "and I trust you."

Her eyes gleamed.

I never told Al what his father did to my mother, and thus to me. I didn't need to. I didn't want to. You don't hurt the people you love.

I had a family now.

I WASN'T TRANSFORMED OVERNIGHT BY Sophie's confession, but I did start to feel there was some good reason I'd been rescued by Al, and I wanted to make him and the other Jacobses proud of me. When I turned eighteen, I found myself outside a downtown storefront, staring at an Army recruitment poster as if I'd been struck by lightning. The Vietnam War was over but had left a bad taste in the public mouth. The Army seemed sinister. People said the generals were all liars, like Nixon, and a career as a soldier seemed foolish. Al had served in the National Guard during college, and struggled with his own hatred of the war machine versus the fact that two of his favorite cousins had been killed in the

Marines, and he had not. "It's not the soldiers' fault that the god-damned politicians and generals sent them over there to kill and be killed for no good reason," he would yell, maybe out of guilt.

I had a simpler view of things.

A young, bulldog-jawed Green Beret looked back at me in the recruiting poster. He wore a full dress uniform, including a sword. The slogan beneath him said BE A SPECIAL FORCES SOLDIER. DE OP-PRESSO LIBER. TO FREE THE OPPRESSED. My spine tingled. I could be a soldier. I could be a warrior. A samurai. A knight in shining armor. I'd free the oppressed. Then no one would ask me how I *felt* about anything, or tell me I ought to learn how to fit in with the ordinary world. Green Berets didn't have to *feel* a certain way, or fit in. They were meant to be different. They only had to do the job.

The job of saving the world.

I walked inside the recruiter's office and joined the Army.

"I finally have a mission," I told Al and Edwina that night. "I'm going to become a Green Beret."

"Is that the best you can do?" Edwina shouted. "You aspire to travel to exotic places and kill exotic people?" Then she broke down in tears. In the four years I'd lived there, I'd never seen her cry before. She had left the DA's office to work as an advocate for a civil liberties group. She'd made a name for herself in city politics. So had Al. He'd won election to the state court. Judge Al, I called him, sometimes. "You have a good heart but a bad philosophy about life," she moaned, "and the Army's going to twist you into someone we won't recognize."

Al was more logical, but just as upset. "I respect the military, Nick, but I don't trust the men who lead it right now. The Army is not the noble way of life you think it is. Besides, you hate rules, you hate living by other people's by-the-books mentality. Then why, in God's name, do you want to be part of the most regi-mented, anachronistic, soulless, brainless institution mankind ever created?"

Whatever I said in return made no difference. I packed my duffel bag and left in the middle of the night while they were asleep. I posted a note for Edwina.

You can throw the coyote skulls away if you want to.

One week after I entered basic training, I got a package from her and Al. It was full of the funny, ordinary things families send to enlisted men — cookies and new socks, a good razor, a box of stationery, and the rosary beads Great-Aunt Sophie had given me.

There was a note from Al in the package. *You think you can get rid of us this easily?* he wrote. *I told you not to underestimate us.* And there was a photo of my bedroom, which had long since ceased to look girly.

Edwina had hung the coyote skulls on the wall.

SEVEN

Weapons Specialist Nicholas Jakobek, that was me. Sergeant Nick Jakobek. Green Beret. Nineteen eighty-one. I was twenty-three years old, six-four and 225 pounds, all of it muscle. Five years into my Army career, and I was happy enough. I hadn't killed anybody yet, but I knew how — I'd mastered a dozen different techniques, aside from my obvious talent with every kind of gun in the U.S. Army's arsenal. I had even begun the slow process of earning a college degree. Whenever I got leave from Fort Bragg, North Carolina, I flew home to Chicago. Al and Edwina still disapproved of my career, so we talked about *their* careers instead. They were moving up the ranks in state politics. There was talk of running Al for Congress.

"Not bad for a dumb guy and a pregnant woman," Al said.

"Fuck you, Papa-san-to-be," Edwina retorted. Then she kissed him. She and Al were in their midthirties, and had been trying to get pregnant for several years. They'd almost given up before they hit the jackpot. Now, Edwina walked like a blond balloon perched on sausages. When I arrived at the apartment that fall, her due date was only two weeks away, and she'd just gone on maternity leave. She commandeered me instantly. "Your mission, Sergeant Nick, is to help me waddle to the park every day for a little exercise."

"Will do. Just don't fall on me."

She said some bad things in Latin.

The next day we put on heavy sweaters and jogging pants, and started along the crowded sidewalk outside the apartment building. Al was in court. Edwina lumbered along with me slightly in front of her, clearing a path in the lunchtime crowds. People tended to step aside when they saw me coming. I could hear Edwina huffing and puffing behind me. "Look how people are dodging us," I said over my shoulder. "They're afraid you'll turn into a human bowling ball."

"Nick." The odd tone in her voice made me turn quickly. She had stopped in the middle of the sidewalk. She pointed downward. Large stains were spreading down the legs of her dark sweats. "My water broke. Call a cab."

She sounded calm enough. I steered her to a lamppost. "Hold on." I flagged a cab, got her into the backseat with her feet propped up, then climbed in the front. "Cook County. Hurry."

"I'm *not* going to the *public* hospital," Edwina complained loudly. "We'll just take our time and cruise over to . . ." Her voice became a sharp gasp, and she clutched her stomach.

"Cook County," I told the driver again. "Fast."

What happened next sounds like a bad joke, but it's the truth. The traffic in Chicago can stop everything but the clock. Our cab got bottlenecked on the way to the hospital, with no hope of moving, and by then Edwina was moaning and punching the back of the seat. "Get on your radio and try to get a cop here," I told the cabbie, then climbed out and went to the back. I opened the passenger door and stared at the soggy crotch of her jogging pants. I could ford a whitewater river with a hundred pounds of gear on my back, live for days in the desert on cactus leaves and my own urine, assemble any rifle known to modern warfare, and pinpoint a target no bigger than an ant's balls. But I had no idea what to do with Edwina's crotch.

"I'm going to have this baby *right now*," she gasped.

"No. Hold on. Think about something else."

"That's not how it works, Nicholas. Get in here and pull these pants off of me."

I knelt between her updrawn legs, hooked my fingers in her clothing, and slid her pants halfway off. Then I stopped.

"For godssake, get my panties off, too! I don't care if you see my ass and the entire theme park of wonders in its vicinity! Just get my clothes off!"

"All right. Calm down." With a few quick tugs, I jerked everything to her ankles, then tried to look only at her face.

Flushed and panting, she jabbed a finger toward her thighs. "I think the baby's head is crowning! Tell me what you see!"

I started sweating. My hands trembled. I gently pried her thighs open and studied the bulging, heaving scenery between them. Edwina screamed and grunted. The baby's bloody, filmy skull appeared. "I have eye contact," I said loudly.

Edwina yelled, groaned, arched her back, and convulsed. "Put your hands down there. Catch the baby!"

I cupped my hands in place, and by God, a miracle occurred. A tiny girl filled them, wiggling just a little. Edwina collapsed, moaning and gasping and trying to lift her head enough to see what—who—I held. "Hand me the baby . . . slowly . . . Nicholas. Gently."

"I've got her," I said. "Don't worry."

"Her. *Her*." Edwina made a crooning sound. "A *girl*. I have to tell Al we have a *daughter*."

I carefully balanced the infant on Edwina's chest, forgetting all awkwardness, cupping the baby's butt in one hand to hold her steady and smoothing the blood and goo off her face. She opened sleepy-looking eyes and seemed to gaze right up at me. I was her first sight in the world. "Hello," I whispered.

"Hello," a big, burly cop said behind me. He peered into the backseat. I tried to shield Edwina's nudity with the baby and my hands. The cop grinned. "Hi, Mrs. Jacobs. Charley Grimoldi. I testified in the Lakenhower case a few years ago."

"Hello, Officer Grimoldi. Will you get me a paramedic, please?" Edwina sounded totally calm again. Good ol' Edwina. I was still trembling like a leaf. My baby cousin and I continued to look at each other. Yeah, I know babies can't see very well when they're born, but she could sense my intentions, I'm sure. In her heart, she was the first human being who looked at me with nothing but trust and curiosity.

"Relax, Pal," the cop told me. "Help's on the way. Be here in a second."

But I continued to hold the baby. Edwina reached for her, stroking her head fervently. "Oh, oh, oh. Move her up a little more, Nicholas." I helped Edwina sit up. She curled her hands around her daughter. "How perfect she is, Nicholas. How perfect. Thank you for helping her into the world."

She cried happily. The baby mewled.

I smiled.

I STOOD ALONE OUTSIDE a hospital entrance that night, smoking a cigar Al had given me, watching in satisfaction as silver curlicues of my own breath rose in the cold night air. The sounds of the city seemed full and rich around me. Life. "Hey, Doc Jakobek," Al said as he joined me. He was giddy with excitement, grinning and slapping me on the back.

I shrugged. "I just played catch."

He put an arm around my shoulders. He had to reach up to do it now. "Shut up, Sergeant. Accept some praise." He looked at me with somber affection. "I thank you, Edwina thanks you, and your new baby cousin thanks you."

"Don't tell Edwina, but I hope I never see her crotch again."

Al laughed until he cried. "Come on inside. We have something to tell you."

I cast wary glances at him as I followed him indoors and rode an elevator to the maternity ward. Edwina smiled at me wearily from her bed in a private room. She snuggled the baby, swaddled in a blanket. Al sat on the edge of the bed beside them. I stayed back, almost standing at attention. They were a threesome. They needed their privacy.

"We've named her," Edwina said.

I grunted. "Good. I won't have to call her 'Hey, you.' "

Al and Edwina traded a tender look. "You tell him," Edwina said.

Al nodded and looked at me. "Her first name's Edwina. For guess who?"

"Makes sense."

"Her middle name is . . . Margisia. For her aunt. Your mother."

I took a few seconds, glancing away, exhaling, then looking back. "That's good, too."

"But of course, she's special. She needs three given names. So she'll be Nicola, too. In *your* honor."

I had to look away again, this time for longer. A few deep breaths, and then I stepped over a little closer to them, and gazed down at the baby. "Edwina Margisia Nicola Jacobs." I spoke her full name aloud — christened her, in my own way. "Eddie," I decided.

"Eddie!" Al agreed.

Edwina rolled her eyes. "Edwina Junior is not going to be called Eddie!" And off she went on a long yatter about Eddie's future and how undignified to be nicknamed something that sounded like a shortstop or a bookie while Al just sat there, nodding patiently, and I reached down, very carefully, and touched the tip of my forefinger to the tip of Eddie's soft nose. I made her a promise.

I'll keep the world safe for you, Little Girl.

NINETEEN EIGHTY-FOUR. I was now First Lieutenant Nick Jakobek, fresh out of officer's training, with a newly minted bachelor's degree, too. An officer *and* a college graduate. I credit Eddie for that phase of my life. Her birth and the three peaceful years that followed it made me feel new inside. Although it was only temporary.

Al and Edwina doted on Eddie, and so did I, in my own way. She was a doll. She had big blue eyes and golden brown hair, a compromise between Edwina's blond and Al's dark brown. As soon as she began to talk, she named me *Nicky*. I often didn't see her for months at a time, but all I had to do was walk in the door again and she'd come running to me with her arms out. "Nicky!" And I couldn't resist picking her up and hugging her.

"Not a bad kid you've got there," I told Al and Edwina.

They weren't fooled. "Get out of the damned Army," Al lectured. "Find a wife. Settle down. You love kids. Start planning to have some."

None of that was in my cards. I slept with the kind of women who moved fast and left damage behind. I could deal with them. I understood them. They were dependably undependable. Plus I couldn't imagine having children of my own to protect. A kid deserved total love and devotion. I was afraid to love anyone that much. Eddie came close enough.

As often as Al and Edwina still tried to talk me into marriage and out of the military, they now talked about changing their own lives, too. Al's work had taken a dark turn. That spring, a prominent Chicago judge was convicted of accepting bribes. Al had helped gather the evidence against him. My uncle had been working undercover with the Justice Department since not long after Eddie was born. Edwina would have been right in there with him, except for the baby.

"One of us has to stay alive for Eddie's sake," she said.

The level of corruption was a wide, stinking pile of shit. Judges, court clerks, police officers, lawyers—all exposed as thieves.

"They're an embarrassment to the system and a threat to the basic integrity of the law," Al said. "There's a lot more work to do before the mess is cleaned up. Twenty or thirty powerful people could be indicted before this is over."

"You could get yourself killed," I countered. "I wouldn't be surprised if somebody out there doesn't suspect you of being the snitch."

"Who, me? I'm just a do-gooding state court judge. Not worth the trouble."

That summer, someone pinned a note to the windshield of the small sedan Al had bought after years of smog-conscious dedication to buses and trains.

You're going to die, you sneaking rat bastard.

I quietly requested extra leave and came home for a month. Every morning I walked Al and Edwina to a cab outside the apartment building, and every evening from the courthouse to a cab to go home. In between, I sat on a bench across the street from Eddie's day nursery. "This is ridiculous, Nick," Al said gently. "You don't have to worry. We have police protection. Besides, it was an idle threat."

"No threat is idle."

"Look, I can take care of myself. You just keep an eye on Edwina and Eddie for me. I have to work this Saturday. Take them to the park."

"I think they should stay indoors."

"I think," Al countered, "that you won't want to be locked indoors all day with a busy three-year-old and Edwina, who's gnashing her teeth because she's worried about *me*."

So we went to the park.

THAT DAY WAS BRIGHT and hot, the park's trees shimmering in the breeze, making my skin crawl with every rustle of their leaves. Eddie tossed sand in a play pit and chortled at Edwina and me. We sat a few feet away on a bench. I kept one hand near the small automatic pistol hidden inside my pants pocket. "I want more power over the lunacy of life," Edwina said. "Al and I aren't making enough of a difference. We *swore* we'd make a difference."

"Why do you care so much?"

"My mother and sisters have no agenda beyond their next manicures. My family owns business interests that pretty much fuck their employees up the ass. I promised myself I'd never settle for that kind of status quo. But over the past few years, I feel that I've been doing just that, in a way. I've been settling. Marking time."

"You have a kid to worry about now. Maybe you're just scared that this sting operation will get Al hurt."

"No, it's not just that. I'm tired of seeing drug addicts go to prison instead of into rehab. I'm tired of watching Al sentence battered women to jail after they shoot the men who beat them up. He hates it, but the law's the law. I'm tired of all the stupidity that exists in the system. I can't fix it at this level." She rubbed a line of tension between her eyes. "Some influential people have been talking to Al about making the leap next year. Running for Congress."

Al. A congressman. I took a moment away from scanning the soft green landscape around us to look at her askance. "I think *you* should run for Congress. You're a winner, Ed-winna."

She smiled. "In a different world, I'd be a politician. But the truth is, Nicholas, women are still at too much of a disadvantage, and I don't come across as *demure* enough to win votes. Besides, I never do anything unless I'm aiming for the top. If I went into politics, it would be with one goal in mind for the future, but that goal would be impossible." She paused. "I'd want to be President."

"Go for it. If you win, you could make me a general. I'd be happy to salute you."

"I think I'd order you to leave the country. You've seen my vagina."

I coughed and changed the subject. "So, if *you* don't run, you think Al could? Be President, that is. Someday?"

She didn't hesitate. "He will be."

The way she said it gave me goosebumps. I didn't doubt her. I stood, feeling odd, sensing some electric fate in the air, as if Edwina had set destiny in motion and it was up to me to make certain nothing interfered. "I'm going to walk the perimeter of the park again. I'll be back in two minutes." I pointed to the baby bag she held on her lap. I had hidden a pistol in it and instructed her to keep one hand on it every time I left her sitting there.

She groaned. "Not again. I'm not meant to play Rambo." She stood, too. "You're giving me the creeps, or I'm giving them to myself. Let's go home." She hung the bag on her shoulder as I scooped Eddie up. "Nicky," Eddie squealed, and kissed me on the cheek.

We headed along a shady sidewalk that bordered the park beside a quiet back street. Edwina reached up and smoothed her daughter's sunny brown hair back. "Nicholas, I'll tell you a secret. And you can take this one to the bank, just like my prediction about Al." She paused. "Someday, my daughter is going to be the first woman President."

I looked from her to Eddie, who patted me on the nose. "If that's what Eddie wants."

"She will."

In terms of family ambitions, Edwina might have been getting in over her head. I made a mental note to speak up on Eddie's behalf when her mother insisted she start campaigning for election.

Probably in kindergarten.

I saw the rusty van from the corner of my eye when it was still fifty yards behind us, moving slowly. Maybe it was the way the driver curled in a little too close to the curb. Maybe it was his suspiciously slow speed. I didn't wait to find out if I was wrong. "Take Eddie and run for those trees over there. Don't ask questions. Go. *Now*." I thrust Eddie into Edwina's arms. Edwina took one glance back at the van, clutched her daughter, and sprinted for a stand of firs. The van roared and sped up.

I saw only one person up front — the driver — but for all I knew, others were hidden in the back. The driver wasn't making any subtle moves. He steered the van over the curb and onto the sidewalk, heading straight for Edwina and Eddie, who wouldn't make it to the trees in time. I sprinted toward the van, pulling the automatic pistol from my pocket as I ran.

The driver swerved as I slid to a stop twenty feet in front of him, with the pistol pointed at his windshield. I had time for one shot. I pulled the trigger, and the van's windshield exploded. The van careened sideways and plowed into a lamppost.

"Get down! Stay down!" I yelled to Edwina, who'd made it to the grove of firs by then. She ducked under their branches, then dropped to her knees and huddled behind a tree trunk with Eddie wrapped in her arms.

The van's driver moved sluggishly inside the cab. He wasn't shot, just stunned. Pebbles of windshield glass covered him. I launched myself at the van's back door, jerked it open with my pistol raised, but found no one inside. Next I ran to the front passenger door and tried to open it, too. It was locked. The driver blinked hard and dragged his left hand over his forehead, where the windshield glass had left small, bloody divets. I pounded my left hand on the rolled-up passenger window while I stepped on the running board. "Don't fucking move," I ordered, and thrust my right arm, holding the pistol, inside the blown-out windshield frame. I leveled the pistol at his head and continued pounding on the passenger window with my hand. He inhaled sharply and came to life. He lifted something from a jumble of old towels in his lap. He pointed a gun at me, and fired.

The concussion from the close-range blast hit me like a slap. The window glass exploded, just as the windshield had, with a force that flung my left hand and arm backward. I stumbled off the running board, dazed, covered in glass, my head ringing with the gunshot. The driver shoved his door open and jumped out, still holding his pistol. He ran for the street.

I followed.

I caught him from behind in the middle of that quiet, civilized lane. He was a few inches shorter than me, but thickset, a body-builder. Even so, he didn't stand a chance. I dropped my gun. Out of my throat came a guttural sound I still hear in my dreams some nights. I caught him around the head from behind. I put one hand under his chin, and the other at the back of his skull. If my damaged left arm hurt, I didn't notice. I channeled all my strength into the job I had been trained to do. I twisted his head.

And broke his neck.

He collapsed at my feet without a sound, twitching, dying. I stood over him victoriously, breathing hard, my feet braced apart, my hands held out slightly from my sides, open and flexed. I could kill him again, if I had to. I wanted to.

The scent of blood began to clear my mind. I stared at him. He'd stopped convulsing, yet blood dripped on his face. I frowned. The blood dripped from *me*. I raised my left hand slowly, and stared at it.

My little finger was gone. He'd shot it off.

"*Dear God,*" Edwina said hoarsely, behind me.

I turned slowly — bloody, maimed, peppered with glass. She stood on the far side of the van with Eddie burrowed in her arms, crying. Edwina kept one hand over Eddie's face to shield her from the sight of the dead man. And the sight of me.

For the first time since I'd known her, I saw disgust in Edwina's eyes. And I saw fear. She'd never feel the same about her and Eddie's safety in public again, but she'd never feel the same about me again either.

I was a killer. It had come easily.
And she was afraid of me.

⁂

"HOW ARE YOU feeling?" Al asked quietly. He'd come back to my hospital bed late that night while I tried to sleep.

"Fine," I lied. I rubbed my eyes with my good hand. The other one was bandaged like a mitten, and the whole arm had been bound in a sling. My face was speckled with small cuts from the glass. I brooded less about my hand than about what I'd become, what I'd done. I didn't feel guilty, and that scared me a little, but then it made me angry, too. I had killed a man who intended to harm the people I loved. Why should I feel anything but satisfied?

"Do you want me to sit here with you?" Al asked. "I'll get a cot. I'll stay all night."

"You need to be home with your family. And you need to spend your time fielding more phone calls from the reporters." Newspaper and TV people were crawling all over the story of the attack and Al's undercover work that had provoked it. He and Edwina were big news now. So was I, but not in a good way. The bastard son of a troubled mother the Jacobs family didn't like to discuss. The Green Beret who had killed a civilian in cold blood.

"You're my family, too," Al countered. That old battle. "You saved your aunt and your cousin's lives today. My wife's life. My daughter's life." Al laid a hand on my good arm. "And you had no choice about the rest of what happened. It was self-defense."

I didn't tell him what I'd seen in Edwina's eyes. I doubt she'd have admitted it herself. And I didn't tell Al something else, either. I could have let the driver go. Let him run. Called the police—they'd have caught the dumb fuck easily. I could have knocked him out, held him down, waited. But I didn't. I killed him. Al and Edwina were telling everyone my actions were self-defense. Maybe true, in the technical sense of the term. No one was going to prosecute me. No charges would be filed. "Yeah, it was self-defense," I said slowly.

Al nodded, his face a little strained at my tone. "You don't have to justify it. He had a gun. You couldn't tell whether he intended to turn around and shoot you again. For all you knew, he intended to go after Edwina and Eddie again. You wrestled with him. You didn't mean to kill him."

I said nothing. *Goddammit, Al, you're the one with the conscience, not me.* Al didn't want to admit that killing could be a good thing, purely and simply, that the man who had tried to hurt his wife and baby deserved to be executed, along with whatever goddamned corrupt judge or lawyer or high-ranking cop had hired the hit. "I intend to find the person who sent that man," Al said now. "And I'll put him away for the rest of his life."

Put him away. All neat and clean, a prison sentence, by the books. No, he didn't want me to confirm that I'd killed for him and Edwina and Eddie, not in self-defense but in revenge, and that deep down, he was glad.

"Go home," I said. "I think I can sleep again. I'll see you in the morning."

He stood. He laid a hand on my hair, as if I were a kid. "I hope you sleep well. Edwina and Eddie and I love you, Nick."

After he left the room, I cried.

BILL SNIDERMAN WAS thirty-eight and looked like a balding Bill Cosby, already showing more forehead than hair. He had the top-dog attitude of a successful man who collected enough money as a corporate attorney to afford politics as a hobby. He'd already made his name as a savvy advisor in statewide campaigns and civil rights debates. He and Al and Edwina had been friends since college. He'd tried to dissuade them from taking me in as a kid. He sat in a chair beside my hospital bed that morning, smoothing the perfect creases in the knees of his thousand-dollar suit.

"What?" I said. "No candy? No flowers? No 'Hope You Find Your Finger' card?"

He threw down a newspaper. "I always knew it was just a matter of time before your uncle's enemies dragged you out from under your rock to hurt him."

The paper fell open to a column by Haywood Kenney. By then fleshy little Kenney, the crime reporter, had become a fleshy, round-faced political columnist. His sprigs of brown curls were already starting to recede, so his forehead showed between the individual wavy hairs. The meatpackers called him Pube Head, but his readers loved him. He'd been fired from the *Tribune* for rigging a story to make it more dramatic, but now his freelance column was syndicated in newspapers all over the midwest, and he hosted a popular talk-radio show about politics on a local AM station. He had never stopped dogging Al and Edwina, waiting for revenge. Now, he began to take it.

BLEEDING-HEART AL AND HIS PERSONAL ASSASSIN ESCAPE MURDER CHARGES, the headline over Kenney's column read.

"This is running in five major newspapers in Illinois today," Bill Sniderman said. "Whether it's true or not doesn't matter."

I stared at the paper grimly. "I know."

"I don't like you, Nick. I never have. You're bad luck for Al. Bad mojo. Bad karma. An albatross around the neck of his political future."

"Tell me something I *don't* know."

"He's going to run for Congress in the next election. I'm going to manage his campaign. The publicity he and Edwina are getting right now makes this the perfect time for him to launch his political career. Edwina and I have mapped out a plan, and it *will* work. He'll serve one term in Congress, then run for the U.S.

Senate. He'll serve two, maybe three terms in the Senate, and then run for President. And he'll win."

"Sounds simple."

"It will be. He's a good man, a man people naturally like and trust. He's the best candidate I've ever seen in my life—squeaky-clean, wholesome background, loyal as a dog, a good husband, a good father, a great public servant. I'm not thrilled that his family's Polish Catholic—too ethnic, you know, and that's tricky—but I can work with it. Edwina's pilgrim credentials and all-American blue blood make her the perfect partner for him. She can get things done, and she's one thousand percent behind him. And of course, Eddie's the cutest little promotional asset in the world."

"Don't talk about Eddie that way."

The tone of my voice made Bill swallow hard. "Sorry. Of course not. Al and Edwina don't look at her the same way I do. You should hear them talking this morning. They're afraid to show her face in public again. I'm worried that they'll be over-protective of her."

"Maybe you can convince them to put her in a nice, safe cage and let voters pay a quarter to look at her."

Bill stared at me. "Let's confine the topics to *you*, okay? All I have to do is eliminate anything and anyone who screws with Al's perfect image. *You.*"

"Aw, Bill, you're flattering me."

"Listen. You'd do anything for him and Edwina and Eddie. Don't bullshit me, I know how you are. Like a wolf protecting its den. Good. Then protect them by going away. Stay out of their lives. Find yourself a nice, quiet hole to crawl into. In another part of the world."

"I'm betting Al doesn't know you're here."

He stood, looking nervous. "No."

"Good. No need to tell him."

Bill exhaled. "I'm glad you agree. He'd be mad as hell. He's loyal to you. Sentimental. That's what makes him so appealing, but it could also ruin him."

"I know."

"Then you'll heed my advice?"

I nodded. "I'm already working on it."

"You're his Achilles' heel. Get out of his spotlight. And stay out." He studied my face and adjusted his silk tie with a nervous flick of one hand, as if thinking of broken necks.

But I was only thinking of loneliness.

A MUTUAL FRIEND AT Fort Bragg made the contact for me, and they sent someone the next day. My life changed that quick, as if the right people and the right moment had been waiting for me out there in the shadows, until I admitted where I belonged. The visitor was only forty, if that, square-jawed and lean, wearing a major's uniform. He had eyes like something that hunts in the woods when the moon is out. Eyes like mine, in fact. He showed me a clean-cut Army ID taken when he was a raw private during the early years of Vietnam. "Just want you to see that we all start out looking like Boy Scouts," he said. "Back then I thought I could save the world just by keeping my underwear clean and waving the flag."

I said nothing for a few seconds, as I finished buttoning the shirt of my uniform, using only my good hand and never asking for help. In years to come, the memory of that pressed shirt — with its stiff cloth torturing the small cuts the flying glass had made on my arms and the smell of new beginnings rising like an antiseptic from the material — would always make a hollow sensation in the pit of my stomach. "You're in luck, Sir. Nobody has to tell me that idealism alone won't get the job done."

"Let me ask you something. When you snapped that man's neck, you knew exactly what you were put on this earth to do, didn't you? You took care of God, country, and family. All in one snap of a brutal motherfucker's spine. Hmmm? God, country, and family."

"Not in that order."

"Whatever inspires you. Fine. We live in a brave new world, Mr. Jakobek. Global. Nuclear. The rules of combat are changing. The enemy isn't marching across a battlefield. He's squatting in a cave or an office somewhere with a satellite phone and a computer and access to weapons we don't even want to think about. To Mom and Pop America, the technology-inspired world seems civilized and quiet. But all the murderous, crazy shit of mankind is still going on out there, and all the killing fields are still open for busi-ness—armed with global capabilities now. Only people who un-derstand that—and who are willing to crawl under the rocks and get dirty if they have to—will choose who owns the future. Us." He paused. "Or Them."

"I accept your invitation to transfer to your group, Sir."

"Good. We'll take care of the details in terms of paperwork. Welcome to your new line of work, Captain Jakobek. Congratulations on your instant promotion. You're now part of the behind-the-scenes war the Army doesn't admit openly and the American public doesn't fund—knowingly—with their tax pen-nies." He paused. "Any questions or second thoughts?"

"No, Sir. I know what I'm doing. I'm fully aware that your people operate below the radar. All I want is to do my job with-out being a burden to my family."

"Secrecy, Mr. Jakobek—" he paused to smile—"is our best weapon."

I couldn't agree more. That afternoon I boarded a plane leav-ing Chicago, leaving the States, heading anywhere and every-where else on the planet. When you look into the dark, what looks back at you? It might be the unhappiness of someone you love but can't help, or it might be the sickness of a stranger who wouldn't mind killing that someone. Or both. You either hunch down and wait for the fight to come for you, or you step into the darkness with your fists up. I'd decided to do whatever was necessary to guard the people I loved against the evil out there, beyond the light.

The letter I left for Al and Edwina summed up my decision this simply: *If you need me, I'll always be out there. I'll do anything for you and Eddie. Just call me.* Al and Edwina wrote back: *When these people are done with you, we won't even recognize your good heart. Will you come if we need you? Of course. And we'll always be here for you. All you have to do is come home. We'll wait.*

So would I.

EIGHT

Barbara Walters still hadn't called, the Marines hadn't stormed my front flower beds, and the killer relative of Eddie Jacobs — one Nicholas Jakobek — hadn't even bothered to phone ahead. I liked to know when presidential hit men expected to arrive on my doorstep. It was only polite.

Oh, there were lots of other phone calls coming in — from the President's aides in Washington, D.C., various Jacobs family members in Chicago, and a hoard of the First Lady's high-toned relatives in Maryland. All these people, asking to speak to Eddie, being upset when Davis refused to wake her up, and telling me I was responsible for her well-being.

"I haven't misplaced even *one* presidential daughter during apple season yet," I said, and put Smooch in charge of taking messages after that.

U.S. Secret Service Agent Lucille — now fully, in southern tradition, identified as Lucille Olson, one of two Olson daughters from a farm family in Minneapolis, Minnesota — guarded my front door. *Guarded* it. Eddie Jacobs needed protection from terrorists, stalkers, kidnappers, and God-alone-knew what other threats a presidential daughter fell heir to, including, apparently, a runaway romance with a fellow Harvard student. I looked around my home with a sinking sense of security, as if the scum of the earth might rise out of my flower beds and rush the antique front door with its brass apple knocker.

Up at the gate, Lucille's fellow Secret Service agents loitered unhappily beside their hulking SUVs. Logan, big and beefy and gently immovable, stood guard before our locked entrance with his tan Stetson on the roof of his patrol car and a fried apple pie in one hand. We had the same reddish-brown hair and green eyes. He was a little baby faced, but strong of character and deep of spirit. A tall, good-looking McGillen, like me.

"Pies, boys?" he called slyly to the agents. They didn't take the bait.

No need to worry that Logan would crack under the pressure, though I was a little worried about his vulnerability where Lucille was concerned. Logan and Lucille had circled each other like antsy house cats when he stopped by the house to introduce himself. He asked her the caliber of her handgun and offered her a fried pie. She shook her head but eyed him with an arched blond brow. He eyed her likewise. He had no idea how to flirt with an armed woman, but it was clear he might try. My brother, a lonely and gallant homebody, had lost a beloved young wife to cancer after only two years of marriage. They'd met while he was overseas in the Army. He doted on their five-year-old daughter. We all did.

She was the sixth Hush McGillen. We called her Hush Puppy.

Puppy sat in the patrol car at the gate, pretending to color a coloring book but darting looks at the agents across the road. "Morning, Puppy," I cooed, leaning into the open window and smoothing her dark hair. She smiled, turned her face up, and let me kiss her on the forehead. "Morning, Aunt Hush."

"I'm going to take you to my house and feed you some of the apple-cinnamon buns cousin Laurie's testing for the catalog. Then we'll put *Harry Potter* on the VCR. Or you can read through your books. You know, I'm ordering you the whole *Detective Girls* series next week." Hush Puppy had a pink, girly bedroom at my house. I'd decorated it especially for her. She stayed with me whenever Logan was out of town on county business. "And I'll set up the Go Girls game on your computer, if you want to play it," I coaxed.

But none of those enticements worked. Her face went somber. "Aunt Hush, I'm too old to treat like a baby. I need to stay up here and watch what's going on."

"Oh? Why?"

"Lucille looks like a lady wrestler, and I think she's gonna throw Daddy for a loop."

"Honey, I expect Lucille could wrestle a full-grown gorilla if she had to."

"She could sure wrestle Daddy. He just stared at her with his mouth open when they met. I think he'd let her win." Hush Puppy looked wistful. "Do you think she has any little girls I could play with?" Puppy was lonely for playmates and sisters.

"I don't get the feeling she's married or has any children, Honey. But she's sure tough enough to be a mother."

"Ahem," Logan said.

I moved away from Puppy's earshot. "How's it going?"

"You're about to have thirty employees lined up outside this gate. What do you want me to do, Sis?"

I handed him a boxful of fried apple pies. "Feed them. Let them in. Tell them to meet me at the main barn and I'll tell them . . . something. Not the truth. Not today. We're opening this farm today just as if nothing's happened."

"There's a problem." He jerked his head toward the stoic group of agents watching us from across the road. "These boys tell me we can't open the gate. They won't stand by and let it happen."

My blood went cold. "You're kidding."

"Orders of Lucille."

Logan set the plate of pies on a gatepost. Across the road, the agents craned their heads and sniffed the fried apple–scented air, but didn't budge. "Tough people," my brother said dryly. "Sis, they're just playing nice for now. We're gonna be in over our heads soon." He hesitated. We both glanced at the patrol car to make certain Hush Puppy had her head down over her coloring book. Logan looked at me somberly. "Not much makes me worry," he said. "But I don't like the idea of outsiders getting too curious about us."

My heart in my throat, I nodded. "Things will be okay by tomorrow. I promise you."

"If we don't get this gate open, the whole county's going to know something funny's going on. *Today.* There'll be a lot of talk. A lot of questions."

That was it. Done. "I'll be back in ten minutes," I said, "with Lucille."

"OPEN THIS GATE," I ordered.

"No, Mrs. Thackery. I can't." Lucille stepped between us and the gate and refused to move. Logan held up the key to the padlock. "Come on now, Lucy," he crooned in a drawl that could congeal mustard. The morning sun glinted off his patrol car. Hush Puppy gaped at the three of us from an open window. Lucille's fellow agents inched toward us across the road. Logan and I gave them a hard look, and they stopped. Then Logan turned a softer gaze on Lucille. "Agent Lucy, you make a mighty appealing barricade, but step aside."

Lucille ignored him and looked at me. "It's a very bad idea to allow huge crowds of strangers near a member of the President's family. Crowds are unpredictable and impossible to fully control. I can't allow this gate to be opened until I speak to my superiors — and to Eddie's parents. I've alerted everyone to the situation. We need to wait for them to contact us."

"Eddie is sound asleep and will stay inside my house, safe as can be. Nobody knows she's there except us. Nobody is going to know."

"This will be resolved soon. Postpone your opening day until this afternoon at least."

"Not going to happen."

"Then I'm not moving." She planted herself at the juncture of the gates, and rested her hands on the padlocked chain.

Logan sighed. "I'm not sure I have the authority to arrest you, Agent Olson, but I hope you won't hold any grudge if I *tackle* you."

"If you do, you'll be wearing your badge someplace it doesn't fit well, Sheriff."

Logan looked impressed. The cell phone on my belt began to chime. I clamped the phone to my ear. "Sweet Hush Farms."

"This is the White House calling," a woman said. "The First Lady's on the line. *Please* hold."

I cupped a hand over the phone. I didn't have time to think about who or what or why. No nerves. The tornado had landed. "You got your wish, Lucille. It's Edwina."

Lucille stiffened. "Please don't call her that, Mrs. Thackery. A word of advice. Always refer to her as 'Mrs. Jacobs,' or 'Ma'am.'"

I didn't have time to say that the honor would have to be reciprocated. Logan and I traded a wide-eyed look. *Be nice,* he mouthed. A crisp, female, uppity East Coast voice poured into my ear. "To whom am I speaking?" it demanded.

"This is Hush McGillen Thackery."

"Shush, this is Edwina Habersham Jacobs. I'm calling from England, so bear with me. I have five minutes before I speak to Parliament."

"Well, you better talk fast then."

Silence. I had stubbed my toe on her goodwill already. "All right, Shush."

"Hush."

"Shush?"

"Hush."

"Shush."

To hell with it. "Your daughter's just fine. I give you my word."

"She better be. The Secret Service assures me she's safe, no thanks to your son."

"Now hold on —"

"I understand you're being less than cooperative."

"Under the circumstances, I think I've been a model of good citizenship."

I heard her rustling papers. "You operate some kind of small family farming business, I gather."

My world stopped. "You . . . have notes on me?" I said slowly.

She ignored me. "I want you to listen to me. I know what's happened is very strange and exciting to you and your relatives on the farm, and I will be the first to admit my daughter owes you an apology for involving your son, Euell —"

"Davis." I felt numb.

"Your son, Ulysses —"

"*Euell.* Euell Davis. We call him Davis. I said, 'Do you have notes on me —'"

"Davis." Her voice held a distinct edge now. "Davis is, no doubt, a fine young man, although I believe he's insinuated himself into my daughter's life with far too many expectations —"

"Whoa. Back up. You spied on my son, and now you're spying on me. Is that right? But you have the gall to criticize us?"

"Mrs. Thackery, I'm not going to discuss any personal issues with you, but I will say that I have been completely aboveboard and legitimate in my gathering of information about the strangers who surround my child — as I'm sure you can understand, given her status in the world. My daughter is a thoughtful and caring young woman who is under a tremendous amount of very public pressure and is very vulnerable to exploitation."

Fury began seeping into my blood, along with the fear and that feel-your-way-along sensation of the unknown. Like walking barefoot in a dark pond, I was aware that poisonous snakes might slither around my feet with every move I made. "So you think my son's some kind of social-climbing Romeo who conned her into running away from college with him?"

"No, no, now, I'm only saying that a secret summer romance has to be kept in perspective—"

"It must just fry your grits that your daughter didn't tell you about him. I didn't know about the romance either, but at least I didn't spy on my son to find out."

"I didn't 'spy' on my daughter—nor have I 'spied' on you, beyond acquiring the most public facts about you. An entire team of professionals is assigned to keep track of my daughter's every move. For her own good. Her current behavior is simply an unfortunate aberration, and I am trying to protect her any way that I can."

"It's a little late, since she's *aberrated* right down the Eastern Seaboard and into my hollow. Now she's *co-aberrating* with my son, in my house."

"Shush, you've obviously had a difficult morning. I'm sure you lead a very quiet life, and I promise you that the President and I will help you and your son get back to your ordinary daily routines very, very quickly."

"That's good, Mrs. Jacobs. Since you're so condescending in your appreciation of me and my routines, I'm going to hand this phone to Agent Olson. Lucille. We've taken a liking to her already. So I'm going to hand my phone to Lucille, and if you will, just tell her to open the gate to my farm so I can sell some apples today. You and the President are keeping up with the government's business despite this problem, and I'm keeping up with mine. As soon as my gate's open, you and I can have a nice long talk about our children. All right? Just tell Lucille to open my gate."

Silence, round three. But I could hear her breathing. "Shush," she said slowly, "if I wanted, I could be sitting in your . . . little farmhouse . . . right *now*, and your entire property would be cordoned off like a nuclear waste site. But instead, it is my fondest wish — as I'm sure it's yours — that I not disrupt your life, and that we put this episode behind us. No one in the public or the media ever needs to find out about this little escapade. All right, Shush?"

I let out a long breath. "*Edwina*," I said loudly. *Ed-weena*. "Edwina, you tell Lucille to open my goddamned gate, or I'm calling CNN."

Lucille winced and began warning me with her hands. *Mrs. Jacobs,* she mouthed. *Not Edwina. No first names. Protocol.*

"Now, calm down, Shush, no need to get the media involved—"

"Edwina, tell it to Lucille." I held out the phone to Lucille. "Edwina wants to talk to you."

The Secret Service agent looked from me to the phone as if it was electrified, then slowly lifted it to her ear. "Mrs. Jacobs, Ma'am? In Mrs. Thackery's point of view, the issue always comes back to her gate, and I am very sorry . . ." Her voice trailed off. When I craned my head, I could just make out the mad-bee buzz of Edwina Jacobs's voice. Lucille nodded, cupped a hand over the phone, and spoke to me. "If I open your gate, will you allow me to post my people at your house until Eddie's safely moved elsewhere?"

"Yes." Anything to resolve this.

Lucille spoke to Edwina again. "We have an agreement. I'll confirm that with my office, Ma'am, but yes, Ma'am, of course, Ma'am."

Lucille handed the phone back to me. "Mrs. Jacobs wants to talk with you again, Mrs. Thackery."

I put the phone to my ear. "Edwina, thank you very kindly. I never had any intention of exposing your daughter and my son to the gossips of the world, so you've got nothing to worry about."

"I don't care what your intentions are. I'm getting my daughter *out* of there." Edwina Jacobs spoke in a voice that could slice rock. "And if you let so much as one word about her situation leak to the rest of the world, or any harm comes to her—if so much as one hair on her head is ruffled—I will *personally* make certain that the entire bureaucracy of the federal government crawls up the ass end of your business, your financial accounts, and your family. In other words, *I will fuck up your life and the life of your overly ambitious son and the lives of your entire apple-picking hillbilly clan.* In the meantime, you already know the President and I are sending someone to bring Eddie *home*." She was yelling now. "A trusted family member! He'll arrive there in a few hours! I urge you to stay out of his way and treat him with more respect than you've shown *me!*"

"Send him. Glad to have him. But you keep your nose out of my business, my life, and my son's life. Or I'll come up there to Washington and kick your ass."

Silence. We both drew in deep breaths as the enormity of what we were doing sank in. The First Lady of the United States and the First Lady of Chocinaw County had degenerated—in their very first conversation—to the level of street hoochies at a gang initiation. "Good-bye," I said quickly.

"Indeed," she answered, undone.

I stuck the phone back in its holster on my belt. Logan and I stared at each other. "*I'm sorry.*"

"You could be arrested for what you said to her, Sis."

Lucille nodded in unhappy awe. "Mrs. Thackery, it's a federal offense to threaten the First Lady." She paused. "If I had heard you do that, I'd have to react."

"Thank you. Now open the gates." I sagged. There was nothing else to do at the moment.

I watched as Lucille stepped aside and Logan unlocked the broad, pretty, hopelessly ineffective gates. We swung them wide. Almost immediately, Lucille's fellow agents went to their SUVs and climbed in. They drove through as if they'd never doubted they'd be allowed. I put a hand over my stomach. I needed more apple slices.

The world had come to my doorstep in ways I'd never imagined. It was quickly invading my home and taking full seed in my life and the life of my son. I would reap the harvest I'd sown, as we all do, sooner or later.

Apple season had begun.

I could only wait for fate, the future, and Edwina's hit man to arrive.

LIEUTENANT COLONEL NICK JAKOBEK. Retired. Not a bad career path: Put in your twenty-plus years; leave when your uncle runs for President. Try to keep an even lower profile than nearly two decades of overseas special operations assignments gave you. Then fade further from sight when your uncle wins the White House. Helluva pension system. Obscurity and notoriety. I'd learned to deal with it.

I was the presidential relative Al's political enemies loved to talk about. Haywood Kenney brought up my Chicago history and military career regularly. I even had a nickname among his newspaper readers and the listeners of his nationally syndicated radio show. *Mad Dog Jakobek.* That was me. Pure proof that Al's views on any issue, including the military, crime, punishment, drugs, sex, family life, raising children, and international relations (take your pick), could be analyzed through the lens of some nasty family baggage. Me.

It didn't help that nobody in Al's camp invited me to photo opportunities during the campaign or the inauguration or at any presidential event afterward. Not that Al and Edwina didn't ask me personally, and sincerely. But I knew my place — I knew what would hurt their image in public. Me. They fought the good fight their way. I fought it mine.

Some of Al's enemies swore I was dead. Not Kenney — I was

more valuable alive, to him—but according to others, I didn't even exist anymore. My death happened during an illegal covert government operation in either (take your pick) Nicaragua, Bosnia, or Iraq, and then Al ordered a cover-up by either (take your pick) the Army, the CIA, the FBI, or Strangers Wearing Dark Suits Who Really Run this Country.

WANTED. DEAD OR ALIVE. BRING PROOF, EITHER WAY.

The truth was that I moved around a lot after leaving the military, so much so that sometimes I had to ask myself where I lived. Where I was. Where I was going. I was still looking for some brand of peace and satisfaction I couldn't quite name. Counting coups, counting souls, counting backward over the past twenty-plus years, I tried to remember who I was before I killed that first time in Chicago. That first time. Key words.

Funded by your taxpayer dollars but without your explicit permission, I had spent almost twenty years teaching our friends in other countries how to kill their fellow citizens. I protected them while they did it, and occasionally, when needed, I killed their enemies alongside them. Through rebel skirmishes and civil wars and secret military actions and politicians' lies about the world's dirty work, I did my job. I saved a lot of lives but I slept at night with the images of the people I couldn't help. A bloodied old woman by the roadside in Sarajevo. A little boy lying dead in the desert with his feet cut off. A battered family carrying their home on their backs in Afghanistan. As long as I was nothing but my memories, I didn't know where I belonged.

And so maybe there was no place to go.

I'd gotten used to being needed by other people but never really liked by them, if that makes any sense. Not liked for ordinary reasons, at any rate—not just for the sound of my voice or the way I looked while I slept. I'd never been the center of anyone's life. Didn't think I knew how to be. I kept searching for the souls I'd taken. Including my own. So far, no miracles.

Then I got a call from good old Bill Sniderman. I was in Texas at the time, teaching paramilitary techniques to officers from a South American country I won't mention. There was good money to be made as an ex–military man, training other soldiers how to kill. Until that phone call. "The President and First Lady need you, I'm sorry to say," Bill told me. "Eddie's in trouble."

"I'm on my way," I said.

NINE

By midafternoon more than two thousand customers crowded my apple barns and pavilion, all unaware that the daughter of the President was hidden in my house. Nearly three dozen McGillens and Thackerys — likewise clueless — were hard at work taking care of those customers. Logan directed traffic at the public gate, and Lucille still commandeered the front walkway to my big porch. WDAL, Dalyrimple's AM radio station, broadcast live coverage of opening day at Sweet Hush Farms from a booth overlooking the festivities. So far, there hadn't been one sign of the man Edwina Jacobs had vowed to send.

Eddie, meantime, slept in my son's bed. Fully dressed, but still. Davis paced the hall outside.

I stood by, watching him. "Where is this presidential kneebreaker? If she were my daughter, I'd be here by now or my personal goon would be here, and *you'd* be in deep trouble."

"Her parents can't just drop everything to take care of family problems. Eddie understands that. In fact, she counted on it. She *wants* to be left alone. She wants to have a normal life. Even if her parents run the country."

"Just remember that *I* have this *farm* to run—maybe it's not a whole country, but to me and most of our family, it's the whole *world*."

"I know that."

I walked to the stairs and halted. "You think long and hard about how your decisions affect all the lives around here, and you be ready to take responsibility when Eddie's relative gets here to deal with you."

"I'm a man," he said quietly. "I'll take care of it."

He sounded so certain. He had no idea how afraid I was for him and his sake. A man? My son? I had given birth to a full grown man? I hurried down the stairs, pounding a fist on a smooth oak banister carved with apple blossoms.

"Come on, hurry up," I said aloud to the faceless stranger traveling my way to add more trouble to the day. "Come on and fight."

⁊◍

"COLONEL JAKOBEK?"

"Yes?" I looked up from a map of the Georgia mountains. The White House aide who'd met me at a Colorado airport stood by my seat, holding a large file folder. We were in a private jet somewhere over the midwest. "The First Lady says this should give you some background on the Thackery family."

I frowned, took the folder, and flipped the cover open to a color photograph of a tall, green-eyed woman in a tailored blue business suit with a knee-length skirt and pearl buttons on her sleeve cuffs. Sounds prim, but she wasn't. Not her, not me, not my reaction. I took a breath. "Who is she?"

"Davis Thackery's mother. Hush. One of those Appalachian folk names. Hush McGillen Thackery. She's named after her family's apples. A variety of apple they created. The Sweet Hush."

Hush McGillen Thackery. Sweet Hush. Named after an apple. Mother of a grown kid at Harvard and head of a small family empire. How old was she? I checked a sheaf of notes behind the photograph. Only forty. Started young. I looked down at stunning green eyes, a strong, classic face, and hair the dark copper-brown color of polished teak in an opium parlor. She wore it pulled up with a heavy silver clasp that couldn't quite keep it under control. The conservative blue skirt and tailored jacket couldn't quite keep her body under control either.

The aide sat down across from me with a stack of notes on his lap. "That photograph was made in a hallway at the state capitol in Atlanta, Sir. Mrs. Thackery serves on the governor's resource committee for the state agricultural commission. She represents the apple farmers."

"Apple farmers have political issues?"

"Everyone has political issues, Sir."

Hush Thackery posed next to some pasty-faced state rep with a bad comb-over and a loud tie. He looked like a used-car salesman trying to sell an old Buick, and she looked as if she wasn't buying. "She's also done some lobbying for the state apple grower's association," the aide went on. "She was president of that association for five years. She's a member of the board of the national grower's organization. And in her hometown, Dalyrimple, she virtually *controls* the chamber, the council, and the county commissioner. Most of the local officials are relatives. Her younger brother's the sheriff. Sweet Hush Farms is the county's biggest employer and largest single tourist draw."

Not your average small-time farmer with an attitude. Ambitious? Willing to encourage her son to make a play for a famous girlfriend? Possible.

I flipped through a full-color catalog advertising dozens of baked, canned, sun-dried, caramel-dipped, homemade apple products, all available via an 800 number with overnight shipping, year-round, twenty-four/seven. I stopped on a color photograph of Hush Thackery among her apple trees and mountains. She was dressed in faded jeans and a soft white sweater, her long legs braced apart, that dark hair draped over her shoulders in thick waves, her arms around a basketful of apples. Her hands, spread lovingly on the basket's coarse wicker sides, were strong and square. She looked out at the world somberly, but smiled. I felt her smile where it did me no good.

"She's something of a legend, Sir," the aide said.

"Tell me about her kid."

"The perfect son." When I arched a brow, the aide nodded. "Perfect, Sir." He handed me a list of Euell Davis Thackery Junior's accomplishments. *All-American farm-boy genius,* I thought. I studied a photograph from the Harvard annual and saw a good-looking kid with dark hair and his mother's calm stare. Trouble.

"Tell me about the father," I said.

"Local hero."

"Is there anyone in this family who isn't a saint?"

"Sir, I can only report the information. The facts."

"Information isn't facts. It's just the window dressing." I exhaled. "Anyway, so tell me what we know about Davis Thackery's saintly old man."

"Davis Senior. Big Davy, some people called him. Stock-car racer, businessman—owned his own racing team, partners in a truck dealership on the interstate, devoted father, great husband, churchgoing pillar of the community. Beloved. His racetrack fans built a monument to him on the mountain where he died. He was racing down the mountain. Trying to break a local speed record."

Dead? This interested me more than I'd admit. "So the saintly Mrs. Thackery is a widow?"

"Yes, Sir. Five years. She and her husband were considered the perfect couple." He handed me a newspaper clipping. "Here's a picture of her husband from the county newspaper." The aide smiled. "A small-town rag called the *Dalyrimple Weekly News.*"

DAVY THACKERY WINS DIVISION CHAMP TITLE AGAIN AT CHOCINAW RIVER TRACK. I studied a tall, grinning, dark-haired man in muddy jeans and a major belt buckle who stood in front of a mud-spattered sedan. His son, then a lanky teenager, grinned beside him, with one arm looped over his father's shoulder. A crowd of fans clustered in the background, waving. Hush Thackery was nowhere to be seen. Just an oversight? I was looking for trouble. Weak points. Vulnerability. Hoping?

I continued to study her picture. Great husband, great son, great all-American success story. All I had to show for my own life was a houseboat on loan to a family I'd befriended somewhere along the Amazon River in Peru, an apartment on Chicago's tough south side that I hadn't visited in years, and the coyote skulls, somewhere in storage. I was forty-four years old that fall, weighing in at six-four, two hundred and thirty pounds of hard-assed gristle, complete with acne scars and a nose that had been badly broken twice, once in Bosnia, another time in Afghanistan. And of course, I was still missing the little finger on my left hand.

So I wasn't exactly a poster boy for anybody's American Dream. I still had no children and still said I never wanted any, but kids saw through me the way cats head straight for people who swear they don't like cats. I'd never been married either, but didn't regret that at all. My kind of woman was reliable. I always picked the ones who needed protection. Usually from themselves.

Eddie, thank God, thought I had spent my career pretending to be Harrison Ford in a Tom Clancy movie. I sent her the occasional photograph of me in a tux posing beside ambassadors and their socialite wives. To Eddie, I would always be the hero who had saved her life when she was a baby. The man who swore he'd make the world safe for her.

Now I looked at Hush Thackery's photographs again. This woman didn't have to ask for help keeping her world safe. I laid the photographs aside, frowning.

The aide approached. "The First Lady feels you need to be aware of Mrs. Thackery's uncooperative and threatening attitude —"

"Give me specifics."

"She had a confrontation with Miss Jacobs's Secret Service detail over access to her house and farm this morning. And a confrontation with the First Lady as well. She threatened to call the media. Resorted to blackmail, or at least threatened to."

"Who won?"

The aide coughed again. "Mrs. Thackery."

I picked up Hush Thackery's orchard photograph. *Always keep your eye on the mother.* I studied her objectively, or tried to. *All right, so you know how to take care of your own. Good. But I'm the one they send when they want people to be afraid.*

And I'm sorry, but you will be.

I STEPPED DOWN FROM the jet at Dobbins Air Reserve Base outside Atlanta. An aide handed me the keys to a hulking camo-green Humvee with government tags. "We thought you'd want this, Sir," one said.

"I'm not invading a foreign country. Just driving into the mountains above Atlanta."

"There're places in those Appalachian hollows where they still threaten to feed strangers to the pigs, Sir."

"I'll take my chances with the pork. Get me a rental car."

The land at the northern cap of Georgia rose above Atlanta like the hump of a big animal, until I felt as if I were driving up the backbone of a sleeping bear. The Georgia interstate began to flow through shoulders of big hills covered in hardwood forest tinged with the first gold and red of autumn. The mountains rolled across the horizon in giant hummocks, looking old and placid compared to the raw Rockies. I was fooled into thinking they seemed tame.

DAVY THACKERY FORD TRUCK, NEXT EXIT, a billboard blared in big letters beneath a life-size painting of a blue-and-white stock car with THACKERY RACING on the door and hood. CHAMPION OF THE DIRT TRACK. I turned off the interstate, past a sprawling dealership doing brisk Saturday business next to a diner and a gas station. Thackery's stock car—real, not a painting—sat out front atop a broad concrete platform. Several people were posing beside the car with their kids, taking pictures. Even dead, Hush Thackery's husband drew a crowd.

Frowning, I steered the rental car along a shady two-lane heading toward a heaped-up skyline of mountains that closed in too quickly. The Appalachians suddenly wrapped themselves around me. I felt as if I'd been swallowed.

VISIT FAMOUS SWEET HUSH APPLE FARMS, 10 MILES, a large, well-kept sign in red and white told me from a landscaped clearing framed by two apple trees picked clean of their lowest fruit by four deer that didn't bother to run when I drove by. SEPTEMBER TO NEW YEAR'S. A CHOCINAW COUNTY TRADITION. And then another sign. HISTORIC DALYRIMPLE, SHOPS, INNS, FINE PEOPLE. THE HEART OF SWEET HUSH APPLE COUNTRY.

Now I understood. I was in a separate *country*. The Civil War hadn't settled that issue, at least not around there.

I guided the sedan up the first of many inclines that began to curve along mountain ridges and skim their edges like icing on the edge of a tall cake. Another sign appeared, this one draped in honeysuckle vines. ENTERING CHOCINAW COUNTY. WE WELCOME YOU TO THE HOME OF THE SWEET HUSH APPLE. And below that, in bright DOT orange: STEEP GRADES AND DANGEROUS CURVES, NEXT TEN MILES. I held the steering wheel lightly, watching the edges of the road fall off into space. THIS WAY TO HUSH MCGILLEN THACKERY AND A DOWN-HOME APPLE-PIE WORLD SHE AND HER FAMILY CONTROL WITH A LOT OF PRIDE AND NO APOLOGIES.

All the warning signs told me so.

Twenty minutes later I officially drove off the map into some no-man's-land at the top of Chocinaw Mountain. I brought the car to a stop on a patch of gravel beside a steel guardrail, then walked over to a view of endless, undulating mountain valleys and round, wooded crests. The view was so beautiful it hurt.

I don't know what made me stop there. The sheer loneliness of the place, probably. A flash of sunlight on polished surfaces caught my eye, and I looked over the guardrail, a hundred feet down. A rough but calculated rectangle of polished granite as long and wide as a car stood on end among the native boulders and rhododendron like a huge domino. An inscription was carved on the gray obelisk in tall, deep letters meant to be easy to read even from the roadside a hundred feet above it.

DAVY THACKERY
1960–1997
HUSBAND, FATHER, HERO
HE DROVE FAST, HE LIVED LARGE, AND HE DID US PROUD
ONLY A MOUNTAIN COULD BEAT HIM

Jesus Christ. This must be where Hush Thackery's husband had died, trying to set a land–speed record on a mountain road that could sling a car off the way a dog shakes a flea, even at normal speeds. I walked back to my tame sedan, looked at it a second with a prickle of competition on the nape of my neck, and decided I should have driven the Humvee. Nothing like two tons of all-terrain domination to impress the hell out of a family who thought driving off a cliff was heroic.

I turned and looked at the steel guardrail and the sheer drop-off, then up at the blue sky where a single hawk hung on a current of air, and finally at the unbroken panorama of wild, lonely mountains heading to the horizon. Hush Thackery's hero husband hadn't died well or easy. He'd died alone and bleeding and broken on the side of this mountain. She must have wanted to tear her heart out.

I stopped cold. Eddie could have ended up on the rocks down there, too, thanks to Davis Thackery Junior. A black mood slid up behind my eyes.

You are in a world of trouble, Junior.

When I reached the bottom of the mountain, I turned the car sharply at a lazy intersection in the middle of the woods. A green metallic county marker said MCGILLEN ORCHARDS ROAD. A bright,

141

handsome, red-and-white sign pointed the way to SWEET HUSH FARMS.

I drove fast along the orchard road, until suddenly it burst out of the forest. I was surrounded by fields that filled a long, narrow gap between the mountains. The entrance to Sweet Hush Hollow. Hundreds of big orange pumpkins dotted the rows of vines. A wooden sign along the road said PICK-YOUR-OWN PUMP-KIN FESTIVAL, OCTOBER 1–31, SWEET HUSH FARMS. Then the pumpkins gave way to regimented fields of neatly tended ornamental pines. A sign said CUT-YOUR-OWN CHRISTMAS TREE FESTIVAL, NOVEMBER 1–DECEMBER 24.

The road plunged into the forest again, flashing through sunshine and shadow, and my hands tightened around the steering wheel. Cars began to meet me going the opposite way, moseying at lazy speeds. Suburban cars and vans, well-kept SUVs, all filled with parents and children and grandparents and fat family dogs, ambling through the late-afternoon shadows of an early fall day. Their contented faces flashed by me. They'd been drugged with apples. They'd be easy marks for the pumpkins and the Christmas trees.

I traveled backward alongside that parade of pleasant and secure Americana making its contented pilgrimage home from Sweet Hush Farms. Suddenly the woods opened into a broad valley, and I was forced to slow down. A rush of apple-scented fall air filled my lungs through the car's open window, and afternoon sunshine blinded me. I pulled over to the mown roadside and stepped out again. I took a few deep breaths, calming down.

Apple orchards covered the valley. A patina of purple-gold afternoon light made me think of old paintings and soft beds. The red peaks of a large farmhouse roof and stone chimneys showed among trees at the valley's distant backside. Up front, good-looking barns and parking lots sprawled among orchards just beyond the road where I stood. There must have been two thousand people there that day, wandering between the pretty barns and shops and a pavilion filled with apple bins, or stretched on blankets under apple trees. The sound of a bluegrass fiddle and the low, sweet drawl of an old mountain song came up to me on a gust of breeze. Musicians commandeered a small stage in the pavilion, and craft tents dotted the area around it. Chocinaw County sheriff's deputies and teenagers wearing neon safety vests directed traffic with equal authority, as if life were so easy a teenager armored in only orange plastic could control it. The warmth of the sun crept over me, and the scent of the apples, and the music. The music.

So this was the hidden queendom Hush Thackery ruled. Shangri-la, southern style. Somebody's fantasy. Not mine. I couldn't believe it really existed.

Take Eddie home. Get the hell out of here.

And don't look back.

⸙

"WASPS!" HUSH PUPPY YELLED. "Wasps, Aunt Hush! The yellow jackets are after me!"

I heard her screaming as I headed down the front path from the house, intending to drive back up to the public barns. I pivoted and ran up a dirt lane to a gray, weathered barn that looked as if it had grown out of the ridge behind the house. This was a real barn, over a hundred years old. "Do you need help, Mrs. Thackery?" Lucille yelled. She and three of her fellow agents shared surveillance of my flower beds, driveway, and front veranda. But they were no match for swarming wasps. I shook my head and kept running.

A shortcut across a tumbled row of fieldstones sent me straight through the barn's tall, shadowy side entrance and into the sifted sunlight and sweet-hay scent of the old structure's past. Two large tractors vied for space in the old mule stalls alongside tillers, plows, and a big wagon I'd bring out for mule-drawn hayrides as soon as the weather turned crisper.

"Over here, Aunt Hush!" Puppy shrieked. "I'm in the corn crib!"

143

"I'm coming, Honey! Stay put!" I dodged between aging, oak-slat bushel baskets stacked head-high like upended ice-cream cones. Dozens of yellow jackets swarmed in a corner streaked with sunlight through the rough barn walls. Puppy rattled the wood hitch from her safe place on the far side of the crib's heavy plank door. I could just make out the crown of her dark, wavy hair in a crack above the cross brace. Her blue eyes peered through a smaller horizontal crack below. "I was chasing Toad the cat, and the yellow jackets buzzed out of their hole in the ground." Her voice, a six-year-old's treble squeak, rose even higher on the word *hole*. She began crying. "Aunt Hush, I'm not cut out to be the sixth Hush McGillen. I don't have sugar skin. Those jackets stung me on my finger!" She sobbed. "I might as well be like anybody else!"

"Baby," I crooned, "the wasps just haven't figured out who you are yet. Now, when I say, 'Go,' you open the door and step out, and just walk slowly out of the barn. And you go get Gruncle Thackery and tell him to bring a smoker can from the hive shed." We had smoker cans for working the honeybee hives in the orchard. Smoke was the only thing that could drive the yellow jackets off my skin. "Don't run. Just go down to the public barns and find Gruncle. All right?"

"All right."

I stood before the swarming, yellow-and-black wasps with their ferocious stingers. "It's me," I said softly to the insects. I pushed up the cuffs of my sweater to my elbows, then held out both hands with my fingers spread, said a small prayer, and stepped into their midst. Slowly, the yellow jackets lit on me. Within less than a minute, they covered my hands and forearms like a living pair of gloves. I could feel their tiny pressures on my skin, their tickling, tasting insect mouths. A dozen or so floated upward to my face and hair, settling on my cheeks, my nose, the scar below my right eye. I could feel one tickling his way along the crescent of sensitive flesh. *Davy hurt you, but we never will.*

After another few seconds, not a single yellow jacket remained in the air. The entire nest was enamored of me. I still had the knack for charming them and the bees, even if the rest of my life had begun to buzz out of control. "Puppy?" I said in a low voice.

"Yes?"

"Go."

The crib door creaked open on its old iron hinges. Puppy eased her head out, looked at me wide-eyed, then crept into the open. She'd seen me do this before — tame the wasps and bees — but still, she stared in awe. "I'll get Gruncle with the smoker can," she whispered. She sidled about ten feet through the stacks of bushel baskets, then broke into a run and bolted out the barn's side entrance.

I stood there, alone in the slivers of late afternoon sunlight, my skin a magnet for creatures who had a place and a purpose no less than my own in the creation of life's fruit. I blew out a slow breath, then whispered to them, "I've got lots worse to be afraid of than you right now, little fellows. And I think you know it."

I sat down slowly on a low wood bench near where I kept my grandfather's carving tools, carefully rested my elbows on my knees so no wasps would be mashed in the process, then turned my wasp-decorated face up to a shard of light. Like an apple tree in springtime, I was being pollinated. A sense of expectation rose like goosebumps on my spine. My skin bloomed strangely. I was here for a reason of some kind. Outside the barn, carried on the softest wind, came the whisper of the ancient Great Lady.

Be still and your trees will bring you new life.

AFTER I DROVE PAST the public areas of Sweet Hush Farms, I entered the orchards, and everything of the outside world disappeared behind me. Even the quality of the light deepened, as if I were being drawn down a well. The trees crowded so close that the leafy tips of a limb, weighted with apples, knocked on my window. *Let us in. You can't win in a fight against the all-American fruit.*

145

The road narrowed to a single car–width of gravel lined with golden flowers of some kind, and the mountains threw afternoon shadows across my vehicle, changing the light even more and warping my perspective and sense of time. I tunneled through lifetimes and apple trees. *This is a wormhole in the universe,* I thought. *I'll come out in some other dimension.*

Maybe I did. The orchards opened up and suddenly I stopped at a weathered gate and fences with split-rail crosspieces. Not worth a damn for keeping anything or anyone in — or out. But pretty. Beyond the gate, up a rise of lawn and terraces outlined in mossy stone walls overflowing with browning flower beds and shaded by big oaks going red, sat the big, handsome house with a red-peaked roof and gray stone chimneys, a broad veranda draped in vines, and a front door of dark, ornate wood and stained glass. Apples were carved on the newel posts of the front steps. Apples were carved in the door. Apples glowed red in the stained glass panels.

Apples everywhere.

Three Secret Service agents came down a walkway of old stone hooded by snowball bushes big enough to hide behind. The place was a picturesque minefield of security risks. I got out of the car and nodded to the agents. They looked like solid, clean-cut family men — the Service's typical choice. None of them knew me on sight, and each kept one hand near their gun holsters as they walked my way. I had that effect on family men.

"Stop right there," one called. "Do you have business at the house?"

I nodded, looking past them. I spotted an old barn and some other outbuildings beyond the woods, a glimpse of small pasture, and more orchards behind it all — hell, orchards from there to forever, an army of apple trees, bending and rising with the valley floor. A wave of apples. I was surrounded. I laid a hand on the locked gate as the agents reached it. "I'm Jakobek," I said, and pulled my credentials from the pocket of old khakis. An agent took the open wallet and studied it. His and the others' expressions changed to relief, or at least recognition. "Colonel. Sorry to stop you." They'd been told to expect me. Be careful what you wish for.

"No problem," I said.

"Colonel," Lucille Olson called. She strode down the stone path and out of the shadows of the subversive shrubs. Al and Edwina had asked me what I thought of her before she was put in charge of Eddie's protection. I'd looked at her records, looked at her training, then went to her and asked one question: "Why would you risk your life to protect Eddie's?"

Lucille Olson had stared me straight in the eye. "Because when I was growing up in Minnesota, my sister was raped and murdered by a stalker. I can only deal with that memory by making sure it doesn't happen to someone else. I have to believe I can make a difference."

I told Al and Edwina they could trust her with Eddie's life. She'd never allow herself to let Eddie down. I understood the mentality.

"Agent Olson, where's Eddie?"

"In the house, Sir." She unlocked the gate. "Upstairs. Sleeping all day. She's had stomach flu, nausea. Nothing serious, although I tried to persuade her to let me call a doctor. No go. Davis Thackery is sitting with her. Can't pry him away. I'm glad you're here."

I walked through the open gate, already moving swiftly up the path toward the house. "Be ready to go when I come back with Eddie. Have a doctor waiting at the airport. I don't expect this to take long."

"I don't think you understand . . ." She hurried alongside me. "Eddie's not that easily persuaded right now."

"She'll listen to me. Is Hush Thackery here? I want to talk to her first. A little protocol. You do the introductions."

"Well, actually, she's . . . we have a situation . . . she's in that barn over there, but I'm not sure what—"

"Y'all have to help me find my gruncle and get the bug smoker!" a small voice cried. A tiny, dark-haired girl in jeans and

147

a Barbie shirt bounded down the hill, clambering over the stone rims of terraced flower beds, a mound of wavy hair dancing as she hit level ground, her face streaked with tears. With that radar kids have for me, she headed straight my way, snared my hand, and tugged. "Excuse me, Sir, but I need a ride to the front barns to get Gruncle Thackery and tell him to bring the bug smoker! My aunt Hush is covered in a whole swarm of yellow jackets!" She held up a red, swollen forefinger. "Look what happened to me! I got stung by just one of them!"

Aunt Hush. Covered. Swarm. Stung. Those were the words I heard. I bent down to the kid, gripping her small hand carefully. "What's your aunt Hush doing right now?"

"Waiting for help! Hurry! They're all over her!" She pointed toward a barn roof peeking above distant treetops. "Over there!"

"I'll take care of her."

"Promise?"

"Promise."

I scooped my hands under her armpits, picked her up, turned, and handed her bodily to one of the men. "Find Gruncle, who-ever that is. I'll go to the barn."

The agent looked toward Lucille. She nodded. "Tom, Hernando, you stay here." Then, to me, "I'll go get her son. And call an ambulance." Lucille bolted for the house, pulling a cell phone from her pants pocket.

I ran up the terraces, jumping fieldstone borders, then climb-ing through late-blooming azaleas, low jungles of lavender mums, and the sharp, browning fronds of summer irises. I reached the oak trees and sprinted beneath their red-tinged limbs, heading for the weathered barn beyond the small pasture. Through a dark opening at the barn's side, I heard no screams and saw nothing but filtered shafts of afternoon sunlight. But I had a mental image of Hush Thackery being stung to death in some freak accident that would turn this peculiar day into a nightmare.

WHEN I WAS JUST a tiny girl, a few years before my father died while digging up blackberry briars in the orchards, he took me and Mama over to Dalyrimple to see the Fourth of July parade, courtesy of the Chocinaw County VFW, a borrowed color guard from the ROTC unit at North Georgia College, and the Chocinaw County High School Band, playing loud and slightly off-key Sousa marches. The town was as old as the gray bricks of the courthouse, shaded by hickory trees that would thump a child on the head in the autumn with nuts as hard as opinions.

Farlo Dalyrimple's dachshunds slept safely in the lazy streets, looking like furry sausages who moved only when someone honked at them. Ancient Ulaine Dalyrimple Baggett, who taught music for free to the poor mountain kids, including me, kept the town's slow tempo from the front porch of her grandson's hardware store. In the late 1960s, Dalyrimple was Mayberry.

We sat on the edge of the porch, Mama on the left side of Mrs. Baggett's rocker, Daddy and me on the right side. Mrs. Baggett sang "May the Circle Be Unbroken" in a low alto, and I harmonized with her. As we sang and watched the parade, fat bumblebees began to bumble over to me from Mrs. Baggett's rosebushes. I didn't yet know I had sugar skin, but I wasn't afraid of the bees, having already learned that most never stung me.

One by one the bumblebees settled on my hair and face, while Daddy, Mama, and Mrs. Baggett watched the parade, unaware. Suddenly Mrs. Baggett stopped singing and said in her calm, crackling old voice, "John Albert McGillen, your child's sung the bees in for a landing."

Daddy and Mama swiveled quickly to look at me. I sat there, as calm as a calf chewing its cud, with several dozen tubby bees clinging to my face and hair. Mama said not one word but reached for a pair of small American flags Mrs. Baggett had stuck in a flowerpot full of geraniums. "Excuse me, Mrs. Baggett, but I'm going to use your flags to shoo these bumbles off Hush."

"No need," Daddy said. Worn and lean, with dark auburn hair sliding back from his forehead like a retreating fire, he had the warmest smile of any man in the world, and a nature so quiet bees lit on him, too. He pulled a long-stemmed pipe from the breast pocket of his blue-checkered Sunday shirt, packed it with tobacco from a leather pouch in his trousers, lit it with a stick match he scratched on the inside of his leathery palm, and exhaled a slow breath of smoke over me.

The bumblebees ambled away in duets and quartets of winged whirring. "Listen to them harmonize," Mrs. Baggett said. "John Albert, you're a wonder. You made the bees sing, too."

My heart swelled with the amazement of small miracles and the awe the luckiest children feel for a parent at least once in their lives. *Daddy saved me.* A permanent stamp of McGillen bee magic already existed between my father and me, but that moment sealed it. He smiled at me, then faced forward to watch the parade again, while Mama exhaled with relief and replanted Mrs. Baggett's small flags in the geraniums.

Mrs. Baggett, the last, grand keeper of southern womanhood in the tradition of spiritual song, bent over the arm of her rocker and beckoned me with a finger as gnarled as the branch on my own Great Lady. When I edged close, she said softly, "Your daddy's a bee charmer, like you. Any man who can charm bees and wasps has a soul of special courage and mighty kindness. You remember that. Always be on the lookout for a bee-charming man. He has a special sort of music in his heart."

I put a hand to my own heart, and nodded. A small, rebel bumblebee returned and lit on my hand as I made that vow, overhearing it so it could be told to bees the world over. But Mrs. Baggett died the next spring without further counsel to me, and Daddy a few years later, and then Davy came along, and my vow was broken.

I had never found a bee-charming man.

Until the day, that fall, when Nick Jakobek arrived.

I HEARD THE RUNNING footsteps. *That's not Gruncle,* I thought. *And not Davis. Davis runs like a giraffe. Slow and gallumping.* I turned my head carefully so as not to disturb the half-dozen yellow jackets that clung like pets to my cheeks and forehead and near the corners of my mouth. The barn's side entrance made a tall, clean rectangle of gray logs framing the blue-pink afternoon light outside like a bright window in a dark room. Forced to sit still, I felt hypnotized by the contrast of light, the footsteps that couldn't belong to my elderly Gruncle, and the slow thud of my own heart. Hither and yon, a small yellow jacket lifted off my covered hands and wrists, seeking a new location on my skin, fitting himself in among his crowded brethren on the pew of my arms. Like a church choir caught in the spirit, they moved to their own rhythm. Mrs. Baggett would have been proud of them.

The footsteps halted. The strong silhouette of a man suddenly loomed in the entranceway's frame of light and trees. I saw his long legs spread slightly apart, his arms splay by his side in readiness, all of him backlit against a coppery blur of the distant house oaks. The yellow jackets shifted ominously.

He took a step forward. "Hold on, there," I called in a low voice. "Be still or they'll come after you."

"How badly are you hurt?" His voice was deep, calm, not southern, but still. A good, strong voice. I wouldn't forget it, or the way he asked that question.

"I'm not hurt at all, thank you. I just have a talent for attracting wasps and bees." I blew out gently as a small wasp tickled my lower lip. It inched away. Chill bumps washed over my skin. The stranger moved forward, walking carefully for a tall man. I opened my mouth to warn him off again, but the words never came out. He stopped in a finger of sunlight.

He looked down at me with a kind of wonder.

And I looked up at him like a child in church.

He had a stark and rugged face with no small share of wear and tear on it, a thick crown of hair more black than brown, and dark eyes that reduced the world to me. Only me. He raised a hand to his chest and slid his fingers into the breast pocket of a rumpled flannel shirt that was tucked into old khakis, which hung over scuffed hiking boots. He pulled a long cigar from the pocket, at the same time gracefully extracting a silver lighter from a front pocket of his pants. I watched him flick the cigar's cellophane wrapping aside and nip off the puckered end with a quick tug of his teeth.

I held my breath.

He slid the cigar tip between his lips and teeth, cupped one large and capable-looking hand around the stogie's business end, thumbed a flame from the lighter, and lit the cigar with the calm ceremony of a man who knows just how much breath it takes to coax fire and tobacco together in a dance. He blew out, and a soft gray cloud of sweet-scented smoke floated toward me. "Let's see what we can do," he said. He eased forward and knelt down on one knee within arm's reach of me.

The slanted sunshine cast one side of our faces in light, the other in shadow. I glimpsed him down inside himself and liked what I saw, or thought I saw. Trust rose between us like the bubble in a carpenter's level. We had a balance, just temporary, perhaps, but enough to tame this moment. He drew in on the cigar, then exhaled a slow breath of aromatic smoke through the rush of air from his lungs, enveloping me.

The yellow jackets didn't so much as buzz at him.

My heart settled back against my spine in wonder.

I had finally met a bee-charming man.

The yellow jackets began to lift from my skin. I raised my hands. Dozens of them ascended and drifted in the smoke, more lazy than annoyed, floating on the currents of this stranger's breath until they followed the smoke between a crack in the wall boards and disappeared. I never took my eyes off the stranger's face, until suddenly I realized my hands and arms were empty.

He lifted his left hand and curved it near my cheek to guide a new breath of smoke from his lips. A few wasps still crept over my skin, stubborn. I leaned toward him with my face tilted into the sweet cloud and the scent of his breath, and he moved a little nearer, too, until we could have kissed. That close. I felt the warmth of his skin near mine. That close. He sent small puffs of air, slow exhalations, against my eyes, my cheeks, and finally, when there was only one last yellow jacket tickling the corner of my mouth, he leaned in one degree more, his gaze shifting from my mouth to my eyes, and blew one last, small stream of air directly into my parted lips. The tiny wasp drifted upward and disappeared into a slot of sunlight between the old barn boards.

We didn't sit back at a safe distance. We looked at each other with a frowning mix of affection and surprise and sexual heat. I think we both knew, at that moment, that we were going to cause each other joy and misery. In more ways than one.

"Why aren't you afraid?" he asked.

"Of the wasps? Or of you?"

"Both."

"I trust the wasps' opinion of you. And *they* trust you."

Something came into his eyes, wishful and hard. "Mrs. Thackery," he said quietly. "My name's Nick Jakobek, and I'm here to take Eddie back where she belongs."

I drew in a hard breath and nodded. "Good."

AND SO A FALL that had started in a Texas military compound had come down to this: There I stood, in a friendly barn in Georgia, a part of the world where I knew more about stereotypes than actual human beings, surrounded by antique farm equipment and the scent of warm apples and sweet hay and mountain air, watching an incredible woman calmly stare at me from her seat on a carving bench, where she'd been covered in small yellow bees. No. *Wasps.* I didn't even know the right term for them. Only their danger. Hush McGillen Thackery wasn't the most beautiful woman I'd ever seen in my life, but she was the hardest to look away from, starting with that moment. I was aroused, and I was awkward, and I was surprised. The fact that I could hide all that turmoil doesn't mean it wasn't there. The rescue and the name-less introduction and the helpless bondage of desire between strangers. All there.

Like the yellow jackets, I wanted to know how she tasted, and why she made me like her so easily.

And why she said what she said about Eddie.

And just why, in general.

❧

THERE WAS JUST ENOUGH time for Nick Jakobek's dark eyes to color with puzzlement—I guess he expected me to covet a pres-idential daughter—when the rattle of a heavy can broke the spell. I stood as if we'd been caught doing something wrong. Jakobek stood slower, eyes shuttered. He had better control of his weak-nesses than I had of mine, or less pent-up frustration. His sex life probably did not center around a vibrating massage pillow.

Be that as it may, to my horror, Davis and Eddie stood frozen in the barn's doorway. Davis bent and picked up a long-nozzled can wisping soft white puffs of smoke. "I know who you are, Colonel, and I know your reputation, but you can't intimidate me. Or my mother."

Jakobek said in a low voice, "Mr. Thackery, you and I need to talk in private, before you jump to any more conclusions about me or about my intentions." His intense stillness raised the hair on the back of my neck. I watched the slightest flex of a sinew in his neck and the tight posture of his body—the set of his shoul-ders, the casual, strong parentheses his big hands made, hanging deceptively calm alongside his lean hips.

I intervened quickly. "There won't be any conversations with-out me present, you hear?"

He looked at me for just one second, frowning. "I'm not here to hurt your son. You have my word. I'm here to get answers. And to make certain Eddie's safe."

"Fine. But there'll be no confrontations between you and my family."

154

He nodded just slightly. I had been saluted, but with conditions.

"I'm being discussed," Davis said tightly. "Not consulted."

Eddie held out her hands to Jakobek. "*Nicky*. Please don't tell me that Mother and Dad asked you to come get me, and you *agreed*. Not you, too. *Not you*. Planning to order me around? Treat me like a child who has to be rescued? Lecture me?"

"I'm here to find out if you're all right. That's all."

"Then I'm fine. Your question is answered."

"You look sick and scared to me. What you've done makes no sense. I just want to make certain you weren't . . . coerced."

"Coerced?" Davis said in a low voice. "You're accusing me —"

Eddie laid a restraining hand on his arm. "Nicky, people have turning points in their lives. Moments in which everything they've been told to think about themselves and their place in the world suddenly no longer fits. When a moment like that occurs, a wise person knows to turn down a different path. That's what I've done, Nicky. Made a quick but infinitely wise decision to leave behind the trappings of a life that had stopped being my own."

"Your folks never pushed you to live in their spotlight."

"Oh, Nicky, of course they did. A child can't escape a light as bright as theirs."

"They've done everything to protect you."

"I know, and I've always felt like a bird in a cage."

"That still doesn't explain making a run down the East Coast with your Secret Service contingent in tow. Why? You and Mr. Thackery couldn't get on a plane and come to visit his mama?"

"Mother," I corrected stiffly. "His *mother*."

As Jakobek gave me a quizzical glance, Davis stepped forward. "Eddie was tired of having every move reported to her parents. No grown child of a President in the past fifty years has been watched the way she's been watched."

"The world isn't as safe as it used to be, Mr. Thackery."

"My mother spies on me," Eddie announced. "Did you know that, Nicky?"

Jakobek frowned. "Your mother is tough, but she's too honor-able to do something like—" He hesitated, frowning harder. "Your mother has good reason to be a little overprotective after what happened—"

"Nicky, don't tell me this started when that man tried to kill us. I've heard that for years, but I just don't think it excuses her. She's become hard and angry and mean-spirited, Nicky. All these years I've watched her grow more sarcastic and less flexible and more tyrannical as Dad moved up the ranks in politics and our family became even more of a public target. But she *really* started to change when I turned eighteen and Dad won the election. In the three years since then, *all* of Mother's controlling instincts have converged on one goal—keeping Dad and me under her thumb."

"Keeping you both safe," Jakobek corrected.

"Well, it's too much. I've been forced to make this drastic change in order to escape from her. And I think Dad will under-stand."

"Maybe. Maybe not." Jakobek turned his hard scrutiny to Davis. "In the meantime, Mr. Thackery, you have a lot of ex-plaining to do."

"No, respectfully, Sir, but what Eddie and I have done is none of your business. She wants you to leave."

"That's not going to happen."

"Yes, it is."

"Whoa," I said. I stepped between them. "Davis, the man's here to talk, and he's representing Eddie's family, and you owe him that courtesy. Eddie, I know you're so mad at your mother you can't see straight, but you can't refuse to at least hear out her messenger." I raised my voice. "And there'll be no more ultima-tums issued, except by *me*. Or else."

Eddie shook her head. Her eyes glowed with tears as she gazed at Jakobek. I had no doubt in my mind of her affection for the big, brutal-looking man they'd sent to fetch her. Was he a killer? Maybe. But he was a bee charmer, too. And that took kindness.

"Nicky, I'm sorry, but you can't tell me anything I don't already know." Eddie wiped her eyes. "I'm not going anywhere with you, and I'm not even going to continue this conversation. You obviously don't understand my motives, and you assume I've made a foolish choice simply because it's not my typical behavior." She pivoted and walked out of the barn.

Nick Jakobek started after her. Davis blocked his way, fists clenched. "She *asked* you to leave her alone. Now, I'm *telling* you."

"Mr. Thackery—"

"Stop patronizing me with that tone of voice. I won't back off."

Jakobek held up his left hand, the forefinger pointed at Davis's livid face in an almost elegant gesture of warning. I got one glimpse of that hand, noting the shocking imbalance of the missing little finger, before Davis exploded. I grabbed for him as he lunged at Jakobek with a fist drawn back. Nick Jakobek caught him by the wrist, spun him, and let go. In the next second Davis went stumbling into a stack of bushel baskets, scattering them everywhere and plowing face first into the barn's clay floor.

My lungs echoed the guttural whump of his expelled breath, and I put a hand over my stomach. Jakobek looked up at me. The expression in his eyes wasn't cruel. "I don't want to hurt your son."

"Do you think I'll *let* you?" Fumbling at a front pocket of my jeans, I pulled out a shower of ma huang tablets and a small enameled pocketknife I always carried. I jerked the blade open, leaned in close to Jakobek's face, wound one hand in his flannel shirt, and thrust the three-inch sliver of sharp steel in front of his eyes. "Touch him again and I'll core you like a baking apple."

A kind of appreciation came into Jakobek's eyes. Not that I frightened him with my tiny prick of a paring knife—hell no, I didn't see a shred of fear. But respect, yes. "Then you have to calm him down."

"I can calm myself down," Davis said. "A mouthful of clay

makes a good tranquilizer." He sat up among the baskets, his face speckled with red dirt. Blood trickled from his nose. Suddenly his gaze swiveled to the barn's entrance. "I'm all right," he called hoarsely.

Jakobek and I swung around to see Eddie standing there, white as a sheet, clutching her stomach. "How could you do this to him, Nicky?" She sank to her knees.

"Eddie!" Davis yelled. He leapt to her side, sat down close to her, and held her forehead in one hand. She vomited a thin stream of water onto the barn floor.

"Dammit," Jakobek said under his breath. "I don't know how to handle this kind of thing."

"You're not the only one," I told him. "I don't understand what's happening or why any more than you do."

Davis took Eddie in his arms as she coughed and retched. "We've been married since last spring," he finally said. "And Eddie's three months' pregnant."

TEN

A blue-and-gold autumn sunset lowered a lonely mist over Chocinaw, Big Jaw, and Ataluck Mountains that night, filling the Hollow and making Lucille's crowd of Secret Service agents squint unhappily into the foggy shadows. Davis and Eddie secluded themselves in his upstairs bedroom, where both phoned friends and relatives with the news of their marriage and baby. Smooch sat, dumbfounded, in my log-cabin office behind the house, fielding phone calls from stunned McGillens and Thackerys. Logan trailed Lucille through our commercial buildings, trying manfully to impress her while she scrutinized the alarm systems and made notes and tried to avoid being impressed. Hush Puppy sat with Smooch in the office, too fascinated to do more than listen and watch in speechless awe.

And I had barely recovered enough to do more than walk the floor.

Nicholas Jakobek took over my living room, where he paced before the fireplace with some kind of high-tech security phone to his ear, listening more than he spoke, the set of his big shoulders tired when I spied on him from the door to the front hall. I could not imagine what Al and Edwina Jacobs were saying to him. I heard him reply once, the timbre of his voice deep and a little warning. "They recited vows they wrote themselves and signed a one-paragraph marriage contract Eddie cooked up. No, they don't have a ten-dollar government license or the Pope's blessing, but whether we take the marriage seriously or not, *they* do."

I admired him at that moment. How many men are willing to tell the President and the Pope to back off at the same time? When Jakobek put the phone down and caught me in the doorway, I didn't bother apologizing for eavesdropping. We were beyond simple courtesies at that point. "Homemade vows or not, Jakobek, you're right. They're not backing down. At least not until the excitement wears off."

"Eddie was raised to honor her word."

"That's how I raised my son, too. And I'm sure he's sincere."

"What about you?"

"About marriage vows? I believe in them for the long haul."

"That's an interesting way of putting it. But my question is, 'What do you intend to do about this situation in the short haul?'"

I felt my face grow hot. He inspired awkward, or maybe honest, misinformation. All right. "I intend to honor a simple but ironclad rule for keeping a family together. I'm duty-bound to welcome a pregnant daughter-in-law no matter what the circumstances, and keep my mouth shut for the good of my grandchild. Even if I think this marriage is impulsive and naive and probably doomed."

Jakobek walked over, studying my face the way a lost man reads a map to find the quickest way home. I almost backed away. I almost leaned toward him. He stopped no more than hugging distance from me. "I like your brutal and dutiful honesty," he said.

"I'll take that as a compliment."

"It was."

I left the living room with the tip of my tongue clamped between my teeth.

Blind. Ye be blind, who would see-eth the most. So quoteth I of the self-named Reverend Betty Passover, pastor of the Gospel Church of the Harvest in Song, Chocinaw County's tiniest church but, in my opinion, its most profound. Blind. I had never looked at Eddie Jacobs and considered the obvious maternal reason for her hair-trigger stomach. I hadn't wanted to think in that direction. I had pulled a shade of hope over my mind's eye. Now I stood in the light.

Not Eddie Jacobs. Eddie Jacobs Thackery. My daughter-in-law. Pregnant with my son's child. My grandbaby.

Up at the public barns, my workers were cleaning up and shutting down for the night. Normally, I held a meeting at the end of opening day to toast everybody with fifty-proof applejack and review the sales record. For the first time in twenty years, I canceled the meeting. As soon as I figured out what to do next, I'd have to talk to everyone about the wife Davis had brought home. I'd have to feign support and happiness.

The truth?

I saw Davis's choices through the narrow view of my own impulsive marriage to his father, and so I feared the worst. I wanted to keen in biblical fashion and slash my breasts.

But I had to keep a close eye on Jakobek.

EDDIE WAS PREGNANT. Pregnant. My kid cousin. The little girl I'd held at birth. Going to be a mother.

Al was headed back to the States on *Air Force One*. Edwina was on her way from England. "Edwina can't talk about this anymore right now," he said hoarsely. "She's too upset. We both are. We want to be there this instant. But we can't be. Thank you for going. Do you know how guilty we feel, not being there?"

He had just the usual job responsibilities — the Middle East, a small crisis, threats to world peace. "I'm not a good stand-in," I admitted, "but I swear to you Eddie's safe, and I'll keep her that way."

"What do you think of this Thackery? Your gut-level first impression."

"Smart. Naive. Cocky. Loves her. Wants to do the right thing."

"And his family? His . . . irascible mother?"

I spent about ten minutes talking enthusiastically about Hush Thackery, until I realized how much I'd said and how quiet Al had become. "I'm asking you to stay neutral," Al said slowly. "Are you . . . all right?"

After a silence of my own, I said, "Al, I'm always neutral. And I'm always all right."

A helluva lie.

That night I stood in Hush Thackery's upstairs hallway, looking at the closed door to the bedroom where Davis Thackery and Eddie had shut us all out. I tossed my duffel bag on a twin four-poster in a room about the size of a closet. A good copy of an eighteenth-century Warford landscape was framed on the wall. Apple pickers in English orchards. The room was the last outpost at the end of the upstairs hall with a tall window. I picked it because I could check the backyard from the bedroom window and a side yard from the hall window. Vantage points. Davis's bedroom was only two doors down, across a width of Turkish rug with apples in the design.

His mother's big bedroom was just beneath mine, downstairs. Hush Thackery, posted at the gate to her home. Guardian of her nest. Keeper of family pride and die-hard morals. She slept alone down there, standing guard. I'd do my best to keep her world safe, too.

And I'd think about her sleeping alone.

Lucille Olson called me on the secure phone she'd set up. "Mrs. Thackery has left the house and disappeared into the back orchard. I think she's upset. Someone should follow her. She told me to make myself at home. I don't think she meant it. Colonel, will you go check on her?"

By the time I said yes and turned the phone off, I was already heading downstairs.

I HID MYSELF UNDER the Great Lady as a huge orange harvest moon rose among milky purple clouds, and there I broke down. I squatted on my heels in the moon-dappled darkness, hugged my knees to my forehead, and sobbed. The scent of the earth and the night wind and the apples above me wafted into my brain, lifting wisps of the scent from Jakobek's cigar from my clothes and skin and memory. The Great Lady showered me with a few of her red autumn leaves.

There is a season for letting go and a season for starting over.

"I *can't* let go of my dreams for Davis," I countered. "God, I made the best of what you handed me and I made sure my son grew up respecting his father and I hid the truth about our fights and Davy's women and how much he disappointed me and how much I disappointed him, all so our son would grow up seeing how a man and a woman ought to treat each other — all so Davis would have more choices and make smarter decisions than his father and I did. Are you telling me it's *smart* for him to marry a girl who has nothing in common with his own people? Are you telling me it's smart for him to leave college and come back here with a baby on the way and the *whole world watching*? God, do you *want* everything I've built here to fall apart under that kind of scrutiny?"

No answer. You can't grill God for explanations as if He were the defendant in the trial for your life. I dried my eyes with the sleeve of my sweater and got to my feet, shoving the Great Lady's lower branches aside. She was trying to tap me on the shoulder and tell me to keep my own counsel. "Why should I listen?" I said hoarsely. "No one seems to be listening to *me*."

"I am," Jakobek said. He stood out in the open alley between the trees, whitewashed in the moonlight.

163

I froze. "How long have you—"

"Long enough. Sorry."

The night breeze ruffled his dark hair and pulled at his loose, earth-hued clothes. The fruit-heavy trees seemed to sway toward him, catching at him with their finest little branches. Goosebumps rose on my skin. Davy had never looked right, with his smirk and his leather and his smell of motor oil, among the trees. But Jakobek did.

I moved forward, holding a small apple I'd snared off the Great Lady. I stopped in front of Jakobek and thrust the apple into his left hand, then clamped his callused fingers over it, taking little care to be discreet or gentle. If he was uncomfortable about his disfigured hand, my touch didn't register any regret. Gripping his hand inside both of mine, I tilted my head back and looked up at him with feverish anger and sorrow and hope. "I know the difference between rotten and ripe, and I'm an expert on the difference between an honest man and a liar. In my version of the Garden of Eden, Eve made it her business to grow the apple of wisdom and never be fooled by a snake again. Which are you, Jakobek? The snake or the apple?"

"Both." He looked down at me with troubled eyes. Most men didn't have enough words for what they felt, and most women had too many. "If you've got anything else I need to know, *tell* me."

"You've already heard more about my marriage than any other person on the face of this earth." I paused. "More than my son has ever so much as suspected."

"I'm not interested in exposing your personal secrets." He turned the small, helpless apple in his maimed hand, examined it, then put it in his shirt pocket. "We're in this mess together. If you work with me, I'll work with you."

Without another word, he pivoted and walked back through the alley in the moonlight toward the house, taking the apple of temptation with him. I stepped out in the light and stood, awed and afraid, as I watched him cast half in light, half in shadow again.

🍂

JAKOBEK LEFT FOR Washington the next morning before dawn. Neither of us said another word about the things he'd overheard regarding Davy. I prayed he'd forget. I knew he wouldn't. Maybe he thought it was all just the soap-opera mumblings of an unhappy widow. I hoped so.

Eddie Jacobs Thackery, my pregnant daughter-in-law, slept in Davis's upstairs bedroom under a silk coverlet in the company of two cats and Davis's favorite dog, an old mixed beagle he and his father had found as a puppy at the Foggy Top Dirt Track in northern Alabama. Davis had named the dog Racer. Racer snored on the First Daughter's feet. Davis, grim faced and silent, watched over her from a corner rocking chair surrounded by his books, computers, stuffed deer heads, and framed pictures of him and Davy standing beside stock cars. The room was a young country-boy college student's bedroom. *Not a husband's,* I told myself.

Not a father's.

🍂

I STAYED IN A HOTEL when I went to Washington, never at the White House. My own choice. The White House was Al and Edwina's world, not mine. I stepped off an elevator into the family quarters, carrying a huge wicker basket. I set it on a gilded table.

One of Edwina's staffers came out of an office. "Colonel, Mrs. Jacobs will be with you momentarily." She stared at the basket. Twenty pounds of Sweet Hush Farms fried apple pies and apple muffins and apple fritters and apple fruitcake and God alone knew what else bulged inside tight, shrink-wrapped plastic beneath a fat red bow. Hush had asked me to present the food to Edwina. "She may laugh at it or she may spit on it,"

Hush said, "but we share a grandbaby, and I have to send a gift. It's another of my rules."

"I'll get it there," I said. "And she won't laugh at it. I can't promise anything else."

"You're loyal," she said, staring into my eyes, searching down behind the corneas, looking for the real me. Like a threat, or a question.

I looked away. Facing guns in a jungle somewhere was easier. "I'm trustworthy. A regular Boy Scout."

"We'll see."

"What's that, may I ask?" the staffer questioned, sniffing at the basket.

I told her. Her face neutral, she probed the cellophane wrapping with a fingertip and read the labels with an arched brow. "Has this homey little offering been cleared by the Secret Service?"

"Lucille Olson watched Mrs. Thackery pack it. Yes."

"I thought this woman had employees to do her menial work for her."

"It's a gift. Personal."

"Is this Thackery woman\presentable? Somewhat educated?"

"Why don't you call her and ask her? She'll be happy to hear she's up for evaluation. After being spied on by Edwina and her minions."

"I've never appreciated your morbid jokes."

"I'm not joking."

She left me in a breeze of expensive perfume and disapproval. I nodded to Secret Service agents who nodded back as I walked into a sitting room Edwina had decorated in country style — French country. "I had to exile my beloved Louis the Fourteenth collection to Mother's estate," Edwina had said. "Our advisors decided it made me look too Marie Antoinette-ish." Only a grass-stained set of golf clubs in one corner and a framed picture of my grandfather Jacobs on the mantel hinted that Al lived in the White House with Edwina.

Her brilliant masterminding of their campaigns and image had put them there, and her protective control over Eddie had been wise — to a point. But she'd gone a bridge too far in fighting the fear I'd seen in her eyes that day I killed the man in the park. Her cynicism and distrust had spread. It included Hush and Davis Thackery now.

I scowled at myself in a gilded mirror. As I straightened the wrinkled jacket I'd pulled out of my duffel bag, I discovered something in the pocket: a slice of apple wrapped in cellophane and a torn piece of Sweet Hush Farms business stationery. I unfolded the slip of paper and saw Puppy's big, scrawled, first-grader lettering.

THE BEES SAY U BEE LONG 2 US OK?

Standing in Edwina's sitting room, I folded Puppy's note carefully and saved it in my pocket, then unwrapped the apple slice and ate it in small bites. The sweet juice spread over my tongue. *Hush* had grown this apple. Hush McGillen Thackery, with an emphasis on *McGillen*. She had fostered the tree and ripened the fruit and maybe even picked this apple with her own hands. Then she'd carved it and handed it to her niece to hide in my pocket like a communion wafer. Shape and form and spirit and hunger.

A door opened on silent hinges, and Edwina walked in. The tailored blue dress suit she wore cinched her like a store mannequin, and her mound of blond hair didn't move. She was fifty-five years old and welded into the armor of campaigns and fundraisers and political maneuvers and the career of a glorified hostess. That was the price she'd paid for standing behind Al instead of in front of him. I missed the cheerful Edwina from those early years, before she saw what it would take to survive public life.

"You never sit," she said. Red-eyed and hard-soft. Never athletic or svelte but strong. "Sit, Nicholas," she ordered. "For godssake, someone in this family ought to do what I tell them to for once."

"Too much toile makes me nervous." I nodded at chairs covered in the patterned green fabric.

She smiled bitterly and shook her head. "How many heterosexual career Army officers know their French fabric prints the way you do?"

"I'm retired. I may become a decorator. I need a job."

"Oh, no. You'll never really retire, Nicholas. You'll die fighting for some good cause far from home and trying to prove something that can't be proved. What the hell were you trying to prove with this?" She indicated the gift basket.

"Mrs. Thackery sent you a gift basket. I don't care what you do with it, but I'm telling her you like it."

"Will she believe you?"

"No."

"Then don't bother. I hate the woman. And she hates me."

I nodded. "Let's talk about Eddie. What does Al say?"

"He's tearing his hair out, naturally." She groaned. "Our pregnant daughter is in Georgia, *non communicato*. And you're the only pipeline of information we have. So you tell *me* what I should say to Al about these people who've taken my daughter away from me, Nicholas. Tell me about Davis Thackery. And about *her*. His mother."

I held out the last bite of apple. "Try this."

She frowned at the sliver of white-and-red fruit on my palm. "In an hour I have a photo session with the United Women's Independence Coalition or the Save the Marine Mollusks Foundation or whatever the fuck I have to do next. I don't keep track of half the pose-and-smile appointments on my party schedule. But my lips are ready, regardless." She pointed to her perfectly outlined mouth. "I can't eat. Not hungry, anyway."

"You want to know what Hush Thackery is made of? Who she is and what her life's about? It's all there." I nodded to the slice.

She stared at me. "They're brainwashing you."

"Try the apple."

Edwina placed the nibble between her teeth, bit down without passion, and chewed. Her eyes brightened, then narrowed. She spit the chewed pulp into her hand and dropped it in a crystal vase of white roses. "What's your point?"

"These people care about what they create. They work hard and seem honest. I'm just telling you. The apple. It's good."

"My daughter is pregnant and married and I want to crawl in a hole and scream. Don't give me a slice of apple and tell me you've had a blinding flash of insight and her choices are all right."

"Eddie thinks she's following her heart. Whether she's right or not, she needs you and Al to support her choice."

"No. She has to come to us."

After a long moment, I said, "She's your kid. She's pregnant."

Edwina swayed, her eyes wet, her mouth hard. "My mother didn't admit me to her home or speak to me for two years after I married Al. It was excruciating. This isn't easy for me."

"Then why do you want to treat Eddie the same way?"

"My mother was right. At the time. Right that I was making a foolish choice, marrying beneath me, endangering my reputation and my future. Thank God, she was wrong about Al. Do you think I understood her wisdom at the time? Not at all. I loved Al, but when I married him it was for the wrong reasons—sentimental romance, idealistic dreams, and frankly, the joy of getting laid. I was lucky he turned out to be more than just good-hearted and good in bed."

"Eddie's your daughter," I repeated. "A kid needs a mother's loyalty."

"Don't you think I know that?" Edwina put her face in her hands. "What am I supposed to do? Encourage her to ruin her life?"

"Maybe she hasn't. Davis Thackery might be worth the trouble."

"Oh? So far he's only demonstrated a knack for luring one of the smartest, most sensible, most career-oriented young women on the face of this planet into bed—and getting her pregnant.

And she *let* him. *My* daughter — who I taught about birth control from the time she was old enough to understand the show-and-tell routine using anatomically correct dolls at the women's clinic. *My* daughter — who at twelve years old sincerely came to the philosophical conclusion that virginity and chastity are empowerment issues worth defending.

"Any young man who is manipulative and sly enough to confuse her on issues that were bedrock values in her life and in the community of family and friends Al and I surrounded her with — any apple-farming stud who could wreak havoc on my . . ." her voice quavered . . . "my wonderful baby's common sense . . . and sidetrack the future that meant everything to her —"

"That meant everything to *you*," I corrected. "If you cut Eddie off, you'll be sorry. You'll be wrong."

"No. She'll come home. You'll see. On my terms."

"What does Al want to do?"

"We're discussing it. I told you, he's letting me handle things."

I thought, *This is the man who tracked me down in a Mexican hospital when I was fourteen. This is the man who brought me home and made me feel welcome. He won't leave his daughter out in the cold.* "Meaning he's mad as hell at your attitude."

Edwina advanced on me with manicured nails up like claws. "He wasn't there that day in the park when we nearly, when you . . . she is my daughter, and I can't forget —" Edwina's voice rattled, and she paused to collect herself — "goddammit, she agreed to make something of her life. Goals, Nick. Specific goals. We agreed she'd put off marriage and children until she'd established herself in public office. What is she going to do with a baby at her age! And some unproven nobody for a husband — Nicholas, this marriage isn't even legal. If she'd only come to me the moment she found out she was pregnant, I'd have helped her avoid this mess."

"If you're talking about bullying her to have an abortion," I said slowly, "maybe that's why she didn't come to you, and maybe that's why she won't talk to you now."

Edwina froze. "I'm not sure what my counsel to her would have been," she said in a low, even voice, "but I don't deserve your insinuations. I am pro *choice,* Nicholas. Not pro abortion. Pro *choice.*"

"My mother had no choice. I vowed I'd make that up to her."

"It's not the same situation."

"To me," I said very quietly, "it is."

I STOOD. THEY SAT. Edwina and her advisors, a mafia of Habersham cousins and smart friends and political aides with nice hair and polished fingernails — twenty people filling a small conference table in the west wing of the White House.

The topic: Hush Thackery and son. Pros and cons. Their mixed-race background had potential. "Colonel, does she look Caucasian or can you tell her grandmother was Native American? Is that an issue we need to address? Or perhaps we can exploit it to our advantage." A black staffer asked the question without a trace of irony.

"She has red hair and green eyes," I said. "She smokes a Cherokee pipe, earned a degree in business at night school, and raised a son who was willing to get his ass kicked for Eddie's sake."

"A smoker," one of the minions said, and wrote the information down, frowning.

"Religion?" another said, reading some notes. "Davis Thackery attended something called the Gospel Church of the Harvest in Song as a kid. His mother was and is a big contributor. Nondenominational. Self-styled, unaffiliated. A woman pastor."

"Snake handlers?" someone asked, nervously twisting a two-hundred-dollar gold ink pen. "Speaking in tongues? Faith healing?"

"Singing," I put in. "Yesterday the Reverend Betty and her gospel band were at the pavilion singing 'May the Circle Be

Unbroken.' Hush Thackery sings with them. And plays the wash-tub bass."

"The what?"

"Overturned metal washtub, heavy cord attached to the center of the bottom, stretched tight to a pole. Put one foot on the washtub to anchor, pull the pole back with your left hand, pluck the cord with your right hand. Sounds like a bass cello if you know the technique. Hush Thackery knows the technique."

"Appalachian hillbilly music," someone said, and made a note.

"We need a photo op. We have to get you and the President to-gether with the new in-law, Mrs. Jacobs."

Edwina nodded. "All right. I need to assess her in person. Rattle her cage. Show her who she's dealing with."

"I don't think she cares who she's dealing with," I said.

"Nicholas, you're no judge of women. This is one who doesn't need rescuing. She's no Cinderella."

I turned from the window where I'd been watching garden-ers cut the green grass on the lawn. "What's that supposed to mean?"

"Attack me, Nicholas. Go ahead and tell me I'm an evil bitch and I've violated some code of honor by scrutinizing every bit of information I can learn about her. Consider the fact that she can easily access excruciatingly detailed public information about our family, Nicholas. Besides — why are you defending her?"

"Because she's given you no reason to attack her, and for better or worse, Eddie's part of her family now. So you're at-tacking Eddie's mother-in-law. It's not good for Eddie." *Because I'm tired of being cynical about people,* I added silently. *Because Hush Thackery is no ordinary person. Because I want to believe in her.*

Edwina stood. "I won't let my daughter be blindsided by shabby in-laws. I'll make a deal with you. You get Hush Thackery to meet with Al and me, and we'll see if her reputation holds up under a little gentle interrogation. If she's as righteous as you seem to think, she'll come through with flying colors."

"You're on," I said.

"EDDIE JACOBS DOESN'T REALLY want to stay here," I told Smooch. We stood outside the back windows of my house, looking up at Davis's windows. "She's not an apple farmer. And Smooch, it's not as if she's homeless and destitute. Her parents *run the country.*"

Smooch leaned close and whispered, "But think about the publicity this farm would get if she stays for good."

"Stop saying that."

We heard a rustling noise in the shrubs at the corner of the house. A Secret Service agent worked his way around the edge of my wicker-filled back porch, peering into large clay pots filled with yellow mums, then parting the limbs of the huge hydrangeas that sheltered several windows. "They're like raccoons," I whispered to Smooch. "You turn your back and they creep right up to the door."

The agent waved at us. "Just a routine assessment, Ma'am," he called. Continuing to move along the back of the house, he scrutinized all the first-floor windows.

"You need locks on those windows," Smooch whispered back anxiously. "He doesn't like that they don't have locks. Look, he's making a note on his pocket computer." She clutched her chest harder. "They have a file on you. And your house. You need locks."

"I don't need locks. I have deer rifles and a shoot-to-kill attitude." Big talk. I wiped my mouth with the back of one hand. All that day I'd tasted fear like a sour kiss. How much would these people want to know? How much did they already know? What might they tell, if they did know? What would Jakobek do?

Smooch, steeped only in ordinary terrors, grabbed my arm.

173

"Hush! All the guns are locked up in Davy's gun cabinet, aren't they? The Secret Service will ask! And they'll want to see the licenses!"

I chewed my tongue. "Let them look. I don't give a damn." Like most of the respectable citizens of Chocinaw County, Davy had been a card-carrying member of the NRA and a rabid foe of gun licensing. His arsenal hailed from local gun shows where crewcut men with skull tattoos took cash money under the table, no questions asked. I looked at Smooch grimly. "I guess this means I better hide the Uzi and the anti-aircraft missile."

"Don't joke!"

"Eddie Jacobs won't be here long enough for her people to squabble with me over the second amendment."

"I'm telling you—"

"Shhh. Look at him now. I swear."

The agent had discovered the doors to my root cellar. He stood with his hands on his hips and frowned down at their aging oak frame. He even toed the wood and tapped the shiny, corrugated tin covering it. Smooch sighed. "He doesn't like crawl spaces and cellars and hidden holes under old farmhouses."

"Then he can go to hell. This house was built by Liza Hush over one hundred years ago of *hard* chestnut and creek stone and tough oak planks. I've put a new roof on it and redone the plumbing and the electrical and that's even new tin on those cellar doors. This house is *solid*."

"Hush, the Secret Service doesn't care about any of *that*. You're talking about decoration, not security." She wrung her hands. "They want bullet-proof glass and infrared sensors and reinforced titanium doors and satellite tracking systems and implanted ID chips and antibacterial—"

The agent opened the cellar door, then looked over at me. "Mind if I take a look down there, Ma'am?"

"Go ahead. But pull out your gun in case you're jumped by giant spiders. And keep an eye out for falling jars of canned applesauce, because the shelves are overloaded. I don't think you'll find anything else sinister, but then again, a cousin of my great-grandfather's disappeared around here in the 1930s and the old folks still claim his wife killed him for cheating on her. They say she buried the body somewhere here in the Hollow. So yell if you spot a skull."

He nodded without a trace of humor, then disappeared down the heavy wooden steps. Smooch had turned pale white. "Don't talk that way! It's like at the airport security check-in. *You're not supposed to joke with them!*"

"How can I take these guys seriously when they think terrorists are hiding in my mums and stalkers are holed up in my cellar?" I shook my head. "Save us from the government."

"If you read thriller novels like I do you'd know all the things evil, crazy people try to do to the President and his family. Somebody could sneak up here and hide a *bomb* in your flowers. Or shoot us all with a high-powered rifle through the old wavy panes of your downstairs windows. Or hide in the cellar and grab Eddie when she walks out to the backyard to watch the sunrise over Ataluck. Hush, the world outside Chocinaw County is just filled with loonies who think of those things, and we can't be too careful, even for one day!" Smooch's blue Thackery eyes radiated sincere concern and filled with tears. "I spent all these years thinking up ways to lure customers to this farm, and I've set up the best fall marketing campaign we've ever had, and I don't want it ruined by terrorists!"

I put an arm around her. "Now, look here. We've survived early frosts, late harvests, stem fungus, recessions, kitchen fires, broken-down delivery trucks, the years when we worked for nothing and had nothing in the bank at the end of the season, and the bad wishes of all those folks who said we'd *never* convince people from Atlanta to drive up here from September to January to buy apples. We'll survive Eddie Jacobs. And I promise you, we won't tangle with any terrorists and we won't get in trouble with the Secret Service."

"You forgot the worst thing." Smooch dabbed her eyes and sighed. "You survived losing Davy."

I froze, then recovered with a quick nod. "That goes without saying."

Smooch sighed again. "I wish I had a man right now. Someone who'd tell me not to worry my pretty little head."

"No, that never works."

She nodded wearily. Small and curvy and fluffy and still desperately needy even at the seasoned age of thirty-six, she'd rejected every man who'd wanted to marry her. It was my fault, in a way. Like everyone else, she thought my marriage to her brother had turned out to be a match made in heaven. We'd inspired her high standards, she said. I gave her a guilty hug. "We're *survivors*. And we have too much work to do to waste time on this kind of teary chitchat."

She drew herself up. "You're right." Smooch trudged inside, then returned, hugging her laptop computer with a phone cord dragging behind it. "I've been doing some research on Eddie."

I groaned. She sat down on a wooden garden bench with apples carved on the back, then hunched over the laptop computer like a brown-haired poodle searching for treats. Gold crosses and fake diamond studs flashed in her earlobes as she typed and thumbed the mouse button. A late summer butterfly lit on one of the dozen delicate gold necklaces she wore. Smooch looked like she ought to be managing a dime store, but she was, in fact, a marketing and computer wiz. "She's a role model," Smooch said in a conspiratorial drawl. "That's what Eddie Jacobs has always been called. Role model. Look here." She pointed at the laptop's screen. "Voted the most admired collegiate female by the readers of *Independent Girl* e-zine. And when her parents were campaigning for the White House? 'Hand the votes to daughter, Eddie,' the *New York Times* said. 'Eloquent, smart, and serious. A role model for—' there's that role model thing again."

"I get the picture."

"She wrote a *book* when she was eighteen! I mean, really wrote it, not just put her name on it. *Chick Power* was the title. 'A book-length essay on the value of chastity, independence, education, and self-determination for young women.' Chastity! With her folks being liberals and all. Chastity! Who'd have thought it! My God, Hush, that book was on the bestseller lists while her folks were running for the White House! She was a hit author. At only eighteen!"

"Some ideas are only worth a penny a bushel even when they're written in a book, Smooch."

"*She's a role model,*" Smooch insisted. "Picture this." She spread her hands as if framing a headline. "SON OF FAMOUS APPLE FARMER RESCUES FIRST DAUGHTER FROM LIFE IN FISHBOWL. READ THE DELICIOUS DETAILS AT WWW.SWEETHUSHAPPLES.COM."

I looked at her until she blushed. She bent over the computer and refused to look at me again. "It's my job to advertise our apples. Anything that sells apples is okay by me. I'll say no more."

"I'll hold you to that promise." I walked into the house. My grandfather clock ticked among fine lithographs of antique apple varieties in the living room, my cats hunkered on the polished oak floor of the kitchen to lap at the water in their apple-red ceramic dishes, and my opening-day paperwork and notes still lay stacked on a claw-footed walnut table by the back door to the porch, where I'd left them on my way out to pour wine on the unsuspecting roots of my life.

The phone sang.

"Number seven," Smooch said, following me inside. She'd kept track of the calls in the past hour.

People on the President's staff. People on the First Lady's staff. They were all polite, but they all spoke to me slowly, as if I were Forrest Gump, and they called me by my first name, as if they obviously had the right. They all continued to say the same thing. *Let's just keep this quiet until the President and First Lady can resolve it with Eddie in private.*

177

I couldn't agree more. "Sweet Hush Farms," I said grimly into the phone.

"Rush, please."

"*Hush*. Hush Thackery. Speaking."

"Hush, I'm Mrs. Habersham-Longley. I manage Mrs. Jacobs's hometown office in Chicago. I'm her younger sister."

"Nice to meet you." So Edwina Jacobs hired her own kin, the same as me. My hometown office, for the record, was on the other side of my goldfish pond, in the first Hush's log cabin. A small dog and four cats were asleep in a bed of yellow autumn mums beside its porch.

"Now, Rush, let's just chat—"

"Excuse me, it's *Hush*."

"I'm so sorry. Hush. Hush. I have a typo in my notes."

"You have *notes* on me, too? Where did *you* get *notes* on me?"

Smooch pointed to one of the gold apple studs in her ears. "Ask her if she'd like some complimentary Sweet Hush Apple fourteen-karat earrings from the gift shop—"

I made a slashing gesture. Silence. Smooch sighed.

"Hush, there's nothing sinister going on," my caller soothed. "I just want to confirm some information about you. After all, you're something of a local celebrity, we understand. Listed with your county chamber of commerce, and the state small business association, and the state apple grower's association, and—"

"Are you people *investigating* me?"

"Well, no, it's just that, *of course,* there are security issues when a relative of the President's is involved."

"Let me tell you something. All you need to know is that Eddie is upstairs in my house right now with my son waiting on her hand and foot. She's safe as a bee in apple honey. Nobody on this farm is going to harm so much as a hair on Eddie Jacobs's head, and we're not going to let any strangers get within ten feet of her. I'm not taking any more of these phone calls."

"You can't be serious. Now, Hush—"

"Don't you people have first names, too?"

"I'm . . . Regina. Regina Habersham-Longley."

Regina and Edwina? What was the third sister named? Vagina?
"Habersham-Longley. With a hyphen?"

"Yes, why?"

"I'm keeping notes on you."

"Are you being sarcastic, Hush?"

"Around here, we call it 'giving tit for tat.'"

"My point, Hush, is that we wouldn't want to exploit the
President's daughter, now would we? We wouldn't want word to
get out to the public in the wrong way. We wouldn't want the
media to descend on your farm and start asking questions.
Because frankly, we don't know if this marriage is serious, and perhaps it can be resolved without anyone outside our small group
ever knowing there is a problem."

"*Regina,* I'm not sure what insults me most about what you
just said, but let me make my point of view real simple for you:
My son says he and Eddie Jacobs are married. I may not be happy
about that, but my son's not a liar. Now, out here in the boon-
docks where we ordinary people live, the parents of a girl who's
run off and gotten married will call or come by to visit the parents of the boy who's run off *with* her. I've granted the Jacobses
some leeway because they were out of the country when this
started. But you give me their phone numbers, and I'll call them
for a chat."

"You know it's not that simple. You can't just call—"

"Oh yes, I can. I pay my taxes."

"Look, I'm sorry. I'll see what I can do, but—"

"All right, then. In the meantime, I've got a business to run
and no more time to waste. You tell Eddie's parents to call me.
We'll keep things quiet in the meantime. This is a family matter,
and I'm not talking to anybody else but them."

"You're joking."

"Don't bet on it, Regina. You have a nice day now, you hear? And
by the way, if I find out you people are researching confidential ma-
terials such as my credit history and family medical records, I'll hire

the biggest, loudest civil liberties lawyer I can find, and your hypo-critical bullshit about privacy will hit the fan. Good-bye."

I tossed the phone in the sink. When the Dalyrimple city coun-cil had leased land for a microwave tower just outside town, I'd been one of the first Chocinaw Countians to buy a cell phone. Anything that put me in faster communication with the world of apple customers was progress to me. The cell phone, the Internet, high-speed computer invoicing, and overnight delivery services were all glorious.

"They put the world just outside our doorstep, and all we have to do is say, 'Hello,' " I'd told everyone who'd listen.

Now I wished I could hide myself, my son, and the Hollow in a cloak of old-fashioned backwardness. I wanted the world to go the hell away. I paced the floor.

Smooch retrieved the phone. "I bet we get interviewed on the *Today Show*."

"No."

"Lord, Hush, look at the bright side. I'm gonna be an aunt! And you're going to be a grandma. Granny Hush. Ol' Gran-mammy Hush. Grand-muther Thackery. And you'll be the mother-in-law to *the President of the United States' daughter*. My God! Think of the publicity we'll get for Sweet Hush Farms! Think of the money we'll make! Big Davy would be so proud! He always said Davis Junior had the Thackery charm with women and the McGillen head for business. But to win the President's daugh-ter! Oh, Hush . . ." I looked at her so hard she flattened her mouth, adjusted her gold necklaces, and jammed a pocket com-puter in her jeans. "I'm going down to the public barns to check out the graphics on the new labels for the apple fruitcakes. I'm wasting my time trying to understand you. Your son married the President's daughter. Most mothers would be happy." She halted, then stared at me with a wounded expression, chewing a thought, then spitting it out as if it hurt her tongue. "You're acting very strange, and I know why. That damned Jakobek blew the yellow jackets off you. And you *let* him."

I stopped pacing. "What's that supposed to mean?"

"It's just that . . . he's . . . Hush, you don't keep up with politics and gossip, yes, I know, but for godssake. Don't you ever listen to Haywood Kenney on the radio?"

Haywood Kenney's nationally syndicated radio talk show was broadcast from coast to coast every day for three hours. He wrote books, made TV appearances, drew crowds when he spoke. He was a self-made so-called political commentator. Huh. He hated Al Jacobs and Edwina Jacobs and every aspect of the Jacobs administration since Day One Amen. I considered him a bigmouth of mean-spirited halfwit ideas and a scrawny show-off in expensive suits, with hair like the thin brown fuzz on a monkey's balls. "No, I don't listen to him," I said, "and what's that bullshit artist know that's not a half-lie or pure hearsay?"

"Kenney knows *everything* about Al Jacobs's family! From way back! He was there twenty-something years ago in Chicago, when Al's nephew — this Jakobek — killed a man with his bare hands. Hush, it's a *famous* story." She related the drama of Jakobek's defense of Edwina and baby Eddie. "Kenney says Jakobek just *slaughtered* the guy. Kenney calls Jakobek 'Al's Psycho Killer Nephew.' He says Al Jacobs pulled strings to get the Army to transfer Jakobek out of the country and keep him from being prosecuted for murder. Kenney says he's been sent on shady missions all over the world ever since. Like he's not much different than a hired gun. The government sends him in to assassinate people and stuff like that. That's what Kenney says."

The skin prickled on the back of my neck, but I flung out my hands impatiently. "What's that got to do with him and me and the yellow jackets right now, Smooch?"

"You shouldn't have let a stranger blow the yellow jackets off you, that's all. He's not the kind of man who does honor to . . . to Davy's memory."

I gave her a stunned, then narrowing look that said she'd crossed the line into Nobody's Business but Mine. "If you think

181

I've dishonored your brother's memory in any way over the years since he died, spit it out now."

She went wide-eyed and teary. "You know I think you've been a wonderful wife! You know I've said you ought to get out more and date a good man! But . . . you *knew* this Jakobek was coming here to cause trouble . . . to mess with Eddie and Davis and try to break them up . . . so why were you *nice* to him?"

"Nice? I threatened to core the man with my paring knife."

"*You let him blow the yellow jackets off you.*"

"Did I have a choice?"

"All you had to do was wait for Gruncle to bring the smoker can. And you're not afraid of the yellow jackets, anyway. There was no need for you to accept Jakobek's help! He's the enemy, Hush. Don't encourage him."

"So far, I'd say he's been tough but fair, and we have to work together to—"

"To break up Eddie and Davis so Davis will go back to Harvard?"

My livid expression must have answered her question. She fled from the house. I sagged.

Was that what I wanted? To enlist Jakobek in scuttling the marriage?

Hands shaking, I retrieved a long-stemmed white pipe from the back pocket of my jeans, filled the pipe bowl from a stash of homegrown tobacco I carried in a small leather pouch, lit the bowl of crushed leaves with a Sweet Hush Farms butane lighter, and took a long, soothing drag. Two Secret Service agents, standing outside the window, stared at me.

"Yes, the mountaineer businesswoman who's now Eddie Jacobs's mother-in-law smokes a pipe," I called to them. They coughed politely and looked away.

So, on top of everything else, my sister-in-law didn't trust Eddie's sinister cousin Nick, and Gruncle came to me with a report that no one else in the family trusted him either.

"We know he flirted with you and knocked Davis down."

"No, he did neither."

"That's sure how it sounds. You taking up for the man?"

"I'm only reporting the facts."

"He's here to break up the marriage. What kind of man does that?"

"He claims he's here to make sure Eddie's all right. The same as my concern for Davis. All I ask is that everyone stay calm and withhold judgment and let's just see what happens."

Gruncle looked at me shrewdly. "Better not withhold judgment for long. We're about to get ourselves in a damned mess here. Because if your son thinks you're working with this Jakobek to upend his marriage, he'll never forgive you."

I said nothing, but shivered inside.

"WILL YOU GO?" Jakobek asked again. It was the middle of the night. I stood in my fancily wallpapered downstairs hall outside the red-and-gold bedroom I'd redecorated after Davy died, holding a white chenille robe closed over my blue cotton pajamas while the big man I barely knew stood before me in weathered khakis, worn flannel, old boots, and a hard predatory look in his eyes, asking me if I'd go with him, immediately, to a meeting with the President and First Lady. He had just arrived from Washington. He stood close enough for me to inhale his warmth and feel quietly unnerved by his presence.

"How?" I asked in return. "Where?"

Before he could answer, out of the mountain night outside my house came the rumble of some aircraft. Jakobek looked skyward, as if the creamy plasterboard ceiling of my hallway held clues. "Marine helicopter," he answered. "They'll fly us to North Carolina. A secure estate that belongs to friends of Edwina's. In a town there. Highlands."

"Highlands? *Rich* friends."

Davis and Eddie walked up behind me, sleepy and rumpled,

wearing matching green robes over Harvard T-shirts. "I don't ex-pect you to answer my mother's beck and call," Eddie said.

Jakobek frowned and started to speak, thought about it, chewed some words, said nothing. But I knew what he was think-ing.

I was the mother of the Jacobses' son-in-law. I was Hush McGillen Thackery, with traditions to uphold and manners to tend. And unfortunately, Jakobek knew enough about me to con-trol me. I pulled my white chenille tighter, like armor. "I'll be ready in ten minutes."

Jakobek almost smiled.

ELEVEN

The air in Highlands smelled cool and green, like fresh money. The ritzy little town sat atop a plateau so high in the mountains northeast of Chocinaw County it might as well be in Canada. It had golf courses and art galleries, blue-cold fishing lakes and towering firs and million-dollar cabins outfitted like Adirondack mansions. The names of some of America's wealthiest families were listed on the local tax roles, if you knew where to look for them. In a few hours, when the shops opened, Mercedes and Jaguars would line the streets.

But the town was quiet under pretty street lamps when our motorcade swarmed through. Motorcade. Yes. Me and Jakobek in a black SUV driven by a Secret Service agent, with more black SUVs in front and back. Jakobek looked unconcerned in khakis and a pullover sweater—whatever he carried in his duffel bag, none of it was formal. After exactly ten minutes of complicated debate (wear your best dress suit; show them you're sophisticated; no, show them you're so sophisticated that you don't care what they think, so wear jeans, like somebody from New York or California), I had compromised: good jeans, four-hundred-dollar

Italian pumps I found at a suburban Atlanta consignment store for fifty dollars, and a navy cashmere sweater I bought at full retail for a speech to a regional meeting of fruit vendors. I twisted my hair up in back with a black clasp, and slapped on just enough expensive makeup to give me the melted look of a teenager after a long, sweaty dance party. Helicopters, by the way, are hell on personal decor.

"Colonel Jakobek," I said as we drove through the pitch-tar darkness of mountainous North Carolina, "if Al and Edwina Jacobs look their Sunday best at four A.M. after all we've been through in the past two days, I'll kiss their ring fingers and admit I should have voted for them."

"Trust me," he answered, "you have the advantage. They've never met anyone like you."

I shrugged off the compliment, assuming it was one. I was trying *very* hard to trust him, considering that he hadn't left me a whole lot of choices.

Our motorcade purred out of Highlands into the black shadows of winding mountain lanes and paved driveways snaking off to either side, disappearing past handsome, locked gates tucked deep into hundred-year-old oaks and massive hedges of rhododendron, the larger-leafed cousin of Chocinaw County's delicate evergreen laurel.

Secret Service agents met us at one such gate and waved us through. I wrapped my hands tighter around my purse as our cars curled up the hidden drive and on to the wooded knoll of a stone-and-wood estate home easily big enough to swallow my farmhouse twice, with room left for dessert. Agents in sweaters and slacks accessorized with little machine guns stood just outside the edges of the lawn's landscape lights. To say it all felt surreal was a given. Other agents hustled to the SUV I shared with Jakobek, opened my passenger door, and said, "Ma'am," in the toneless way of law officers giving a traffic ticket.

But Jakobek waved them away, and by God, they moved. As he escorted me up a cobblestoned walkway to a long veranda, I wondered if Al and Edwina Jacobs, my First In-Laws, were sneaking looks at me through one of the shuttered upstairs windows. "If this were a cartoon," I said to Jakobek under my breath, "I'd look up and see Edwina glaring down at me, and laser beams would shoot from her eyes."

"I've been hit a few times," Jakobek replied, and stepped in front of me.

On that note, the big home's front doors swung open. Two agents emerged, holding the doors wide. There stood a middle-aged couple dressed in casual clothes and sweaters as if planning a game of golf at the club: him, tall and lanky with dark, somber eyes and a ruffled tug of hair going silver; her, short and stocky with smart, serial-killer blue eyes and a short poof of medium blond hair. I gazed up at two of the most famous faces in the world. The President and the First Lady of these United States.

Thank God, at first glance they looked just like ordinary people.

My ribcage relaxed. I held out a hand and climbed three stone steps carefully. "Al. Edwina. I'm Hush McGillen Thackery, and I've come here to tell you that I don't like what our kids have done any better than you do, but you have my word your daughter will get nothing but fair and kind treatment in my home. And that my son is a good young man you can count on. And finally, I've come to say that y'all are welcome in my Hollow anytime, as far as I'm concerned. The rest is up to you and Eddie."

No one breathed for a second. The agents stared at me. Beside me, Jakobek stepped up and stood close, as if planning to plead my case if the king ordered me beheaded. Edwina's eyes narrowed to slits. But Al, good old Polish-American Aleksandr Jacobs of Chicago, Illinois, Jakobek's uncle and Eddie's father and Leader of the Free World, nodded, accepted me in some way that went beyond words, then held out a lanky hand and said quietly, "Hush, you're even more impressive than Nicholas described. Now, let's go inside and talk about our idealistic children and grandchild-to-be."

Edwina smiled.

I didn't trust it.

☙

AL, EDWINA, AND I sat on handsome leather couches around an antique coffee table that probably cost more than all my heirloom living room furniture put together. We pretended to sip coffee. Jakobek kept his distance, standing over by a window with his arms crossed and his big shoulders loose, his legs apart and his back to the outside world. A protector's stance. A loner's.

On Al and Edwina's faces I saw everything I felt—worry, love, frustration, shock. I didn't doubt they were loving parents who had been slapped in the head and knocked off balance. I knew I looked the same way.

"We agree then," Al said. "We believe this marriage has very little chance of succeeding, but we'll present a united front of support."

I nodded. "I swear to you both—I'll do everything I can to help mend the breach between you and Eddie. And as I said before, you'll always be welcome at the Hollow."

"Thank you," Al said. Beside him, Edwina nodded and smiled some more. I didn't believe her attitude for one second. But I admired Al Jacobs, the way he spoke to me, the solid and deliberate kindness of him. Al gestured around us. "I doubt you'd want us there during your peak business time. The friends who own this estate outfitted it especially for my visits. There are more security systems in these walls and on the grounds than you can ever imagine. That's what it takes to guard a President, God help us. With the state of the world the way it is today, my own daughter is in danger every time she's in my presence. I put her in jeopardy just by being in the same room with her. She may be safer in your Hollow than anywhere else in the world. We have to admit our daughter hated the spotlight, and that she has good reasons for wanting to live her life—and raise her child—far away from us."

From the corner of my eye, I saw Edwina's face tighten like a wrung towel, the fake smile stretching to its limits. I stood. "Edwina, can you and I take a walk? We need a private mother talk. Can we do that without setting off alarms?"

She stood. "Only the man-made kind."

I nodded. A high-voltage power line held less danger.

OUR WALK CONSISTED OF moving stiffly, side by side, in the cold predawn mountain air, down a manicured path lined with land-scape lights, then into the forest to a small gazebo next to a koi pond with a natural rock waterfall. "I like fish," I said. "I have a pond in my backyard."

"I know," she said.

She knew. Nosy high-toned bitch. We stood there in the gazebo with only the path lights to brighten the darkness and the splashing fountain to keep the angry silence at bay. "Don't step off the path," Edwina finally warned. "There are infrared sensors everywhere."

As if she might make me run. I hunched my shoulders. "I don't doubt you live in a glass bowl and everyone around it is armed with rocks. But is all of this high-tech paranoia really necessary?"

"Last week, in Israel, a man tried to plant plastic explosives in the cars of my husband's motorcade. The Secret Service caught him. And that's just the latest incident. My husband risks assassination every day."

"You mean those stories don't show up in the news?"

"Of course not. It happens all the time. The incidents aren't publicized. The public *rarely* finds out about an attack on the President unless the situation explodes in front of television cameras. That's why most of the world's most profound political, social, economic, and military secrets *remain* secret. It's the relatively petty little *personal* secrets that escape. Those can be excruciating, but they hurt only the people closest to their epicenter."

"I'm sorry. I can see that you're worried. Scared."

"Scared? No. *Horrified*." She pivoted toward me. "There is evil in the world that can't be reasoned with. I believe that more and more as time goes by, and I'll do whatever it takes to protect my family as best I can. Nicholas has always understood that the ends justify the means. He saved my and Eddie's lives years ago because he didn't hesitate to kill for our protection. At the time, I was shocked and confused by his brutal judgment. I was naive. I doubt he'd believe me if I told him so. But he was right."

A chill ran down my spine. "You see me and my son as one more threat you have to deal with. And you'll do whatever it takes to make sure we don't hurt Eddie."

"That's absolutely correct."

"All right, so let's cut to the chase. Just between you and me. What's said here goes no farther. You're smiling for your husband and saying all the right things, but I don't buy it. Talk."

She walked around me, studying me, deciding what to risk, circling me. I turned with her motion the way a cat swivels when another cat stalks it. "Just between us?" she said.

"You have my word."

She halted. "I intend to find out everything about you. Every nasty little family secret that might crop up to hurt my daughter's good name. Every embarrassing weakness I can use to persuade her that she doesn't want to be part of your family. Because above all, I want my daughter to be so disillusioned by her new husband and his in-laws that she bolts from this marriage. I want her and my grandchild safely under my wing. I want her future restored as quickly as possible."

My head buzzed. "Go on," I finally said.

"We live in a world where nothing's a secret, Hush. Al and I have been humiliated more than once by the media. Hounded. Our most harmless personal intimacies detailed. Al's sister had an ugly, unfortunate history . . . and so does Nicholas. Private matters, but we can't keep them private. No one is safe anymore. Medical records. Police records. Financial records. All can be had at the click of a button on a computer. God help those of us who

190

show our faces above the crowd. The Japanese have a saying: The nail that sticks up gets hammered first. It's so true. You have my sympathy. But you also have my warning. Don't fuck with me, Hush. And don't try to hide any secrets about your life. Because if they come back to haunt my daughter's good name, I'll have no mercy."

She stepped close to me. "You have to tell me, Hush. Tell me everything I *don't* know about you. Tell me if there's anything you've had to hide. Maybe I can help you."

"I don't trust you enough to trust you any more," I said. "So I'll take my chances with what's left of my privacy."

She stiffened. "I'll do whatever it takes to get my daughter back and protect her best interests. Even if it means sacrificing you and your son. Make no mistake."

"I've only made one," I said. "And that was coming here with the idea that we could make friends."

HOODED BY THE BLUE, predawn light, I drove to the top of Chocinaw Mountain after returning from Highlands. A cold breeze and the eternal stillness of bedrock surrounded me. The scent and feel and loneliness became the endless dome of the world. I parked a truck with a HUSH license plate and walked over to the steel guardrail without spiritual or material protection. Any early-morning neighbor headed for the flatlands outside these mountains would have recognized me and my car, but might only mention to family and friends how Hush was up on Chocinaw speaking to Davy's spirit, telling him about the amazing new circumstances of our son's life. Seeded with the right mix of hearsay and assumption, gossip could work in a person's favor. I had been fearfully lucky in such regards over the years.

But my luck had run out.

I stared down through the boulders and laurel at the tall granite stone that marked Davy's death place. He still might drag Davis and me down there with him, but I'd be damned if I'd let him do it without a fight. I climbed over the guardrail, snagging my nice pumps on the blunt rocks and twisting branches off the laurel, losing a shoe but not even stopping to hunt for it in the dim light. I scrambled down a hundred feet into the maw of that rough divet in the mountainside, seeing the ghost of Davy's body twisted inside his high-powered car.

When I'd found him that day, I reached one hand inside and spread my fingers across his face, stroking the cheeks and lips of the handsomest man in Chocinaw County, the dead face of my lover, my enemy, my husband, the other half of my son. "Oh Davy, I'm sorry it turned out this way," I whispered.

And I cried. There was no doubt in my mind he'd killed himself because I'd found out things about him he couldn't abide any better than I could. After I'd abided so much else, and he'd let me.

Now I reached the bottom of the ravine, soaked in sweat, sprinkled with debris, heartsick and scared and furious. "Dammit, Davy." I drew back one arm and slapped the towering granite monument so hard my bones jolted. Pain shot up to my right shoulder. Holding my arm, I sat down at the marker's base, then hunched over and rocked slowly. My shoulder ached and my head swam. Another day was starting and I could only get up and keep going.

I didn't hear Jakobek until he laid a hand on my shoulder. "Easy," he urged.

I shrank back in fury and humiliation. "Don't touch me. Stop tracking me everywhere. And don't tell me I can trust you either."

He dropped to his heels in front of me, his expression dark and bewildered. "I don't know what Edwina said to you, but it's nothing she shared with me. Or the President."

"I don't believe you."

"You told me you're an expert at picking out dishonest men."

"That's not quite what I said."

"It's what you *meant*. Look at me. Tell me if you really think I'm here to spy on you, to hurt you, to hurt your son. I could have done a thousand things differently, if I wanted to strong-arm you. Or him."

"I've heard you're no better than a cold-blooded professional killer. Are you? A heartless killer?"

The air stilled between us. "Not heartless," he said quietly.

That needed a breath or two. Then, "Did the President and First Lady send you here to scare me and my son if need be?"

"They sent me to do whatever needed doing, if Eddie was in trouble."

"But you don't approve of the marriage any more than they do. Any more than I do."

"From the day Eddie was born, I swore I'd protect her. That includes protecting everything she holds dear — meaning her new husband and his family. As long as she wants to be your son's wife, I'm here to support her. And since you're her mother-in-law, you're part of the package." He paused. "Maybe I want you to think as highly of me as your yellow jackets did."

"I don't know *what* to think."

He blew out a long breath. "Tell me what Edwina said."

"It's confidential."

"That bad?"

I couldn't cover my misery quickly enough. He studied my face and said, "Goddammit," softly. Before I could say anything else, he stood and helped me up by my good arm. He began brushing leaves from my hair, saying nothing, frowning down at me and studying my expression for clues to my changing moods. A mystery himself. I should have been afraid. Tall man, still a stranger, careless but precise and so quiet even the mountain had not been able to hide me from him.

The wind rose, curling around him and me, singing coldly to bring us together for warmth. I looked up at him feverishly for a moment, then turned and climbed the boulders and laurel with bad grace, clumsy without both shoes, my injured shoulder feeling torn. Jakobek climbed behind me. I stumbled and felt his broad hand bracing my back.

When we reached the roadside, he vaulted the guardrail, then picked me up and lifted me over it. I'm not a delicately sized woman, and he startled me with his easy strength. He didn't set me down immediately, and I didn't ask him to. He stood there, holding me, looking at me, and me at him. "I want you to believe in me, and I *need* to believe in you," I said.

"Someone needs to."

"That's a strange answer, Jakob."

"What did you call me?"

"I . . . can't keep calling you by your last name. *Jakob* has a biblical ring to it. *Nick's* too hard. Maybe if I give you a spiritual-sounding name, you'll prove you're a spiritual man, Jakob."

"It's a deal."

"All right. We're in this together, Jakob, just as you said the other night. I'm not willing to work against my son's marriage, even if I think I'm doing it for his best interests."

Jakobek nodded. "Then we're a team. We support the marriage. We let it run its course. We don't get in the way." He hesitated. "And we don't let Edwina get in the way either."

The quiet that settled between us was as bewildered and potent as any silence could be. The rising wind pulled at us, and I heard my husband's sharp spirit in it. "Put me down now," I ordered quietly. "And leave me to drive myself back when I'm ready. I came up here to talk to my dead, Jakob."

He nodded, set me down, and stepped back. "Just remember. He's dead. But I'm alive. And I listen."

TWELVE

One hour of sleep, ten cups of coffee, a pack of herbal wake-up pills, a double dose of prescription arthritis medication for my arm, a cold slice of apple pie, and one long, sobbing shower. Yours truly, the new mother-in-law, was finally ready to fake happiness. Jakobek wisely kept to himself.

"Thank you for meeting with my parents," Eddie said quietly. "Nicky says it went diplomatically."

"We agreed to support your decisions."

Eddie sighed. Davis frowned. "We didn't expect everyone to jump up and down with joy, but a little enthusiasm would be nice. I'm telling you, if you want us to leave —"

"No. This is your home. You can stay here. And that's final."

I walked outside. Eddie and Davis followed. I spread a handful of pellets on the water of the small pond beneath the backyard trees while they stood awkwardly by, trying to be nice to me by following me around and saying the right things. The rising sun cast beautiful streaks across the shallow, shimmering water. Davy had built the pond for me as an anniversary gift, complete with two small gold-and-white Comets that quickly, under my care, grew to a foot long each, and began breeding more Comets, which I sold.

"You're greedy, Mother Nature," Davy said when that happened. "You can't allow a single living soul on this place to just *be* for the sake of pleasure. It has to make money or make you proud. If you could figure out how to make a profit off 'em, you'd have given me more children by now."

"Mother?" Davis said. "Are you all right?" Pain shot up my injured arm; remembering Davy's words, I flinched and dropped the bag of pellets. Davis retrieved it for me. "Are you having trouble with your bad shoulder?"

"A little. Just the usual."

He turned to Eddie. "Mother went deer hunting with Dad not long before he died. She slipped and fell out of the hunting stand. He carried her two miles back to the truck. Never left her side at the hospital. Sat by her day and night here at home. Mother says she'll never forget that time they spent together, or how he took care of her."

Eddie looked from him to me with gleaming eyes. "What wonderful memories you must have of Davis's father. Those are exactly the kind of memories Davis and I expect to build here."

I only wished the hunting story had been true. I put my hands on my hips and took several deep breaths. "Let me get something straight here. You two are planning to go back to Harvard after the baby is born, aren't you?"

Davis said nothing. Eddie smiled sadly. "It's not what we want anymore. Either of us."

My skin shrank, and fairy lights danced in front of my eyes. I sat down on a bench and dropped the fish food again. This time, Davis didn't bother to pick up the bag. He sat down beside me. "We're asking you for jobs here at the farm. Jobs, and a home here for us and our child, and a future helping you build an even bigger future for the family business. You've always said this business would be mine someday, if I wanted it. Well, I do. Let me start working in that direction."

"We have so many ideas," Eddie put in eagerly. "So many projects and dreams and plans. I want to get to know *real* people, Mrs. Thackery. I want to make a difference in a community where I'm appreciated for my own skills and hard work, not the fame of my parents or their political power. Please don't be disappointed by our decision not to return to Harvard. A college education cannot possibly replace life experiences."

I nearly choked. What I would have given to have their opportunities in the great wide world—to be their age again, with no mouths to feed but my own and no apples waiting impatiently for harvest, and no responsibilities except to chase a young soldier named Jakobek—strange, how that thought got in there. I loved the Hollow, but I would have loved Harvard, too. And Jakobek.

"Mother?" Davis asked again. "Are you all right?"

I shook my head. "If you want to do justice to this legacy, then go out there in the wide world and make yourself so smart and important you'll be able to come home someday and take care of this land *forever.* Not just grubbing along one year at a time, or even one generation at a time, the way we've always done. Davis, you can't give up all your other opportunities to settle here *now!*"

"I don't need a degree to run a successful business, Mother. You're the perfect example of that." He paused. "What it boils down to is this: We're asking for your blessings."

"You'll have to earn them."

"Then we will."

And I may have to earn them all over again myself.

EDDIE SPOKE TO HER mother and father by phone. "Yes, Mother, I believe you when you say you're happy for me. No, Dad, I don't need for you to visit me. Yes, I believe you want to. But you'll draw a mob of reporters and so much security you'll disrupt apple season. And I'm fine. Don't worry. I love you, too. I'm glad we've come to an agreement on my choices."

At the end of the conversation, she put the phone down and

cried. "I would have liked for Dad to walk me down the aisle, I admit," she moaned while Davis hovered over her, saying soothing, husband-type things, which didn't help. Jakobek and I traded troubled frowns.

I pulled him outside to the veranda. "It may be a lost cause, but I have to attempt some kind of normal routine — for their sake as well as mine. I'm putting her and Davis to work. It's what they want, but it may not be what they expect. Certainly not glamorous. I'll give her a kitchen job, in the Barns. She'll be out of public sight and the work isn't that hard, physically. Just boring. You have a problem with that?"

"I'm all for it. Boring work is safe work. All right, so what about me? How do I earn *my* keep around here?"

For one split second my eyes betrayed me, and I gave him a once-over that could rightfully be interpreted the wrong way. By the time I caught myself, he had returned the favor. He leaned against one of the veranda columns with just enough humor in his eyes to give me an easy out. "Is that job hourly or by the week?"

I arched a brow. "That job's only in your imagination, Colonel."

"Seriously."

We'd pretend the moment hadn't happened. All right.

"You want work to do, Jakob? I'll give you work. Put you on the payroll. Farm chores, shipping, packaging, loading apples. Gruncle is in charge of all that. So do whatever Gruncle tells you to do. Are you willing to salute an old man who's bad tempered and unreasonable?"

"I've had a lot of experience. I've been in the Army. Consider me hired, Mrs. Thackery."

I ASSEMBLED FAMILY, employees, Davis, Eddie, Smooch, Logan, and Jakobek in the apple-sorting room of the public barn. More than forty people stood among the alleys of wood-framed con-

veyor belts and crates and rinsing shelves and steel channel-ways
that guided fresh-picked Sweet Hushes into plastic bags and small
shipping crates and pretty little oak-slat baskets that would be
wrapped in apple-red cellophane with red bows on the tops for
the retail shelves. The barn's wall vents channeled the smell of
fried apple turnovers baking in the ovens of the kitchens of the
barn next door. The piney scent of wood shavings rose from the
old-fashioned floor beneath our feet. Life was good and fragrant,
at least in my apple barns.

"I have some wonderful news," I lied to the whole crowd,
looking out on old and young faces wreathed in red Sweet Hush
tractor caps or hygienic red Sweet Hush logoed hair bonnets atop
a human quilt of crisp white Sweet Hush Farms aprons over blue
jeans and flannel shirts with Sweet Hush Farms crests—a dear
and loyal and hardworking crowd of people who glanced with
grim wonder from me to the somber Jakobek, then to the bravely
smiling Eddie and the stern Davis, who held Eddie's hand and
stood at attention.

I told them bluntly. *Meet Eddie Jacobs Thackery. Yes, just as
you've heard. Eddie and Davis are married. They're going to stay
here for the season and work with us. And yes, there is more good
news. As y'all know, I'm going to be a grandmother.*

Tentative hands clapped slowly, while all eyes went from me to
the newlyweds to Jakobek and back to me again. Davis clamped
his mouth tightly at the less than enthusiastic reaction of his family and stared straight at the offenders, a muscle flexing in his
cheek. "We came here to be part of the family and the community and the legacy my parents have built with your help. I know
you'll love Eddie and make her feel welcome. She wants to be
treated like anyone else. I expect . . . no, I know . . . that you'll
treat her with friendship and respect."

He told them all he had come home and given up Harvard
gladly to help me run the family business, but when he said that,
some of his younger cousins—who idolized him and his adven-

tures in the world — shook their heads. Some of the less polite old men and women wiped tears of disappointment off their faces.

Others glowered at Eddie as if she were five-foot-seven inches of skinny, seductive ruination — and a damned liberal Jacobs to boot. Their resentment included the towering, rough-faced Jakobek. He had bloodied Davis and blown the yellow jackets off me. Tribal symbolism brought my relatives' defenses to the surface — a stranger had walked into the kingdom, thrown down the prince, and tried to seduce the widowed queen. *Hamlet* by way of the Hollow.

I knew what I had to do, like it or not. Family harmony requires as much grit-your-teeth maneuvering as any political campaign, and often just as much spin doctoring on the truth. I went over to Eddie, pried her hand out of Davis's grip, and gave her a ceremonial hug to warn all my relatives I had accepted her. She uttered a small cry of surprise, then wrapped her arms around me and whispered brokenly in my ear, "Thank you. I won't let you down."

"Share the favor. Introduce your cousin Jakobek and give everyone a dose of sweet talk on his behalf," I whispered back, "or they'll hoist him on his own petard."

She gave me a bewildered look but faced the audience. "You are all such a legend to me. Davis has told me all about his family and this wonderful place and his love for the land and for his mother and the memory of his father and for the proud business they built together. I come from a legacy of strong family values, too. I respect what you've all accomplished. I'm here because I want my life choices to reflect the same values.

"In that vein, I want you all to meet the relative of mine who has come here solely for my benefit, solely to represent my parents, who could not be here today. I asked Hush to let me introduce him personally." Eddie held out a hand to indicate Jakobek. "My father's nephew, my first cousin, and . . . and surrogate older brother and —" her voice broke gently — "one of my true heroes, along with Davis: Lieutenant Colonel Nicholas Jakobek, retired from the United States Army."

Jakobek sank his big hands in the pockets of his rumpled trousers and nodded to everyone, but still managed to look stiff and worldly and as sweet as a rottweiler behind a security fence. He stood before my suspicious family in khakis and old flannel, as simple as any of us, but not like a one of us, not like anyone we knew, a wolf in apple farmer's clothing. He inclined his head in acceptance of the introduction. "The President and First Lady send their hellos," he said. "They intend to stay on top of this situation."

This sounded more like a threat than a kindly message from new in-laws. Mutters of concern went up. Jakobek frowned and looked at me for advice. "It's all right, Jakob," I whispered. "Around here, men are expected to shoot something or drive too fast or get drunk to show they care. You don't have to make a big, sloppy, sentimental speech. But you might want to make up something about 'best wishes' or such."

He turned back to the muttering crowd. "And they look forward to meeting all of Davis's family and friends. They . . . send their best wishes."

The mutters faded, but people still regarded him suspiciously.

Jean Fruitacre Bascomb, an aging cousin to my grandmother on her father's side, stepped forward with a look of rheumy impatience. Lima Jean ran the kitchens. "Sweet Davis," she said to my son in a voice cracked like old paint, "your mama came to us over twenty years ago with this crazy plan to build barns and sell apples to rich fools from Atlanta. We stuck with her, and she was right. We believe in her and she hasn't ever let us down. You look around: You see old people with pensions and insurance. You see young folks with college money. You see mamas and daddies taking care of their kids in comfort. All because we stuck together — and all because of your mama. Don't mess with that. Don't come in here and give up on your college and show off a famous wife and say, 'I'm a man and I'm an apple farmer and

I'm here to run things.' You've got to earn the right to stay here. It's not about what you've given up. It's about what you've taken on."

"Yes, Miss Jean, I know," Davis said stiffly. "I'm not here to ask for handouts."

"Good. You won't get any. Your mama didn't ask for any, and look what she's built up for us all. And you, Miss Eddie. You look like a fine, smart girl to me. I didn't vote for your daddy but I've got nothing against him, except his politics. But are you born in the ways of an apple? Are you for us or against us or just don't give a damn one way or the other?"

"I'm *for* you," Eddie said fervently. "Ma'am, I am the daughter of a woman who believes wholeheartedly in the fair and just treatment of all human beings and the daughter of a man whose family built a proud American dream that began with nothing but the clothes on their backs at Ellis Island."

"Big talk," Jean said gently. "But it doesn't pay the bills."

My gruncle, an old, troubled warrior hunched inside a white Sweet Hush sweater and baggy dungarees with rolled-up cuffs, stepped out of the group and pointed a bony finger at Jakobek. I gestured for the nearest great-aunt to ward him off, but it was too late. "Let's get down to the dirt. We've heard what you did when you got here, Boy!" Everyone under sixty was a boy or a girl to Gruncle. "We don't like strangers who take liberties with our Hush."

"Hold on, everybody. The man took no liberties," I announced. "My liberties are safe and sound, so let's just calm down."

"But the man hurt your *son,* Girl! Are you gonna look the other way on that insult, too?"

"Gruncle, I was a witness to what happened and I'm here to tell you the Colonel deserves no blame. The incident was between him and Davis. They've made their peace, and it's nobody's business but theirs." I paused. "Davis is a grown man. He can take care of himself."

"No, it's *family* business when a dangerous honcho sets up housekeeping right in our own yard! I've heard about this Jakobek on Haywood Kenney's radio show." Gruncle glared at Jakobek. "The President has kept you out of sight all these years for a *reason*, Boy. What devil do you dance with, Boy, and what misery are you gonna bring into our midst, *and how many people will you admit you've killed*? Did you kill for mean avarice or did you kill for God and country, Boy?"

"My cousin's a hero," Eddie said. "I assure you his reputation has been twisted and —"

"I don't care about God or country," Jakobek interjected quietly. We all went stone-cold still and looked at him like small creatures hearing the high hunting call of a hawk. Eyes narrowed. Hands went to Bible verses in shirt pockets and flag decals tucked into wallets. Opinions hardened. Jakobek looked back with the quiet of a statue in a war memorial. He would not be moved.

"What *do* you care about?" someone called.

Before he could answer, a distant rumbling outside grew loud enough to grab our attention. Lucille and her fellow agents rushed to the barn's big plateglass windows, cupping their hands over their eyes and looking upward. Jakobek and I followed, and then everyone else, until we were all gazing outward and upward anxiously. A small, blue-and-white helicopter approached over Ataluck's wooded ridges. Jakobek turned to Davis and Eddie. "Move her back from the window."

"Yes," Lucille agreed quickly.

Eddie stiffened. "No. I refuse to react as if I'm always a target for every lunatic and monster in the world. Not anymore. Here on this farm I'm as safe as —" Davis picked her up and carried her to the center of the barn, then set her down. She frowned and looked up at him in wounded surprise. "Et tu, Brute?"

"I support your stand on the issues," he said, "but not your stand by the window."

"It's a camera crew," Lucille called. By now the helicopter was only a hundred feet over the farm's public yards, and I could see the logo of a cable news network, one of the sleazier ones, if that's not redundant. A cameraman, harnessed to the copter's open door, hung out in the air, filming the Barns and orchards. I grabbed Logan by one arm. "They're invading our privacy. They're trespassing. Nosy sons of bitches! They can't do that."

"What do you want me to do, Sis? Shoot them down?"

"Hell, yes."

Jakobek walked to a set of large double doors while we were mewling among ourselves, and the next thing I knew he opened the doors and stepped outside, reached within his shirt, and pulled out a kind of sleek, long-barreled automatic pistol. I rushed out behind him. "As mad as I am, Jakob, I didn't really mean to shoot at the damned helicopter."

"Are you willing to bluff?"

"Bluff?" I gestured at the cameraman. "He's filming every move you make. Don't provoke him."

"He's not just filming me." He glanced at me pointedly as he jacked the pistol. "He's filming *us*. I'll take care of this. Go back inside."

After a moment, I shook my head. "No, let's scare the SOB together." He smiled, raised the gun to the sky, and aimed at the helicopter. The cameraman scooted inside the open door like a Florida beach crab backing into its hole. I caught one glimpse of the wide-eyed pilot mouthing words I didn't need to hear to understand.

The helicopter rose quickly and disappeared back over the horizon. Everyone crowded around Jakobek and me, looking at him with troubled respect. A feeling like guilty, excited fingers crept up my spine. He lowered the pistol and slid it back inside his shirt. "I take care of my family," he said. "*That's* what I care about."

He turned and walked through the crowd. Everyone made a path for him. Including me.

Eddie exhaled a soft, keening sound. "Maybe I shouldn't have encouraged Davis to bring me here. I'm so sorry my introduction was marred by an attack on the very autonomy and privacy that makes this Hollow such a sanctuary."

A strange thing happened. My family — all ornery, independent individuals, fiercely patriotic on many levels, passionate about family loyalty and homestead defense and the sanctity of the land, but still reeling from Jakobek's dramatic demonstration of the right stuff on behalf of kith and kin — suddenly took a second look at Eddie Jacobs and saw instead Eddie Thackery.

At the very least she was Davis's wife, the mother of his child, in need of sympathy and protection whether she'd earned it yet or not. As her dowry she'd brought a strong male cousin, this Jakobek, a man willing to speak his mind and point a gun at trespassers and damn the consequences. If he did dance with the devil, at least he made the devil let him lead.

"I'm so sorry for the disruption," Eddie said again.

Davis wearily put an arm around her. "It's all right, Honey."

"No, it's not. I have lived with the limelight all my life, but I won't subject your family to —"

"Time to get to work," I said. "Eddie, Davis — both of you are on my payroll. We have apples to sell. You can't get squeamish on us now. We need you on the job."

Davis gave me a look that nearly melted the anger between us. Eddie put a hand to her heart and smiled. The family nodded. One of the Thackery aunts — a big, fleshy mama with hands that could peel a bushel of apples faster than a machine — plopped a Sweet Hush baseball cap on Eddie's soft brown hair. "I claim her for the kitchen. We're short a hand in the production line for the apple fritters. I got over four hundred units to package before the UPS man makes his pickup tomorrow morning." Everyone watched Eddie with held breath. The President's daughter. Working on the fritter line.

"I'll be happy to perform kitchen chores," Eddie said earnestly. "When I was growing up, Mother and I studied culinary arts with some of the finest chefs in the world. We used to spend an entire week every summer at the French Laundry in California, actually working as assistants to the owner. My father would play golf at one of the local clubs during the day and the three of us would share the most wonderful meals at night. Cooking was our special family hobby . . ." Her voice trailed off and tears gleamed in her eyes as the memory of happier times with her estranged parents sank in. She quickly wiped her face and gazed at Davis with poignant self-discipline. "What's a fritter?"

As he explained the nuances of fried apple slices to her, I turned and looked after Jakobek. The wide autumn majesty of the mountains framed him as he walked up the gravel road through the parking lots. He idly tapped one hand to his right leg. Four of the farm dogs, two cats, and a black-and-white baby goat that had escaped from our petting barn followed him with the devotion of simple beings, sensing kindness as well as strength.

I found myself touching my fingertips to my throat and my lips in fevered wonder. Following him, too, but without the courage to admit it.

LIFE IN THE HOLLOW would never be the same, and that day had proved it.

Lucille set her agents up at motel rooms and inns throughout the county, but she herself rented a basement apartment at Logan's pragmatic cedar-wood bungalow on a winding back lane in Dalyrimple. How that arrangement came to be agreed upon by my brother and Lucille, I didn't ask. Puppy latched on to the big blond woman with immediate affection and nicknamed her Lucy Bee. The newly monikered Lucy Bee was spotted sitting on Logan's front porch on crisp afternoons wrapped in an apple-woven afghan, reading to Puppy from one of Logan's hunting magazines. "Bambi—Stew, Steak, or Roast?" was probably the topic. Puppy, regardless, was enthralled by Lucy Bee.

We kept Eddie out of sight in the kitchens and the back barns and the house for her own good and our sanity, a situation she accepted graciously, to her credit. Dozens and sometimes hundreds of people called the farm every day asking to speak with her, claiming to be friends, or shouting obscenities or stupid comments into the answering machine of my office. Love it or hate it, she was famous and infamous.

And now, so were we.

PART
TWO

THIRTEEN

The footage of Hush and me standing shoulder to shoulder in a potential surface-to-air attack against the news chopper made the rounds on national television. Kenney told his national radio audience I needed to be checked for rabies — and that it appeared I'd already infected Eddie's new mother-in-law, too.

"I want you to know how sorry I am," I told her.

"I can take the heat," Hush said, but didn't look happy. She was standing in the middle of a warehouse-sized storage barn at the time, surrounded by big wooden crates full of her apples, one square, strong hand on the controls of a mechanized pallet mover, the other palming a walkie-talkie. Cool air hissed from big refrigeration units on the ceilings. The crisp scent of apples by the thousands surrounded us. Her commerce and command of that whole apple world hypnotized me. "Two-point-five pounds per unit at thirty-five per case," she drawled into the walkie-talkie. Click. To another question: "I'll double-check our contract with the U-Market phone-order people on that." Click. And to someone else: "Eighty-six the caramel-dip station until we test the propane line under that kettle."

211

Every five seconds one of her employees radioed with another question. She talked into the walkie-talkie and worked the pallet and looked at me with exhausted hospitality. "I can take the heat," she repeated. "You didn't twist my arm."

"Maybe people think I did. How *is* your arm?"

"Fine." Hush said nothing else, just studied me with her haunted green eyes, the thin crescent of the scar showing pale against the ruddy color of her cheeks. A chill went down my spine. The arm. I'd keep that subject in the back of my mind. Something about it worried me. "So I'm persona grata, at least with you, these days?"

"I take the yellow jackets' judgment seriously. And Puppy likes you. She's no pushover." She paused. "And then there's the baby goat."

Which had followed me into the barn.

A good distraction. I looked down at the little black-and-white kid. It nibbled my pants leg. "Animal magnetism," I said, feeling the need to diffuse some things going on inside me. "It's a gift."

"Yes, it is," Hush said without joking. I looked at her seriously. She frowned and looked away. Davis's voice came over her walkie-talkie. "Mother, I've asked Aunt Smooch to field media calls. They're coming in on an average of one per minute. From all over the world. Uncle Logan has turned away two satellite trucks, but that won't stop print journalists from slipping by him disguised as customers. They're probably already roaming around the Barns. I'm telling everyone to say 'no comment' if a stranger asks about Eddie. That includes you, Mother. Agreed?"

"No comment."

"All right, you hate this. I'm sorry. The chaos is going to be worse than we expected. But Jakobek's stunt didn't help. The President's sociopathic relative shouldn't threaten to shoot down a cameraman."

Hush met my eyes with unblinking challenge, knowing I could

hear every word she and Davis said. "I think Jakobek knows it wasn't good public relations," she said to her son, "but it sure was effective. Jakobek's the least of my worries. And he should be the least of yours."

"I'll ask him to leave, if you want me to. It's what Dad would do, I suspect."

"If I want Jakobek to leave, I'll ask him myself. Thank you, though."

She clicked the walkie-talkie off. Swoops of root-red hair dangled from a clip on the back of her neck. Her body shifted in waves of breasts, hips, long legs. She swayed like a tree hit by a strong breeze. I couldn't take my eyes off her. "At least you know where you stand with him."

"Was your husband proud of you for not needing him?"

Her back stiffened. After a long pause, she spoke. "You already know the answer to that. But Davis doesn't, and I intend to keep it that way."

"Consider it done," I said. And I left her there, steeped in the privacy of her apples.

WHAT WAS I SUPPOSED to think when I drove up from the front barns one afternoon to unload stacks of paper files and computer discs for an evening in my log-house office, and there was Jakobek on the front walkway with some tall, scruffy, gray-bearded stranger dressed in faded overalls, a floppy green Army jacket, and a tractor cap with a logo for the Chicago Bears on it?

"This is a friend of mine," Jakobek said. "I picked him up outside town today. He could use a meal. Do you mind if I bring him into the house?"

Jakobek didn't have any friends that I knew of, and he wasn't the turn-the-other-cheek type who assumed the goodness of his fellow men. Nor had he demonstrated any interest in letting strangers waltz up to my house or my family. And certainly not a disreputable old bum, and certainly not near Eddie. I was speechless. Lucille stood on my veranda, and I looked at her.

"Eddie's not here," she said. "So I have no problem with giving this gentleman some limited access to your house."

Knock me over with a feather. This was not typical Lucille behavior either. Still, I had no reason to think up wild scenarios and suspect other goings on. Plus I had been raised by a father and mother who quoted the Bible on entertaining angels unawares and lived by the "do for the least of men as ye would do for me" rule.

So I stepped up to the visitor and held out a hand. "I'm sorry for hesitating. Our situation is a little unusual right now, but I've never turned away a guest, so welcome to my home. I'm Hush McGillen Thackery."

"Thank you, Ma'am, for your kindness." He solemnly shook my hand. *Clean hand, for a bum,* I thought.

About that time, Eddie and Davis drove up in a farm truck. They had worked all day in the kitchens. They were dusty with flour, and smelled of apples and cinnamon. Both wore old jeans and soft T-shirts under heavy sweaters. Eddie's stomach made a gentle mound under her clothes, and her face glowed. Davis smiled and pulled a blue bandana from her soft brown hair. Flour poofed in the cool air. She laughed.

The old-man stranger—who hadn't given me the courtesy of his name, I was about to point out—went as still as a stone and watched them as they came up the path between my azaleas, holding hands. She looked like a sugar-dusted angel.

I didn't know what to make of the old bum's interest in my son and his famous wife, but it was too intense for my comfort. "Jakob?" I said to Jakobek in high-pitched warning. But he watched the old man and Eddie without any apparent worry, and so, I noticed, did Lucille.

Eddie smiled at the visitor politely, but then her smile froze. One hand rose to her throat. She made a soft, happy, crying sound. Davis turned to her, frowning. "What's wrong, Honey—"

"Nothing. Nothing at all. I should have known Nicky would find a way to . . ." Crying, smiling, she rushed toward the lanky, bearded old man in overalls and threw her arms around him. He made a soft noise and wrapped her up in his own arms, and they swayed.

She plucked at his fake beard. "*Dad,*" she cried. "You look like the guitarists in ZZ Top."

I almost sat down in the azaleas. Jakobek took me by one arm and held me up. His mouth curved in a quiet, satisfied, wolf smile.

The President stood safely and secretly in my yard.

TEARS WERE SHED, tender, private conversations were held, Edwina was discussed, and Al stiffly told Davis he had a major deficit of goodwill and respect to overcome.

"I know that, Sir," my son answered quietly. "But the path to the highest good for a family, a community, or a nation is not necessarily the simplest one, nor is it likely to win easy praise."

"Are you quoting to me from my own speeches?"

"Yes, Sir."

"Which one was that?"

"Your speech to the National League of Families. Two years ago."

"How many of my major policy speeches have you read?"

"All of them, Sir."

"Why?"

"You're Eddie's father. I wanted to understand your view of the world."

"And?"

"I'd like to take the fifth until you decide you like me anyway, Sir."

Al laughed.

It was a good meeting. I was proud of Davis. But as for the rest of the conversation, and our children's future . . .

"I think I'll go back to Tel Aviv and work on world peace," Al said wearily. "That would be simpler."

Al could only stay an hour before Jakobek took him back to a helicopter somewhere Jakobek didn't discuss. "The media starts to get itchy after a few hours corralled in the press area at Camp David," Al explained. "I'm supposed to be spending the afternoon in consultation with the Chinese trade minister. We'll make an appearance together tonight at a press conference and announce the details of a new trade agreement."

"So . . . what's the Chinese trade minister doing right now?" I asked.

"Playing golf with Edwina and the Vice President."

"My God."

"Yes. Edwina's a shark if any betting money's involved, and the Vice President has a bad slice. I'm a little worried."

Al and I spent a few minutes by my goldfish pond, sitting in old Adirondack chairs, smoking. Me, my long pipe. He might as well see. Him, a cigar purloined from Jakobek. Peace-pipe smoking. Curls of smoke from our different families twined together over the water.

"Thank you for taking care of my daughter," he said. "I wish I could explain the problem between her and her mother. I can only assure you that my wife was not always so difficult on the subject of what's best for Eddie."

"A lot of water has passed under that mother-daughter bridge. You can't change the flow."

"I wasn't there the day a man almost killed Eddie and Edwina. If it hadn't been for Nicholas . . . Edwina has never quite gotten over the fear she felt that day, and what she saw Nicholas do, and what it showed her about the realities of the world into which we'd birthed a daughter. She's protected Eddie obsessively ever since, and so have I. But I do it with more diplomacy, I guess."

"Daughters cut their daddies more slack than they do their mothers. Just as sons forgive their mothers easier than their fathers."

"You can be proud of your son. I have to give him a hard time. It's my duty as Eddie's father."

"I totally agree. Give him hell."

"Everything Eddie tells me about him seems sincere. My daughter *does* share her thoughts with me. We *are* close. Despite what this current circumstance indicates."

"I understand. And for the record, I'm getting them back to Harvard as soon as possible. Somehow. I swear to you."

"We'll work on that plan, yes. Don't let my wife know, but Eddie tells me she wants to attend a state college down here eventually and switch from criminal law to civil. Needless to say, fine-tuning fat-cat contracts for big oil companies is not the idealistic legal career my wife envisioned for her."

"I'm afraid I know where this idea of Eddie's comes from. It's not about working for the fat cats, Al. It's about working for *me*. Or rather, working with Davis. They plan to build a 'diverse conglomerate,' they call it, with Sweet Hush Farms as its core company. So Eddie plans to do all the legal work for our family empire. I felt like the godfather when she told me that. Evil, but proud."

"I see. Do you *want* your apple business turned into a conglomerate?"

"Not particularly. Apples don't need to take over the world, Al. They *are* the world. My world, at least."

"Eddie tells me you're a model citizen. And that your husband was beloved by everyone who knew him — most of all, his own son. I know you're proud."

I changed the subject. "Tell me about Jakobek, please." I paused. "What is he?"

Al knew exactly what I meant. "A fighter, a loner, a lover — by that I mean a man who loves deeply — and a hero."

"Where'd he go all those years after he left Chicago? What did he do, exactly, for the Army?"

"He went anywhere no one else wanted to go. Places you don't see on maps. He fought for people we're not supposed to fight for. Alliances our government can't discuss. People who need help below the radar of politics. I used to think he had a simplistic view of good and evil, but I've had to make hard decisions since then, had to send people into battle, had to send people to kill other human beings. The subtleties fall by the wayside when the consequences are life and death."

"But why did he leave his family behind to do that kind of military work? Why did he go so far away from people he obviously cares about?"

"I'm not sure. After he killed the man who attacked my wife and daughter, he wasn't the same. None of us were. I think he felt even more outcast. Nothing Edwina and I could do or say had an effect. Nicholas doesn't talk about his feelings or motivations very often. He simply does the job he feels needs doing. He doesn't confess his sins, and he doesn't ask for forgiveness. Or praise. Or understanding. If he needs us, we don't know about it. But if we need *him*, he's there."

"He needs you, trust me. He's got a good heart. And he *is* a family man."

"I've heard Nicholas called a lot of things, but you're the only person who calls him that."

"I have it on good authority."

"Oh?"

"From the wasps."

"I'm not even going to ask for an explanation, Hush. But I believe you're right. Try convincing *him*, though. My worst fear is that he'll never find any place to feel at home, or anyone who can settle him down. That he'll die alone."

A chill went through me. "No. That can't be allowed to happen to him."

"Although, I have hope. I've never seen him like this."

"Like what?"

"Happy."

"He's happy? What makes you say that? How can you tell?"

Al just looked at me and said nothing.

Presidents are cagey that way.

SEPTEMBER FADED INTO October. My relatives now had a collection of headlines from major newspapers and supermarket tabloids. Heady stuff for people whose main publicity had involved being blurbed in the genteel travel pages of *Southern Living* or the trade columns of *Apple Grower's Digest*.

THREATENED CAMERAMAN SEEKS TRAUMA COUNSELING—
PLANS TO SUE PRESIDENT'S CONTROVERSIAL NEPHEW AND
EDDIE'S MOTHER-IN-LAW
EDDIE JACOBS IN SECRET MARRIAGE THAT STUNS COUNTRY
STRAIGHT-ARROW FIRST DAUGHTER PREGNANT,
HIDING IN SHAME
SON OF APPLE FARMER STEALS MISS AMERICAN PIE
EDDIE'S PICTURE-PERFECT LIFE A COVER FOR FAMILY FEUDS
"JACOBS FAMILY VALUES SHOW FAILED LEADERSHIP,"
OPPONENTS SAY
PRESIDENT LOCKED IN MIDDLE EAST TURMOIL WHILE
FAMILY COLLAPSES AT HOME
EDDIE'S NEW HUSBAND A BRAINY, BRAWNY BUBBA WITH
RACE CAR LEGEND FATHER

I tried my best not to read the stories or listen to the commentary on television or, God forbid, to hear Haywood Kenney's goddamned talk show on the radio. But I couldn't help myself. *Hotpants Eddie and Her Hillbilly Harvard Boy*, he called Eddie and Davis. He aired daily skits about them, always with nasty asides about Al Jacobs's administration and personal values.

Jakobek walked in my office one afternoon and caught me throwing my desk radio against a wall. I think being surprised in a fit of helpless rage upset me as much as Kenney's attack on my son. But Jakobek said quietly, "Radios bounce. I know from experience." He picked up the radio, set it back on my desk, and tuned it to a soft jazz station.

I swayed, hands knotted, tears of fury just behind my eyes. "I could kill him."

Jakobek took me by the shoulders. "Kenney's too worthless to kill. I decided that a long time ago. He's not worth what it would take out of you."

"I need something to take my mind off this. I feel like screaming."

"I have a solution."

He kissed me.

Quick and urgent, and very, very dangerous. I didn't need much provocation, so within five seconds I was definitely kissing him back, holding him by the shirtfront as I did, pulling him closer.

We halted in the middle of the desperate need to do worse. Self-discipline is deadly. My skin felt scalded and ripe; the details of him were seared in my body. His face was flushed and he already had one arm wrapped hard around my shoulders. We looked at each other without mercy. "We just can't," I whispered.

He nodded. "But I'm not sorry."

And neither was I.

WHATEVER JAKOBEK HAD DONE in his past as a trained soldier, he was now armed primarily with a flute, a camera, and my complete attention.

He played the softest, most mellow melodies on his flute at dawn, then walked downstairs with big, quiet feet, as if tracking me in my own kitchen. He worked alongside my people from daybreak until well past dark without a complaint. He pulped apples in the bakery, loaded delivery trucks, and hoisted autumn pumpkins into the backs of SUVs for blushing soccer moms and pale, computer-company dads who stared at him the way small house dogs might watch a pit bull around their females. Most of all, he shadowed Eddie and Davis, with a pistol hidden inside his shirt. The government agents deferred to him with the subtle ease of command. Even Lucille, a fierce leader, gave him a pass.

"He's been everywhere in the world," she told me. "Rumor has it we're safe in this country today because of things he did."

"I feel safe," I replied.

Except when I thought of him over me, in bed.

I'd had plenty of offers from men since Davy died, but not many worth the effort. I loved men, the idea of men, and I did want one, a really really good one. But that kind was hard to find, and the rest were like puppies with cute eyes and big feet; I just knew before long they'd outgrow their charm and be knocking over my furniture and barking at the moon. I wasn't real comfortable picking and choosing; I could never turn a stray away or get rid of it once I'd taken it in. I knew that about myself, and so I avoided making a choice. Otherwise I'd have had men all over the Hollow, running around my feet, needing to be fixed.

"Need to cut back, find that puppy a home," I overheard myself say as I stood at the kitchen sink.

"What puppy?" Smooch asked from the table. She looked at me suspiciously. "You all right?"

I turned around and she frowned at me. "Just working in my personal kennel," I said.

I wandered my dark house like a sleepwalker that night and finally headed down a short foyer into a living room of soft leather couches and little end tables with glass apples for feet and a big stone fireplace mantel decorated with Davis's academic plaques and sports trophies, beneath a portrait he had paid some artist to paint. It had come from a photograph of his father and me at a country-club dance a fruit wholesaler had sponsored down in Atlanta. Davis had been so proud to give us that portrait for our wedding anniversary one year. In it, his father looked down at the world like a handsome and successful family man, dressed in a tuxedo. I looked glamorous and happy in a green silk ball gown. What a lie.

But in a corner of the wall, half hidden behind a peace lily in an old clay pot on a primitive pine washstand that had been Mama's only family heirloom, hung an old black-and-white photograph of her and my daddy on their wedding day. They looked dirt-poor and run-down. Mama was fourteen and pregnant with me. Near that picture was a framed snapshot of me, pregnant, with Davy Senior and the beat-up, juiced-up Impala. A scrawny teenage girl with auburn hair and gunslinger eyes, next to the gunslinger. I'd hung both those pictures in my fine living room near the big portrait so I'd never forget the truth.

I turned on a lamp and halted, startled. Davis and Eddie were asleep on the couch, her head on his shoulder, oblivious to the lessons learned from two generations of young marriages and hard times. Just . . . happy.

"Here," Jakobek whispered. He had followed me. He had a crocheted throw in his hands, trying not to look whimsical with yarn apple trees blooming under his callused fingertips. I nodded, and together we gently covered the grown children before us, then slipped out of the house.

Desire is warm and pulsing, a living, invisible force with tendrils as tough as the ivy that had taken over one side of the house. It had already latched itself to my skin, and to Jakobek's. Something we'd just have to deal with, but I didn't know how.

I grew into wanting Davy over years of childhood friendship. By the time we had sex, we were carrying more baggage than most teenagers, and then the next year we were the parents of a baby son. Since Davy died I'd never met a man I had trouble forgetting. Until now.

Jakobek and I drank apple wine at a campfire near the goldfish pond, sitting carefully on opposite sides of the fire, but watching the stars together.

I DREAMED THAT NIGHT about a soldier I killed in a place I won't name. It's enough to say my men and I wiped out a small group in hand-to-hand combat, bloody and personal. It was one of the last missions I took part in before Al announced his campaign for President and I left the Army. After the fight we limped among the bodies, retrieving any ID we could find. I staggered over a dead boy—he couldn't have been more than fourteen—and when I felt inside the pockets of his Russian-made camo jacket, I found a mangled snapshot of a pretty girl with the hood of her cloak pulled aside and long, black hair streaming around her smile. Her name and a word that meant *my betrothed* were written on the back.

She'll always wonder how he died, I thought. I stood there, holding that picture in my bloody fingers and feeling like my heart would empty all my life onto the ground and no one would know either. An enemy was made up of forces too strong to be left alive—men who dealt in death, who did harm to innocent people. That boy had only been their slave, not one of their kind. I thought about him and his widowed girl for weeks after that. To be in love so much that you carried a picture of her with you when you fought. And when you died. I tracked her down at her family's home and sent the photograph through a local man I could trust. I included this anonymous message: *He was brave. He was a soldier. He thought of you.*

When I woke up from that dream, I searched my duffel bag for the folded picture of Hush in her orchards. I took out a fat leather passport wallet I carried on me wherever I went, and tucked her photograph among the cards and credentials that told every country in the world who I was.

He was brave. He was a soldier. He thought of you.

ON SUNDAY EVENINGS, after the hard work of the weekend was over, we often built a bonfire in a clearing of the orchard and sat around, a dozen or so of us — employees, family, and me, all tired and dusty and smelling of apples — while a huge kettle of stew or chili simmered on the fire. We'd eat and sip coffee and discuss the weekend's profits and problems. Hold our postgame debriefing, like a football team. Sometimes someone would play a guitar. Sometimes we'd sing — mostly old Appalachian hill music, twangy and almost Celtic in its rhythms, comforting in its basic philosophies.

At first, everyone was shy around Eddie at the campfire. Then one Sunday she suddenly burst into an off-key rendition of "Staying Alive," while Davis stood solemnly and did a John Travolta disco move. Everyone fell over laughing. Even Jakobek smiled.

"She's a good girl," one of my cousins whispered.

I nodded.

One by one, everyone drifted away until only Jakobek and I were left by the fire. I watched with helpless appreciation as the shadows and firelight played across his face and body. He stood and looked down at me, then gauged the privacy of the surrounding night around us. "I have something for you. I'll be back in a minute."

I sat forward anxiously on an old wooden bench and hugged myself inside my wool jacket. He disappeared into the darkness. He was gone a long time, and when he returned he carried a soft leather briefcase. Its sides bulged. He sat down on the earth next to my feet, opened the briefcase, and pulled out a thick file.

"These are Al's medical and financial records. No one outside the family ever sees these. No one. You want to know about his prostate trouble? His bad investments? Read it here." He laid the file on my lap, then pulled out another. "Edwina. Antidepressants, anger-management counseling, plastic surgery." As I sat there in speechless silence, he pulled a third, smaller folder from the briefcase. "Me," he said, and laid that file atop the others on my knees. "Documents on every assignment I've ever had in special operations, including some in places our government swears we never go. Hand that file to the right journalist and international relations would never be the same."

"Why are you doing this?" I finally managed.

"Because it's the only fair thing. You feel violated by Edwina's tactics. You're right. Here's a little bit of payback."

"Jakob, I—"

"Read the files. What else you do with them is up to you."

Trembling, I gathered the files in my arms, stood, and went to the fire. One by one I burned them. Jakob moved close beside me. I felt his gaze on me. I watched his file go up in smoke. "I know all I need to know about you from the yellow jackets," I said.

IT TOOK ME A FEW DAYS to get my equilibrium back after the file incident, though I doubted I'd ever really get both feet balanced on ordinary earth again, not with TV vans parked at the end of the farm's driveway and people still jumping ass backward in excitement over Eddie, and my deep problem with being the center of scrutiny, not to mention my bad relationship with Edwina. And of course, what was happening between me and Jakobek.

Smooch still disliked him, and the rest of the family remained wary. Davis said little but clearly considered Jakobek bad news — and a threat to his father's place in my life. Sons don't deal well with their mothers' other lives as women, no matter how much they claim to be at ease with the idea, and no matter how good a man the mother picks out to replace the father.

Jakobek was a good man — kind, strong, funny, and smart. He read thoughtful novels, he sweated well, and he was apt with the blue-collar rituals of the men in my family, yet there was an elegance about him, the hint that he was comfortable in the company of fine things and ideas. He was old enough to appreciate the sanctuary of me and the farm, young enough to take me away from it if he wanted. He had a prime man's body, fleshed out, hard but cushioned, going craggy in the face, his skin burnished with a patina of textures, his hair still thick but coarse. I didn't want a smooth piece of fruit; I liked my apples unpolished, more sensation for the lips. When I'd kissed him he'd tasted full and rich and able.

Not that I could let myself take another bite of that forbidden fruit.

I swore it. I swore. I really did.

"HAVE YOU SEEN Jakobek?" I called to people out the window of a white-and-red Sweet Hush pickup truck. They shook their heads. Everyone in town knew him, just as they knew Eddie. I swung the truck into a space in front of Dalyrimple Hardware and Garden and called out the window to other passersby as they came out of small shops around the square. "Have you seen the Colonel? He came up here with Davis and Eddie to go shopping."

To act as Eddie's bodyguard, but I didn't mention that. Eddie hated being trailed by Lucille and Crew. So instead, sometimes she was trailed by Jakobek. At least he didn't dress like an off-

226

season golfer. I chewed my lower lip and watched puffs of my own breath in the chilly October air.

Where was he? I hated when people didn't carry cell phones.

I sat there in the truck, muttering to myself ("The irony, Jakob, is that you're never off my mind, but I can't get you on the phone. Why can't you be psychic? Oh, yes, that's what I need — a man I can't stop thinking about who's psychic.") as he walked up from behind, so I didn't see him until he suddenly stood by the open window, watching me quietly with a small smile. It was one of those moments when you catch someone from the corner of your eye and instantly form your mouth into a fake shape, as if you were just flexing your jaw and not holding a one-woman conversation about him. I feigned looking in the rearview mirror and checking my lipstick, except I don't wear lipstick to the hardware store. Those days, I barely had the wits to remember deodorant. I wanted to sniff my armpits quickly, but there was no delicate way to fake that.

"I heard you thinking," he said. "Anything wrong?"

"There's a tractor trailer in my yard. From Washington. Filled with wedding gifts for Eddie and Davis. A tractor trailer, Jakob."

He frowned. "It's Edwina's work. She's trying to make nice with Eddie and rub your nose in it."

"Well, she did a good job."

Just then, Eddie and Davis walked out of a shop called the Baby Boutique, their arms full of packages. They saw me and smiled. I looked at Jakobek. "I gave Eddie a shopping spree at the Baby Boutique." I paused. "I should have given her the entire store."

I WAS RIGHT TO FEEL upstaged. Inside the tractor trailer was (among hundreds of other forwarded gifts) a sterling-silver, elephant-shaped soup tureen with ruby tusks from the king of Thailand. A major movie star had sent an entire twenty-piece place setting of the finest monogrammed china. The CEO of a multinational conglomerate sent a small, framed sketch of some scraggly olive trees. By Picasso.

And let's not forget the presents from Edwina and her rich relatives. Silver services and crystal stemware and fine linens and heirloom furniture and more. And a secretary—human, that is, not the wooden kind. She recorded all the gifts and managed hundreds of thank-you notes while Smooch, Eddie, and Davis prowled through stacks of beautifully wrapped boxes and crates. Smooch routinely clutched her chest and squealed. Eddie's own gasps of delight made a steep contrast to Davis's deepening silence.

Jakobek and I stood outside the trailer's open back. "This isn't good," I whispered.

He nodded. "It's never good when a man realizes it would take him a year's salary to buy his wife the solid-gold teapot her aunt gave her for fun."

"Look what my aunt Regina sent me," Eddie said happily, coming to the open back door to hold up that gleaming, gold teapot. "Isn't this just . . ." She looked at Davis, and her voice trailed off, then, "Isn't it just *so* ostentatious? I love my aunt Regina, but this thing is absurd."

Davis eyed her with pensive gallantry. "Maybe we can install a special simulated wood-grain shelf for it when we can afford our own house trailer."

"The teapot really is hideous," Eddie insisted, trying very hard to look sincere. "And most of this other frilly *accoutrement*—well, it goes back, you understand? Mother will have it stored, donated to charity, whatever. Some of these items definitely qualify as political gifts, and they have to be accounted for—"

"No. It's all yours, Honey, and you shouldn't feel odd about it."

"It's *ours,* Davis. Not *mine.* Ours."

He shook his head. Stubborn pride had set in. Eddie's face

began to color. I leaned close to Jakobek and whispered, "We have to do something."

"Lock it up," he called. Everyone looked at him, startled. He nodded. "Lock it up in storage. Send the thank-yous, then decide what to do with everything later."

Eddie nodded. "That's a wonderful idea, Nicky. Very practical."

Davis shrugged. "Yes. I just need some time to think about this. Absorb the idea of it all."

"Sweetie, I understand," Eddie crooned.

He took her in his arms. "If you want the teapot, you keep the teapot. We'll get a *real pine* shelf for it." She laughed. Davis and she kissed.

Jakobek and I looked at each other with grim relief. "Damn Edwina," I said.

FOURTEEN

Edwina wasn't done. She had allies.

Jakobek and I came in from the front barns one cool, golden October afternoon to find Smooch and Gruncle staring as several Japanese gentlemen unloaded crates from a delivery truck parked near my goldfish pond in the backyard.

"They're bringing you gifts from the Emperor of Japan," Smooch whispered. "Lucille cleared them for delivery. But I don't know—"

"Goddamn sneaky, murderous Japs," Gruncle said, and Smooch had to lead him inside the house before fifty years of Asian-American diplomacy went up in the flames of an old fighter's memories.

The spokesman of the Japanese contingent bowed to Jakobek and me. Not quite knowing the protocol, I followed Jakobek's lead and bowed back. "Let me go get my son and his wife—"

"Oh, no, Ma'am." The man spoke perfect English with a charming Japanese accent. "These are presents for *you*, Mrs. Thackery—you are the much-admired mother of the groom, a business lady of immense respect. The Emperor has been reading all about you. He and his wife would be so grateful if you would accept this token of their esteem." He opened a packing container and I looked down into water containing two daisy-yellow koi fish. I knew enough about koi to recognize championship markings. "They're beautiful. But I can't—"

"They need to swim freely in their new home, Mrs. Thackery. What a shame to leave them and their friends in these cramped containers much longer. Not healthy for them."

"Accept the fish," Jakobek whispered.

"I am most grateful," I said awkwardly, and bowed again. "But they wouldn't be safe here. I lose about five fish a year."

"Lose?" the Japanese spokesman said, frowning.

I leaned close to him, as if the fish might overhear. "To hungry raccoons."

"Oh!" He brightened. "Mrs. Thackery, my men and I can build an excellent antiraccoon fence around your pond." He paused. "But if I may—what is a *raccoon?*"

JAKOBEK AND I STOOD in my downstairs guest bath, a tiny space containing cast-off marble tile I'd found at a quarry up in North Carolina, a sparkling white commode, good oak cabinetry burnished by my housekeeper's weekly waxing, a white porcelain sink, antique apple botanicals in applewood frames on green-apple–flocked wallpaper, and now, on the back of the commode, a small ceramic statue of a monkey wearing a fedora and an overcoat. Edwina had sent it. "A mother-to-mother gift," her card said. "Enjoy."

"She sent me a statue of an ugly monkey dressed like Humphrey Bogart at the end of *Casablanca*," I said. "What the hell is *that* supposed to mean?"

Jakobek rubbed a trace of a smile off his mouth before he answered. "I think it's a special piece made by an African sculptor she likes. Probably worth a lot of money."

I looked up at him quietly. "This is the artistic equivalent of giving me the finger. Jakob, there's a raunchy old saying among country folk: 'Either shit gold or gild your turds.' This is Edwina's way of saying her world is filled with treasures, of saying to her daughter and my son, 'Look what you can have if you'll just come over to the other side of the fence.' Or worse, 'Eddie, look at the world you could have if you leave your husband.' "

Jakobek looked at me with quiet confidence. "So what will Hush McGillen Thackery do to set the record straight?"

I knew a challenge when I heard one.

"THIS IS GOING OVERBOARD!" Davis yelled above the rumble of a dozen two-ton, open-air fruit trucks. Eddie pressed her hands to her throat. Dressed in a Gucci sweatshirt and overalls, with her pregnant tummy beginning to show, she looked so young and vulnerable. "Hush, you don't have to send an extravagant gift to my parents! My mother was just trying to provoke you!"

Well, it worked, I thought as I climbed to my feet atop a mountain of apples feeding into soft beds of wood shavings padding the trucks. I surveyed the storage bins in our main barn. Nearby, Jakobek guided a conveyor belt filled with red apples into the next truck. "These apples aren't just a gift," I called down to Eddie. "They're messengers. They'll remind your mother that you are the fruit of her womb. Now, here's my question to *you:* Are *you* willing to go along with the apples?"

She looked from me to Jakobek, and her eyebrows arched. "I believe you've been scheming with Hush to get me to visit my mother."

"I don't scheme," he said with a straight face.

She turned to Davis. "What do you think? Should I visit her? Will it look as if I'm caving in and I need her approval?"

Davis gestured toward two tons of apples. "No, I think it'll look like you want her recipe for apple cobbler." She smiled anxiously. He took her hand. "Let's visit your mother. She's already demonstrated her approval with all those gifts."

"Oh, Davis, you're right."

"Then we'll go."

He and she burrowed their heads together and nuzzled each other.

I crawled down from the truck, scowling dramatically when Jakobek handed me a bandana to wipe my eyes. "They live in a blissful fog of romantic ideals," I whispered.

He folded my tearstained bandana and placed it carefully in the chest pocket of his work shirt. "Good for them," he said.

THE CARAVAN OF Sweet Hush Farms trucks made national news for an entire day as it wound from the mountains of northern Georgia to the soft coastal highlands of the Carolinas, Virginia, and finally, Washington, D.C. Smooch saved a few apples to auction on eBay. Souvenir hunters had already stolen the Hollow's mailbox and the handsome road signs leading drivers to us from the interstate. Our apples were collectible, too.

Once the Secret Service cleared us to enter, we parked the caravan on the long front drive leading up to the White House. Jakobek got out and leaned against the lead cab, his hands encased in heavy work gloves, his face sanguine. I sat atop the mound of apples on that lead truck, ruddy from the autumn wind, trying not to shiver despite a heavy jacket and blue ski pants. Edwina—and an entourage of her open-mouthed staff—came out to do the niceties.

A White House photographer snapped pictures. Edwina smiled up at me. "Well, if it isn't 'Johnny Anna Appleseed.'"

At that moment, Eddie and Davis stepped from the cab of the truck behind mine. "Mother," Eddie said softly, and began crying. Edwina ditched me and went to her child with her arms out. I sat back atop my apple mountain and looked at Jakobek, who stood on the driveway below me, gazing up at me with an expression that heated my skin. He gave me a thumbs-up. I nodded.

I had bested Edwina. I had shown her up with grace and style and cunning. Because I'd brought her a better gift than anything she'd sent me.

Her daughter.

※

"OUR WORK HERE is done," Jakobek said. "More wine?"

"Absolutely."

He poured a rich merlot into my half-empty goblet, then his. We clinked our glasses over plates of prime rib and grilled salmon, toasting the delivery of Eddie to her mother. A beautiful panorama of nighttime Washington and the Potomac River spread out below the windows of our hotel room. Well, *my* hotel room.

Oh, Edwina had insisted we stay at the White House, but no, there was no way in hell I'd sleep beneath her roof. Al was in China, so I didn't have to worry about offending him with a no-thank-you. So I told Edwina I'd stay out of the way. She deserved some quality time with Eddie and my son. I emphasized *my son* in a tone that warned her she'd better treat Davis well. To her credit, the evidence I saw left little doubt of that. Even after she restored a certain cold dignity about Eddie's surprise arrival, she looked happy to meet him.

"Your son's safe with me," she shot back.

"Stop frowning like that. You'll need more Botox injections in your forehead."

A little nugget from Jakobek. She didn't have the gall to ask where I'd learned it, though she turned and looked hard toward Jakobek, who pretended to study the Washington Monument.

A good day, all in all.

But then people discovered Jakobek and me in the lobby of the hotel and came over for my autograph. No one had ever asked me for my autograph before, and I wasn't giving it now. More than that, people recognized Jakobek, and not in a positive way. During the ten minutes we stood at the front desk waiting to check in, a half-dozen brave and obnoxious souls stared at him fearfully. I could see the quiet resolve on his face, the faint, cynical humor of being looked at like a guard dog who isn't supposed to roam free in public.

So I made a big show of being unnerved by the autograph thing, and asked Jakobek if he'd mind eating dinner with me in private. He immediately discerned that I was doing it for his sake.

"If you think I'm going to be stoic and turn down an invitation to go to your room," he said, "you're wrong."

At least we understood what we were getting into.

"Feel good?" he asked when we were finished eating. The mood between us suddenly went very quiet, very intense.

I laid my napkin atop my plate. "Very good."

"This is the first time we've gotten to sit down at a meal together — alone."

"It was wonderful. So pleasant it . . . makes me nervous."

"You make things too complicated. Me, I like simplicity." Smiling a little beneath serious eyes, he gestured at his empty plate. "When I'm hungry, I say so." He let those words settle into the deep pulse of sexual energy we shared. His smile faded. "When I look at you, I'm starving."

He had me, in that moment. He had me right down where I lived and breathed and didn't need to think. He had me in ways that whispered, *He's a blessing, and you've earned him.*

"Jakob," I groaned.

He rose halfway out of his chair, and I rose to meet him.

Someone knocked at the door.

Eddie and Davis stood there. She'd been crying. Davis looked angry. Behind them, Lucille and her agents gave us tired nods.

"I've had more than enough visiting time with my mother, thank you," Eddie said. "We can go home now."

IT HAD TAKEN less than three hours of face-to-face conversation for the small bombshell to fall from Edwina's tongue. She'd been careful at first, bless her paranoid little heart, to make the kind of small talk any doting mother would make. Was Eddie eating a healthy diet, how was she sleeping, did she feel good in general, and how did she like the obstetrician she was seeing down in Atlanta? It was a doctor I'd suggested, a friend.

Yes, fine, fine, and fine, Eddie had answered firmly. Everything was fine.

But then Edwina slipped up and said, "I understand your physician is *quite* an amateur gardener in her spare time, and that's how she and Hush met. When Hush conducted a state Gardening Society workshop on growing the old southern apple varieties."

At which point, Eddie froze. "How would you know that, Mother, since you and Hush barely speak and I've never told you the story of how they met?"

"Oh, well, I . . . now, listen, I'm sure you *must* have mentioned that bit of information, I mean, such an innocent little anecdote—"

"Oh, *Mother.* You checked out my doctor, didn't you? You *investigated* her. *You're still spying on me.*"

And all Edwina could do, caught like a motherly rat in a maternal trap, was admit it.

I almost felt sorry for her, except when I thought of the night Jakobek and I had lost, driving apple trucks back to Georgia instead of making good on the promise of a hungry heart.

FIFTEEN

With the reconciliation of Eddie and her mother on hold again, life in the Hollow settled back into its extraordinary ordinary routines, and neither Jakobek nor I ventured near the subject of what had almost happened in Washington. We had a dull brand of self-control that said we wouldn't touch each other with his unhappy niece and my wary son under the same roof with us. When cooler thoughts prevailed, I told myself Edwina had saved us from starting something that neither of us knew how to finish happily. He wasn't an apple farmer. I was, and always would be. He'd spent twenty years traveling the world and lived out of a duffel bag. I'd been rooted in one place all my life.

Not that I liked Edwina any better for taking that night from us.

Jakobek said nothing, but didn't have to. He loaded apple crates with a grim vengeance; he commandeered the final autumn mowing of the orchard alleys atop a tractor dragging a wrathful Bush Hog blade; he was up in the coldest dawn and outside in the darkest night, working harder than any person on the farm except me, impressing my relatives beyond any possibility. But he wasn't doing the work to win their favor. He was doing it to forget that night we'd lost.

And so was I.

DURING AN AVERAGE FALL SEASON, Sweet Hush Farms welcomed about five hundred visitors a day during the week, two thousand on Saturdays, and a thousand on Sundays. Thanks to the national blitz of news and gossip about Eddie's marriage to my son, our average jumped to two thousand customers per weekday and five thousand on the weekends, both Saturday and Sunday.

The profits were astounding. The work was backbreaking. Smooch, who avoided Jakobek and was still prickly with me, nonetheless reveled in her role as marketing director of the Eddie Jacobs Thackery show. Eddie graciously ignored the fact that she was valuable. Davis grimly pretended nothing was wrong and spent hours at the computer in his and Eddie's bedroom every night, where she and he conferred on a business plan that they said would launch Sweet Hush Farms into the new century. During the day Davis loaded baked goods into our delivery trucks while Eddie made fritters and pies and caramel apples and threw up nobly and won over all my relatives with her good-natured smarts.

She was the talk of Chocinaw County, and despite my efforts to sanctify our relationship by not making money off her, the money rolled in. "I don't mind being your celebrity cash cow," she told me gently. "It comes with the territory."

"I mind," I said. "You're my daughter-in-law."

She hugged me. And I hugged her back.

Eddie's community impact came home to me in a big way at the November meeting of the Chocinaw County Chamber of Commerce. Our restaurants, our little country inns, and all our shops had prospered mightily since September, with the overflow of curiosity seekers lured by Eddie.

So Eddie received a key to the county, along with a plaque

thanking her for representing us to the world. "I'm very honored, but all I've done is make fritters," Eddie said with a smile to two hundred leading citizens packed into the sanctuary of a local church.

They laughed and applauded. Davis grinned at the reaction. Lucille and her team watched discreetly from the vestibule and the choir loft like armed angels. Jakobek, dressed in corduroys and a brown leather bomber jacket, sat beside me in a pew, drawing stares from everyone, and not approving ones. When Bernard Dalyrimple, a brief, discreet, pleasant-enough man-friend and business partner, leaned over to me and whispered, "You're looking good. Call me," Jakobek turned slowly and stared at him. Bernard sat back and swallowed hard.

And God help me, I enjoyed that.

THE MORE I FELL IN LOVE with Hush—without much hope that we'd ever get past the canyon of family duties and role-model dignity we were trying to pull off with every shred of self-control we had—the more I wanted to take her picture. The one hidden in my wallet wasn't enough. She seemed planted and ripe and full and . . . I searched for some old-fashioned word . . . bountiful. I liked the language of old books, gallant language, elegant, courtly. I kept wrapping myself in new layers against the cold. Forewith or anon, sooner or later, I had to expose my skin to something or someone extraordinarily warm.

Hush.

"What are you doing?" she asked in the apple barns, the orchards, sometimes on her own front porch.

"Taking your picture. I take pictures of everything and everyone around here. You're my favorite, though." I paused. "You and the baby goat."

We could joke about ourselves, if there were goats involved.

That weekend I caught a pair of teenagers trying to steal the goat, who'd become my closest friend. I'd named him Rambo.

They were locking him in the trunk of their mother's Lexus when I reached them. "Hey, Dude, we just wanted something from the presidential collection," the lead asswipe said. I shook the kid hard enough to rattle his teeth, took the keys, set Rambo free, then turned the pair over to Hush's brother.

"Nobody gets our goat," Logan said, red as hell, and dragged the little bastards off to find their mother.

I carried Rambo up to the house in my arms. I locked him on the back screened porch with a pan of water and a loaf of apple bread and said, "Stay put, you stinking SOB." I walked back to the public barns smelling like the third day of a goat-shit marathon.

Rambo chewed a two-foot hole in the screen door and followed me to the open pavilion, where I was walking among the produce stands. "Jakobek, your friend's back," called a McGillen cousin with her hand over her smile, and everyone laughed. I found a length of twine, tied one end around Rambo's neck like a collar, and tied the other end to my belt. "He's a trained security goat," I said. The little bastard stayed on the leash as proudly as a poodle at a poodle show.

At the end of every Sunday, Hush gathered her whole crew and they voted on the best employee of the week. The prize was a free dinner for two at the Apple Valley Inn on a small lake outside Dalyrimple and an enameled lapel pin of an apple with a gold star in the center. Some workers at the farm wore dozens of best-employee pins on red vests or the fronts of their baseball caps.

That Sunday, I won the pin for rescuing Rambo.

"Just smile and act pleased," Hush ordered quietly, as she handed me the prize pin in front of everyone. She didn't expect me to indulge their tradition and put the silly pin on. I attached the apple pin to the breast pocket of my work shirt. "It's an honor," I said. "My goat and I thank you."

Everyone applauded. Hush smiled at me with the off-kilter brand of approval she got on her face when she thought no one might catch her looking pleasantly surprised. I invited her to share the prize dinner with me the next night, and, sitting at a table overlooking the little lake, we talked about everything and nothing and we wrapped ourselves around each other without even touching. We drove back to the farm with enough heat between us to warm the cold autumn midnight.

Davis and Eddie were sitting on the front porch, wrapped in blankets, waiting for us. "You kids stayed out past your curfew," Davis said dryly.

Hush went to bed in a brusque mood, and the evening was over.

But God help me, I had never had a better night.

Or a pet goat before.

THEIR NAMES WERE Marcus, Simon, and Bill. Three cocky, good-hearted, but hell-raising Harvard men who had been Davis's best friends since his freshman year. They couldn't have been more different from him in background, race, or religion, but under the skin they shared the same solid bone structure: Family, Faith, Friends. All three had wandered in and out of the Hollow with my son for the past few years, so when they showed up after dark one Friday in an old blue van, waving champagne bottles and hooting that it was time for Davis's better-late-than-never bachelor party down in Atlanta, I gave each one a hug.

Eddie, however, was not so understanding. She confronted Davis in my kitchen while Jakobek and I sat there at the harvest table, nursing glasses of predinner wine and pretending not to listen. "Are you planning to go with them to some strip club?" she demanded.

Davis stared at her, open-mouthed. "*No*. The last time I went to . . . well, it was a long time before I met you. No. Why in the world would you think—"

"Oh, I see. Then the four of you are just going to a bar and get drunk?"

"We're going to one of the clubs in Buckhead and eat dinner and have a few beers."

"*Get drunk*," she insisted. "Get drunk and pretend you're not a married man and father-to-be who spends his days defending a wife who's alone and depressed, a wife who hasn't spoken to her own mother in weeks, a wife who knows you hate being trapped inside all this ridiculous publicity we get, a wife who feels very, very deserted right now."

"Deserted? The whole world watches you. You're a local hero. My mother makes you homemade applesauce — and she doesn't just do that for anybody."

"You're changing the subject! You're going down to the bars in Atlanta to drink and smoke and ogle the girls. Not the pregnant girls. The slender girls who don't vomit every morning." And crying, she went upstairs.

Davis looked stunned. "I just want to have some beers with my friends."

"You're talking to a pregnant wife full of hormones," I countered. "You don't stand a chance in that battle. I'll cook for you and the guys. Break out the beer and the smokes. Have your party here. Include Eddie in it." My memories of life as a pregnant wife with a wandering husband wouldn't allow me to take his side.

"No, I'm going down to Atlanta and enjoy a night out with my friends. Friends who knew me before I was a joke in the national media." He shut his eyes, took a deep breath, then looked at the ceiling as if talking to Eddie in the rooms above us. "I'm going because *my wife should trust me.*" Then he scowled in my direction. "And you ought to *encourage* her to trust me, Mother. You always trusted Dad, even though he was away from home a lot."

I kept my eyes on my wineglass and struggled for the right words, the right lie. Jakobek came to the rescue. "I'll go with you. Be your designated driver. Spy on you for Eddie. Keep you straight." His mouth curved in what might be a smile — or not. With Jakobek, it was always a little hard to tell.

"Forget it, Colonel. I don't need a chaperon. Or a body-guard."

I lifted my gaze to Davis. "You always tell me what your father would do. I'll tell you what he'd do right now. He'd consider his wife's feelings. He'd invite his wife's relative to go out with him, just to make her happy. He'd compromise."

I struck home. Davis chewed his tongue for a few seconds, then nodded to Jakobek. "Consider yourself invited, Colonel. I'll go upstairs and tell Eddie."

After he left the kitchen, I settled my gaze on the wineglass. I heard the clink of Jakobek's glass as he set it aside and the soft rustle of his khakis and flannel as he stood. "Quick thinking," he said.

I raised hard, tired eyes to his somber ones. "Please go and take care of my son. What he thinks his own father would have done is a fantasy I want him to keep."

Jakobek touched a single blunt fingertip to my cheek, stole the tear there, and nodded.

NO ONE—LEAST OF ALL Hush—asked me to play daddy to Davis. Davis sure as hell didn't want to admit that anyone but his old man had a place in his mother's life. Listen, I'd have been the same way, if my mother had lived. So I cut Davis a lot of slack.

Racers, the bar's name said in big, gold-neon letters. The decor was an ad for NASCAR—racing memorabilia and posters, with a few hanging ferns thrown in for the ladies. The bar sat just off the main drag in Buckhead, a section of Atlanta that had gone from quiet and old-money rich to noisy and new-money show-off. On a cold weeknight in November, the crowd was fairly tame—well-dressed students from the universities, a couple of recognizable Braves outfielders, some rap-music execs wearing heavy platinum chains, and a sprinkling of good-looking girls trying hard to be Britney Spears. The music was loud and the beer was imported. I sat by myself at a small corner table, sipping something dark and

Irish while I read a book I'd borrowed from Hush's library. *Apples: A History of the World's Oldest Fruit.* I was engrossed in a chapter on horticultural grafting methods when some drunk kid young enough to be my son walked by and yelled over the music, "Jesus Christ, Dude, you're *reading* about apples in here?" and laughed.

In the meantime, Davis slouched over a table across the room with his buddies, ignoring a ten-dollar hamburger and a six-dollar beer, and generally looking miserable. The buddies were whacked enough not to notice, and spent their time whooping at racetrack videos on the bar's billboard-sized TV.

So it was an uneventful night for the first hour or so, until Davis's crew got the bright idea to move on to louder pastures. "Get the limo, Jeeves, my dear man," the buddy named Marcus said to me, grinning and throwing a pudgy hand on my shoulder. Buddy Marcus looked like a little black Buddha wearing glasses. He was a law student from New York. Buddy Bill was a skinny, Lutheran economics major from the midwest, and Buddy Simon, also an economics major, had been the only Jewish guy in his California town to win a state wrestling tournament. "Yeah, Jeeves, our dear man," the three echoed.

I liked them. They were harmless and cheerful and had never had to hurt anyone. I felt like a hundred-year-old sergeant in charge of baby recruits. "Shut up and try not to puke on your way to the car, assholes." In return I got a happy chorus of "Yes, Sir, Lieutenant Colonel, Sir," and one-finger salutes as they staggered out a side exit. They were so drunk they forgot Davis, who stayed behind to pay the bill. "Follow your platoon and make sure they don't get run over," I told him. "I'll take care of the bill. Happy birthday."

"What's happy about it? My wife's mad at me, I don't have anything in common with my buddies anymore, and my mother is just waiting for me to admit I should never have left college and come back home."

"Tired of loading crates of fried apple pies for a living? Good."

"No, I'm tired of my mother not taking me seriously as the heir to the family business. Last week I handed her a ten-year company goals outline and she said, 'That's nice. Can you have the new caramel kettles scrubbed out and set up by nine in the morning?' I gave her a master's thesis on small-business management and she gave me a scrub brush."

"Ever notice that your mother's usually up to her elbows in work? That she falls asleep in front of her fireplace at night with a heating pad on her shoulder? That she's out in her office before dawn? Pay attention to what she's trying to show you, Davis. She works like a dog. She's probably scrubbed more caramel kettles than you can count. Are you willing to work that hard? Do you love the farm that much? That's what she wants to know."

"I see you've paid an awful lot of attention to my mother's daily schedules. Especially how she falls asleep and how early she gets out of bed. Back off, Colonel. A lot of men have tried to get close to my mother. She's ignored all of them. Nobody can live up to my father, in her eyes. So don't try to bullshit her *or* me. Your motives are showing."

"Hey, it *is* him!" someone yelled. "Yeah, that's him. Hey, *you*. Aren't you Eddie Jacobs's husband? Hey, *Mr. Jacobs*." Laughter followed.

Davis and I did a slow half-turn toward a tableful of knuckle-draggers in college jerseys, including the young dumb fuck who'd laughed at my reading choices. "They're not worth the trouble," I said. "Let's go. *Now*."

"No. I've been a joke in public for months. At least here I get a face-to-face rebuttal."

"There's no point in wrestling with a pig. You get dirty and the pig just likes it. One of your mother's sayings. Let's go."

"Stay out of this. And don't quote my mother to me."

"You've got a pregnant wife who doesn't need to see you with your teeth kicked in. Words don't mean shit. Take the abuse like a man."

"Dammit, you don't listen, do you? Don't tell me how to take abuse—and don't tell me how to take care of my *wife* either. You don't know what a wife needs. You treat women like a Special Forces mission—quick in, fix their problem, quick out. And don't tell me what a *man* does. My father was a *man*—he knew people looked up to him, and he took care of us, and he gave his life to make his name mean something to people. You haven't got the *heart* to be a man like him."

He walked over to the group. I debated my next move and decided to stay put. I faced a lose-lose situation at that point. "My name is Thackery," Davis said to the strangers, his voice dropping into a mountain drawl. "And if you *dazzlin'* mental giants can't remember that, it's your dumb shit problem, not mine."

"Don't get pissy, Man. Hey, you're famous, that's all. You fuck the President's daughter. Hey, Man, is her ass smaller than her mama's?"

End of conversation. It was all fists after that.

"NICKY, YOU WERE SUPPOSED to take *care* of him."

Eddie glared at Jakobek as she held a washcloth to my son's bleeding mouth. We sat in the kitchen. Bloody ice water dripped on the floor. I carefully planted two ice packs on Jakobek's outstretched hands. Other than raw, swollen knuckles, Jakobek didn't have a mark on him. Davis, however, had a bloody mouth and a black eye. "I got to him after the first two punches," Jakobek said. "No one laid a hand on him after that."

"Because they couldn't reach me," Davis mumbled. "I was on the floor."

"They knocked him *out?*" Eddie moaned.

"Down, not out," Jakobek said.

Davis coughed. "Same difference." He squinted through his swollen eye. "Thank you, Nick."

"No problem."

Nick. We'd made a step forward. I looked at Jakobek gently.

"You left six young men clutching various injured parts of their bodies and dragged Davis out before the police came. But the fight won't be any secret. People recognized Davis. I'd better call a lawyer."

I started to get up, but Jakobek slid an ice-covered hand over my arm. "I've got a good one lined up already. I made a call on the way home."

"Who?"

"Al. And he called the Attorney General."

I sat back down. I didn't know whether to laugh or cry. Wherever my first lawyer, Fred Carlisle, rested in some bourbon-pickled afterlife, I hoped he appreciated that moment.

Later that night, after Eddie led Davis off to bed, Jakobek and I sat across from each other at the harvest table. Under the low light of an overhead lamp, I guided Jakobek's big, beaten hands into a crockery bowl filled with a warm gruel of apple vinegar and crushed tobacco leaves. "The old people swear this concoction will pull the sting out of a hurt. The *stang*. That's how they say it. The *stang*."

"Maybe I need all the stang I can hold on to."

"Oh, you've got plenty of stang left, take my word for—" I stopped, the flirtatious words censoring themselves, but also silenced by Jakobek's serious expression. "Jakob, what's troubling you?"

"I let Davis walk into that fight. He was giving me some shit, so I let him take a couple of punches before I jumped in. I apologize."

I bent my head and considered my words carefully. Then, "Nobody else would have taken on six beefy drunks for my son's sake. Thank you. You've got nothing to feel bad about. You've shown a lot of patience with him. Thank you."

"My job is to protect people. That's all I'm good at."

"You make it sound simple. It's not. And it's not all you're good at."

A potent silence grew between us. Jakobek cleared his throat.

"On the way home, Davis said his old man would have fought for him the way I did."

I made a soft sound. "He paid you a great compliment, then."

"I don't think we're ever going to be *pals*. He believes I'm moving in on his father's territory." He looked at me meaningfully. "Says you've never looked twice at another man, and I'm wasting my time."

I felt the heat rise in my face. "I've had plenty of offers. I accepted a couple of them, here and there. Davis doesn't know that."

"Bernard Dalyrimple."

I sat back. Managed not to stammer. "Sweet, divorced. Decided I was too scary behind closed doors."

You can see yourself put a gleam in a man's eyes that, in return, sinks down where you live and melts you open. I saw that look come into Jakobek's eyes. "Let me make up my own image," he said.

"You'll have to. I'm blushing."

"Then there was this J. Chester Baggett I've heard about."

I sagged. Chocinaw County's state representative had been sweet, and widowed, and very religious. But he was very lonely, like me, at the time. "I lured him into sin and felt bad about it later. We're still friends. Stop. I won't discuss this anymore."

"Not all men are scared or religious."

"But most men want to run my business for me. They think they know best. Or they think they deserve more of my time than the farm does." I paused. "Are you, by the way? Chasing me?"

After a moment, Jakobek said quietly, "I thought that was obvious. Are you chasing *me?*"

I pulled my hands from the bowl and got up from the table. "I think that's pretty obvious, too. But I also think it would be a mistake for us to catch each other. In a lot of ways, we have nothing in common."

"Nothing. Right."

I hurt him. He hurt me. We looked at each other for a second, full of regrets, then both of us retreated. "Good night," he said grimly.

"Good night."

I bumped my bad shoulder on the door frame to the back hall on the way out, rushed to my bedroom, and sat on my shower floor a long time, hugging my knees and wincing. I couldn't love any man wholeheartedly. Or couldn't admit it to him if I did. Davy's *stang* was still inside me.

But I wanted Jakobek. He wanted me. Without a word of invitation or a hope that the situation would ever be simple enough for us to indulge ourselves. I laid in my bed, curling up tight, then stretching out, touching myself, touching myself again, crying into my pillow a minute later. I could only imagine what Jakobek was doing to himself in the small bedroom directly above mine. In the morning, we'd be polite again.

But that night wouldn't be forgotten.

UPSTAIRS, I WAS DOING exactly what she imagined me doing. And thinking of her all the time.

SIXTEEN

"YOU'LL WORK OR I'LL KICK YOU OUT!" ORDERS EDDIE'S VA-
VA-VOOM MOTHER-IN-LAW. READ HAYWOOD KENNEY'S COL-
UMN AND SEE EXCLUSIVE PHOTOS OF EDDIE JACOBS SLAVING IN
BAKERY OF NEW HUSBAND'S FAMILY BUSINESS

"The manager at the grocery store told me about this before
the newspaper ever hit the racks," Smooch said in a high whisper,
waving a copy of the headline from the doorway to my office.
"Oh, Hush. This had to be an inside job. Look at the pictures of
Eddie! Someone was only ten feet away."

I took the newspaper in my fists. "Buy all the issues you can
find," I said. "And burn them."

Then I was out the door to take revenge.

"HURRY, COLONEL," a man called as I jumped down from a Sweet
Hush Farms delivery truck. "She looked mad." The crowd standing in front of the autumn pumpkin decorations and rocking
chairs under the sidewalk awning of the Dalyrimple Diner backed

250

away from me and pointed inside. "Her brother'll be here in a minute," someone else called. "He was way out near the north end of the county on a call. That's why we phoned the farm. Figured you'd get here faster."

I shoved my way past double doors sporting flyers for the high school production of *Bye Bye Birdie* and a string quartet concert sponsored by Sweet Hush Farms. I dodged empty tables covered in plastic, red-checked cloths. Thank God the lunch crowd had already left and only a few employees had been on hand when a middle-aged McGillen cousin named MerriLee had run inside, screaming, with Hush following at a calm, deliberate walk.

"Like Arnold in a *Terminator* movie," the phone caller had warned.

Two waitresses and a manager stood by a door to the kitchen. "The walk-in cooler," the manager said, and pointed. "Hush herded her in there and slammed the door. Hush knows the layout of this diner, you know. Her mama waited tables here years ago. And Hush is a half-owner now, along with Bernard Dalyrimple. They dated some, but we don't think you have anything to worry—"

"Tell me the gossip later," I said. Jesus, Hush and I were an item. By then I was already in the back storage room. Hush, dressed in dusty jeans, loafers, a flour-dusted plaid shirt, and a cinnamon-stained apron, braced one hand against the cooler's closed steel door and bent her head close. "MerriLee, you tell me who else was involved in taking and selling those goddamned pictures of my daughter-in-law to Haywood Kenney, or I'll turn this thermostat so far down they'll have to thaw you with a blowtorch."

From inside the cooler came muffled sobs. "If we hadn't taken a few pictures, some stranger would have, sooner or later. We didn't tell Mr. Kenney what to say about them. At least, I didn't. Daddy talked to him."

Hush leaned closer, bent her head to the cooler's steel door, and shut her eyes. "That greedy, vindictive son of a bitch. And Kenney, too."

I put a hand on the lock. "Davis and Eddie are still over in Dahlonega having lunch at the college?"

She nodded. "Lucille's with them."

"Good."

She slid her fingers under mine and pushed the pin further into the lock. "MerriLee?"

"Yes?"

"I don't ever want to see you or your family at the Hollow again. Never."

"Hush, you can't banish us, you can't banish your own —"

"I have to take shit from strangers, but not from my own kin. You betrayed my trust. No second chances."

"Hush!"

Hush walked out with me behind her. "Leave MerriLee in there for another ten minutes," she told the manager. "I don't want her on the phone to her daddy right away. I plan to surprise him." We went out the front doors. The crowd parted.

"Did you put the fear of God in her?" a woman asked.

"No. The fear of *me,*" Hush said. She halted. "Jakob, there's no point in adding more public controversy to what you've already got. Stay here. No hard feelings."

"Those photos of Eddie are my concern, too. So no, I won't let you go alone. If this is about family, then . . . I'm part of it."

After a quiet, potent moment under the avid scrutiny of the crowd, Hush nodded. "I'll do the talking. You stand behind me and do the scowling."

"Agreed."

I steered the big red-and-white delivery truck through a town square draped in big shade trees turning gold in front of little shops and park benches and all the things we like to believe small-town America looks like. Sometimes, a town fits the image.

HISTORIC DALYRIMPLE, a sign said. Coated with Sweet Hush Farms enterprise and the money lured in by visitors to Sweet Hush apple country, Dalyrimple was real.

"That way," Hush said, jabbing a flour-dusted finger up a knoll. A modern complex, consisting of a handsome brick court-house, the county jail, and the county library, shared the hilltop with more big, golden trees; lawns being mowed one more time for the season by an old man who waved at us; and a life-size bronze statue of a pretty pioneer woman in long skirts, striding into the unseen future with a bronze basket of bronze apples in her arms.

PLANT. GROW. HARVEST.

DONATED BY HUSH MCGILLEN THACKERY FOR

SWEET HUSH FARMS

I read that inscription as Hush strode up the steps ahead of me into our own unseen future. "You look good as a statue," I said.

"I paid for it, and I posed for it." She paused. "And next week the grocery store tabloids will probably say I'm as *hard-hearted* as it."

I followed her inside the courthouse and down a hallway honey-combed with little offices behind doors with open blinds. GOD BLESS AMERICA AND CHOCINAW COUNTY decals dotted the hallway windows. "My daddy's first cousin Aaron McGillen is the county commissioner," Hush explained. "I got him elected because he's a tightwad and a sly manager, and that's a good thing in county government. But not in a family."

She threw open a pair of double glass doors and strode into an anteroom where a young secretary said, "Cousin Hush, Ma'am, uh, Ma'am," to which Hush said, "Take a bathroom break, Chancy. You never saw a thing."

The girl grabbed her purse and left.

We walked into the office beyond her desk. A lanky, prim-looking older man immediately glowered at us. His desk plaque said AARON MCGILLEN, COUNTY COMMISSIONER — HONEST BUT TOUGH.

"I know what you did," Hush said. "And there was nothing *honest* about selling my daughter-in-law's privacy."

"Don't you stand on your high horse and look down at *me*. You make money off Eddie Jacobs hand over fist."

"You betrayed my trust and embarrassed me."

"You can't control the truth anymore. And you can't maneuver all the gossip to suit your own purposes. The *facts* are a big, dark, festering cloud of smoke pouring out of your chimney and threatening to burn your home down. People are starting to smell the stink. Welcome to your own dose of that 'open public scrutiny' you bragged about a few years ago when you 'exposed' me for inviting the immigration boys to take a look at your Mexican apple pickers. I tried to enforce the law, and you made me look like a monster."

"Because those Mexicans work harder for their pay than any people I've ever seen in my life and I wasn't about to let them be bullied on account of laws that are mainly a bunch of racist hogwash."

"You're *above* the law. That's what you've *always* thought." He pounded his desk. "But don't cry now that the world's knocking on your door to learn all about you. You've always acted like you know what's best for everybody around here. You've run this town and this county and you even think you run *me*. So I'm not *about* to stand by and watch you add to your power base now that you've got a gold-plated celebrity daughter-in-law to give you even more clout. I'm going to cut your personal tree down to size for the good of this community! And there's only one way to do that — by showing people what you and yours are really like."

"You attack *me* all you want, Aaron, but if you —"

"I may not be able to cut you off at the trunk, but I can sure lop off your branches."

"What is *that* supposed to mean?"

"Logan's so-called wife, for one thing. A wife nobody ever met or spoke with on the phone or—"

"She was German. She *died in Germany* when Puppy was a month old and Logan was still stationed there in the Army. Everyone knows that."

"No, everyone *says* that because you told them they'd *better* say that. Even though there's not *one* picture of Logan's wife anywhere to be seen, and no visits from her family to see Puppy, and just no trace of her at all. I'll tell you what people think your brother *really* did. They think he knocked up some gal over there and she didn't want the baby but you *made* him bring his little bastard home and do the right thing."

Hush was electrified. She hunched over his desk. "If you ever say anything to hurt my brother or Puppy I'll—"

"Hush," I said. Her name, an order, a quiet heads-up. *Walk softly and keep your threats to yourself.* I had been standing there just wanting to take her relative by his collar and slam him against a wall, but now I thrust an arm between her and him, pried her back from his desk, and said, "Talk is cheap."

She looked at me with feverish understanding, but also with a kind of *Help Me* expression in her eyes I'd never seen before, and it shook me up—although for once I was in territory I knew how to handle. Women who needed help were my specialty. "I'll take care of it," I said. I didn't know how I'd take care of the situation, but that didn't matter. A good bluff—just like with the cameraman in the helicopter—often produced more results than real action. "No need for you to worry about your cousin Aaron," I said to Hush. "I'll handle him."

Aaron leapt to his feet. "Are you threatening me?" he yelled. He'd taken the bait.

Hush searched my face for clues. I held her tight with an arm around her shoulders, squeezing silent signals that she interpreted rightly as a code to stay quiet. I looked at Aaron. "I don't make threats."

"You *are* threatening me." His face turned white. "Get out of my office."

"I'm going. Hush, too. Come on, Hush."

Aaron turned whiter, trembling. "You think I'm going to put up with that kind of sinister attitude? Goddammit, I'm *not* afraid of you."

"We're going. I said I'd handle this problem for Hush, and I will. Nothing else to talk about."

I saw the whites of his eyes. "You just keep your distance, Mister! The bet is that Eddie and Davis's marriage won't last a year, and the day she leaves here for good, we'll never see you again. You're nothing but a trained attack dog, and you can't stifle—"

"Enough," Hush said. She backed from the room, pale and stiff, pulling at me to follow.

I just looked at Aaron McGillen one more time, and pointed a finger at him. Just pointed. He sat down hard in his chair.

I turned and strode after Hush. She rushed to an exit and outside onto the building's lawn. Without warning she pulled the skirt of her flour-speckled apron to her mouth, bent over the shrubs along a small parking lot, and vomited. I scanned the area in case anyone walked out of the building, then took the bundled apron from her and stuffed it in a tall trash can nearby. "Let's get you to a water fountain."

"Thank you. For everything. You're amazing."

"He was an easy target. Next time I'll recite the alphabet and really scare the shit out of him."

"No. I can't provoke him." She swayed. Her eyes were whip-hard and pained. She dragged a hand over the back of her mouth.

I stared at her. "Are you telling me that what he said about Logan and Puppy is the truth?"

"No."

"Then—"

"I can't talk about this, Jakob. That's all. Don't ever ask me. Ever."

The hackles rose on the back of my neck. Surprised, confused, and, all right, wounded, I could only stand there with one hand out, asking for something and getting nothing. "Aren't we way beyond the point where you won't trust me with information about your life and your family?"

"There are some things I'll *never* discuss with you or anyone else."

I took her by the shoulders. "What kind of game are you playing? Don't you understand that Haywood Kenney is looking for *exactly* the kind of trash you don't want him to know? Do you think he won't find it?"

"You sound like Edwina."

"She warned you?"

"For my own good. 'Tell all. To me, Edwina. Confess your sins. Your family's sins. For your own good.' That's just plain bullshit."

"She was right."

Hush stared at me, took a big, symbolic step back, and said softly, "She doesn't really know *anything* about me and my family, and neither do you. And I intend to keep it that way."

"Then I see where I stand with you. Nowhere."

She vomited in the shrubs again, refused my help getting into the truck, and didn't say another word as I drove her back to the Hollow.

Nowhere.

EDWINA WAS ON the phone immediately.

"Is this the best you can do — your relatives creep into the work area where my daughter is 'slaving away' and snap secret pictures of her? Is this how your family takes care of its own? *Is this how you take care of my daughter?*"

I had no comeback for that. I had failed to protect Eddie. My family had failed to protect Eddie, too. "I apologize," I said wearily. "You have every right to be angry."

Fortunately, Edwina was so shocked she simply said, "Well . . . good."

And I hung up.

&

I HAD HURT JAKOBEK BADLY, and I hated that, but there was nothing I could do short of tell him truths I could not bring myself to speak out loud. Things that were buried inside me so deeply that I had to believe nothing and no one—not even the Haywood Kenneys of the world—could dig them up unless I spoke first. All I had to do was keep the faith—the faith and the silent strength and the terrible, lonely endurance I'd learned all my life from my stoic trees, my gallant soldiers, and the Hollow itself.

But forces had already been set in motion. My luck really had run out.

&

"HUSH, IT'S ALL RIGHT," Eddie begged, following me into the pavilion. "Really. Don't. Please."

"Mother, stop," Davis ordered. "You're overreacting."

Jakobek stood to one side, his eyes shuttered, watching me. Smooch, as agitated as a yellow jacket in full sting mode, paced the sawdust floor. Logan clasped his Stetson in one brawny hand and traded worried frowns with Lucille.

I faced every soul who worked for me. There had been a lot of muttering about Aaron and MerriLee, about kicking Aaron out of office and ostracizing MerriLee, but I'd said, *No. No. I banned them from the Hollow. That's enough.*

But it wasn't enough. Kenney and his kind were moving in like vultures. A few silly photographs of Eddie making fritters wasn't the issue. What Kenney might do *next* was the issue.

"This farm is closed as of today. I won't risk any more publicity. I don't know who to trust right now. I will not allow my family to become laughingstocks. I don't give a damn what Haywood Kenney said about *me,* but no one is going to abuse the image of this family and this farm. You'll all get paid for the rest of the season. We'll start again next spring. Close down the kitchens, put the apples in cold storage, and go home. This year's apple season is over."

People cried. They tried to talk me out of it. It was only November. "All of this over some pictures?"

Davis and Eddie said in unison, "This is our fault."

I grabbed them in a hug. "No. This started long before you were born."

That made no sense to them, but the harvest cycle of truth and sacrifice and secrets made perfect sense to me.

I left everyone standing there and walked back to the house.

BY DECEMBER THE FARM was stark and quiet and a stranger to us. It felt less safe, not more, with the crowds vanished, the gates locked, the Barns quiet. My fears infected everyone.

Davis started carrying a pistol inside his shirt, like Jakobek. Lucille added security dogs to our routines. German shepherds snuffled their way through my house and barns twice a day. All the farm's mail was scanned, irradiated, then opened in a shed by people wearing latex gloves. I agreed to some other measures, too, and soon a number of my wavy-glassed old windows leaned against each other in the cellar so that tinted, bullet-proof windows with unbreakable frames could take their place. As if any of that would keep Haywood Kenney out.

Eddie stood at those windows with me, looking out sadly. "What a naive little girl I've been," she said quietly. "This beautiful old Hollow is just like the rest of the world. Only as safe as the feeling in my heart."

I put an arm around her. "We have to carry our security around *with* us, like the shell of a turtle. Always setting up housekeeping wherever we end up for the moment, always trusting that we've brought what we need to keep us safe."

She smiled a little. "But you've never lived anywhere else."

"Apples are hard to carry on top of a turtle shell."

She leaned her head against mine. "What should Davis and I do now? Rethink everything we've planned?"

"No. Wait and rest, and listen for answers. Because apple trees talk to us, you know."

"*Hush*." She chuckled.

"They do."

"Then I'll try to listen."

She put my hand over her abdomen. I felt my grandchild move contentedly.

Safe inside our shell.

I SAT IN THE LOFT DOOR of the old barn late one cold, starry night. Just sitting.

Of course, Jakob tracked me there, and without a word, sat down next to me.

"I couldn't breathe indoors," I said. A half-moon and millions of bright stars filled the soft black dome of the sky without even a hint of the world's lights leavening the mountain rims in any direction. We were alone on the planet. Him, me, and a weight of wordless dread that made me shake. "I don't know what to do, Jakob."

"Yes, you do."

Tell me what you're hiding, I thought he was about to say, but instead he pulled me into his arms and held me. He stroked my hair and said nothing—just held me close. And we kissed. It was as simple as the night, as complicated as the night sky. A sense of dread began to creep under my skin again. All my mountain sayings and superstitions and old ways and new ones could not stop that feeling. "Something terrible is going to happen out there in the dark," I whispered, nodding toward the world beyond my mountains. "Something's waiting."

"I've known that all my life," he answered.

I had always sold apples as if they were protective talismans I sent out into the world. But I dreamed at night of terrible trees growing from seeds I didn't willingly spread and couldn't reclaim. Flashes of the strangling dread came and went; I knew what it was — a premonition. The world was catching up with all I held dear. The threat wasn't necessarily the haters and the lunatics, but the past, the past. In ways no fence or weapon or guard could prevent. I watched the phones as if a single call would electrocute me with no warning.

A few days before Christmas, it came.

SEVENTEEN

I know when women are hurting. It doesn't take an extremely sensitive man to recognize the pain in another human being, but considering my background, I'm more of an expert than most men. I knew something had happened to hurt Hush more than her secrets had already hurt her.

As I lay in my bed in the room above hers, I heard the faint ring of her bedroom phone through the floorboards. I listened to her pace the floor for hours after that. I got up and moved restlessly, too, my bare feet creaking on my own floor, and she stopped moving.

She heard me. I heard her.

But she didn't ask for my help. And I didn't know how to give it. Or why she needed it.

"Goddamn," I whispered.

I didn't sleep much that night. In the kitchen the next morning, I couldn't move fast enough to corner her before Eddie and Davis came down. Davis made breakfast for Eddie. Hush made breakfast for Davis, and for me. Eddie and I did the dishes after we all finished. The four of us had a system. In just a few months, we'd become a family. I'd never even tried to tell Hush what those times meant to me.

"I'm going to Chattanooga for the day," Hush announced. "I may not be back until tomorrow morning."

"To see Abbie?" Davis asked. Nothing his mother did seemed to startle him ever since her bizarre decision to close the farm early and turn it into a fortress. He and Eddie remained full of guilt over their effect on life in the Hollow.

"Yes. She's having some problems with her husband. I have to go." She kissed Eddie on the top of the head, ruffled Davis's dark hair, avoided me, and left the kitchen.

I sat there with my hands making empty gestures around a plate of pancakes she'd fixed for me. "Abbie?"

"Old friend of my folks. Abbie's husband and my father were racetrack buddies. Her husband has money. A lot of money. He invested in Dad's team." Davis dug into his own pancakes while Eddie picked at a bowl of cereal with one slender hand. The other rested protectively on her bulging stomach. She had asked me to feel her baby move the other day. I'd started to lay the maimed hand on her, then switched and used the other one. Didn't want to scare the baby. I felt it kick. "He knows kung fu already," I said.

"Oh, Nicky, you sweet old soldier." She had laughed, and hugged me.

"Old friends," I continued prodding Davis.

Davis set a stone keg of syrup between us like a boundary marker. The look on his face said, *Stay out of my mother's business.* "Mother's loyal to her *friends.* She drops everything if Abbie needs her."

No, I thought. *She drops everything when Abbie calls her in the middle of the night and warns her.*

ACROSS THE MOUNTAINS, just over the Tennessee line, I bought coffee and an apple at an interstate convenience store, sat in my car holding both on my lap with my eyes shut, then bit into the apple just to remind myself that the world outside the Hollow held no protective magic. No sweet burst of pleasure on my tongue. I was out here all alone with everyday apples, waiting for the hammer of God to fall on me and mine.

On better days, I loved Chattanooga. The historic old city was a monument to its Old South heritage but no fool for the past. Friends of mine had been instrumental in turning rows of decrepit warehouses along the broad Tennessee River into a neighborhood of shops and restaurants. The soaring glass roof of the Tennessee Aquarium gleamed nearby, overlooking the river. I met Abbie on the aquarium's top floor.

FROM THE MOUNTAINS TO THE SEA, an educational display said. The mountain habitat smelled of laurel and moss, water and earth and rocks. Otters played in a stone grotto. Behind walls of glass, turtles and trout and large-mouthed bass swam among huge logs and rushing currents. This part of the aquarium always made me think of the Hollow, wild but protected.

"Hush," Abbie whispered, crying, and we hugged each other tightly. She was ten years younger than me, but we looked alike. Auburn hair, green eyes, tall, but not delicate. There the sameness ended. Her voice was far more citified than my country twang could ever hope for; she had a master's degree from Vanderbilt; she came from banking money and silver-spoon pedigrees; and her husband, Nolan, was heir to one of Tennessee's biggest insurance brokerages and a major behind-the-scenes player in state politics. Abbie devoted her time to their riverside mansion and their two baby boys.

We bent our heads together in a dark alcove of wood and vine, high atop that man-made planet. "They called me," she whispered hoarsely, clutching my arm, holding on. "Haywood Kenney's people. One of his assistants. The woman said, 'We understand from certain sources that Eddie Jacobs's late father-in-law led a double life. And that you were having an affair with him when he died. We have witnesses. Evidence. Is it just coincidence that your husband is a major fundraiser for President

Jacobs in Tennessee?' I told her that had nothing to do with anything, and I didn't know what she was talking about. 'Davy Thackery has been dead for over five years. His wife and I are dear friends. I've been married to the most wonderful man in the world since then.' She said, 'Come on, now. What does the President think of this old soap opera, now that his daughter has married Thackery's son? Mr. Kenney would like you to comment, that's all. Tie all the loose ends together for his audience. You can't hide. You might as well talk to Mr. Kenney. If he found out about your connection to Eddie Jacobs's in-laws, the rest of the media won't be far behind. And maybe there's more to the story, hmmm?' "

Abbie sagged against me. I held her up. "Abbie, they've put two and two together and come up with five. Idiots. It doesn't mean —"

"Oh, Hush, all that matters is that they're sniffing out the truth, slowly but surely." She raised her head and looked at me with haunted eyes. "They'll find out the rest. Hush, Nolan knows the truth, but my children —" she looked around furtively, though we were alone — "Hush, I don't want to see *any* of my children suffer because of this."

"No." I heard my own voice like an empty echo. "No, I won't let . . ." I put a cold, sweating hand over hers where she held my arm.

"What can we do?" she moaned.

"I have to think it through. I don't know yet."

"The terrible thing is, this is all my fault. Nolan and I can survive. But your relationship with Davis and —"

"It's not your fault. It's mine, maybe, for believing a golden rule I made up when I was too young to know better."

"Your rule?"

"Give people a good story and they won't care about the truth."

"Oh, Hush. That's true, most of the time."

"All right, we'll talk more when I come up with some ideas."

"Please don't leave me alone with this dilemma."

"I'll be at the inn. Close by." The fake mountain atmosphere and the truth and the past and the future suddenly stole my air. I pulled at the soft collar of the leather coat I wore. "I have to get outside. Have to go. I'll call you later. Let me know if you hear anything else today. I'll come running."

She hugged me. "Hush, I'm so sorry."

I should have hated and envied her for what her dalliance with Davy had done to my life, but she'd only made foolish mistakes, just like me when I was young. In a way, *because* of me. Davy had picked her out of a crowd when she was barely twenty-one and ripe for trouble. He'd chased her because she reminded him of me when I was baby-soft and easy to charm. She was the only one of Davy's women I didn't want to kill on sight.

I made the right noises, said the right words, but began to mourn inside. *Sorry* wouldn't get the job done.

I'M A TRACKER. I followed Hush to Chattanooga, watched her go into the aquarium, waited outside in the cold December morning, watched her walk out. She was dressed in a long coat, soft tan trousers, a white blouse too thin for the temperature. She must have been freezing, but didn't seem to notice, or care. The wind of a bright blue mountain day whipped her coat away from her as she crossed the plaza outside the aquarium, her head down, her fists shoved into the coat pockets. Thinking. Walking blindly. I hunched my shoulders inside my heavy down jacket.

You're cold. I'll give you my jacket. Look up. Look for me. You know I'm here. You knew I'd follow you. I always do.

I trailed her down a quiet street in a historic district of nice shops. She turned toward the river and I turned, too. The city had transformed an old, narrow car bridge into a pretty walkway over the water. Goosebumps rose on my skin as she strode out on that long span of girders and concrete in the icy wind. The bridge was empty that morning. Even the hard-core walkers and joggers stayed away.

She walked without seeing until she was nearly halfway across, then stumbled to a side rail and held on with both hands, breathing hard as she stared down at the smooth, gray sheet of the Tennessee River passing deep and slow and deadly, yards below.

I closed the distance between us in only a few seconds, barely enough time for her to hear me running. She turned around, swaying, not startled so much as ready. I took her by the shoulders. "If you go, I go over with you."

"*Jakob*." Looking up at me with affection and anguish, she cupped my face between her ice-cold hands. "What are you doing here?"

"I don't give up. And I won't let go of you."

"I wasn't going to jump. I was thinking of who I'd like to *push*."

"Then tell *me*, and I'll throw the bastard over *for* you. You *want* to trust me. You wanted me to follow you from the farm. I'm here. Talk to me."

With the slow melt of defeat in her, the giving up of hard defenses and bone-tired pride, Hush shut her eyes. "Abbie was my husband's last girlfriend." She paused, her throat working. "And the mother of his other child."

"Puppy," I said automatically.

She nodded, and for the first time since I'd known her, she looked hopeless.

All I could do was pull her close and hold her.

THERE WAS A PRETTY INN near the historic district, perched high on the bluffs above the river. Each time I visited Abbie, bringing her new pictures of Puppy and little stories to tell about her everyday life, I stayed at the inn. I paid cash for my room, registering under a fake name. I took every measure to keep that life separate from my life in the Hollow. I had to protect Davis. Protect Puppy. Protect Abbie and her husband and their baby sons. Protect

Sweet Hush Farms and all it stood for. And yes, I had to protect me, too.

Hush McGillen Thackery couldn't keep her husband in her own bed, and finally he left her with another woman's child to raise in secret. She didn't even tell her son he had a half sister. Some legend. A lot of people would be happy to spread that news.

So in Chattanooga I called myself Ms. Ogden. Patricia Ogden. The inn's owners prided themselves on remembering my name, adding me to their guest book, inquiring about my relatives. I'd made up an entire family history for myself.

"I always come home from my visits to Abbie and scrub like a leper," I told Jakobek. "Trying to get back down to the skin of Hush McGillen Thackery, the honest woman I claim to be."

"You look honest enough to me," he said. "A mother taking care of her son. And her son's half sister. That's what I see."

"The road to hell is paved with good intentions, Jakob."

"Been there," he said.

I sat outside on the inn's veranda alone while he went inside to register. I was too shell-shocked to do more than stare at the winter hedges and Christmas garlands wrapping old, wind-twisted oaks in the yard. A broad vista of river and hills, homes and shops and traffic and everyday life, moved slowly in the distance. High places. A view. I had picked the inn for that.

When Jakob came back outside, he rested a hand on my shoulder and shook me just a little. I was dazed. "You sure you want to stay here?" he asked.

"I can't go home until I decide what to do. I have to have a plan. Get myself together so I can say the right thing. Only I don't know what the right thing is. Do I tell more lies to Davis? Hide the truth from Puppy for the rest of her life? Or do I do nothing and hope the shit diggers like Haywood Kenney won't find out about Puppy and tell the story just for the sake of gossiping about Al Jacobs's in-laws?"

"The world's changed since we were kids. People aren't shocked by anything."

"Not *my* people. And not my son."

He squeezed my shoulder. "I have a stake in this, too. Whatever hurts Davis, hurts Eddie."

"I worry about that all the time. I . . . like her, Jakob. No. I *love* her. She's my daughter-in-law and I love her."

"And she loves you."

We sat there, letting a cold wind curl around the simple core of my family, something I desperately wanted to preserve. I made a keening sound, and Jakobek pulled me to my feet. "Let's take this inside. We'll talk. We have a room with a fireplace. We're Mr. and Mrs. Johnson. Bill and Patricia. I told them you married me, Ms. Ogden. They think I teach at a military college they never heard of."

I focused on the soft give of my kneecaps and the tremor in my hands. My throat ached. I'd corrupted even Jakobek, lured him into my cover-up. "Bill, you married a woman who seems to be falling apart."

"Mrs. Johnson doesn't fall apart."

I took the challenge. We went inside.

I SAT ON THE ROUNDED EDGE of a deep burgundy couch before the room's fireplace, hugging myself and staring into the flames. The room was decorated for Christmas, with a Victorian-themed tree and the scent of pine from garland on the mantel. The furnishings were elegant and feminine and plush — a lot of brocade, lace on the white pillow shams, amber lampshades with beaded fringe that reflected flecks of rainbow color on the high, patterned ceiling. A fantasy. I liked my fantasies. I was losing them.

My life with Davy flowed out of me in words as ruined as a melting honeycomb. I'd never told another soul the ugly facts I told Jakobek on that long day into evening. He listened, as quietly as a ghost, in a tall armchair by the hearth, leaning forward, his eyes never leaving me, his elbows on his knees, his big, crude, gentle hands hanging in thin air, ready to help me if there were any way, which there wasn't. Shadows grew around us and the night came. Jakobek poured tea from a wicker hostess cart the owner brought up. It was all I could do to swallow from the cup he handed me.

"I found out about Abbie a little over five years ago, just after Davis left for his first year at Harvard," I told him. "Heard a rumor, went to find her. I always kept track of my husband's girl-friends, just to make sure they wouldn't cause trouble for me and Davis. I didn't play nice with them, Jakob. Every time I found one, I did my best to scare the hell out of her. I tracked Abbie down and just flat *told* her: 'You touch my husband again and you're dead. Do you *want* to die?' That had always worked with his other girls. But this skinny, prep-school southern belle, this rich girl — and she was *just* a girl, fresh out of Vanderbilt, then — she looked at me with big, sad eyes and answered, 'Except for the baby, I'd tell you to go ahead and kill me.'

"Except for the baby. A baby. Davy's baby. He'd gotten this college girl pregnant. I could have killed *him. Except for the baby.*

"Abbie didn't want to have an abortion, but she didn't want anybody in her family to know she was pregnant either. She wanted the baby, but then again she *didn't* want it. Said she was going out to California to stay with friends and give the baby up for adoption when it was born.

"I went home and cornered Davy. He said I refused to have more children with him, and how he had always wanted more, so that was my fault, too. I told him no, he'd done *me* out of having another child, because I'd be damned if I'd fight him for the soul of a second child the way I'd fought him for Davis." I stared into the fire. "To make a long story short, that night we fought about everything our marriage had been and would never be. It was the worst fight of our lives — a knock-down-drag-out battle."

Jakobek said quietly, "That was when you tore your shoulder."

I couldn't bring myself to answer outright — to admit I'd lived with a man capable of throwing me down my own back stairs. Jakobek shifted slightly. I didn't have to admit it. He knew. When I looked at him, his eyes were nearly black.

"I'm not a doormat, Jakob. I fought back. Don't feel sorry for me."

"I never do," he said quietly. Lying. A gallant man. "Keep talking."

"I hit him. Hit him right in the face with my fist. How dare he twist what my pride and hard work had built for him and our son as well as me. I tried my best to hurt him."

I paused. "And he hurt me back. I ended up in the hospital emergency room, and I told everyone I'd fallen during a hunting trip." I stopped again, flexing my hands in front of the fire, pulling back into the shadows, feeling Jakobek watching me even more intently. "Davy was inconsolable. He felt bad about what he'd done to me, bad about Abbie, bad about her baby, but worst of all—he didn't want Davis to find out and hate him. My husband had his own kind of honor.

"He didn't say a word when I told him I wasn't going to let his girlfriend give my son's half brother or half sister to strangers and never know how or where or *if* that child was raised kindly. A few hours later, he drove up on Chocinaw. His accident was deliberate, Jakob. No doubt in my mind. He killed himself up there."

Jakobek stood. "Some debts of honor can only be paid back one way."

"I didn't want him to die. Does that make sense?"

"Things are never simple. Yeah."

"Abbie showed up at his funeral. I spotted her in the background, crying, looking like hell, this . . . rich pregnant girl, all alone . . . hiding her stomach in an oversize cashmere coat and grieving for my husband. I wanted to hate her, but I couldn't. So I helped her. Came up with a plan. Logan was on his way home from the Army, in Germany. His wife had died—he really did have a sweet German wife, Marla, when he was in the Army—and I told him about the baby. And Logan, God bless him, Logan said, 'If you'll help me, I'll take the baby. Marla and I wanted kids so bad we didn't know what to do. She'd want me to raise this baby. Please.'

"So that's how it came to be. This perfect little baby girl came home with my brother, and people accepted our story about her being Logan's daughter. Our state rep, J. Chester Baggett, helped me get the right paperwork — a foreign birth certificate, all that — and I announced that Logan's little girl was Hush McGillen the Sixth. Hush Puppy. Puppy. End of story."

I put my head in my hands and sat in silence, rocking a little. Jakobek dropped to his heels in front of me. "Look at me," he ordered gruffly.

When I did, he smoothed his fingers over my hair and my damp cheeks. Straightening me. Righting me. "You're going to go home tomorrow and sit down with your son and tell him the truth — tell him, before anyone else gets the chance."

"The truth? Tell him I didn't have the guts to be honest with him about his father and me from the day he was born? A son has a right to expect better from his mother. Wouldn't you?"

Jakobek grew quieter, his face hard, pensive, sad. "Let me tell you," he said quietly, "the truth I live with. The truth about my mother."

WHAT I HAD KNOWN about Jakobek — what was said, what I'd heard, and what the paid liars like Kenney told the world about the President's darkly constituted nephew — went up in the smoke of the inn's Victorian chimney that night. Jakobek described his childhood in ways that turned my stomach over and drew my sorrows through the fine sieve of his loneliness. The flat timbre of his voice said he wanted no one to call it a sob story. He gave me the facts. But they were brutal.

"Don't do that," he said softly, as I sat there listening with tears on my face. "You don't want anybody's pity. Neither do I."

"I don't feel sorry *for* you. I feel sorry *with* you."

And that was the truth. I felt sorry *with* him. Sorry for what life does to us, starting when we're young and completely defenseless, the shame of that. A shame on the families that let it happen, and on the societies that let it happen, a shame on the ordinary pettiness of ordinary life. Children suffer and then grow up hardhearted as a result, ready to hurt the children who come behind them. It's a miracle when a soul shines through the loss and defeat. It's a time for celebrating. An unexpected harvest is the sweetest.

I knelt in front of Jakobek, just as he'd knelt in front of me. "You have nothing to feel bad about. I was right to believe in you, like the yellow jackets — although I tried to resist. I've been fooled before. But not this time." He lifted his head and looked at me.

The mantel clock slowly struck ten in the darkness above our fire. I stood, touched his face, then went to the bath, did not turn on any light, and waited in the shadows with a Chattanooga midnight gleaming through a stained glass transom, lighting us with ancient star shine over the old southern river that bound the city. I twisted the knobby faucets of the shower, adjusted the heat, and let the water flow over my hands as if the river itself, warm with comfort, had come inside. I heard Jakobek's footsteps. I felt the depth of his body before he put the careful grip of his hands on my shoulders. Both of us needed to come clean.

"Yes, I knew you'd follow me," I said quietly. "And yes, I wanted you to."

"I've been following you all my life," he whispered.

We undressed each other in the fertile warmth of that winter night.

HUSH AND I DIDN'T trash the room, tear the sheets off the bed, or tie each other to the headboard. We didn't have to. All that chaos, all that energy, all the mind-clearing joy and cathartic lust and tender, intense sex can tear two people apart and wrap them back together without any outward evidence. It's as simple as a kiss, a fast rhythm, a word or two at the right second, her holding me around the shoulders, me bearing down on her and her lifting me up. When we finally had to rest, had to pull the covers up and be still, we tangled ourselves together and breathed against each other like dozing wolves, still ready to attack.

Tell her. Tell her you love her and see what she says. And when she says, 'Thank you, you're good in bed and I enjoy your company,' say, 'Yeah, that's all I meant, too,' and let it go at that.

I love you. Hard words to say and get them right, plus we had enough trouble to deal with already. And besides that, no, I didn't want to know her answer. One of the few times in my life I'd rather stay in the dark.

"I was trying to let you rest," I said once, deep in those shadows. I had been touching her hair, slowly curling just one red-brown swath between my fingers.

"You know you really weren't," she accused. "I've just been waiting for you to admit it." She straddled me, kissed me, and took me in so fast I couldn't ask for forgiveness.

But for the first time in my life, I didn't need to.

IF JAKOBEK HAD BEEN following me all his life, then I'd been waiting all my life for him to find me. He rode high and hard and gentle in the rough spots; he knew what a woman's parts were for, what they liked, what to do. And he knew that sometimes, just the feather touch of a fingertip on the right spot makes a kind of magic. He knew *me,* on instinct. And I knew him.

After all my years of angry sex, no sex, and using sex to keep my marriage intact, for once all I had to do was make love. To love a man. Nicholas Jakobek. Jakob. I didn't know if he would call it love on his side of the bed. I was too afraid to ask him, and maybe he was too afraid to ask me either. We had enough hope to keep us going that night, without saying so. I loved him.

I had known from the day of the bee charming, not needing rhyme or reason, that I did. He bent his head to my breast and took it in his mouth. I called out *Jakob* as I came, and he followed in a rush of motion, the next second.

"You got me," he whispered, as if I'd shot him through the heart.

EIGHTEEN

B y early morning we showered and dressed and touched one more time, then sat on the couch in front of the cold fireplace, separate from each other in the day's light, knowing we had hard times ahead. Regrets and survival are practical matters to be weighed against common sense. I had to risk everything I loved to save everything I loved. "I'll talk to Abbie first," I told Jakobek wearily. "Then I'll go home to the Hollow, sit Davis down—just the two of us—and tell him the truth about his father, and our marriage, and Puppy. Beyond that, I have no idea what will happen next."

"No one ever does. But you're doing the right thing."

I looked at him dully. "Oh? I'm not being brave, and I'm sure as hell not feeling noble. If I could go on hiding everything, I would. But dear God, it's better that Davis hear the facts from me than from some reporter."

Jakobek nodded. "Let's go, then."

"You'll talk to Eddie? Help her to help my son understand I never meant any harm by hiding things? I don't want Eddie upset either. I don't want her to think she married into a family of nasty secrets and false honor."

"All families have their nasty secrets and false honor. Look at mine. Look at me."

"Jakob, there's nothing nasty or false about you. You're the most die-hard *true* man I've ever met."

He cleared his throat and changed the subject. "I'll talk to Eddie. She's a strong girl. Stronger than I realized — stronger than Al and Edwina realized, too. She has a lot of compassion in her. She'll be all right." He paused. "*They'll* be all right. Her and Davis. They're good together."

"They're young. They think love conquers all. They're wrong, but I'm glad they think so."

"You're saying *we* know better," Jakobek said, watching me.

Never read too much into a man's words — or too little. Analyzing my night with Jakobek would be a job for other nights, maybe the lonely ones, if and when he went on his own lonely way. "Yes," I said finally, hurting, searching, unsure. "*We* ought to know better." He and I traded a long look, then he just nodded. He didn't know what else to say, and I didn't know how to listen.

Neither of us was brave enough to admit loving someone is as simple as saying so.

Downstairs in the inn's small lobby — an emotional wonderland of soft Christmas lights and decorations that made me ache with fears I couldn't describe — I laid our door key on the owner's desk while Jakobek walked out onto the cold, sunlit veranda, carrying my small overnight bag for me, reaching for the stub of a cigar he always seemed to have on him. I moved slowly, reluctant to get on with the day, staring at the handsome bronze room key, old-fashioned and sturdy. Traditions. Values. I wished I could put a solid lock on my family's future.

I heard a soft sound outside, as if a large dog was scuffling in the dried oak leaves that matted along the inn's front walkway. I glanced dully through the glass panes of the front doors and halted, stunned. Davis stood in the yard, swaying, his face furious but tear-streaked, one hand still drawn back in a fist. Jakobek stood with his legs braced apart and his back to me. He drew one hand across his mouth. I saw blood on his fingers.

The breath clotted in my throat. I rushed outside, dropping the coat I held over one arm, flinging myself between Davis and Jakob. Blood smeared Jakobek's lower lip. He rubbed it off with the pad of his thumb. "You've needed to punch me since the first day," he told Davis.

Davis stared at him bitterly. "Don't patronize me. That's for sleeping with my mother." He shifted his father's blue eyes to me, full of fury and pain. "And for helping my mother hide the fact that everything she taught me about love and marriage and my father's honor is a lie."

Dear God, he knew.

WHILE JAKOBEK AND I had been working out our miseries and strategies and needs the night before, thinking we still controlled the world, that world had gone up in the smoke of sly gossip. The public's right to know is a respectable ideal some of the time, but a sham to cover its greed for trash most of the time. We're so used to treating other people's lives like entertainment that personal privacy doesn't mean a damn thing and the facts mean even less.

As Eddie dozed in their bedroom upstairs at the Hollow with a baby magazine on her stomach and yet another firm, pleading letter from her estranged mother in one tearstained hand, my son had gone downstairs, past one of Lucille's men posted in the kitchen, to get himself a glass of milk. Jakobek's unexplained night out didn't worry him; he had no idea Nick had headed for Chattanooga, too.

His cell phone rang. Eddie had programmed it to play a few bars from "God Didn't Make the Little Green Apples." Davis searched out the song. He'd dumped his phone on a table by the back porch door, which was lined in garland and apple ornaments. It lay among work gloves, a box of custom-made koi food courtesy of the Japanese royalty, and a file folder stuffed with Davis's meticulous shipping report on the orders of Sweet Hush apples, apple products, and baked apple goods throughout the fall season. Even though we'd closed the farm two months early, we'd broken all our previous sales records.

Frowning, looking at an apple wall clock where the stem pointed to midnight, he dug the phone out. After several months spent dodging crank calls from strangers and questions from the media, plus guarding new, unlisted numbers the Secret Service set up for every phone in the house except the Sweet Hush Farms business lines, Davis didn't suffer phone in fools lightly. "Davis Thackery speaking. My wife's asleep and it's midnight. Whoever you are, you're calling my private number and this better be important."

"Mr. Thackery," a smug male voice said, "this is Haywood Kenney, calling from Chicago, and I'd say that you may want to wake your wife up. Because, Mr. Thackery, I'm about to tell you a story about her in-laws that she might want to comment on before I put it on the air, nationwide, in the morning. I certainly hope so."

And my son could only stand there, listening in speechless horror, as the lurid details of his father's life spilled out. When Kenney told him Puppy was his half sister, Davis said, "I have to go," laid the phone down, and turned to find Eddie behind him, floating like a soft, pregnant vision in a long flannel nightgown with tiny apples on it, something I'd given her. She stared at him anxiously. "Who's calling? Is everything all right?"

My strong, grown son couldn't bring himself to answer. He sat down in a chair his father had built from apple wood and I'd proudly carved so apples spilled across the lattice of the back — the fruit of his parents' roughly partnered hands — and he put his head in his own hands, and he cried.

JAKOBEK STOOD THERE IN Chattanooga with blood on his mouth, one hand on my shoulder, the other on my son's — who let him offer silent comfort that way, now that blood had been shed and his father had been turned into a tainted ghost. "Where's Eddie?" Jakobek asked quietly.

"On her way to Washington." Misery was written in every inch of Davis's body. "She believes none of this would have happened if she hadn't married me. She blames herself for the public exposure of my family's secrets."

"Go after your wife," I said.

"Believe me, I am. As soon as I get some answers from you." He swayed. "Did you love Dad? Or was that all just a lie, too?"

To have your son say something like that to you is a small death inside you. I hugged myself, pulling my heart into a tight, numb block. "It was no lie. I did love him."

"You wouldn't let anyone so much as steal an apple from you, *but you let Dad screw other women?*"

"There were years when he reformed, and years when I needed him. And years when we slept on opposite sides of a king-size bed and never so much as touched by accident. Do you think marriage is simple? Do you think there's an *easy* explanation for any of this? Marriage isn't something you do just because you love someone. Or even if you don't. Your father and I were never meant to be together, but we became partners. We became *parents*. We didn't have to be happy together. We just had to raise a son who could count on us to be there for him. And we did."

"You could have told me! There were so many times when I wondered why you didn't go with him on the race circuit, and why I never saw the two of you hold hands or kiss. I thought you were . . . dignified. God."

"Your father wanted you to grow up with two parents in the house just as much as I did. He and Smooch got hurt so badly as children; your father knew how it felt to be a kid with no real home and no parents to depend on. And I knew how that felt, too, in my own way, losing my father young, and then my mother when I was barely grown. Would you have been happier if you'd grown up with divorced parents like half the other kids your age? Would you have been happier growing up with parents who fought in front of you and a father you only visited according to some schedule set by a judge?"

"There's a lot more to the issue than that. How could you justify not telling me about Puppy! You would have let me go on not knowing I have a *sister*. I had a right to know that. *She* had a right to know I'm her brother."

"I made the best decision I could at the time."

"Because Dad wanted to raise her but keep her identity secret out of respect for you and me? Because he wanted to take responsibility?" Davis looked desperately hopeful. I hesitated, searching for the right words. That silence gave me away. Davis groaned. "Dammit."

"I'm sorry. But *I* wanted her. And your uncle Logan wanted her. She's loved and wanted and she has a good life, Davis, but now she has to be told that Logan isn't her father and that her real mother gave her up for adoption. Would I do anything different if I could keep her and you from learning about all that? *No*. I wouldn't change one damned thing. You turned out fine and God help me, if what I did made you the man you are today, then I can't swear to you I'd go back and make different choices. Look at you—you're smart and thoughtful and you know how to love well and you married a great, smart young woman—"

Davis exploded. "Don't you understand? Yes, I married Eddie because I *love* her. Because I wanted the romance my parents had. What am I supposed to tell her now? That everything I based my ideals on was an act you and Dad made up to lie to the rest of the world—including *me*?"

"You tell her you were raised *right*. You tell her the whole point was to teach you to expect better than your own parents had. You tell her you married her for love and respect and partnership because we taught you to. Those things are *real*, Davis. Whether your father and I practiced what we preached or not, what we *preached* was the *truth*." I reached for him. He held up a hand and stepped back. Tears still streaked his face, and mine. I moaned. "Do you really *hate* me?"

The wind seemed to rise on those words. Jakobek tightened his grip on my shoulder, warning me. Davis swung a hand at the cold breeze, staggered, then made an ugly, broken sound. "Right now, Mother, I don't know how I feel about you."

He turned and walked away. My legs folded and I sat down on the pathway of the inn, with only Jakobek's quick hold on my blouse collar to slow me down. I watched my son throw himself into the farm truck he'd driven. I watched him disappear up a Chattanooga street lined with handsome winter trees that seemed to toss their branches in the opposite direction of home.

Jakobek dropped to his heels beside me. "Come on. I'll help you get inside." He pulled me to my feet and guided me to a small couch near a glittering tree of tiny Victorian angels. I sat down and shut my eyes. "What have I *done?*"

Jakobek bent over me, cupped my chin in his hand, and raised my face to his. "You gave your kid a father to love. You gave Puppy a father to love. I never even learned my own old man's name, but all my life I've known he was out there, somewhere, not knowing about me, probably not caring. Trust me. Mothers owe their kids a father. You did the right thing."

"If you really believe that, then follow Davis," I whispered. "Follow him all the way to Washington. Take care of him and Eddie. Try to talk to them. I have to go back to the Hollow and take care of Puppy. *But you take care of my son for me, Jakob.* Please."

"Of course." He spoke with the quiet sadness of a soldier who knows that what he does best is not pretty. "We're a team, re-member?"

I continued to sit without moving, dazed. My hard work, fero-cious pride, and good intentions had failed to keep my family safe. My good stories had been exposed as wishful thinking. My reputation had been peeled away. My legend had been pared down to a rotten core. *My son hated me.* The flesh of my flesh, hating me.

"Mrs. Johnson, is everything all right?" the innkeeper asked.

"My name's Hush McGillen Thackery," I answered. "And as soon as I can remember why that still matters, I'm going home."

IT TOOK EVERYTHING in me to leave Hush there, looking the way she did. Yes, I knew she was the kind of woman who could take care of herself and everyone around her. If I'd tried to take care of her any more than I already had, she'd have told me to get out. She only needed one thing from me, and I respected her choice on that: her son.

I'd go after him and act as his mother's voice until he was ready to listen to Hush himself. In the meantime, I'd tell Eddie she'd married for better or worse, that she was no more to blame for what had happened than anybody else was, and that all the gray areas between trust and loneliness were worth the trouble. I was suddenly an expert on love and marriage.

Not that the realization didn't come too little, too late for me.

AL AND EDWINA WERE packing to leave Washington for Christmas at one of the Habersham homes belonging to Edwina's sisters when the news broke about Kenney's radio program. They got a full briefing from their staff as Kenney went about the business of broadcasting the so-called *sordid* connection between the President's new in-laws and the wife of a big-money Jacobs supporter in Tennessee. "Did you have any inkling of this?" Al asked Edwina.

"I knew Hush was hiding something. I'd done some . . . research. I warned her to tell me the details, so I could help her. She wouldn't."

"Of course she wouldn't!" Al yelled. "I wouldn't either, if someone was spying on me! God, I'm ashamed of you!"

Having Al — her devoted Al — ashamed of her accomplished a rare thing. Edwina, the killer shark of motherhood and politics, the toughest woman I knew except for Hush, burst into tears. Al was so startled he hugged her, but at the same time he said with a no-bullshit-Chicago-butcher's-son voice, "Some things are going to *change* around here."

And she nodded against his chest.

I walked into the White House's family quarters as Al and Edwina met Eddie and Davis at the doors. Edwina's face was puffy but composed, and she opened her arms wide. "Oh, Honey, welcome home. And come here, Davis. It's so wonderful to see you again. I'm so sorry for everything."

She enfolded the very pregnant, very upset Eddie in her arms, then the grim-faced but gallant Davis, while Al frowned and I watched from the sidelines. Davis turned and stared at me like stone. "Mother sent you after me?"

I nodded. "And I'm not going anywhere until you listen. So get used to me."

Eddie protested in a soft voice, "Nicky, this is one problem you can't solve by guarding us."

AT THE HOLLOW, in Dalyrimple, and all through Chocinaw County, news of Haywood Kenney's radio show spread like a fast infection. Smooch was the first on my doorstep, running into the house, her dark hair a wild jumble, a fat blue ski jacket wrapped around her sweater and jeans like a bulky shawl. "We'll sue that bastard for lying about my brother that way! I'm calling a lawyer! Who does he think he *is* — and where did he get such a pack of lies! My brother may have been wild when he was young, but to claim he had other women after he married you . . . and this Abbie . . . claiming Puppy is my brother's baby . . ."

Her voice trailed off. She stared at me. I stood in the middle of the kitchen floor, barefoot, my hair tangled worse than hers. I was dressed in old jeans and a sweatshirt, a wad of Christmas garland in my clammy hands. Don't ask me why I was putting up more decorations in a house already covered from roof to basement in holiday finery. I only knew I had to keep moving and stay focused on any small chore I could find.

"I left you a message," I said. "And I've called Logan. He'll be here soon. With Puppy. We have to find some way to tell her what's happening."

Smooch dropped her coat on the floor, leaned heavily on a kitchen chair, then sat down slowly as I grabbed her by the arm and helped her. She never took her eyes off me. "Are you saying—Hush, are you telling me that what that man says about Davy, that it's *true?*"

I sat down beside her and tried to hug her. "I'm sorry."

She turned away from me, burrowed her head on her arms atop the harvest table she had given Davy and me as our tenth anniversary present, and sobbed. "Y'all were my role models. All these years I've been looking for a man to marry who met the standards you and Davy set. Do you know how many men I've turned down because I wanted the perfect marriage, like you and my brother?"

"I'm sorry. You don't know how sorry I am."

"It was all a fairy tale!"

"I wish," I said, "life was that simple."

An hour later, I had Puppy crying, too. And Logan. And me. And Smooch again, who hovered around us like a churchyard wraith, wringing her hands and moaning. Logan sat there at a loss for words so deep he could only let tears run down his face. "Baby," he said hoarsely, watching Puppy huddle in my arms, "it's okay."

"But I don't *want* a new daddy," Puppy sobbed. "And how can I have a mama named Abbie when my mama is supposed to be in *heaven in Germany?*" She raced upstairs with Smooch close behind, heading for the small, pink, pretty bedroom I'd made for her so lovingly in her father's house. Logan and I heard the door slam. His big shoulders slumped. Dressed in his sheriff's uniform, with his hat lying on the floor between his big, solid feet, he bent his head and said nothing, wiping his eyes. I sat down beside him, crying so hard I couldn't speak either. I draped an arm around his shoulders. "Bubba Logan," I said finally. "Bubba Logan, I'm so sorry."

"Before—" he struggled for a moment—"before Lucille left with Eddie, she said it'll be more than a one-man job to get Puppy through this. What do you think she meant by that, Sis?"

I stared at him. "She means she loves you and Puppy and she wants to come back here and take care of you both. All you have to do is ask her."

He pondered this revelation for a good minute. "Thank God," he finally said.

I had done a little good at least.

But then, there was the rest of my family to deal with. Strange and wondrous people, those McGillens and Thackerys. Except for Aaron and his crowd, my relatives showed up without calling, without asking, without judgment. Over forty of them gathered around me in my kitchen, packed in like seeds, waiting. I stood at the head of my table. "I used to tell myself that what kind of marriage Davy and I had behind closed doors was nobody's business but ours. I used to think we were doing our son—and our family—a favor by putting on a big show of happiness. Y'all came to depend on that image of us so much. This farm depended on it, too. The business. Every time I set up a deal with a fruit wholesaler or grocery-chain buyer—especially in the early years, when everyone outside Chocinaw County said I'd never make the Hollow's orchards pay again—I'd think, *If they smell any weakness on me, these businessmen will say, 'She's just a gal who can't even hold up her own household,' and turn their backs.* I couldn't let those men, or anybody else, suspect that Davy and I weren't really a team.

"So I put on a show. And Davy did, too. He wanted you all to think we were a perfect couple. Your respect was important to him. Our son's respect was important to him. He lived for that. I

286

want you to know that . . . he always tried his best to do the right thing by me and by Davis, and when he found out he was going to be a father to another woman's child, he . . . did the right thing then, too."

All right, I lied on that count, unless you took it to mean that by killing himself, Davy had been honorable. A good story. A gift to Davy. And to Davis. And to Puppy. "He did the right thing for his baby girl. Puppy is Davy's daughter by default, yes she is, but that doesn't matter. She's part of this family, and he intended to honor that. And I know he'd tell you to honor that, too, in his memory."

I paused, working hard not to cry. They'd seen me cry so rarely over the years that I thought it might scare them. Then, "Look, I'll understand if some of you don't want to work for me any-more. I can't abide a liar — can't abide myself, right now. There'll be no hard feelings toward any one of you who doesn't want to be associated with me."

Gruncle squinted at me with eyes like dark, cool marbles bur-rowed in crinkled paper. "Oh, hold off the pity talk. We know the score. Davy was a show-off and a big talker and a ladies' man and a racetrack hero. Yes, he was a good daddy and a strong friend and a good enough husband to play-act with you, for your sake and the sake of his son. But if you think we all didn't *know* you were holding up his reputation without much help from him, then you must think we all were just blind."

"You knew . . . what?"

"God love him, we knew he was weak to the core. That's what we knew. He decided when he was a kid that he was mad at the whole world and could charm the whole world and the world owed him a free pass. I watched him struggle with his own nature over the years. I always knew you and Davis were the glue hold-ing that effort together for him, and I figured any time he wasn't here in this Hollow with you and Davis, well, that he let the worst side of his nature get the best of him."

Everyone nodded. But deep in the crowd, Smooch covered her

face and cried, while several Thackerys and McGillens hugged her or patted her. The truth settled in me. I could feel the weight of it shift from my head down to my heart, making me light enough to sway but too heavy to fall. Balanced, maybe. I had my family's sympathy, but it came at the price of my pride. All those years I'd thought Davy and I had everyone fooled. No.

Sad and empty and lost without that armor of assumptions around me, I said, "Well, there's not much else to discuss then. I appreciate y'all's support. Excuse me now, I have to go see if I can get Davis on the phone. Try to talk some of the anger out of him."

Gruncle frowned. "You gonna try to get him and Eddie back here full time?"

"I don't expect to, no."

"Then what about Jakobek? We got used to him."

"He was here for Eddie's sake. I don't know." I sagged a little. "I don't expect him back."

"At least you could depend on my brother to *always* come back," Smooch said loudly. Angry, flushed, she looked around at our relatives as if betrayed. "Maybe he wasn't all that we wanted him to be. *But he kept trying.* That's what marriage is really about—partners who stick around and keep trying to make it work. I threw away chances at happiness because you sold *me* a fantasy, Hush." She looked at me with more sorrow than anything else. "I'm leaving this place. I quit."

People moaned and said things like *Now, that's just talk*, and shook their heads, but I didn't doubt her. "Smoochie, your job will be waiting if you change your mind, and please do."

"I'm sorry, but I won't."

She burrowed her way through the crowd and disappeared. The sound of the front door slamming behind her made my bones crack together. Everyone sighed and made small, crying sounds, but spoke not one word. It was one of those moments when no one wants to say *anything* else; they just want to get as far away as they can from the sadness. I sat down at the table, staring at my hands on the heavy, polished wood while the whole crowd eased out of my house.

When I finally looked up, I was all alone.

CHRISTMAS CAME IN Washington. I called Hush with a daily report—brief, five minutes, nothing personal. She was hanging on by her fingertips and didn't want sentimentality to gum up her effort. I understood but still had to fight an urge to call her every hour—and *talk* for an hour. Strange urge for a man who had never been a talker before. Soldiers with no war to fight are speechless; soldiers, put in tame times, armed only with words, are silent and invisible. Wanting to talk was my punishment for all the shut-up years I'd lived. I was doomed to be a soldier, a loner, an unspeaking human eyeglass looking into the dark, waiting.

She might not know it, but she was waiting with me.

CHRISTMAS. I SAT IN the living room all day before a cold fireplace, listening to the answering machine pick up. My relatives kept calling, asking how I was. They wanted to visit. We usually held big Christmases at the Hollow, but not that year. Finally, I put a message on the phone.

Nothing to report. I just need to think. Merry Christmas.

I waited for Jakobek's daily call. When it came, I wrapped one arm around my head and burrowed on a corner of the couch with my legs drawn up and the phone tight against my ear. Jakobek's plain and deep voice, penetrating far down inside the baby curl I made of myself, kept me going. He admitted Davis hadn't softened but said he, Jakobek, would not give up. He was at my service. He was with me in spirit.

I wanted him to talk to me forever.

"EDDIE? COLONEL? I just resigned from the Service. I've come to say good-bye." The day after Christmas, Lucille stood in a hallway of the family quarters, carrying a flowered luggage bag. Flowered. "I'm going back to Georgia. I've got an interview with the GBI. As a field agent maybe. Sheriff McGillen put in a word with the bureau for me."

Eddie looked from her to me with shock. "Nicky, did you know about this?" I nodded. Eddie turned to Lucille. "Why are you quitting? Whatever the problem is, I'll talk to your bosses on your behalf. You can't leave me. I think of you as . . . Lucille, *why?*"

"Let me ask you first — why are you happy to be here, instead of at the Hollow? After all you went through to get there and prove a point about how you intend to live your life?"

"I proved that point. Now I have to take responsibility for the damage I've done. I don't belong at the Hollow — not as a person just hiding out there. I only brought the wrong kind of attention to it. I realize that now. Davis and I are partners. We can live anywhere. Be safe anywhere. We're . . . we're turtles. And we listen to the apple trees for advice." She paused. "Don't try to understand. I'm quoting Hush's philosophy."

Lucille smiled. "Good. You've got so many dedicated people looking out for your well-being. And you've got a husband who loves you, looking out for you. I'm convinced of that now. So, there's a . . . a time when it's time to move on." She paused, then said gruffly, "Sheriff McGillen needs me. His daughter needs me." Her voice became gentle. "I have another girl to look after, you see?"

"Oh, Lucille." Eddie hugged the tall, brawny blonde. "What I started to say was this: *I think of you as a sister.*"

"Then I've served your purpose and mine, too." Lucille backed away, clearing her throat, sniffing away tears. "I need a moment to speak to the Colonel, please."

Eddie nodded and left us alone. Lucille held out a hand. We shook warmly before she laid her message on the line: "Colonel,

290

people like you and me need to find a good purpose and a good home, or we'll just wander in the dark all our lives. We need to understand where we're needed most — and who *we* need the most." She stared at me pointedly. "And then we need to have the guts to say so. I've done it. You can, too."

"Saying it is one thing. Being afraid it won't be said back is another." I shook her hand and let it go at that.

COURAGE AND CHOICES and lost chances. I thought about all three when I took a walk in the city that afternoon. "No, thanks," I said to the Secret Service agents who dutifully offered to trail me, then ducked out through a guard gate. I was tall and obvious in some ways, but just another man alone in others — old khakis, a heavy shirt, my apple-red Sweet Hush Farms employee pin tacked inside the lapel of a long gray overcoat, my secret. I shoved my hands in the overcoat's pockets and, head down, tried to walk off the past, the present, the future.

I think I covered most of the city on that bright, cold December afternoon. I walked in the shadows of the monuments and the Capitol building; glimpsed my own frown in the windows of small shops; jaywalked through the city's dangerous, spokes-on-a-wheel intersections; filled myself with the cold scent of the Potomac, flowing to the Atlantic.

A chant began to cycle through my mind.

God, country, apple pie.

Hush.

Late in the day I looked up from tracking the rhythm of my own shoes on the sidewalks, and I halted, surprised. I'd made my way back where I started. The White House made its famous cameo behind the famous fences that fronted the famous lawn and the famous avenue with its huge concrete planters and other security blockades disguised as ornaments, its lanes shut down to vehicle traffic, its sidewalks barely hospitable to visitors, under the eyes of guards and cameras. Al had a grim habit of telling historical anecdotes about the White House — how in the early 1900s the public came to picnic on the lawns every week.

"What will it take to return the world to that state of grace?" he liked to ask.

"A time machine," I liked to answer.

I never told him the barricades and fences and armed guards at the gates bothered me, too. I was a soldier — a hard-ass, hard-line, guards-and-barricade-loving, take-no-prisoners American samurai. I wasn't supposed to be bothered by the symbols of protection — or the fear that inspired them. But I was.

I nodded to the guards at the gatehouse. They nodded back and prepared to let me through. But I lingered on the sidewalk, frowning at a crowd of tourists milling in front of the high, ornate fences, snapping pictures. They gazed lovingly at the country's symbolic home, behind bars.

"We should plant some more public lawns around here," I said to the guards. "And I think it would be nice to put some apple trees in those big planters."

"Colonel?"

"Apple trees. Apples. The all-American fruit. Apples are welcoming. Apples mean home and family. People would appreciate the idea of them."

They traded cautious looks. "Is everything all right, Sir?"

No, *nothing* was all right.

The thing in the dark, looking back at me, had finally arrived.

The hair rose on the back of my neck one second before I spotted him. He was a huge, sloppy man, maybe four hundred pounds, and a good six inches taller than me — a hulk in baggy camo pants and an old Army jacket he'd cut apart and spliced with brown material to make it several sizes too big, even for him. Dark, dirty hair straggled over his shoulders. Greasy black stubble didn't help his look. His expression was angry, hurt, confused. His eyes had the kind of sweaty stare no one wants to face.

Maybe a veteran, I thought. *Not old enough to claim Vietnam, but could be the Gulf War.* Or maybe he was just a miserable, fucked-up bastard who'd been through wars in his own mind. He waved his arms suddenly, scattering a flock of startled tourists. Then he threw back his head and yelled at the sky.

"I'm going to blow up this goddamned fence. I'm going to walk onto my property and go into my house and see the President! I have a right! I have the power! I don't want to hurt anybody! Everybody get away! Look." He opened the jacket and turned in a circle. His belly was wrapped in packets that could be high-tech explosives or a few pounds of harmless potter's clay stuffed into sandwich bags.

The tourists screamed and ran.

"Stay away!" he yelled at the guards. "I've got this, too!"

He shook his right arm. A long butcher knife slid out of the Army jacket's dirty, patched sleeve. He caught the handle in a palm the size of a dinner saucer, then held the long knife up. His hand trembled. "Stay away, and you won't get hurt," he bellowed toward the guards and me. Our eyes met. His filled with tears. "Stay away," he moaned.

He's not threatening us, I thought, as my skin slowly tightened with his pain. *The poor fucker is trying to protect us from himself.*

Behind me, the guards pulled their guns and began radioing for assistance. I knew what was about to happen. They'd tell him to drop the knife, and when he didn't, they'd wound him with a bullet to the legs. If he was too drugged, too psychotic, or just too stubborn to go down for his own good, they'd shoot him again. And they'd kill him.

No.

I slowly walked toward him. The guards went ape-shit. "Colonel, Sir, Sir! Come back, Sir! Sir!" I held up a hand for quiet as I stepped over the boundary between the light and the dark, into the shadows that had swallowed the huge, desperate human soul staring back at me. "What do you think you're doing, Man?" he yelled. His voice broke.

"You talk. I'll listen."

He stared at me for a good minute, then waved the knife

wearily and began to tell me stories. Slowly at first, then faster. Words gushed out of him. Part of my brain tuned into the sirens in the distance, the tense conversations of the guards behind me, the scuffle of feet as both uniformed and plainclothes Secret Service agents took up places on the street with the soft stealth of hunters. If he made one wrong move, he'd die.

No. I wouldn't let him.

Not much of what he said made sense — he offered no profound ideas or hints of genius, no clues to who he was or what had brought him there to commit public suicide. Just misery and confusion and bitterness and fear. The faceless things that lived in the darkness with him, with me, with us all. He was the soul behind every human being I'd killed in battle, right or wrong. He was the stalker in Chicago. He was the father I'd never know, the brothers I might have, somewhere. Part of him was Davy Thackery, and part of him was me.

He was death. And he was redemption.

Finally his voice dropped off in a groan, and he began to sob. "How are we supposed to know what to do, Man? I came here to ask the *President*. He knows. He's *got* to know."

"I can tell you what he'd say. He said it to me once, when I was lost." I eased up to him. "*Let's go home.*"

"Home." His shoulders sagged. A sigh of relief came out of him. The hand holding the knife dropped loosely to his side. "Okay, Man." It was that simple.

I put one hand on his shoulder to keep him still as I reached for the knife. His head jerked up as one of the guards made a sudden move. His eyes shifted wildly toward the motion. His knife hand moved with a convulsive swing.

"*Down,*" I ordered. I tackled him low around the bulk of the explosives. He stumbled and fell, with me on top of him. The knife came up with uncanny precision. I wasn't sure I'd been stabbed in the chest until I began to gasp for air and realized the blood soaking his Army jacket was mine. He lifted his head, saw what he'd done, and moaned. "I'm sorry."

My vision began to cloud. I put a hand on his head, protecting him.

"Hush," I whispered.

"Okay," he whispered back, misunderstanding but getting the point. He stopped struggling. So did I.

Hush.

NINETEEN

I sat with Puppy in a big rocking chair on the back porch, holding her against the cold afternoon air. I'd wrapped a warm afghan around us; apples marched along the weave. She burrowed her head into the crook of my neck and I rocked her, kissing her dark, Thackery hair. "Tell me again who I am," she said in a small voice.

"You are the *sixth* Hush McGillen, and the *second* Hush McGillen Thackery," I whispered. "That makes you very special, and that's all that matters."

"Are you sure?"

"Yes, Honey, I'm absolutely certain. People are born to be whoever they want to be. It's all in how you tell your own story."

We heard footsteps. I set her down and she ran through the house to the front foyer, with me following anxiously. When she saw Logan and Lucille, she halted. Logan looked down at her with red-rimmed eyes. "How's my baby after talking to Aunt Hush?"

"I'm still the sixth Hush McGillen, Daddy."

"Absolutely."

"But I'm a Thackery, too. But I don't have to change my name. Names are just the stem on the apple. They hold it on the family tree, that's all."

"That's right, Baby. That's the whole point, Baby. Yes. You're Hush McGillen. You're my Hush Puppy."

"And it's okay for Davis to be my big brother."

"That's right. It's fine."

"He sent me this heart by special delivery." She lifted a tiny, gold, heart-shaped pendant. "And he called me on the phone and said he's glad I'm his sister."

"He's a good big brother."

"You sure you still want to be my daddy?"

"Yes, Ma'am. Always. Now and forever."

"Good!" Puppy launched herself at Logan, and he swung her into his arms and held her like mad. Crying, she hugged Logan's neck and reached out urgently to touch Lucille's damp face. "Lucy Bee! You're in the *Secret* Service. You never cry!"

"I'm not in the Secret Service anymore. I'm out in the open now."

Her expression fell. "Are you crying because I'm going to see Abbie? Because you know she's my mama?"

"I'm not crying because you have a mama. I think it's wonderful that you're going to meet your mama and get to know her."

"But then I'm going to come right back home with Daddy."

"Absolutely."

"Aunt Hush says I can pick any mama I want to. I can have more than one."

"You bet."

"So I need a mama *here*, too." Puppy gulped back tears. "Do you want to be it?"

"Yes! Oh, *yes*, Puppy. I'd be so honored."

"Okay." Puppy placed the palm of her hand on Lucille's hair as if christening her. "I name you—" she whispered—"Lucille the Number-One Mama."

Lucille dissolved into stalwart, unblinking tears. Logan put his arm around her solidly, and she stood at attention beside him, then submerged herself in his bear hug, engulfed by his arms, with him and Puppy inside hers.

I wiped my own eyes and left them alone with their moment. I walked out on the back porch and gazed at the old orchard, a winter scene of dormant life. I could just make out the silhouette of the Great Lady tree. She whispered to me. *See what strong roots you've set, and how these trees of yours stand strong together.*

I nodded. Puppy would have more questions as she grew up, some of them painful, but she'd be all right. She'd be all right because I'd planted her where she belonged. If only Davis could feel that way, too.

And Jakobek.

My cell phone sang, lost somewhere in one of the porch's flowerpots beneath a mixture of mulch and pinecones sprayed gold for Christmas. I shuffled the golden cones aside with slow hands, raised the phone to my ear, and leaned on a porch rail, a tired old woman at only forty.

"Hello?"

"Mother."

My son's somber voice drew me up straight and young again. "Davis! I'm so glad you called—"

"It's about Jakobek," he said.

JAKOBEK WAS STILL IN the recovery room when I arrived at the hospital in Washington that night. He had suffered a punctured lung and tremendous blood loss from two arteries the knife had sliced. He was lucky to be alive, the doctors said after surgery.

"Alive," I whispered, and leaned against a wall. "Alive."

The Secret Service controlled all access to that wing of the hospital. I'd gotten to the surgical floor, but they wouldn't let me see him. "We have orders from Mrs. Jacobs to keep everyone out of the recovery room," they said politely.

Edwina.

Al was in China for more trade talks, so Edwina had commandeered Jakobek's situation and was with him in the recovery room along with some of the Jacobses' relatives and a priest — that last news nearly folded my legs until I learned the priest was a family friend just leading a prayer for Jakobek's swift recovery.

I made my way down a corridor, searching for a water fountain. I turned a corner, and Davis met me. We stared at each other sadly, mother to son, son to mother. "I'm glad he's going to be all right," Davis said. "I mean it."

"Good. How are you?"

"I have a question. When you hurt your arm and Dad took you to the emergency room, was it really an accident?"

"Oh, Davis."

He shut his eyes, exhaled, then opened them with a hard, new gleam in the irises. A shiver went up my spine. I watched my son age into true manhood, with all its tempered joys and accepted disappointments. "Everyone's saying the Colonel is a hero."

"I agree."

"But nobody understands why he did what he did. He didn't have to risk his life to talk a stranger into surrendering."

"Yes, he did. Jakobek has instincts about good and evil. Oh, don't look at me that way; I know it's not sophisticated to say there's evil in the world, but there is, and Jakobek recognizes it. He saw that that poor fool was no threat to anybody else, and that there was nothing evil in him. If there's one thing Jakobek believes in, it's justice. There wouldn't have been any justice in letting armed guards shoot a crazy man."

"Then I guess Jakobek really is a hero."

"I doubt he'd use that word about himself."

"Mother . . . from the moment I met Jakobek, I felt he was *real* in a way that Dad hadn't been. I couldn't put that feeling into words at the time. Maybe it was watching your reaction to him, the way you looked at him, the way you trusted his opinion. Now I realize why your relationship with him bothered me so much." Davis cleared his throat. "Because I could never recall you being that trusting with Dad."

"I don't want you to hate your father. He came from a hard beginning, and he was wired for trouble long before you were born. It's a testament to something grand in the scheme of things that he made so much effort to be a good father to you."

"A good father doesn't abandon his other child."

"He didn't abandon Puppy; he just didn't live long enough to do right by her." A small lie, but still. All right, I'd never entirely give up a certain inclination to tell the best story rather than the truth, if need be.

"You really believe that?"

"Yes."

"I'm going to do my best to be a good husband and a good father and a good *man*," he told me. "Eddie and I are going back to Harvard in the spring. Her mother has offered to rent a house off campus for us. With a staff. Bodyguards. We've decided to accept the offer. Do you mind?"

"I'm all for anything that gets you and Eddie back to college."

"Someday, I'll come home. But I have to find out who I am, and I have to make peace with who Dad was. I'll come home when I'm my own man."

"The Hollow and I will be waiting with open arms."

He only nodded. There was a distance between us, a sad coolness, and it would take years to build a new bridge over it. At least we'd started. Part of me wanted to thank Edwina for greasing the path for him and Eddie to go back to college in prosperous security after their baby was born, but part of me wanted to hate her for giving my son more help than I could. And part of me said, *Shut up and accept what's best for him.*

He returned to the White House that night with my blessing. Eddie was under an obstetrician's orders to rest after the upset of hearing that her beloved Nicky had been stabbed. She sent me a sweet note. *Take care of him, please, the way he has always tried to take care of us.* I was supposed to tell one of Edwina's minions to take me to the White House whenever I was ready to sleep. Sleeping in the White House, as a guest of Edwina Jacobs, First Lady of these United States, including Chocinaw County. Hush McGillen Thackery. Edwina's guest.

I would rather eat dirt and shit roots first.

"I want to see the Colonel," I kept saying to everyone in sight. "We're friends. And he's family."

"We have orders," I continued to hear.

"The President doesn't know what's going on here," I countered, "or he'd be mad as hell."

No one spoke up to deny that. They went quiet and looked the other way. Finally I was assigned to a nice young woman on Edwina's staff, who led me to an elevator that would take me up to Jakobek's private room. But Secret Service agents stopped us at the elevator doors. "Mrs. Thackery still isn't on the First Lady's list to be admitted."

The young aide blushed. "There must be some mistake." She went around a corner to place a phone call in private. When she returned she wouldn't meet my eyes. "Mrs. Jacobs says the Colonel is under sedation and sleeping soundly now that he's out of the recovery room. She believes it's best that he not be disturbed tonight. Mrs. Thackery, I'm sorry. Mrs. Jacobs says you're welcome to visit him tomorrow."

I paced. The aide twisted her hands and apologized repeatedly. After I got myself under control, I said, "You go upstairs, Honey, and you tell Edwina that I'm going to sit in the waiting room down the hall here all night, and I want her *to think* about that. I want her to *consider* the fact that every hour I don't get to see Nick Jakobek moves her one notch higher on my shit list, *and so by morning she'll be right up at the top.*"

The aide blanched. "I'll relay the message, Ma'am."

"You do that, please."

I spent the night in the waiting room. Too much pride kept me from calling my own son, at the White House, and asking for help.

THE NEXT MORNING I still didn't get to see Jakobek. Al was flying in from overseas; the media was all over the story of Jakobek's heroism, and the hospital floor where I sat was swarming with even more Secret Service. They sent two agents to get me. "Mrs. Jacobs wants to see you, Ma'am, at the White House."

"I'm not leaving *here* until I see *the Colonel.*"

"Mrs. Jacobs says she'd like to speak with you first. If you'll agree to that, she says she'll permit you to visit the Colonel."

Stalemate. I was grinding my teeth, swallowing my own bile. "Take me to the White House, then. Fast."

On my wristwatch, the stem of a flat gold apple clicked over to a new hour. Edwina had officially reached the top of my list.

THE FIRST THING I noticed, after I was escorted like a criminal under guard through the White House and into Edwina's mauve-and-eggshell, country-French office, was that she kept two rotten apples inside a crystal cookie jar on her bookshelf. Two Sweet Hush apples. She'd plucked them from the loads I'd brought to the White House back in the fall.

She set the cookie jar on her desk like a sacred urn filled with poison and magic. "I kept these apples of yours to remind me that one day they'd be nothing but a dehydrated pile of organic debris," she said. "Apple molecules. That's all. I reduced you, in my mind, to nothing but that, too. Because the thing that has antagonized me the most about you is your absolute courage in the face of adversity. I'm afraid I lost that courage twenty years ago."

"You? You're the bravest woman I've met."

"It takes very little bravery to turn into a sarcastic, controlling bitch. I'm well aware of what I've become. And none too fond of it." She lifted the jar's lid, set it aside, then reached inside and gingerly picked up the pair of soft, brown, wrinkling, rotten apples. She examined them for a moment, then laid them carefully on her desk. "Unfortunately, it appears neither you nor your son *nor* your apples are going to dry up and blow away, so I've *welcomed* your son and will do all I can to make him adore me, Al, and our entire family. He's quite a fine young man, actually. I'm going to enjoy winning his respect and support. Who knows? He may feel far more at home in *my* family than in his own. He has a great deal in common with us, I suspect. Intelligence, education. A sophisticated worldview."

"You can't scare me with these voodoo-mama threats. I've been through the fires of hell with my son. We're welded like steel."

She stiffened. "Why shouldn't I threaten you the way you've threatened me? *You stole my daughter*. You *never* seriously encouraged her to mend the break with her father and me."

"That's a lie, and you know it. You betrayed her trust and she surprised you by being just as stubborn as you are. You don't want to admit you screwed up. Being a mother means half the time we apologize for doing the wrong thing and the other half we spend doing the wrong thing again. You need to get the equation right."

"You practically turned her into a hillbilly. She came home with overalls packed in her luggage. She's developed a fondness for country music and apple fritters. She adores you. You're brilliant, kind, strong, generous. 'Hush does this and Hush says that' is all

I've heard since she returned. *You owe me.* I want my daughter's affection back."

"I want my *son's* back. It'll take time, but I'll get it. Along the way I want you and yours to let go of Nick Jakobek's soul, too. *You're* the ones who nearly got him killed yesterday."

"*What* are you talking about? *You* marooned his soul in your little *apple heaven*. After a few months in your company, he's obviously developed a death wish. Why else would he walk up to a human bomb? If there'd been innocent bystanders to protect, I'd understand. But there weren't."

"Yes, there *were*. That pathetic crazy man, for one. And Jakobek, for another. Both of them—innocent bystanders in the dark, cold pit of the ugliest urges of humanity. If Jakobek let the guards kill that man, he'd have been guilty as charged—a cold-blooded killer, just like people whisper. You've always thought of him that way *yourself,* so don't tell me—"

"Thought of Nicholas as a cold-blooded killer? Have you lost your mind? What the hell are you talking about *now?*"

"In Chicago. When he killed the man in front of you. The look he saw on your face—you were never the same with him after that—you were afraid of him."

"My God. That's what he thought?" She sank down on the corner of the desk, a hand rising to her throat. "I was afraid of the entire *world* at that moment, not of him."

"He didn't know that. He felt like he was everything evil in the world then. Especially after Al made a big deal out of calling it self-defense. He thought Al was ashamed of him."

"My God. Nicholas."

"I haven't taken anything away from him or made him want to give up his life or his common sense. I've just . . . *listened* to him. Maybe no one really gave him the opportunity to talk before, or maybe he trusts me in some way he's never trusted anybody else. Because I don't judge him. *I love him.*"

She stared at me. "You what?"

"Don't worry. I have no idea if he loves *me,* or even if the idea of staying with me and two hundred acres of apple trees and a pack of cranky relatives and my beat-up reputation makes any sense to him."

She stood. "I assure you, Nicholas is *not* cut out to be an apple farmer." Edwina clamped her lips together and gazed into thin air, distracted, frowning. I felt dismissed. I felt insulted. I felt she was probably right about him not wanting to live with me and my apples. But I also felt the time had come to let my fruit make the ultimate statement. *There is a time to fight,* the Great Lady whispered.

I picked up a rotten apple off Edwina's desk. "Edwina," I said evenly, "you need to be ceremoniously christened with the essence of the McGillen family tree." I slung the apple. Gooey, brown, stinking Sweet Hush apple rot spread across her perfect, pale, cashmere-scarved business suit.

She didn't even blink. A tough mother. How I admired her. She snatched up the other apple, drew back an arm, and let me have it across the front of my blazer.

"Same to *you,*" she said.

And then we both looked horrified, as women are trained to do after they've been brutally honest.

And I left.

HE WAS SO PALE, so quiet. I sat close beside Jakobek's bed, watching him sleep in the drugged way of an injured animal, him not even knowing I was there. I cried quiet tears and held his left hand, the damaged one. "An old preacher told me once that the right hand of God commands all that's good and the left hand smites all that's wicked," I whispered. "But I say you've used this hand and your life and your heart and your soul to do good *and* smite what's wicked." I placed a small crucifix of apple wood into his palm, then wrapped the necklace chain around his wrist so he wouldn't lose the talisman. "Jakob, if you can hear me, believe me. *You've earned your blessings.*"

Al came into the room not long after that, and I told him I'd hit Edwina with the apple, and he said she probably deserved it. I never spoke a word about the night before or anything else that had passed between her and me, but he shook my hand and said with a grim gleam in his eyes, "I promise you, this atmosphere of confrontation will not continue. I adore my wife, and I understand her motives, but I do apologize for her behavior."

"Don't apologize. I have to admit something to you. She's tough, she's smart, she doesn't give up. If she ran for President, I'd vote for her."

He smiled. "Instead of me?"

"Maybe you could be her Vice President."

"That's a diplomat's answer."

"Oh? Then you got the last drop of my diplomacy for today." I gave Jakobek a long, painful look. I could feel Al watching me.

"You love my nephew very much," he said.

I nodded miserably. Al put a consoling hand on my shoulder. "Then why not just tell him?"

"On top of everything he's been through, he doesn't need to wake up and see me meowing over him like a cat who's waiting outside the door for him to let me in. If I stay here, that's exactly how I'll behave. I'll embarrass myself and maybe him, too. No, if he wakes up and says he needs me, you tell him I'll come running. If not . . . well." My throat closed. "Well."

Al insisted a Secret Service agent drive me to the airport, but I said no, and so his staff called an ordinary cab for me. Fine. I ought to get back to living my ordinary life and try to remember not only who I had been, but who I should be next. So I sat in the backseat of a smelly city cab, speeding through the countryside, feeling lost and alone. I wanted to turn in the seat and gaze out the back window as the hospital with Jakobek in it faded from view. But I could only go home, start tilling the torn-up winter earth of my life, and wait for spring.

The cab driver turned up his radio. "I'm hoping you don't mind the loudness," he called over his shoulder in a lilting Caribbean accent. "I always listen to Haywood Kenney. He is *the Man*."

Kenney's smarmy voice curled out of the radio from its high, smug origins in his radio studio atop a Chicago office building. "So Al Jacobs's killer nephew pulled this idiotic John Wayne act yesterday," Kenney was saying, "like some kind of dumb-Polack Superman — God, he could have provoked that goofball to blow up a lot of taxpayer property! Too bad the goofball *and* Mad Dog Jakobek didn't end up splattered all over the concrete, if you ask me. . . ."

I pulled out my cell phone and made a call. I hadn't yet caused myself enough trouble for the day.

"I'd like to change my plane ticket," I said. "I want to go to Chicago."

IF YOU ASK ME, I was fated to do what I did. Asia Makumba, in Atlanta, returned my phone call with exactly the information I needed. Media people knew all the trivia about each other. "He lunches at a restaurant called Hallowden's after his show every day," Asia reported. "May I ask what you're planning to *do* to him?"

"Give him a dose of his own medicine."

I walked into the swank eatery that afternoon, and stopped cold at the sight of a huge stone vase on a table by the entrance. It was filled with bare limbs and twigs. I swear to God, they looked just like branches off an apple tree.

I put one hand to my heart in awe. With the other, I broke off a three-foot swath of hard, whip-thin boughs. "Ma'am!" the hostess shrieked. "That's an expensive decorator arrangement —"

"Send the repair bill to Sweet Hush Farms, Chocinaw County, Georgia." I laid a business card on her hostess podium. "And when the reporters ask you about me, you can tell them my phone number and address, too. If everything about my life is public news now, then I intend to make that news work *for* me and the people I love."

I nodded to her and strode past into a crowded, darkly paneled bar with leather couches and billiard tables and the sweet hint of fine cigar smoke and old brandy. It was cocktail time and the place had filled with people, mostly well-dressed businessmen. As I angled between the plush chairs, I bumped against their shoulders, rattled their scotches, and began to draw attention. "Ma'am? Ma'am!" the hostess called, but I'd already shut out her and all other distractions. I was on a hunting trip.

I quickly found my prey.

Haywood Kenney was never handsome, even in his doctored publicity pictures, but in person he looked like he needed embalming—him and his five-thousand-dollar suits and solid-gold collar pins and Italian leather suspenders and his forty-dollar cigars and his trashy radio show, too. He sat among a group of his fat-cat toadies in a step-up alcove that had VIP Table written all over it.

"Haywood Kenney, you sorry, gutless, lying sonuvabitch," I said loudly. The whole bar went stark silent. Kenney looked up at me and gaped. By then I was beside him. The element of surprise. I had to move fast. "My name is Hush McGillen Thackery."

"Oh, Jesus," he said.

"Don't pray for help *now*, you turd on the ass of humanity."

I whipped him across the side of the head with my apple branches, hard enough to nearly knock him off his chair. "That's for what you've said about my family." I slapped him again with the branches. "That's for what you've said about the Jacobses' family, because they're my family, too." *Slap.* "And *that's* for telling the other ignorant, wimpy-assed fools out in the great wide world that Nick Jakobek is a killer and a joke."

By now, Kenney was up and dodging me, shielding his head with his arms, trying to back into a corner of the alcove. "Somebody help me!" he shrieked. Shrieked. An expert columnist on media relations would write later, in the big newspapers, that that squawk of fear might as well be called the death knell of his radio manhood. You don't preach ballsy politics on the air but then hide in the corner of a fancy bar when an outraged mother whips your ass with faux apple branches. His toadies scattered like mealy bugs when you lift a rock. I wouldn't have been surprised if they'd rolled up in tight little balls on the parquet floor.

I shoved their empty chairs aside and cornered Kenney. *Slap*. "This is for smirking at the world from your pissy little ivory tower while men like Jakobek keep that world safe for you." *Slap*. "And finally, this is for abusing the meaning of freedom of speech by turning good people's lives into po'-trash manure for your vicious—" *Slap*—"petty—" *Slap*—"mealymouthed—" *Slap*— "lies." *Slap*.

On that last slap, he sank down to his haunches with his arms wrapped around his head in silent, cowering submission. I looked down at him the way a cat looks at a mouse that's stopped moving. "You just bore the hell out of me," I said. I tossed the apple branches at him, and he flinched.

I pivoted and stared at the crowd. Everyone was standing. In the back of the room, people had climbed up on tables for a better view. I saw a number of eager faces. There was scattered applause.

"If you really mean that," I announced, "then make it count. Turn off his filthy radio show. Tell people the truth behind his lies. And don't laugh at the misery he brings on others. Today it's about me and mine. But tomorrow it could be about you and yours."

They made a path for me. Rhetoric delivered in a southern

drawl with a certain crazed look in the eye will clear the way, most times. I walked out onto a cold Chicago sidewalk, wondering if I'd get arrested for assaulting a national media celebrity before I made it to the airport. A little dazed, I turned vaguely and bumped into a tall, muscular blond woman dressed in a jogging suit.

Lucille.

"I arrived in Washington about the time you were leaving," she said. "The President asked me to keep an eye on you. So I've been following discreetly since you left the hospital."

"I hate to tell you this, but I'm in trouble. I just whipped Haywood Kenney's ass. In public. With witnesses."

"I know." She took me by one arm and gestured toward a dark sedan on the street.

"I've been had," I said.

"No, you've been *protected*," Lucille corrected. "We had a feeling you'd go after Kenney. Actually, Mrs. Jacobs said she'd bet money on it. She has good instincts."

"She's a mother and a lover and a wild woman, like me. She knows what scores have to be settled."

Another agent appeared from somewhere and whisked open the car's passenger door. Lucille pushed me in and climbed in beside me. "Back to the airport," she told the driver. Then she looked at me. "The President and Mrs. Jacobs say they'll personally represent you on the assault charges, if need be."

"Edwina said that? Before or after she cleaned the apple goo off her designer suit?"

"After. And Hush — this is only my opinion as your future sister-in-law, but well —" Lucille cleared her throat. "You just joined the ranks of the Colonel in my hall of heroes."

I shook my head.

Heroes weren't this lonely.

TWENTY

I woke up feeling as if something had changed inside me. Not just because there'd been a slice-and-dice job on my lung and torn arteries. Something more fundamental. I was lighter inside. Groggy, I lifted my left hand to see what tickled my palm. I blinked hard and finally focused on the rough little wooden crucifix dangling from my fingers by a gold chain. Only one person carved something holy out of simple wood. "Hush?" I said hoarsely, and tried to sit up in the hospital bed.

"She went home. She wasn't sure you needed her or wanted her here." Al's voice. He put a hand on my shoulder to hold me still, then sat down in a chair beside me. I laid back weakly. Not need her? I couldn't put into words how *much* I needed her. My throat was raw from the anesthesia tube during surgery. I closed my hand around the crucifix, imprinting Hush on my palm.

Al watched me. "Don't try to talk. Just listen." He told me what Hush had done to Haywood Kenney on my behalf. My brain was slow and my nerves were junked up with medication, but goosebumps spread slowly over my skin. Al went on. "You're her hero. And she's yours. A corny term, *hero*—overused, trivial-ized—but in this case, it's true." He paused, his throat working. "You may think that Edwina and I stopped believing in your basic humanity years ago, but you're wrong. We knew from the day we brought you home from Mexico that you were someone special, someone who understood the world's extremes with a clarity we could only envy. We've disappointed you, but you've never disap-pointed us. You're *our* hero, too."

"Forget it," I rasped. "I've made my peace with what I am. I take care of my family. Can't save the world. But—"

"You've done your job, Nick. Now it's time to save yourself." He studied me quietly. "If you don't love Hush Thackery, that's your business. But if you do, then you need to say so. To *her*. Not to me, not to Edwina. Not to the walls of this room. Not just to yourself. To her." He stood. "Now, get some rest. We love you, Nick." He patted my shoulder and left the room.

I fumbled the crucifix off my left hand, then slowly, methodi-cally, raised the chain around my neck, and fastened the clasp. *Please God, make me strong enough to get out of this bed soon and do what I have to do.*

"Hello, Nicky." Eddie's soft whisper echoed in my ear.

I opened my eyes in the shadows of the room and said, "Hey, Kid. You shouldn't be here."

"They couldn't keep me away, but I promised to only stay a minute. Davis is waiting in the hall. And Mother." She brushed my hair with her fingertips. "When I was little, I pictured you in a knight's silver armor, out in the forest, slaying dragons. Dad was the king of the kingdom you protected, and Mother was the queen, and I was the princess. And I told my friends that there was no reason to be afraid of anything in our realm, because my knight, Sir Nicky, kept all the dragons under control." She smiled tearfully. "Now I know I wasn't just pretending."

"Princess Eddie. I'm still at your service."

"Princess Edwina Margisia *Nicola*," she corrected.

"Poor kid. Saddled with three funky names."

"Nicky. Shhh. I've come to ask you for favors. All right?"

"Just name them."

"Will you be my baby's godfather?"

I was quiet for a long time. "What about Davis—"

"He'll ask you, too. But I wanted to go first."

"I'd be honored." I cleared my throat, looked away, looked back. "And the other favor?"

"I want you to go away."

"What?"

"Go away. Go back where you belong. And don't say you don't know what I mean by that, *Jakob*." She stood.

"I intend—"

"Shhh. Don't say anything at all. The answer is between you and your heart." She kissed me on the top of the head, straightened my covers, smiled, and left the room, walking carefully, her hands spread on her bulging stomach, making a canopy over the child I would happily protect, just as I'd protected her. I shut my eyes for a moment, and when I opened them, Edwina was straightening my covers. "I must really be wrinkled," I said.

"Not yet. But if you wait many more years to catch a wife, you'll have a *very* hard time, because you'll be as wrinkled as a dried . . . apple." She grimaced. "Apple analogies. I'm pathologically obsessed with them." She pulled up the chair and sat down. Her face and attitude softened. "*Nicholas*," she said sadly.

"I'm fine."

"No, you're not. We've let you roam the world all these years without saying the things we should have said."

"It's all right to be uncomfortable around me."

"Uncomfortable? You mean *afraid*?" When I nodded, she sighed. "When Al brought you home to live with us, I admit I was afraid of you. But probably no more than you were afraid of me."

DEBORAH SMITH

"All right. Yes. You scared the *shit* out of *me*."

"But it didn't take very long for me to see that you had a deep sense of honor and an even deeper capacity for honesty and kindness."

"You could tell that from coyote skulls?"

"Yes. Yes, I could." Her quick smile faded. "I'm so sorry Al and I preached our rules of morality to you, when all along you held to a code of duty and sacrifice that went far beyond our simple speeches. Unfortunately, when you needed our support the most, we turned out to be hypocrites."

"No. You were honest. That's why I loved you both. Why I still do."

She wiped her eyes, then reached over and picked up the carved wooden crucifix on my chest. She pursed her mouth tightly. "You'll be singing baritone in the Chocinaw County Gospel Church of the Harvest in Song, if you're not careful."

I started to say something about my future, but she stood. "No need to answer that. And Nicholas? I realize I've turned into a monster over the years. I'm planning to reform. All right? Get some rest."

She turned out the light over my bed and left the room. I lay alone in the dark, amazed. I finally had something to say, but no one would listen. Well, one person would.

I just had to get to her.

We roll back the years sometimes. With a kind of déjà vu, we see a moment in our lives for what it is: a reminder of how far we've come. I was sitting on the side of my hospital bed at dawn, sweating with the effort, using most of my concentration to get dressed. I wasn't supposed to be sitting up, much less packing to leave. I'd managed to put on my old khakis and zip my fly. Next, I fumbled with the buttons on my flannel shirt.

Bill Sniderman walked in. Same dapper bastard he'd been that day at the hospital in Chicago, nearly twenty years earlier. His crisp white shirt was knotted high on his neck. He wore a creased dark suit and silk tie the way a men's store mannequin wears a can't-touch-this attitude. Al's senior advisor looked down his flared brown nose at me with the same shit-sniffing dislike as always. "Disappearing again, I hope, Nick?"

"You're smart for a man who wears his collars tight enough to cut off the blood supply to his brain."

"You don't look too well. Any chance you'll collapse and die on your way to the street?"

"Aw, Bill, don't be shy. You know you'll miss me."

He arched a graying black brow. "I came by to tell you one thing: I've always thought you'd make a good *dead* hero."

"That's sweet. Where were you when I needed my bedpan changed yesterday?"

He held out a hand. "Why don't you go back to your apple-farming woman and stay out of the President's limelight and practice being a good *live* hero?"

We traded a long look. "Damn, I'm starting to like you," I said.

We shook on the news.

Davis walked in, dressed for a long drive in old jeans and a heavy coat. "Ready?"

"I was born ready," I said.

A SAMPLE OF the day's national headlines:

KENNEY FLEES "PO'-TRASH" WHIPPING FROM
EDDIE JACOBS THACKERY'S MOTHER-IN-LAW
KENNEY COWERS. CAN HIS MACHO BIGMOUTH IMAGE SURVIVE?
NO CHARGES TO BE FILED BY KENNEY; SOURCES SAY HE WANTS
INCIDENT FORGOTTEN QUICKLY
PRESIDENT'S NEPHEW "A NATIONAL TREASURE," SAYS CARDINAL OF
CHICAGO ARCHDIOCESE. CONDEMNS KENNEY'S SHOW
And the best of all: TWO RADIO STATIONS PULL KENNEY'S
SHOW OFF AIR. MORE MAY FOLLOW

All great news, but cold comfort on that day after my return home to the Hollow. I shut down the farm and shooed my kin away. A chilly rain drizzled down from a gray sky. Freezing weather and ice were moving in. The most wonderful, terrible apple season of my life was over. I wanted to curl up under a blanket and hug the misery inside me.

A call on my cell phone roused me. "Hush, it's Smooch."

"Smooch!"

"I'm in Miami, just sitting here in seventy-degree weather on a dock waiting to get on a cruise ship to the Bahamas, but I . . . I just can't stop crying—"

"Come *home*."

"I meant to forget all about the past and just find myself a good man on the cruise ship, but then cousin Mayflo called me about Jakobek, and then I saw the news about you and Kenney, and I've been thinking you *really* need me there, I mean, you need a good public relations person more than I need a good man—"

"Smoochie, I have no idea how I'll get along without you if you don't come home."

"I don't know what to say about my brother. I just don't know."

"We'll talk. We'll figure out a way to remember him, the good and the bad."

"Here's the thing—can you still love me like a sister-at-heart if you never loved my brother?"

"Oh, Smoochie. Love is like apples. Every seed is different, even if they come from the same tree. Of course I love you. Of course you're still my sister-at-heart. *Come home*."

"All right, then, all right, Hush." She stopped crying long enough to call across the crowded south Florida cruise-ship pier, "Bring my luggage back, *por favor, Señor!*"

After I got off the phone with her, I went out in the cold, misty weather and walked in the orchards, thinking how I'd managed to keep my family together despite myself. *Plant well and the harvest will be good*, the Great Lady whispered.

"You reap what you sow," I said aloud. "I do know *that*. But what if the only man who can charm my bees hasn't shown any sign of coming back for the next season, or any seasons after that?"

No answer. I was on my own.

I walked a long time, the mist covering me. I grew soggy in my jeans and sweater, just wandering over the old orchards and the terraces of the ancient mountains and the graves of the gallant soldiers, until I made my way down the valley into the new orchards and reached the edges of their shelter. I faced the big, empty barns and empty gravel parking lots and, up the rise to McGillen Orchards Road, the locked gate. Emptiness and isolation seemed to surround me like the fading afternoon light. Barren days and nights waited for me. I sat down at the edge of my orchards among the gloom of day's end and season's end, and cried.

I still had my head in my hands when I began to hear the rumble of large engines. Frowning, I got up and stared at the public road. The rumble grew louder. A parade of khaki-green military trucks crawled into view — about a dozen of them. I stared. The lead vehicle, a Humvee, pulled up to my gate.

Davis got out of the passenger side. My Davis. My son. All right, this was his second unannounced road trip of the year — he'd started and ended the season by surprising me. He didn't see me staring, openmouthed, from the fringe of the orchards as he fiddled with his key ring. He opened the padlocked gates. A soldier in Army fatigues helped him push them aside. Davis and the soldier then climbed back into the Humvee. The caravan — the convoy — rolled slowly down the driveway and into the gravel parking lots.

By then, I was running to meet it.

I slid to a stop about the same time the trucks maneuvered into a cluster. The rumble of engines faded to nothing. The soft, wet whisper of the mountains' breath filled in the silence. Davis saw me and got out again, raising a hand in greeting. He gestured toward a vehicle somewhere near the middle of the group, then walked that way. My feet froze to the gravel.

Men and women in Army fatigues climbed down from the Humvees and transports, some carrying medical equipment, some apparently just along as escorts. They converged on the one Humvee, where someone I couldn't see was being helped out of the back, slowly. That slow-moving man was tall and dark-haired, weathered and scarred. Dressed in an Army jacket, flannel shirt, and old khakis, he waved his helpers away, then turned to face me. He began walking slowly, haltingly, with great determination, toward me.

Jakobek.

I ran to him.

"You shouldn't be out of the hospital, Jakob! Oh, *Jakob*."

"I want to be an apple farmer," he said.

I threw my arms around his neck and kissed him, and he kissed me as he curled one arm around my shoulders and the other around my waist. I forced myself not to pull him too close, thinking of his wound, but he maneuvered me to his good side and we held each other tightly.

"Then welcome home," I whispered.

TWENTY-ONE

One Month Later

The trip to Washington for the birth of Eddie and Davis's baby was Jakobek's first big trip after recuperating from the injury. He had turned out fine, healing in all the important ways. We were getting there — that is, becoming a couple — just as Davis and I were coming to gentler terms on all that had happened, and life was beginning to settle into a new brand of normal. For Jakobek, a month of my home cooking, a lot of doting attention from me and most of Chocinaw County, and just the right mix of soulful conversations and gentle sex had worked wonders. On him *and* me.

The next generation of the Davis Thackery branch of the family was about to be born, not under an apple tree, but in a high-tech, extremely expensive, suburban-D.C. birthing center. Eddie and Davis had chosen the facility because it was near the city and the Secret Service approved. In a special room for younger visitors, Puppy was busy making friends with a half-dozen Jacobs and Habersham kids.

The Jacobs cousins were rambunctious little nose pickers and good-natured wrestlers, but the Habershams were way too clean for younguns under the age of twelve, and a little stuck-up, just like Edwina. "I'm Walford Habersham the Fourth," one boy said grandly when he introduced himself to Puppy. "Are you a hillbilly?" She didn't bat a single, dark Thackery eyelash. She had decided who she would be, and how her story should be told. "I'm Hush McGillen the *Sixth*," she told Walford. "So don't give me any shit."

Watching like a new mother tiger from one corner, Lucille grinned.

Edwina and I stood in a small private waiting room. Waiting. Al and Jakobek and Logan smoked cigars outdoors in the snowy dark. I wanted to smoke my pipe, but had forgotten it in the rush to travel to Washington when the call came that Eddie was in labor. Smooch had stayed behind to answer the phones and plan the press release. She wanted to hold a contest to name a new apple product in honor of the baby. I'd told her no, but she was determined.

Edwina suddenly linked a strong, twisting arm through mine, as if we were girlfriends. "I'm planning a spring wedding for you and Nicholas," she announced.

I eyed her askance. "Well, it's mighty nice of you to let us know."

"What's the problem? You say you're definitely getting married."

"Yes, but I'm not letting you take charge of our wedding."

"You don't want to be married at the White House?"

I stared at her. "Are you kidding me?"

"I don't kid," she said coolly. "I've already asked Nicholas if he'd mind me asking you. He says it's your decision."

I was speechless. Then, "You'll do that for me?"

"No, I'll do that for Nicholas. You're just a necessary prop to celebrate his happiness."

"I see."

She harrumphed and looked away. "Then you'll agree?"

"Edwina, I think you're trying to be nice to me, and all I can say is, it's painful to watch."

"Either accept the goddamned offer or don't."

"I accept."

"Good."

"Thank you, Your Highness."

"Shut up."

We faced forward, both watching the closed doors to the birthing suite. "You're always busy with your apple business in the fall," she said suddenly. "So every year, fall will be my time to spend with my grandchild."

"All right. But I have dibs on *my* grandchild for winter, spring, and the summer solstice."

"Winter, spring, *and* the summer solstice? The *solstice?* Why? Is it some kind of ritualistic apple holiday?"

"In a way. It's the day of the year when the season turns toward harvest time. We have a huge, potluck family reunion outdoors in the orchards, and we cook an old Cherokee pioneer recipe for green apple stew."

"Green apple stew? What happens after you eat a stew made from unripe apples? The entire clan runs the ceremonial 'Diarrhea Road Race'? No. You're not feeding *my* grandchild the fast-trot family specialty."

"Oh, don't be a sissy. I'll send the recipe to your chef. You can test it first. Feed it to some of your serfs or peasants. See if they live. You know. Your usual routine."

She sighed. "Never mind. All right then, the baby is mine from summer solstice to autumn, and through Christmas."

"Whoa. Major holidays are a different negotiation."

"All right, we'll alternate Christmases."

"And Thanksgivings."

"But I always get Easter. You're practically a heathen. You don't need Easter."

"If the Reverend Betty of the Gospel Church of the Harvest in Song heard you say that, she'd put a hex on you."

Al, Jakobek, and Logan had walked back inside as we were talking. "Ladies," Al said, "I need to point something out. The baby has parents who might like to *tell* you when you'll get to babysit."

"No way," Edwina and I said in unison.

Jakobek took me by the arm and walked me down a nearby hall. "Relax," he said.

"I can't. I've never been a grandmother before. How much longer can it take? I think I was in labor with Davis for only five seconds. Or maybe five days. It was all a blur of cold rain and hurt followed by the most incredible joy."

"I was there when Eddie was born. I wish I'd been there with you and Davis," he said quietly.

"That would have been hard to explain to his father."

A poor joke. It quieted us. We held hands in apology, walked to a window overlooking a winter garden, and watched the way a landscape lamp made snowy shadows on a patch of holly shrubs. "I wish you'd been there with me and Davis, too," I said.

"You've always wanted another baby."

I squeezed his hand. "I still have Puppy to help raise. And a grandchild, any minute." I paused. "But yes, I've always wanted another flesh-of-my-flesh baby."

"You'll be forty-one this year. I'll be forty-four. We'd be a little nuts to even think about—"

"Let's be a little nuts, then." My heart raced. We faced each other, trading serious, searching, hopeful looks. "Would you," I whispered, "want to be a father if we could do it?"

He nodded, never taking his eyes off mine. "And you? A mother again?"

"*Yes.*"

"Good."

We both exhaled with relief and bent our heads together. "It may not work," I admitted, crying a little. "But let's plow the fur-row and sow the seeds."

He laughed. "I don't know whether to throw away my con-doms or buy a new garden rake." We held each other, swaying, damp-eyed, smiling, scared, excited. Baby or no baby, it was good to feel fertile again.

"Everyone?" Davis called. "Mother? Where are you?"

Jakobek and I hurried back to the waiting room. Davis stood there, smiling, sweaty, a little pale, his tall, lanky body swamped in rumpled blue hospital scrubs. With Al, Edwina, Logan, and Lucille, we crowded around him.

"Eddie's fine," he said, "and we have a perfect baby daughter."

Applause. Hugs. Tears. Handshaking.

"Our granddaughter," Edwina said to Al, and kissed him.

"My granddaughter," I said to Jakobek, and kissed him.

"My goddaughter," he said to everyone, and kissed me.

A few minutes later, the nurses let us into the private room where Eddie held the sweetest baby girl, wrapped in a pink blan-ket. Without any dignity at all, we pushed in close and whispered and gawked and put our hands over our hearts. Davis sat down on the bed beside her. "Do you want to tell them now?" Bedraggled and exhausted but happy, Eddie nodded.

"Davis and I decided our daughter needs a set of names to re-mind her of her roots."

"Oh, not something to do with *apples*," Edwina moaned.

"No, Mother. Something to represent the strength, and love, and sheer, wonderful stubbornness of her family tree."

"Anything to do with trees is fine by me," I put in.

"Mother, shhh," Davis urged.

Eddie smiled. Looking at Davis tenderly, then down at their daughter, she whispered, "Her name is Edwina . . . Hush . . . Thackery."

Edwina Hush. It was unwieldy, a mouthful, not musical at all. But I loved it. "Hush Edwina," I said softly. "Perfect."

"Edwina Hush," Edwina corrected. "Perfect."

Al began laughing. I looked at Jakobek and saw him trying not to smile. "What?" I demanded.

Al shook his head. "I hope someone comes up with a nickname, or I may have to ask the Supreme Court for a ruling."

YES, EDWINA HUSH WOULD need a nickname. For now, Davis and Eddie were calling her Little Eddie. I suspected that would stick. I didn't mind. I made up my own version. "Little Eddie Hush," I kept saying to Jakobek, with a smile. "Little Eddie Hush. That's not too long a name. When she visits the Hollow, I'll call her Eddie Hush. That's very southern."

Jakobek arched a brow. "It sounds like a jockey or a professional gambler." Laughter spilled out between us.

We drove to Washington well after midnight. The Secret Service had been told to expect us, and they let us onto the grounds of the White House. Jakobek and I walked to a lamplit area approved by the bureaucracy that manages the grand old mansion and its gardens. And there, where it would receive good sun and rain, we planted a Sweet Hush apple tree.

The darkness would not win against apples.

It's good to be famous, the Great Lady whispered to me. *Sometimes we have to let our legends do the work for us, to see if they'll really survive in the hardest seasons.*

Yes, I answered. *They've survived. And bloomed.*

Jakobek clasped my dirt-stained hand in his. "What are you thinking about with that look on your face? Whatever it is, I like it."

"I'm thinking about you. You and our family and this wonderful night and our apple trees, and the bees that are waiting to come to the Hollow in the spring to be charmed by the two of us. Imagine, Jakob. You and me — two bee charmers working in the orchards, *together*. We'll be knee-deep in apples and honey and good times."

He smiled. "We're already there," he said.

ACKNOWLEDGMENTS

I grew up with apples, yellow jacket wasps, and a family full of staunch farmers who risked a few stings every year to turn the harvest of our wild apple trees into civilized victuals. My childhood memories include stirring huge washtubs of sweet apples that had been set out to soak in my grandmother's kitchen and biting into hard, tart crab apples that made my lips pucker. As an adult, my happiest fall excursions have been to mountain apple markets. No autumn has passed without fried apple pies sitting on my dining table, apple bread cooling on my cutting board, and soft brown apple butter spreading like syrup across the biscuits on my breakfast plates.

I have been hypnotized every year by the sight of mountain women peeling bushel baskets full of Arkansas Blacks or Rome Reds under cool October skies; the scent of the apples is so potent that swarms of bees and yellow jackets come to share the fruit, and, hypnotized like me, linger quietly to watch the work. Apples are the most ancient food of life, meant to bring sustenance and peace. Even the stinging creatures know that.

This book is for the grand old apple orchards that have disappeared in the wake of modern agriculture; for the lost names of apple varieties that made a kind of poetry in themselves; and for the remembrance of contented tastes and aromas and textures and moments.

For the apples.

My thanks go to Ann White, Sandra Chastain, and Virginia Ellis for sharing the job of growing this book from seed to fruit. Also many thanks to Ellen Taber for her skillful research and meticulous proofreading, and to Staff Sergeant Lynn Cypert, U.S. Army, Fort

McPherson, and Captain Steven Ray, U.S. Army, Fort Gillem, who advised me on the details of military protocol.

Finally, as always, I couldn't have written this book without the patience of my husband, Hank, the support of my mother, Dora Brown, and the faithful affection of four cats, three dogs, and thirty goldfish.

Well, all right, I'm not quite sure the goldfish care that much.

But they do like it when I toss sliced apples into their pond.

Readers are invited to visit Deborah at her Web site, www.deborahsmith.com.

ABOUT THE AUTHOR

Deborah Smith, a former newspaper reporter, has written eight other novels, including *A Place to Call Home, On Bear Mountain,* and *The Stone Flower Garden.* A sixth-generation native southerner, she uses her pioneer farm heritage as an inspiration for many of her novels. She is married to her childhood sweetheart and lives in the mountains of north Georgia.